W9-BUR-235

KELLEY

ESKRIDGE

SOLITAIRE

An Imprint of HarperCollins Publishers

EOS

EOS

An Imprint of HarperCollins*Publishers*
10 East 53rd Street
New York, New York 10022-5299

Copyright © 2002 by Kelley Eskridge

ISBN: 0-06-008857-5

Library of Congress Cataloging-in-Publication Data

Eskridge, Kelley.
Solitaire / Kelley Eskridge.—1st ed.
p. cm.
ISBN 0-06-008857-5
I. Title.
PS3605.S75 S65 2002
813'.6—dc21   2002025381

First Eos hardcover printing: September 2002

Eos Trademark Reg. U.S. Pat. Off. and in Other Countries,
Marca Registrada, Hecho en U.S.A.
HarperCollins ® is a trademark of HarperCollins Publishers Inc.

Printed in the U.S.A.

FIRST EDITION

10 9 8 7 6 5 4 3 2 1

www.eosbooks.com

For Nicola,
my sunshine

SOLITAIRE

PART I

BEFORE

THE

FALL

1

SO HERE SHE WAS, FRAMED IN THE OPEN DOUBLE DOORS like a photograph: Jackal Segura on the worst day of her life, preparing to join the party. The room splayed wide before her, swollen with voices, music, human heat, and she thought perhaps this was a bad idea after all. But she was conscious of the picture she made, backlit in gold by the autumn afternoon sun, standing square, taking up space. A good entrance, casually dramatic. People were already noticing, smiling; *there's our Jackal being herself. There's our Hope*. It shamed her, now that she knew it was a lie.

She took a breath and stepped into the chaos of color and noise, conscious of her bare face. Most people had made some effort at a Halloween costume, even if only a few finger smears of paint along cheekbone or forehead. Enough to make them unrecognizable, alien. She had a vision of Ko Island full of monsters lurching to the beat that boomed like a kodo drum, so loud that she imagined the huge western windows bulging under the pressure, only a moment from jagged eruption. It could happen. There was always a breaking point.

But she should not be thinking about things breaking, about her life splintered like a bone that could never be set straight. She should wipe from her mind her mother's voice, thin and sharp,

They give you everything and you don't deserve it, you're no more a Hope than I am! She should stop wanting to split Donatella's head open for saying it. And she should not yearn to lay herself in her mother's lap and beg her *take it back, Mama, make it better* while Donatella stroked her hair. What good would it do? Her mother would only find a way to break her all over again.

Enough. She shook her head and braced herself against the jostle of bodies. Fuck Donatella. Jackal would cope. She would find a way to work it out. She was here, that was the first step: and somewhere in this confusion were the people she needed—her web mates, her peers among the second generation of Ko Corporation citizen–employees. Her web was the world. Her web was safety. She only had to brave the crowd long enough to find them.

She guessed they would stake out their usual space by the windows that faced the cliffs and the sea beyond. They would be drinking and laughing, expansive, expecting only what everyone expected—that the world turned, that business was good, that the company prospered and its people prospered with it, flowers in the sun of Ko. With Jackal as the tallest sunflower in the bunch. It was a ludicrous image, with her olive skin and dark eyes, but it was true. Every person of the company—the three hundred in the room, the four hundred thousand on the island, the two million around the world—watched their Hope with a mix of awe and possession, as if she were a marvelous new grain in the research garden, or the current stock valuation. They knew her latest aptitude scores and her taste for mango sorbet. They had opinions about her. They parsed her future at their dinner tables. Is she ready? Will she be a good Hope? Compelling questions for the past twenty-two years, gathering urgency now as Jackal approached her investiture. In just two months she would go to Al Iskandariyah, where the heart of the world government pumped, to stand with the other Hopes in the first breath of the new year, the shared second of their birth. At twenty-three, they would be of age in any society, legally entitled to take up their symbolic place in the global administration. But what was the task? *You are the world builders*, the official letter from Earth Congress read. Jackal knew it by heart; she bet all the Hopes did, the thousands scattered around the planet who had been born in the first second of the first attempt to unify the world. *We honor you as the first citizens born into the new age of world coalition. You are the face of unity: the living symbol of our hope to be a global community with shared dreams and common goals.* That was who she was: the Hope of Ko. The Hope of the only commercial entity on the planet with its own home territory and almost-realized independence from its host nation, only a few negotiations away from becoming the first corporate-state in the new world order.

"Coming through!" a man called as he bumped past her and spattered beer on her shirt. She bit down on the impulse to say something nasty; instead, she ducked her head and stepped back. The Hope must be always gracious. The Hope must show the best face of Ko.

She had been aware for most of her twenty-two years that she carried the future of the company in some way that was undefined, emblematic. She had tried to visualize it. She could see herself in Al Iskandariyah, living in a functionary's apartment near the marketplace with its smells of boiled wool and incense and calamari fried in glass-green olive oil. She could imagine the cool hallways of the Green and Blue Houses of government. But she never pictured herself doing anything. What exactly was a Hope supposed to do? All she was being taught was what any manager at Ko might learn, albeit more quickly and with more personal attention from her trainers; there had to be more to being a Hope than that. She squeezed her eyes shut against the frenzied loop playing in her brain: *no more a Hope no hope no hope—*

Breathe, she told herself. The music seemed louder, the air thicker with sweat and the smell of beer. A new track was playing, that song about fame, and she felt her lips pull back from her teeth. Easy—people were watching. She pulled her jacket tighter around her chest and managed a general nod to as many of them as she could. She had to find the web. Especially Snow. All she wanted right now was someone to be safe with. But maybe she would never be safe again; never safe, never—

"Jackal!" A hand on her arm. "Great, you're here. Hey, they're playing your song." Tiger laughed at his own joke, and she made herself smile even though it was hard.

"Hey, Tiger."

"Where've you been? Everybody's asking for you. Come on, we're over here. I'll get you a drink." Drawing her into the music and the laughter, his body warm from dancing, just a little too close. Another thing to deal with. Later, she thought. First a drink and some space to wind down. And Snow. I'll deal with the rest of it later.

He led her to the back of the room, opening a path with a touch on one person's shoulder, a gentle nudge of his hip to an enthusiastic dancer, a grin and a clever word for all of them as he cleared them from his way. The music battered at her; her heart took up the beat. And there was the web, some dancing in the glow of the sea-refracted sun, some stuffed two to a chair, loud and laughing; a few at a corner table with a pitcher of beer, muttering over a project timeline. Business and life, moving belly-to-belly. Ko might be structured along traditional lines of management, but it was sustained by the webs that cut across hierarchies and divisions, people focused on the company but loyal to one another. As familiar as family. Web mates liked or loved or despised each other, but regardless they made each other successful, and Ko thrived.

"Jackal!"

"Hey, Jackal."

"Hey." She was especially glad to see Bear and Turtle, both good friends, both solid and safe. She smiled, settling into a chair next to them. Bear blinked at her from behind his feathered half-mask, turquoise and scarlet, dramatic against his mahogany skin. "Where's your costume? We should send you back home and make you change."

"She came as an ordinary person," Turtle said, leaning over to hug her. From someone else it might have been a nasty remark. Today, it hurt precisely because it was so earnest, so obviously well-meant. "*Feliz Víspera de Todos Los Santos*," he said with a smile.

"She always looks like that," Mist said. That wasn't exactly nasty, just disapproving.

Tiger had come up beside her with a tall glass of something orange and cold. "Oh, lay off," he said. Then, to Jackal, "Here, try this."

"What is it?"

He gave her a look. "Try it. If you don't like it, I'll get you something else."

She took a sip: lovely, cool orange juice with something warm and rich behind it. "Mmm," she said, nodding. "Good." She took another, larger swallow. "What is it?"

"Brandy and orange juice. My new favorite drink."

"It's revolting," Mist said. Tiger rolled his eyes at Jackal. She raised her glass to him and drank down the rest in one breath, then wiped her arm across her mouth. Turtle chuckled.

"Well," Tiger said. "You'd better have this one too." He handed her his glass.

"Thanks." Another deep swallow, until her stomach felt hard and full, and waves of heat started up her spine. The party rolled around her, music and laughter, people in motion. She wanted Snow. The others were talking over her; as far as she could tell, she'd interrupted a debate about planning the web's holiday celebration. She tuned it out: she didn't care. She didn't mind New Year's Eve; there were no presents to buy, and she liked champagne, and the New Year toast always morphed into everyone wishing her a happy birthday. But she did not expect to enjoy this New Year's. She would be in some official residence in Al Iskandariyah preparing for investiture, unless of course someone found out about her and de-Hoped her, whatever that entailed.

That made her want to cry. She blinked and peered at her empty glass. She could feel Tiger watching; she asked, "Can I have another one of these?"

He studied her for a moment before he answered. "Whatever's wrong, is there anything I can do?"

She gave him a plastic cheerful smile. "Everything's fine. All I need is another drink and to find Snow. Do you know where she is?"

"She's taking around a group of little kid trick-or-treaters. She left about a half hour ago."

Oh, damn, damn, she thought, and knew he saw it. She had been counting on Snow's comforting arm and anchoring solidity. Tiger sighed so briefly that she almost missed it, and it was one more thing she couldn't cope with right now. He said, "Does that mean you're going too, or do you still want that drink?"

Great. Just terrific. Snow was gone, Tiger was hurt, and Jackal felt overwhelmingly tired of all of them, especially her own helpless self. What did people do when they were uprooted, a torn tree tumbling in the funnel cloud? "Drink," she said, ignoring the voice inside her that was saying *be careful, Jackal*. "I'll definitely have another drink."

"Okay," Tiger answered, sounding surprised and slightly mollified. "I'll be right back."

But he wasn't. She could see the crowd around the bar, and she imagined him patiently negotiating a way through the thicket of raucous people because she had asked. *They give you everything and you don't deserve it!* the mother-voice screeched again, rolling over her like the waves she had seen breaking onto the beach as she walked to her parents' house earlier that afternoon. It was a beautiful day: the sunlit asphalt road overhung by brilliant dying leaves and a periwinkle sky, quiet except for the creek at the edge of the property chewing its mouthfuls of silt, and a seagull skreeking toward the sea.

Her mother was in her office, working. She put her cheek up distractedly for Jackal to kiss. "Ren, sweetheart, what a lovely surprise."

Jackal could see that she meant it. That was the hardest part sometimes. She sat on the visitor's chair by the desk, gathering herself. She thought she was ready, although she always dreaded these conversations. When she was little, she had for a time carried school papers and awards home as proudly as a cat with a dead garter snake; but she had learned that Donatella responded strangely to her daughter's success. And this time would be worse. Still, she had to deliver the news, and then do her best not to see her mother's jaw stiffen and her head start to shake very slightly, her gaze flatten as her smile grew wide; Donatella would show too many teeth, and her congratulations would be bracketed by the usual "Well, of course, if they really think you can handle it," or, "Now don't worry, I'm sure they'll give you lots of backup, they do make a lot of allowances for you." Then her father would see her to the door, saying softly, "Of course your mother loves you, *hija*, she's just very competitive by nature," as he had a thousand times since Jackal was old enough to start having accomplishments of her own.

But today Carlos wasn't there, and things went bad right away.

"I have some news to share with you, but I'm a little nervous about it because I think it might put us in an awkward position with each other," Jackal said. She thought it was a good beginning; she'd been working on it all the way to the house.

Her mother turned in her chair so that Jackal could see most, but not all, of her face. It was a power position: *you have enough of my attention to serve courtesy, but I'll be getting back to my very important work in just a moment.* "You don't need to facilitate me, dear," Donatella said, managing to sound both irritated and amused.

"I'm not trying to . . ." Jackal took a breath. "I want . . ."

"Ren, just say whatever you have to say."

She wanted to say, Mama, you're supposed to be such a good communicator, so why doesn't this ever work better? But instead she replied, "Okay. I've been asked to take over a new project in the next few weeks. The Garbo project."

Outside, a bird warbled a few shrill notes.

"I'm supposed to take Garbo," Donatella said.

"The administration has decided it's an appropriate training opportunity for me."

"It's not a training project," Donatella snapped, and Jackal tried not to wince. "It's much too complex for someone at your level. I've been preparing for months. It's my project," she repeated, as if Jackal simply hadn't understood the situation and would become reasonable as soon as the point was clear.

"I'm sorry," Jackal said. "I wanted you to hear about it from me." She meant to go on, perhaps say something like *it's not my fault*, or *please don't be mad at me*, but Donatella rolled right over her.

"This is ridiculous. It makes no sense. It's a huge assignment and you're leaving in a couple of months. What are they thinking?" Her head was beginning to shake. "Neill promised me the project himself. He's certainly not going to like this when he hears about it."

"My instructions came from Neill," Jackal said, trying to make her voice as calm as possible so she wouldn't feed her mother's tailspin.

"There's been a mistake. I'm sure that's all it is. I'll talk to him and get it sorted out."

"Mama," Jackal began, and heard the pleading tone that her mother always seemed to bring out in her, "Mama, I know you're upset—"

"Of course I'm upset! They've got no right! And giving it to you is laughable, you're clearly not ready for it."

Jackal replied, as evenly as she could, "It's true I need to prepare. I don't know much about the background and the particulars yet. I would certainly value your advice." She took another deep breath. "Of course you can talk to Neill, but he said plainly that I will be leading the project. I hope you understand I'm not happy about the way it's been handled. I don't want you to feel I'm taking something away from you."

"You little pig," her mother said shockingly, sickeningly, her voice like flint. "Of course you're taking it away from me. Did you even stop to think about it?" She threw up a hand. "Don't bother to answer. You probably think, oh well, they'll just give her something else. And they will, but not like this one. Not as important. Garbo's getting more attention from the Executive Council than any project in at least the last five years. I've been talking to Neill about it since Phase One started. I've been working overtime to get my other projects wrapped up so I could be ready. I've read every single project report, the minutes of every meeting. And you have the nerve to sit there and say you don't know much about it. But you'll take it. Again. *Again!* Because you're the Hope. No, just be quiet," she said, her voice rising. Jackal was trying to say *Stop, Mama, don't do this.* "And don't look at me like that," Donatella continued, the words foaming out. "Of course it's because you're the Hope. Anything Ren Segura needs, anything Ren Segura wants, whether you're ready for it or not, whether you can even understand it. All of it taken from someone else! Every training opportunity," she spat the words, "every accelerated class, every place at the head of every line, every second of attention could be going to someone who's worked and worked and worked and then has to stand by and see it all go to you because you're the precious Hope. Again and again and again! But you can't have this, you can't! You've had your chances. This is mine!" She was shouting now, her mouth enormous. "It's not fair, they give you everything, everything, the best chance I'll ever have and you don't deserve it, you're no more a Hope than I am!"

And then her mother gasped and put a hand to her mouth, the left hand with the old scar showing stark white: and they sat in awful silence until Jackal said, "What do you mean?"

Born too late, was what it came down to, even after all the careful planning, the induced labor, the drugs, the forceps. They had dragged her out of her mother's womb well past the first second of the new year; her birth, as with all the potential Hope births, recorded by tamperproof time-stamp technology supplied by EarthGov. Which had promptly been subverted by the technicians. "It's Ko technology, after all," Donatella said. "We should know how to get around it."

And so they had, and little Ren grew up and took the web name Jackal and worked and trained and prepared, the unknowing center of an enormous secret, a plan that had seemingly run itself like clockwork for twenty-two years. Until now: until her mother had lost her temper in the one way she never should. Jackal understood why Donatella's voice had changed from fury to fear at the end, why she had followed Jackal onto the front terrace saying "Ren! Ren, wait! Come back and let's hammer this out." But Jackal hadn't gone back. Don't negotiate me, she had thought bitterly, I'm not a fucking business deal. Except she was; and that was the real problem, the bottom line. The company had wanted a Hope badly enough to take the enormous risk of creating one, and the Hope's own mother had destabilized her at this most critical juncture. Ko would crucify her mother if they knew.

And maybe they should. How dare Donatella do this to her, make her so miserable that she could sit surrounded by her web and feel so alone? She had a sudden longing to hurt her mother. Hurt her deep. She imagined herself in some vice president's office telling the story doggedly, piously, saying, "I'm completely on board with this, but I'm a little worried that my mother is so upset." God, it's tempting, she thought.

"What is?" Tiger said, drinks in hand, startling her; she hadn't meant to speak aloud. Can't tell you, she thought, can't tell anybody, and then hoped she hadn't said that out loud as well. "This is," she said as brightly as she could, reaching for the glass.

Around her, her web mates chattered on. She wanted to scream. She wanted to hit something. She wanted Snow to hold her. But she had come here to get centered, so best be about it. She roused herself and waded into the conversation, made herself focus and listen and smile, smile, smile. She shifted so Tiger could perch on the arm of her chair. She recounted for Bear the entire plot of a play she'd seen in Esperance Park, complete with arm-waving descriptions of the fight scenes. She fetched her own next drink from the bar, and commiserated with someone from another web about the stress of the holiday season, her voice saying agreeably, "It sounds like you have a lot on your plate right now," while her head said *you have no fucking idea, sport*.

None of it worked. She knew she had only to say, "I have a problem, I need your help," and she would get everyone's undivided attention, the benefit of the dozens of brains here and the others who were part of the web, whether a mile away or a thousand. But she couldn't do it; she didn't know how to open her mouth and say *I'm not a Hope*. It was like saying, *I am a lie; I am not real*.

"I am real," she told herself. "I am real."

"What?" Tiger asked, leaning in closer, smiling down at her. "What did you say?"

"I am really drunk," she said. "And I am really tired of the whole stupid world and I just want to forget about everything for a while."

"Then let's dance."

"That's a great idea. I'd love to. Umm . . . can you help me stand up?"

He laughed. "Sure."

She took his hand. "Don't let me fall, Tiger," she said. "Don't let me fall."

That night she dreamed of Terry on the cliffs.

They were seven years old, on a school trip to the south coast of Ko on an early spring day. This was one of the few natural parts of the island; the rest was human-made, a project of the company's very profitable custom land-mass construction subsidiary. Ren and Terry scrambled along the cliff's edge with the other children, examining rock formations. They were supervised by teachers and the requisite accompanying parents, including Donatella. It was already clear to Ren that these trips made her mother restless and impatient, and she wished Donatella wouldn't come; not all the parents did, even though they were supposed to take turns. But her mother always put on her best pair of walking shoes and insisted brightly that she was looking forward to it, darling Ren, of course she wouldn't miss it.

Today, Donatella was organizing the parents and teachers as easily as she ran multinational projects; she had completely rearranged the supervising teacher's safety plan and was ordering everyone about. The teacher tried to argue: Ren sighed, and pulled Terry farther along the bluff, farther than they were supposed to go. Behind them the teacher's voice grated against the rocks, and Donatella murmured soothingly.

Ren and Terry dug together for a while, saving the best rocks

aside in a fiber bag, and making a game of pretending that the rejected bits were horrible criminals being forced to leap to their
deaths. The adult voices buzzed behind them.

"Your mom never yells back," Terry said, after a while. He was
smaller than Ren, and even better at math, and the only person she
knew beside herself who had ever stayed up all night just to see
what happened to the moon.

"She doesn't need to yell," Ren answered. "She always gets what
she wants. She calls it clarifying."

"Maybe—" Terry began, and then the cliff suddenly sighed and
slid away from under his bottom, and he went down with it in a
silent, surprised bundle of arms and legs, his mouth and eyes wide.
He broke apart on the rocks as he fell.

The ground under Ren began to shift. Her fear was liquid silver weighing down her arms and legs.

"Ren, get away from the edge!" her mother shouted in her command voice, the voice that must be obeyed. Donatella was forty
feet away, already in motion; but Ren could not move. Down
below, Terry's small body lay in an impossible shape. Another
large section of crust began to slide, and Donatella howled and
threw herself the last ten feet, landed hard on her stomach and
flung out both arms to snatch Ren's wrists as the ground under her
went down in a rumble. Ren hung over the raw new edge and
heard her mother's left hand crackle as one of the big rocks rolled
on it. Donatella turned white and began to pant, but she didn't let
go of her daughter until there were two other adults there to help
lift her the rest of the way.

Surgery restored most of the function of the hand, after endless
weeks of physiotherapy and a confining rehabilitative brace that
made Donatella clumsy and bitter. Ren knew that she was to blame
for her mother's pain, because she hadn't obeyed. And maybe it was
her fault that Terry had fallen. She wasn't sure: no one had told her.
But she knew that she had failed in responsibility.

She decided that she must make sure to never, never forget what she had done. She crept out to the garden and found the largest stone that she could hold with one hand, a beautiful ragged thing of gray and brown. It was a day like a painting: a hundred shades of green in the leaves and grasses and lily pads of the pond, in the vegetable tops waving from the brown grit of the soil; the sky that looked as if one of the blue colorsticks in her classroom had melted across it; the pinks and lavenders and sun-yellows of the flowers whose names she didn't know, that nodded wild and rangy on their thin stalks because her father liked them that way. The pain, when it came, was sharp and orange. She managed to hit her left hand twice before Carlos found her.

"Oh, Ren," he said, after he'd made her an ice pack and wiped her tears. "Don't hurt yourself. That won't help. The only thing that helps is to do better next time."

She waited for him to tell her how, but he only hugged her and said, "Okay?"

She wasn't sure, but she wanted to please him, so she told him, "I'll do better."

2

SOMEHOW LIFE WENT ON IN THE BAD DAYS AFTER HAL-loween. Jackal hung on to her secret. Sometimes it felt like a soft animal biting the lining of her stomach, wanting out. At odd moments, a frightened voice in her head would whisper *They're looking at me funny. Did I say something wrong? Do they know?*

She only had to stay sharp, stay frosty, a little longer. The end-of-year holidays were less than a month away, with the investiture looming behind them, and she saw it as a talisman of sorts: she would be off the island, just another Hope doing Hope things, and it would not be so hard to lie to strangers.

This morning she rode her bicycle from her apartment to the center of Ko. It was a typical early-December day, the blue sky gathering clouds at the horizon, the sun warm on her back as she pedaled. Her route traveled the Ring Highway along the coast toward the south junction, where Fortaleza Road ran north and west into the center of the island and the Ko Prime corporate campus. Although the South China Sea lolled along a reef, salty and shallow, only fifty meters to her left, it was the greenland to her right that she noticed. The hundreds of acres on this part of the island would probably not be developed for decades; the company liked to plan for growth, to marshal its resources early. This wildness was safe for years, perhaps for her whole lifetime, and there was no risk in letting herself believe that these trees belonged to her; the rough trunks, the startling soft meat of a broken branch, the knobbled twigs rising in rows like choirs. The ground belonged to her, the human-made rises and falls of root and rock, carefully random, beautiful. The flowers were hers, stuporous in their mulch: the light and the stippled shadow, the stones and the rich rot underneath them, were all part of this place that felt like part of her. For the few minutes of passing through it, she was drawn into it like a breath.

Ahead, the treeline thinned and Fortaleza Road pulled away from the coastline into a neighborhood of houses that muscled their way out of the rock, built with open spaces and expanses of E-glass to take full advantage of wind and solar energy. Beyond them rose clusters of angled apartment buildings, grouped around common sports and shopping areas—vertical communities, every bit as comfortable and modern as the executive homes. Lately, Jackal had begun to see this as the place where the company lifted itself from the ground like something protean raising a head full of teeth. Everything was constructed and furnished with company-made materials, tools, appliances, fixtures, textiles, electronics, entertainment equipment. The company name was everywhere: KO, the O flattened at top and bottom in the universal symbol for the map of the world. Everyone on the island ate food grown with Ko hydroponics technology, and relied on the Ko network to talk across the street or around the world. Jackal's mother had been part of the team that developed the "Kommunications" name and marketing campaign, and Jackal was certain that Donatella had much to do with the success of the project. Her mother had the temperament of a moray eel, which at first consideration did not seem a good fit with her position as an Assistant Director of Corporate Participation: but Jackal understood that biting down hard and fast was Donatella's path to success. "I'm not there to get my own way," Donatella would say, "just to get results." And recognition: Jackal knew her mother loved her job and the corporate pin she wore every day on her right shoulder. And her father loved her mother, and was made proud by his Dona's pride. They had given themselves to Ko long ago. And then they had given her. Riding between the apartment towers, toward the glass canyon of skyscrapers, one hundred nineteen subsidiaries' world headquarters and the twin executive towers of Ko Prime, Jackal felt two million minds turn toward her, full of Hope.

She still did not know what to do with her tension and fear. They were growing; these days, any small friction could make her cramp with anger. Carlos had called the day after the party: "*Hija*, your mother's very upset about the argument you had. She won't tell me what happened, but whatever it was, can't you forgive her? At least call her and tell her things are all right?" But Jackal couldn't. She wasn't much good at talking to anyone right now, not even Snow, who had been asking more and more often what was wrong. Just tense about the investiture, Jackal told her, and a fight with my mother. Nothing new. She was relieved when Snow said, "I won't push, at least not right now."

She parked her bike and went on with her busy morning of workshops and research. In the afternoon, she went to Esperance Park for the web's monthly game day. She thought games were stupid, mostly because she rarely won. But she knew that failing at something unimportant made people more comfortable with her, so she played. Games were an easy way to fail.

But she should have known better today. Losing wasn't so easy when a person was full to the back teeth with rage, and what had she been thinking, agreeing to play machiavelli with Tiger? In just an hour he had won three consecutive rounds with a speed and a jolly, obvious contempt that humiliated her.

She said as quietly as she could, "Tiger, ease up, okay? You're really sharking me."

"Oh, please," he said. "You're the Hope of Ko and you can't even hold your temper over a game of machiavelli? Good thing the fate of the world didn't depend on you today. You'd have lost at least a couple of fourth-world countries."

He spoke in his smiling, public voice, pitched with just the right tone to send the message *we're only playing here* to the people watching in the small plaza. He made them his audience so easily: they loved him, her web mates crowded around the table, the strangers at a respectful distance enjoying one of the last warm days of the year before the slide into January cold. Tiger was vibrant against the brushed-steel buildings that towered over this end of the park, their banks of mirrored windows washing the warm afternoon light back in dapples over the tended, careful trees: he glowed like a candle, his eyes black-bright against his golden skin. She had a moment of piercing regret that things had gone so bad between them.

"Don't they teach you anything in those process classes?" he was saying. "Feedback is an integral part of improvement, Jackal. You really ought to learn how to handle it." There was a bite to the words, and a challenge; and then he smiled in a way she recognized, and she understood that he was picturing himself on top of her, moving his hips slowly while he held her face in his hands and said—

"Stop," she said.

The smile deepened. "Oh, don't be like that," he said. "I know you like to play." And that did it. Her heart juddered hard against her breastbone once, twice, and Tiger became outlined in crimson, and she let the leash inside her slip: just this once, she thought wildly, just this one time, and lunged across the table, and broke his nose with the blade of her hand.

Ko always moved fast, particularly where Jackal was concerned: Tiger's blood was still damp on her shirt when the assistant showed her into Analin Chao's office in the Executive Two tower. Chao was short and sleek: Jackal gangled over her while they shook hands.

"Sit down." Chao waved her to an armchair that looked large enough for two of Jackal, with an ottoman conveniently canted to one side.

"No, thank you."

"Why not be comfortable?"

The furniture, upholstered in a deep blue fabric, looked slightly worn and indeed very comforting, as if it could cradle all her troubles away. From its corner on the far side of the office, the chair faced a floor-to-ceiling window that looked out to the east coast of the island. It was a clear day: Jackal could see the hazy bumps of the Hong Kong skyline on the horizon of the flat sea. A person could sit in this chair and be safe without being trapped; a person could be wombed here. But she wasn't falling for it. She had studied with the lead designers of Ko's consumer psychology division: they had even used last year's model of this chair as a class discussion topic.

She shook her head.

"Ah," Chao said, "of course, you'd be aware of the subliminals. Sorry, most people don't get that training until director level, at least. How about this one?" She pulled her own chair from behind her corner desk.

Jackal ignored it. She did not like being so easily read, and she was determined not to let this Chao disconcert her. All she wanted was to go home and curl up in a hot bath and be tired of everything. She folded her arms across her stomach, smearing a brushstroke of blood across her shirt along the underside of her left breast. She made no move to wipe it off; Chao was watching everything.

Jackal said, "Dr. Andabe is my usual counselor." That was the right note, just casual enough but still firm. Good.

Chao smiled as if Jackal had said something clever. "Yes, he is," she agreed. "He'll get copies of all my notes, of course. But Khofi is really more of an educational and motivational advisor, after all, and you're certainly past that now, don't you think? Your training is almost finished, Al Iskandariyah is less than a month away. You're about to be officially invested as a world Hope. It's important that any difficulties—" she smiled and opened her hands in a way that made those difficulties shared, "—be resolved efficiently before they complicate your taking up your new position." She sat easily on the edge of the ottoman, waved again to the chair she had pulled out for Jackal.

"Your needs are changing." She spoke earnestly, and her hands traced persuasive arcs in the cool recycled air of the room, pale against the earth tones of the smooth walls and the thick woven rug. "Ko wants to make sure you have all the support you need to make what is, after all, a very important transition. So the executive team has decided that I should be available to you from now until your investiture, at least. To be a resource, help you work out any concerns you might have. Think of me as someone to help you with managing change."

"What's your real job?" She had meant to be assertive, but it only sounded rude. She kept her hands locked around her folded arms so her fingers would not tremble.

Chao answered as if it were a reasonable question. "I'm the Executive Vice President of Organizational Development for Ko Worldwide."

Jackal opened her mouth. Nothing came out, so she shut it again. She was feeling shaky now: the adrenaline hit had faded and left her with a sour stomach and the beginning of a headache behind her right eye. Maybe she should take the chair after all. What was she doing here? Had she hurt Tiger worse than she realized? She had only meant to hit him in the face, to sting and shame him, but even that had gone wrong. There had been no

time to check the damage: two Ko security guards had snapped to
her side like stones from a slingshot, quick enough to push Tiger
back into the chair he'd kicked aside in his lurch around the table,
one hand cupped and filling with blood and the other reaching for
her, the machiavelli tiles scattering across the courtyard.

She wished she could grab the moment back and tuck it safely
into a pocket until the urge to hurt someone had passed.

"Am I in trouble?" she said.

"No one's in trouble," Chao replied smoothly. "But of course
we're concerned. You offered violence to a web mate. I'm sure you
had a very good reason, and I'd like to know what it is so that I can
help you with it."

Jackal thought bleakly, I'm too tired. But she would just have to
tough it out. She would have to find something to distract this
woman who, given her position, was almost certainly a psychia-
trist: something that would keep her from going after the real reason, which had nothing to do with Tiger and everything to do
with being a false Hope.

Chao waited, bright-eyed and relaxed.

Okay, Jackal thought. Okay. She unclasped her arms, and
plucked at her shirt. "Have you got a towel?"

Chao smiled. "Of course," she said. "There's a bathroom right
behind that door. Why don't you clean up and then we'll talk?"

"You and Tiger were lovers," Chao said matter-of-factly.

Jackal shook her head.

"It's in your record."

"We did—It was—" She shook her head again helplessly. How
to explain the horror of Halloween day, the confusion of brandy
and the desperate need to be real again? But she mustn't tell Chao
about Donatella's hideous blunder, or that the rest had happened
only because Jackal was trying to make the bad news go away. Tell

her instead about dancing like a banshee until she had dervished herself into a place where only each single, exquisite moment mattered. That was something a doctor would buy, without looking underneath. Doctors loved the discovery of demons, the moments of *I just wasn't myself*, those revealing truths that rolled over and yawned in the mud of the hindbrain. Jackal gave Chao the glow of the setting sun that stippled Tiger in gold, the way his face had stilled and then hardened when he saw her watching him. The hours after and their awareness of each other, so intoxicating, a different kind of dance. Leaving the group without looking behind her, knowing he would follow; leading him to his own apartment door, waiting, then the sudden shock of him against her with one arm stretched out to palm the lock. And then inside. The sex was a series of strobe moments, mouth here, fingers there, and she flowed through them click click click as if working a string of worry beads to count her sorrows away. Until, between breaths, she stepped off the shelf in her head where she'd been storing herself, came back into real time to find him on her, in her, his breath in her open mouth.

"What happened then?" Chao had prompted her after a moment.

What had happened was that Tiger said, "I can't believe I'm fucking the Hope of the whole bloody world," and she had heard again her mother's voice, out of control, screeching. And she hadn't been able to bear it, she had to get away. He had tried to kiss her as she was leaving and she had stopped him without a word, even when he looked confused and followed her out into the hall, calling, "Jackal, what's wrong? What did I do?" And from then on it was bad between them, just as it was between her and her mother. It was the moment when the world began to rot.

Jackal said, "Nothing happened . . . I mean, we finished, we got up off the floor, I left. End of story."

"Was the sex bad? Did he hurt or frighten you?"

Jackal began to worry with her teeth at a shred of skin beside a fingernail. "It was fine, there's nothing to tell. Really." She could feel the heat in her face.

"Then why have the two of you become increasingly hostile to each other over the last weeks? Today's incident is extreme, certainly, but it's by no means isolated from an overall pattern."

Jackal stayed silent and hoped her face did not show how trapped she felt.

"Perhaps there's some guilt there? Does Snow know about the sex with Tiger?"

"Snow and I are fine, thanks."

Chao's turn to be silent.

"Yes, she knows."

"If I asked Snow why you would happily be having sex with Tiger one day and scrubbing his blood off your hands five weeks later, what do you think she would say?"

Jackal imagined Snow in the womb chair under Chao's surgical gaze. She bit hard enough on her finger to draw blood. "She'd probably say she has no idea. Why should she know? I don't even know."

Chao said "I think you do." It wasn't a challenge so much as a plain acknowledgment, and a promise to return. "But we'll leave it for now," she continued. "We'll talk more in a day or two. I want you to do two things: first, you need to believe that I'm here to help you. I'm completely in your corner. I'll do whatever is necessary to make you all that you should be. Second, no more hitting people. I recognize that you're under stress, but today was a very serious breach of acceptable behavior. If someone is a problem, come to me. I'll fix them."

"No one's a problem," Jackal said, her mouth dry, imagining Chao turned loose on her mother. "I'm tense about the investiture and I drank too much and made a stupid mistake then and another one today. I'm sorry about it. There's no excuse. It's a web matter, we'll sort it out there."

"Fine, if that's what you want. In the meantime, we'll schedule a stress management refresher for you. You'll get an e-mail."

"Fine," Jackal said, with an inward sigh. She hated those classes; they were silly and obvious and only made her more angry. But if it was the price to keep this woman off her back, then she would pay.

After the calm of Analin Chao's office, the lobby of the executive building seemed stuffed with people; thousands of them, moving purposefully in their business costumes as their footsteps and voices ricocheted off the flagstone floors and the six-meter-tall glass windows. Home was a half-hour ride across the island. Jackal stopped, wondering if her bike was still in the park.

"Ms. Segura." The guard had come up in her blind spot. His polite, professional voice matched the shuttered face and the body armor and the Ko Security insignia. "Dr. Chao has asked that you be given an escort to the destination of your choice. If you'll come with me."

By now he would have registered her swollen eyes and the brown blotches on her shirt. He had probably even noticed her bleeding hangnail. He did not touch her, but gestured across the atrium to a set of doors on the far wall. "There's a shuttle van in the west parking lot."

He stepped back slightly to let her walk in front of him. It was important, that difference between following and leading. In Al Iskandariyah she would follow a security escort, depending upon them for her sense of location until she was fully acclimated into the structure of the Earth Government. Then the balance of power would shift so that she would only receive guidance if she asked for it. But Ko was already her place; on Ko, she led. If the guard thought she needed a wedge through the crowd, he would call for support and then wait until the way was clear before allowing her to proceed. But she never had a problem finding a path on Ko. Everyone got out of her way. They smiled politely, maybe nodded, but they never looked too long and they always stepped aside. The problem was that she always had to know where she wanted to go.

People eddied between elevators and escalators and the entrances of the atrium shops, the café that served thick coffee and beignets and never closed. Everyone moved to a purpose, except for one person leaning against a tiled wall near the south tower elevators. Jackal looked again.

She barely noticed as the people-stream opened a channel for her. She simply found the straight line between her and Snow and started walking. Snow met her halfway and pulled her close abruptly, without a word: Jackal stood with her head in the place where Snow's overshirt hollowed against a sharp collarbone.

"How'd you know I was here?" she said finally.

"I always know where you are." Snow squeezed her shoulder. "Bear called me. Come on, let's go."

Jackal straightened and found the guard right behind her. "It's okay. Snow will take me home."

"I was told to accompany you."

She gave him a look. "And I'm telling you that Snow will take me home."

"Ah. Of course. I'll inform Dr. Chao."

"You do that," Jackal said, and took Snow's hand.

Snow hop-stepped to catch up. "He's only doing his job."

"Then he should learn when to stop doing it."

They pushed through the south door into the thin light of the late afternoon. "The look," Snow said, "really works better with just one eyebrow."

"You always say that. I can't help it if I don't have the single-brow gene."

"You seem to have the martial arts recessive."

Jackal sighed.

"Do you want to talk about it?"

And she did, desperately: wanted to open her mouth and let the words fall out, *Hope* and *Ko* and *lies*. And *I'm afraid*. Instead she looked up to the daytime moon blooming over Esperance Park. "Not right now," she said.

"Do you want to go home?"

Jackal shook her head helplessly. "Don't know what I want."

"Doesn't matter," Snow answered. "When we start doing something you don't like, you can tell me."

Jackal stayed quiet and let herself be led to the parking lot. Snow bundled her into the passenger seat of a dormitory car parked in the No Stop zone; Jackal's bike was wedged into the trunk. Snow said, "Don't step on the bag," and in a canvas backpack on the floor, Jackal found two bottles of red wine and four messy sandwiches clumsily wrapped in a kitchen towel.

"Mmm. Where are we going?"

"Well, I thought, it's a lovely December afternoon. You just punched out a web mate and got yourself a ten-second segment on twenty thousand Who's News broadcasts around the world. We have corned beef sandwiches and some not-very-good Australian cabernet." Snow shrugged and looked at Jackal sideways. "There's really no point in trying to do anything sensible. Beach okay with you?"

Jackal felt her shoulders drop fractionally and she grinned, the fierce show of teeth that went with the name and her wild dark hair and eyes. Snow drove silently, her eyes colorless and remote in her pale face. Jackal thought, she's so beautiful.

"Did we just choose our web names brilliantly, or did we all grow into them, do you think?"

That earned her a quick look, and Snow's eyes narrowed as she turned her face back to the road, but Jackal knew that only half her attention was on driving now. Good: she liked making Snow think. She watched through the windshield as the car pushed the road ahead of itself like a dog nosing a ball, unrolling the way to the end of Ko, while Snow tapped a complicated rhythm on the steering wheel and shook her head every so often.

Snow stopped the car on a patch of gravel close to the place where the dunes began their slow hump to the sea. The air was cooler here, slow and full of salt, dark brine on the back of Jackal's tongue. She hoisted the carrybag and Snow pulled a blanket from the trunk, and they turned automatically toward the path that led up to the cliffs.

They spread the blanket by a stagger of boulders that deflected some of the breeze. The sun was setting quickly; Snow dialed her portable lamp to low, so there was just enough light to see the cliff edge fifteen feet away. Jackal ignored the sandwiches and went straight for the wine, then fumbled in the bottom of the bag. "Corkscrew?"

Snow snorted, took the bottle and held it in the crook of her right arm while she tweezered her thumb and index finger around the nail of her left little finger. She tugged hard: the nail extruded a half inch and then folded out of her fingertip like an accordion. She pulled it out to a three inch length and twisted; the sections locked into a smooth spike that she used to slit the foil covering and skewer the cork. She handed Jackal the bottle and worked the cork slowly off her nail, watching Jackal watch her. "It's never too late to be your own best tool," she said.

Jackal raised both eyebrows again. "I don't need a corkscrew that badly."

"It's more than a corkscrew. Anyway, that's not the point."

Jackal turned up her hands in a way that said *Fine, we've had this discussion before*. She drank: the wine made the inside of her mouth feel hollow and large. She settled as best she could against a rock, drank again, rolling the tannin around her tongue and enjoying the warmth of the wine in her chest. They traded the bottle back and forth in silence for a longish time.

"I feel differently about it than I used to," Snow said after a while. She sat opposite Jackal with her back against a squat pillar of stone, her knees drawn up and her head bent. Long fingers of hair had worked themselves loose from the clip she always wore, that looked like carved ivory, the same pale yellow as the hair it bound. Snow didn't care that it shocked people; having assured herself the ivory wasn't real, she had no need to reassure anyone else. Jackal had seen Snow leave people in mid-sentence, or tasks not quite finished, or holomovies just before the final scene, if it occurred to her that there was something else she should be doing. Where her mind leapt, her body followed with a singleness of purpose that had at some point upset almost everyone who knew her. Except for Carlos, who told Jackal, "It's not true that Snow is easily distracted. In fact, I'd say she was the most focused person I've ever met. It just bothers people when she is so clearly not focused on them."

Snow was studying her hand, the little finger and the white oval face of the digital display set into her wrist, that could be programmed to tell her the time and temperature and emergency call numbers for any city in the world. "It was a practical thing," she said. "They're tools, they're useful." She lowered her knees into a tailor's seat and braced her hands on them, fingers splayed, unusually gold in the light of the lamp. "But it turns out it's more than that," she continued slowly, turning her hands in the light. "They make me feel, I don't know . . . elegant, enhanced. Like Jaoli on my team who wears silk panties under her coveralls when she's out installing the power grid in a manufacturing plant. I'm starting to think they make me feel closer to some ideas I have about myself, that I'm competent and also . . ." She frowned, rubbed her fingers together as if she could snap the thought into coherence. "I don't think I'd want something I couldn't use some-how. The cosmetic stuff doesn't work for me. But maybe being able to screw a steel horn into your forehead does the same thing for those folks that my polymer nail does for me. Maybe it gets them closer to themselves."

They had drunk the bottle dry. Snow opened the other; Jackal watched her face, the quiet satisfaction as she made short work of the cork and collapsed the nail back into the bone and steel pocket built inside her fingertip.

"How do you know that's who you really are?" Jackal asked fi-nally.

Snow nodded. "That's the same question as the one you asked before, about names." Jackal blinked: she had forgotten. She was struck again by Snow's ability to connect one idea to another: she imagined Snow's mind as an Escher construct, like the series of waterfalls that flowed back up into themselves, nothing ever lost.

"It's funny that we don't talk about names in the web," Snow said. "Maybe they're just so much a part of who we are that we don't wonder about them. You've always been Jackal to me. I can barely remember a time when you were Ren." She peered at Jackal. "Why did you choose Jackal? You could've had any name you wanted, why that one?"

It was full dark now; still early, but the black sky and full moon and the phosphorescent surf had the feeling of late night, remote and slightly out of tune. It reminded her of a day she had come un-expectedly upon Donatella in one of the corporate offices, and the dislocating instant before her mother recognized her. The night world looked on her with the same blankness she had seen in her mother's eyes.

"It'll start getting cold soon," she told Snow. "Can you feel it coming on? I hated being cold when I was little. I didn't under-stand how other people could bear it. Then I figured out that they couldn't—that's why they put on a hundred layers of clothes and drank hot soup all the time. And I don't like being bundled up, I can't move with so many layers under my arms, and anything tight around my neck makes me feel like I can't breathe. So now being cold is really a choice to not wrap myself up like something that's been rolled in too much dough.

"But I didn't know that when I was little. I just spent months being angry with the weather and with my parents for making me go out in it." She shook her head, remembering.

Snow smiled and passed her the bottle. "I can picture it. Grumpy little Jackal."

"Grumpy little Ren. Jackal came later."

"You didn't have the name, but you were still the person who hated being cold."

Jackal considered this. "Okay," she answered finally. "But it did make a difference about the name. In February after I turned twelve, when it was decided that our web names would be nature-based, my mother started dragging in all the books and holomovies she could find. We went to the zoo and the arboretum seven times that month so that I could make an informed decision."

"Your mother likes to have a plan," Snow said dryly.

"You have no idea. She researched nature symbology in world religions. She dug up information on the way that various animals are regarded culturally by the member countries of the Earth Government Permanent Council. She said that it was important that my name be a symbol that everyone in the world could relate to, could draw some measure of hope from. She even got one of the Jungians from Educational Games to talk to her about the iconic roles of elements and weather descriptives in the unconscious."

"She's got the determination gene."

"She's got it twice. So eventually she drew up a shortlist of names, ranked in order of maximum cross-cultural positive impact combined with religious inferences of leadership, strength, and wisdom. Stop laughing."

"I can't. Really, I can't . . . here, take this before I spill any more." Jackal smiled and drank.

Snow said, "I guess Mouse wasn't at the top of the list."

"Nope."

"Emu."

Jackal shook her head.

"Swamp thing."

"If my mother had her way, you'd be calling me Elephant."

Snow gave a delighted hoot, and Jackal began to giggle helplessly. They ended up on their backs in the sand, heads together, their laughter bubbling up toward the sky. Jackal imagined the vapor of their breath adding a layer to the moon-bright cirrus trails overhead, their merriment carried in the belly of a cloud until it rained down in some far-off spot. Today of all days, I can't believe I'm laughing, she thought. Bless Snow.

"Where are those sandwiches?" she demanded. "I'm starving. Hey, don't drink all the wine."

"So what was wrong with Elephant?"

"You mean apart from the fact that my mother wanted it so bad?"

Snow crooked her head. "Was that it?"

Jackal thought about it around another mouthful. "I suppose it was a little. It wasn't so much that I would have said no to anything she came up with. . . . It was more that all her choices seemed so wrong for me. She kept saying 'Oh, they're only my ideas, little one, you make your own choice.' But it was so clear even then that she wanted me to choose to be an elephant or an eagle or an oak. And I just wanted a name, you know? I didn't want to wear a word like some kind of world responsibility around my neck for the rest of my life. And it was winter, and I was tired of being cold, and I didn't know what I was, only what I wasn't. I sure wasn't anything on her list. So I finally sorted out all the books that described warm-weather climates and fauna, and opened them at random. One of them said that jackals were related to wolves and ran in packs and were scavengers, and it said—I'll never forget this—it said 'The jackal's cry is even more terrifying than that of the hyena.' And I thought, that's what I want. I want to run with my web and be wild, survive anywhere, and I want everyone to get out of the way when I yell."

"Well," Snow said finally.

"I was only twelve."

"A rebel."

"I was just mad at everything." She was getting a crick in her neck; she stretched hard and felt cool air seep into the spaces where her clothes pulled back from her wrists and ankles.

"What do you think a rebel is?" Snow said matter-of-factly. And then, dismissively, surprising Jackal, "Your mother has no imagination. But there's your answer, anyway. You picked a name because it meant something you wanted to be, not something you were. It suits you because you grew into it. Maybe you'd be different if you were Elephant." She unwrapped a sandwich, examined it a moment; then folded back a corner of the bread and began to pick out and nibble bits of corned beef. "Everyone would expect you to be wise and thoughtful. Deliberate. Have thick legs." Snow was piked, Jackal realized, and then saw the second bottle standing in the dead-soldier position in a carefully built dome of sand next to Snow's right knee. "So," she continued, "are you like that jackal in the book?"

"I don't know. I guess I won't know for a while. . . . Have you ever seen someone who looked like they grew into exactly the right face for them? That's what I want. I don't think I have it yet."

"So what does the right face of a Hope look like? Jackal, what's the—oh, here, let me help. Poor baby. I'm right here. Take this, wipe your mouth. Damn all cheap wine. Let's get you home."

She could feel Snow's drunken worry as she drove, trying to

watch Jackal and keep on the road at the same time. Jackal felt dizzy, and when she closed her eyes she saw Tiger, Chao, her mother. . . .

"Stop the car," she said thickly, and Snow made a little sound and wobbled the car to the side of the road. Jackal opened her door and leaned her head out. When she was done, she wiped her mouth on the hem of her tunic even though the cloth was gritty with sand. The cool air on her face did not make her any less drunk, but it steadied her. She put her mother and Tiger and the rest of it back into its particular box inside her, clamped the lid tight. She was so tired.

"Take me home," she said. "I'm sorry I hit Tiger and I don't want to feel bad, I want to go home and have mad sex and then just hold onto you, you're the only good thing in the whole fucking world right now."

"Okay, honey." Snow leaned over and kissed Jackal on the side of the mouth, said pragmatically, "But you'll have to brush your teeth first," and put the car into gear. Jackal leaned back. The night sky above her was clear now: all that joy gone, sobbed up into the clouds that the cold winds of Ko had blown to shreds. Winter was coming.

3

SHE DID NOT WANT TO FACE THE DAY. SHE HATED MORN-
ings, especially the bright, cheerful ones that bustled in before a
person was ready; but the insistent hand on her hip would not let
her fall back into unconsciousness.

"Jackal. Jackal, wake up."

She found herself facedown, so tangled in her sheet that she
could barely move. Her favorite woven blanket, worn from long
use, was wrapped around her. Her feet and calves were rough
with bits of sand, and her throat felt as if she'd eaten a handful.

"How are you?" Snow asked gently.

Jackal thought about it. "Not so bad," she said finally, a little
surprised.

"That's good." Snow stroked her head.

"Can I have just another hour? I didn't get enough sleep."

A wicked smile from Snow. "No one to blame but yourself."

"And you," Jackal said, smiling back. She loved sex with Snow,
the two-step of safety and free-fall, the immediacy and intensity of
their bodies straining and sweaty, hips and bellies and breasts
against each other. It made Jackal feel bigger than herself, larger
in the world. Her body was sore, but her heart was not as bruised
as it had been.

She watched Snow move to the wide window at the east end of the room and open it to a sky like gossamer over the South China Sea, sheets of green-gray clouds lit by stripes of sunlight. A slow, warm breeze brought salt and seabird voices into the room. Jackal loved her window, and the terrace that looked over the sea toward Hong Kong and Kowloon beyond. The entire apartment block curved long and low around this part of the island coast, full of light and space, wood and stone, water and wind, built especially for her web because she was the Hope; like her parents' house close by on the other side of the greenbelt, nestled in the dunes, also beautiful, a special growing-up place for the special child of Ko.

Snow said, "It's after nine. You'll be late for Neill if we don't hurry."

That brought Jackal out of bed in spite of her aches and the need for more sleep. She still remembered the first time she had been punished in school: little Ren, hair windblown straight out from her head, breathless from running but still late, made to stand in front of the class while Mr. Tirani instructed the other children to tell her, one at a time, "It's wrong to keep others waiting." Then she was required to apologize, and thank her classmates for their help. Afterwards, he took her aside and dried her tears, saying, "You have a very big responsibility, Ren, even though you're still a little girl. But we will all help you be equal to it."

Now Tirani was one of the people that stepped out of her way when she passed by; but it was still a lesson well learned. So she rooted through her closet until she found loose khaki trousers and an oversized shirt in burgundy and deep blue, then carried the clothes into the small square living room and dug a clean pair of underwear out of the basket pushed against a wall. She pulled scuffed brown boots with worn heels from under the big chair that was almost identical to the one in Chao's office. These days she liked clothes she could move in without pinching a breast or turning an ankle, that could be pushed up over her elbows or crumpled and stuffed into a carrybag. She followed fashion but never caught up with it—now who had first said that? Someone in the web: was it Bat, or maybe Tiger? No, she didn't want to think about Tiger, his bright blood and the shock on his face.

"Where's my other sock?"

Snow shrugged. Jackal began turning over the chair cushions.

"Get another pair."

"I want these, they go with my shirt." A part of her was surprised to find herself sounding so ordinary, as if nothing much had happened, as if she had not yesterday taken a long step closer to a dangerous edge.

"What's that on the bookshelf? No, the other one."

She put the two socks together just to make sure they matched, and then dressed in a storm of flapping sleeves and a boot that tried to get away and had to be chased across the room. Snow stayed against a wall and watched in amusement as Jackal hunted it down. The boot was dirty, but there was no time to polish it. Maybe no one would notice. Ah, she remembered the fashion remark now: it was Mist, in one of her look-down-her-nose moments. And what kind of a stupid name is Mist, anyway, Jackal thought for the thousand-and-first time. She was sure that Mist would end up in a public-relations job that involved many dinners with competitively dressed people, while the rest of her department did whatever actual work there might be. And Mist would probably come to Jackal for favors, fixes, confident that whatever she asked would be done.

And so it would be. Jackal sighed. Mist was a web mate, and it didn't matter if she was also profoundly irritating. "Say, do you think Mist is the most annoying person in the whole world, or just this part of it?" she asked Snow as she pulled on her second boot.

"I think Mist will be less annoying after breakfast. Bring an apple."

It was a good omen that they found seats together on the bus. She really did feel a little better, as if she'd sicked up some of the poison inside her along with the wine. She still hated the vulnerability and the secrecy; it was almost unthinkable not to share this with Snow, if no one else. But she couldn't risk making Snow a target for Ko. If it came right down to it, she'd give up her mother in a heartbeat to protect Snow. Oddly, the realization made her feel more grounded than she had for a while. She knew what she had to do. She had her priorities. She ate her apple and cautiously allowed herself to feel a bit more cheerful.

Snow was somewhere in her own head, doubtless thinking elegant, complex thoughts. Jackal nudged her with an elbow. "Who's the smartest?" she asked, smacking the words around the last bite of apple.

"This month, I think it's Bat." Snow smiled back. "But you're pretty smart."

"Who's the most likely to succeed?" It was a new question, and she could see the moment of surprise before Snow answered, in a gentler voice, "You are, Jackal. Everyone knows that." Snow took the apple core out of Jackal's hand and dropped it carelessly into her own pocket, and then she leaned in to kiss Jackal. "You'll be a great Hope," she said quietly. "The things you do will shape the world. You are smart and stubborn and brave. Forget about Tiger. Oh, don't look at me like that, I've seen how he rides you. He's an asshole. You're the Hope. Now here's your stop. Go do Hope stuff and I'll see you later."

"You know," Jackal said after a moment, "you just astonish me. Bless you twice. Oh, hell," she added as her stop slid by. She scrambled out of her seat, calling to the driver to wait, and by the time she'd collected herself out on the sidewalk, the bus was purring away and she could only wave after it and hope that Snow saw. If she could have put her heart on a stick, she would have given it to Snow right there in the aisle. But no, she thought, I'll need it if I'm going to do the right things, if I'm going to be a good Hope. I can still be a good Hope. I just have to work a little harder and be a little braver. And I can. I can.

Jackal was the youngest person by at least ten years in Neill's workshop, the only one who didn't have to juggle a full-time job schedule to keep up with classes. Everyone else was a serious runner on the Ko management track, people chosen for perceived long-distance stamina rather than sprinting ability. The company's strategy, Jackal had come to understand, was to offer power to people who were experienced enough to make quick decisions out of confidence in their own reference points, rather than rashness or received wisdom. Youth was almost never an advantage at Ko.

She remembered having this macroscopic realization: it was the first time she had been able to articulate an original perception about the company, about business strategy in general, rather than parroting back the theories of her teachers. Khofi Andabe had grinned with pleasure at their weekly review session. "Good for you, Fraulein Schakal," he said, leaning back far enough in his chair to make it creak in distress. It was his game to name her in the dozen languages that he knew—at their first meeting, when Jackal began her training in earnest at the age of thirteen, he had leaned across his office desk with his square face resting on his big fists and said, "*Eh bien*, Jackal," except that he pronounced it *zhaKAL*. "Zhakal," he had said again. "An unexpected naming, to be sure." Then he had smiled and she had liked him. The years of working together had brought her from liking to trust, and now Andabe was almost like a part of her own web. His approval mattered; she enjoyed making him grin.

Good work, he had said almost a year ago about her new understanding, and the next week had entered her into Neill's workshop series in activity management.

"Khofi, no," she gasped when he told her.

"And why not?"

"I'm not ready."

"Nonsense. I am to say when you are ready, and I have said. Neill has agreed. It is arranged." He wiped his hands against each other and then spread them as if this would show her that the thing was done.

"It's too advanced." God, her mother had only just been through it herself two years ago, after how many years of building an experience base and a track record of successful smaller projects. She'll be pissed, Jackal thought in passing.

Khofi said, "You are ready for this training. It is necessary. You will need to know these things as the Hope of Ko."

"Why?"

"You will understand when you have completed the series, when you have these skills."

"You're supposed to be my advisor. How come you won't ever tell me why I'm supposed to be learning these things? Maybe all the other Hopes are studying macroengineering or combinatorial mathematics or zero-gee furniture design."

"I doubt this, Zhakal."

"Well, then, you know more about it than I do."

Andabe delivered his sigh of disappointment and dismay, a labored, breathy whistle through a pursed bottom lip. It didn't impress her anymore, and she was exasperated enough to tell him so.

"This is how I know you are ready," he said smugly, and that was the end of the discussion.

Two days later she headed through Esperance Park toward the cart of the ice cream man, in his usual place along the grass at the west end of the biggest fountain. He was a Ko employee like everyone else, but he wore his ID skin meld unobtrusively high on his wrist, up under his long sleeves, and behaved instead as if he and his cart had just happened upon this spot for the first and only time in a long and varied journey. His ice cream was rich and surprising, a single, different flavor each day in crunchy brown waffle cones.

Two strangers offered to let her into the line. She refused with a smile and stood at the end behind a man whom she noticed primarily because he was as anonymous as anyone she'd ever seen on the island. Most adults on Ko used clothing to signal their working function or status. She knew enough of the code, from a lifetime's worth of dinners with Donatella, to be genuinely confused by the man in front of her.

He turned around enough that she could see about three quarters of his face: white, no clear ethnic markers. Even his sunglasses were unremarkable. "So, what do you think?" he asked.

It was too late to pretend she wasn't puzzled, so she turned her bewilderment into a smile that was meant to be an invitation rather than a criticism. "I'm sorry," she replied, with just a twist of question at the end.

"What kind is it today?"

"Ah. Well, let's see. He's wearing an orange hat, that's a clue. Could be orange, tangerine, peach melba. I'm always hopeful for mango sorbet, myself."

"Hmm, that's very good," he said, and turned all the way around, twisting the glasses off his face. "The way you finished with that bit about the sorbet, and the head nod, that's good. It gives the other person a way to stop the chitchat right there if they've run out of things to say. I imagine you get more than your share of people who don't know a graceful way out of a conversation. Any rate, you'll be fine."

"I'm sorry?" she said again, and this time it was an obvious question.

"Ah," he answered, and she heard her own vocal strategies done better. "Please excuse me. I'm Gavin Neill, I run some workshops on activity management. You're joining us soon, aren't you? Wonderful. I'm glad we could meet this way, it's so much nicer to have an idea of what people are like before we all start working together." And he told her a funny story about the most unproductive team ever recorded by company measurement specialists. ". . . and instead they ended up with ten thousand cases of canned organic tomatoes."

"Oh, no," Jackal laughed. "What happened to them?"

"I'm sure they're still in the warehouse. The tomatoes, not the team. No one will touch them, they carry the curse of the one hundred percent error rate." Did he mean the team or the tomatoes that time, she wondered, but he only smiled and said, "So, here we are. Not mango today, I'm afraid." He smiled again and paid for his cone, stepped out of line. "Nice to meet you. See you soon." She watched him move away; he walked with his head back as if he were enjoying the day and the tangerine taste in his mouth.

The first morning of the workshop, all the students turned up twenty minutes early. The conference room was spacious, with a long oval table that faced an enormous white board and a series of clean flip chart pads hung around the walls. Giant windows looked out across a section of the corporate complex. Jackal could see into offices in a handful of other buildings: people working, meeting, scribbling on their white boards.

She turned to the food table and poured herself a cup of coffee. The trays of pastries and fruit didn't tempt her—she was too nervous to eat—but food was always a good way of meeting people. There were fifteen trainees in addition to her, all of whom were introducing themselves around the room in the brisk manner that she associated with people bursting with business purpose, as if getting everyone's name was one item on a very long task list. Jackal promptly forgot who they all were, but she could tell they were all, without exception, surprised to find her there. Everyone did the Hope routine with her, deferring to her and speaking in polite, formal sentences that made her feel like a little girl dressed up in oversized clothes: "Well, it's very good to have you with us, Ms. Segura, and may I ask your opinion about quantifying return on investment for corporate training?" When she realized that everyone was still standing only because they were waiting for her to choose her seat at the table, she sighed and plomped her rucksack down at the nearest place. "Look, folks," she said as lightly as she could, "I'm a little out of my depth here and most of you have a lot more training than I do, but I really need this class to help me with my job and it would make it a lot easier if you could just call me Jackal." It didn't really say what she meant, but it seemed to do the trick: the others began to settle down around her, and the talk became less stiff.

One of the junior managers confessed that he wasn't sure what to expect from the training.

"Oh, don't worry," an older woman told him, in a tone that was equivalent enough to a motherly pat on the arm to make Jackal wince. The junior man smiled, although not, Jackal thought, very well. "He's really very nice," the woman went on. "I happened to meet him last week. He attended one of our Renaissance choir performances and recognized my name on the program."

It didn't take long to discover that they had all happened to meet Neill recently. The junior man said slowly, "It seems so manipulative." Jackal, silent and watchful, was inclined to agree, but some of the others argued, including the woman who had spoken first. "Didn't it make you feel better?" she asked. "It certainly helped me walk in here today."

Jackal thought about that: it was true that she'd been less anxious about the workshop since laughing with Neill over the tomatoes. She realized that she had developed a little script in her head of how this morning might play out: herself in a room of strangers, Neill entering, looking over the room, catching her eye and acknowledging her, giving her a metaphorical place at his table. God, I've been rehearsing for it, she thought, and chuckled at herself. She saw the man directly across the table become curious, eyebrows wrinkling over blue eyes.

"I was just thinking it only seems manipulative because he did it with everyone. I bet we all think it was really nice of him. We just expected to be special on an individual level when we walked in here."

"Hmm," he said. "You might be right."

"Tell me your name again? I'm Jackal Segura." She leaned across the table and offered her hand.

"Jordie Myers."

"What do you—" But Neill walked in, and she shut up and straightened in her chair along with everyone else.

He gave a nod that managed to include everyone individually on his way to the white board, where he stopped only long enough to stuff a handful of colored markers into one loose pocket. Jackal ran a hand over her own trousers, cut close out of the dayglo leathers that were still trendy in lots of places, no matter what Mist said . . . she liked the way they looked, but they were tight. She wiggled in her seat, looked at Neill's clothes more closely.

"So," he said, cocking his head to one side and smiling a little, "what have you learned so far?"

No one said a word. It reassured Jackal that managers half again her age would still rather look down at the table than be the first person to make a mistake. Neill let them admire the wood grain for at least fifteen seconds before he spoke again. "Did my mother dress me funny today?"

Everyone looked; everyone laughed tentatively.

He made a face. "It must be something. None of you will talk to me."

And that was all it took to make the group relax; people shifted, reached for their drinks, became engaged with him. "So, what have you got from this morning up to this point? Anything? Jordie."

"Well, we know that you made an effort to meet everyone before the first session."

"Mm hmm," Neill said, nodding encouragingly. He moved to one of the flip charts, wrote *meet in advance* in red block letters. "And what's the benefit in that?" And they were off. Before Jackal had time to become too self-conscious, she was caught up in a six-way discussion of techniques for building a team fast and informally. Neill encouraged everyone's ideas and wrote them all on the flip chart pages, never missing a thought even though he was also playing traffic manager, calling on people in order and making sure they all had a chance to speak. When he put the pen down, there were at least four chart pages stuck to the walls by the adhesive strips on their backs.

He said, "It looks like you learned something after all." Jackal saw how that pleased everyone at the table. And she got the point: in less than an hour, sixteen strangers had generated some four dozen strategies for getting people to be more productive together.

She looked up to find Neill watching her, a brief evaluative look like being brushed with sandpaper. She was suddenly nervous again.

He poured himself a glass of grapefruit juice and found an empty chair near the top of the oval: now he was one of the group. He bent forward, and Jackal leaned toward him with the rest. He spread his hands: his fingers were stained with ink, and he used them to punctuate his words with color.

"You're here to learn what makes an activity successful. So what is it? What are we really talking about here?" He waved at the words on the walls.

"Teams?" ventured a woman with a large mouth and a soft voice.

"More strategic," Neill replied.

"Results," Jackal said.

"That's your mother talking," Neill said.

"People," Jordie volunteered.

"What about them?"

No one spoke. Neill took a moment and a swallow of juice. "What do people have to do with projects?"

Jackal shrugged, confused. "They do the work."

"So what?" he said, pointing a green fingertip at her. "You think that's all there is to it, a bunch of people doing a bunch of work?"

She flushed. "No—" she began, but was interrupted by Sawyer, the one she'd begun to think of as Junior Man. "No," he said, echoing her. "Someone has to tell them what to do."

"Why?"

"Because they might do it wrong."

"People are stupid?"

That upset Sawyer and everyone else: there was a chorus of *no* and *that's not what he meant* while people waved their arms and frowned. Neill sat back and drank more juice and said nothing, just watched while the rest of them wrangled their way through definitions of "stupid" and "work" and then moved on to "management." The talk became less and less controlled, until two or three people were speaking over each other, and two or three others had simply checked out of the discussion altogether. Jordie shook his head, then shook it again: he looked like a kettle building up a snoutful of steam. Jackal ignored the stew of noise for a minute to chart his emotional journey by the changes in his face and body, to recognize the moment he decided that he could no longer sit still. He braced both palms against the edge of the table, squared his shoulders. "Okay—"

The woman on his right, Senior Woman, held up her left index finger in front of his face in a *stop* signal, while she talked right over him: she and a visibly angry woman in a powered wheelchair were engaged in the business equivalent of a toe-to-toe argument, and Senior Woman seemed intent on winning by volume. "Wait a minute," Jordie said, and Senior Woman turned on him and snapped, "Do you mind? I'm not finished here."

Time to move, Jackal thought.

"All right," she said in a moderately loud voice. No one at the table seemed to notice that she had spoken, except Neill. He seemed amused. Jackal wasn't: it had been a long time since she had needed to shout. She waited for Neill to take back the meeting, but instead he slowly leaned back in his chair and played with his empty juice glass, looking for all the world like someone settling in for a good long show.

She took a deep breath and reached for what Donatella called the power voice. "All *right*, people." She knew enough to use her stomach, not her throat, so the sound was broad rather than high, even though a bit wobbly. Some of the people who had been talking trailed off; those who had disengaged sat up in their chairs and looked at her doubtfully. Senior Woman was still yammering on. Jackal exchanged glances with Jordie; he shook his head again.

Jackal stood up and leaned across the table, bracing herself against her hands. Senior Woman sensed the motion and turned to find Jackal close enough to spit on.

"Excuse me," said Jackal quietly, "could I just get your attention for a minute?" When Senior Woman started to sputter, Jackal held up her finger. Senior Woman's lips thinned; the woman beside her smiled down at her own lap.

Jackal motioned to Jordie as she sat down, handing him the heavy silence.

"Okay," he began again. "This doesn't seem very productive to me. Two out of every three meetings I go to are exactly like this, and nothing ever gets done. I'll bet some of us can't even remember our original topic."

A gray-haired man with skin darker than Jackal's said, "I can. It was the question of what makes projects successful."

"Well, this isn't it."

"No," the other man agreed. "This is what screws them up. This kind of thing makes people go out of their way to avoid working with each other."

Neill was listening closely now, his juice glass pushed to one side.

"So part of the trick is to keep them working together." That from the woman who'd been fighting with Senior Woman; she gave her sparring partner a rueful look.

"Yes," Jordie said. "And you can't just bully them into it. Theory X doesn't apply anymore. You have to make them willing to do it."

Neill spoke then. "And how do you do that?"

He waited. No one answered for a full minute.

"That is what you are here to learn," he said. He spoke slowly and deliberately. "There are two things I have to teach you about managing activities: influence and structure. Influence in this context is helping people perceive the work you need from them as meaningful and constructive. Structure is setting up this work in the way that best ensures success and therefore reinforces their choice to do it. Influence and structure," he repeated, and underlined them with ink-fingered gestures: Jackal wondered if she would always see *influence* as a blue stroke. Or perhaps she would just see Neill's face, intent and empty of concern.

"You've just participated in one work experience based on influence and structure, and one that was not. It's up to you to decide which you found more productive. These two concepts will be the foundation of our learning. They are complex skills, both to acquire and to apply. They are the bridge between people and results. They are not theories: theories are garbage and I don't want to hear yours. And they are not negotiable. If you don't see the value, don't return: there will be no hard feelings. Now go off and think about it. Be back here at ten tomorrow morning if you're coming back."

Everyone sat like animals on the road gone lamp-eyed in on-coming headlights, until Neill began shepherding them gently out the door. Jackal found herself with Jordie, Sawyer, the woman with the soft voice, and the woman in the wheelchair, who was called Ng Mai and who expertly steered them to a noodle café about a half-kilometer further inside the complex.

"Well," Jordie said when they had ordered their food and were all cradling cups of green tea. The sun shone warm on Jackal's back. She breathed in the smell of soy and onion that wafted through the swinging kitchen door.

"Mm hmm," Mai answered.

"Instructive," the other woman said, her voice even softer through the steam of the tea.

"I don't like it," Sawyer said slowly. He made a face. "I know, I know, he's the great Neill and I'm a second-tier manager and I'm lucky to be here. My boss and her boss and her boss have all made that very clear." He looked down as he spoke, tracing circles on the plastic tablecloth with his fingernail. "But it's so cold. Influence and structure." He twisted his mouth around the words. "Manip-ulation and control, more like. Let's at least be honest."

Jordie frowned. "But it's not. It's not manipulation. You saw yourself how different it was when he ran the session and when he just sat back. It was better when he did it. It was great. He had, I don't know—he had this vision of how it ought to go and he made it happen." He leaned so far across the small table that he was in danger of sweeping all the cups away, and his hair feathered out of its meticulous topknot. He cares about this a lot, Jackal thought. She tasted it, like something she'd swallowed with her tea: what did she care about that much? It struck her again how much older than her they all were. Did surety of purpose come with age? How do they know what they want, she wondered, watching Jordie cresting on his own wavefront, earnest and emphatic, making even Sawyer smile faintly and reconsider. Jackal already knew she'd go back to the class: Khofi said she needed this to be the Hope, and it was the first tangible direction Ko had ever pointed her in, even if they hadn't yet actually told her where she was going. But there was a destination, and Neill was already beginning to assess her ability to reach it. Those were the sandpaper moments. She predicted her future: a little extra attention, more opportunities to practice, more direct coaching. More praise than the others when it was needed to motivate her. A larger share of criticism, when it was time to refine and integrate her understanding. Neill would make sure she learned.

And she loved it. Even with too little sleep and apple lumps in her stomach, she hurried toward it. The work was like nitrogen in her blood, a fizzing feeling when she did well. Here she felt confident, real. Here she felt safe. When she doubted herself and her ability to play the role that she was being customized for, she pushed herself harder, staked out another skill and skinned it and sucked it from the guts down to the marrow. It nourished her spirit in the same way that Snow sustained her heart.

She ran all the way from the bus. Neill wouldn't wait for her, Hope or not. He always started on time: it was one of what he called the hard rules, the ones with no flex. Middle managers fostered the rumor that he had once opened a strategy meeting at the appointed time, without the CEO of Ko. He was still outlining his role as the facilitator and reviewing the proposed agenda when Smith stepped into the room. Jackal imagined that had been a great relief for the other executives, who were probably trying to decide whether to actually do business without the Chief or to piss off Neill at the start of the most delicate political activity of the Ko planning year. The story went that Neill had peremptorily waved Smith up to the head of the table without pausing his monologue; and that while the rest of the room held its collective breath, Smith had simply smiled in a

way that could have been either polite apology or confident amusement, and taken her seat. Most of Ko scoffed at this as embellish-
ment, but Donatella had been in the room, serving as the meeting's
recorder. Lately whenever Jackal got too scared, she tried to remember that Ko's Chief knew how to smile.

Neill, of course, could smile a dozen ways: that was one of the
skills.

She cornered into the room at three seconds before ten o'clock,
and smiled as Jordie shoved his palmtop aside to make space for
her. She shrugged off her jacket, moving easily in her Neill-
inspired clothes that she now understood were designed to be non-
threatening and comfortable to stand in for hours at a time. She
laughed with Svenson over her breathlessness, and fumbled in her
bag for a disk she'd copied for Allison, a collection of live soleares
flamenco performances that was one of the staples of her music
collection. She loved to share this music with people; she wondered what Allison, with her precisely constructed approach to the
world, would make of the percussive clapping and the shouted en-
couragements that jostled for rhythmic space, wove themselves
into a net that caught the passionate singing and threw it back out
to the listener. "There's ten songs and a history of flamenco with a
bunch of links, and an amazing video of the story of Carmen set
to flamenco, really powerful." Allison was smiling; so was everyone else. "Ah," Jackal said, "I'm being enthusiastic again. Well,
there you go. There's a lot of beauty on this disk, it's worth getting
excited about."

"Nobody's laughing at you," said Jordie. "Near you. We're
laughing near you. Your enthusiasm really comes out when you
facilitate, you know? It makes people want to keep working, just
to get more of that energy splashed their way."

She was so pleased, she was sure it showed in a yellow cloud
around her head like a ring of light. I can do this, she thought. I
can. I can take this to Al Iskandariyah and it'll be mine. She could

almost love Ko for giving her this thing, this balance to the confusion and fear. If this work was really part of being a Hope, then perhaps she would survive to fool the world. Save her family and her web. Maybe even make the CEO smile for her one day. She wondered if she could ever tell Neill how much difference he had made.

And where was he? The digital display over the white board read 10:04, and everyone had begun to shift in their chairs.

The door banged open.

"What's wrong with him?" Jordie muttered. Jackal did not answer: she was too busy staring. She'd never seen those particular lines in Neill's face, and so it took a longer moment to realize that—

"He's sharked," she whispered back. Neill must have heard, the way he heard and saw everything in his territory, but he gave no notice. He took a minute at a window with his back to the room. Jackal knew when he was ready to turn, because his shoulders ratcheted down a notch under his shirt.

"I am late. I apologize." That didn't sound like a word he was used to saying. "I was delayed by an administrative matter. Before we proceed, I want to let you know that unfortunately Mr. Sawyer is no longer with us."

She scanned the room before she could stop herself, as if Sawyer might be there, eyebrows raised with the rest of them.

"Jackal, Sawyer's project passes to you. We'll discuss it this afternoon."

Jackal nodded. Great, more work. She wasn't particularly thrilled with Sawyer right now, but she wished him well. Surely this was not the first time that someone had been removed from a class. Sawyer was a pretty good facilitator, but he wasn't on the team, not really. She hoped he wasn't in too much trouble.

*   *   *

Two hours later, she discovered Neill had actually meant that Sawyer was no longer with Ko.

She learned from the most unlikely source: her father. She and Snow met him for lunch, as they did at least once a week, in the large kitchen at the back of her parents' house. Carlos always cooked: today there was a quiche of scallions and bacon and goat cheese, a bowl of acid-green spanish olives, and a salad of sliced valencia oranges, red grapes, and yellow apple slices. Jackal watched him conjure the preparations so that everything was ready together, with just enough time left to pour cream over Snow's fruit, the way she liked it. It was all delicious: the meal; her father's favorite dishes with an Etruscan pattern in blue and burnt umber; the cool green light that hung lazy in the kitchen, slow-moving like the goldfish in the pond outside the window; her father's laugh, even though Snow's joke was told all backwards; Snow herself, awkward in motion as always, scattering bits of quiche onto the table.

She blinked. Her father and Snow had stopped talking and were staring at her.

"Not hungry?" Carlos asked.

She blinked again, then shook her head vigorously. "No, no, it's great." She spiked a huge mouthful of fruit to prove she meant it. Then she replayed the last ten seconds of conversation in memory. "You said something about Sawyer? Which Sawyer?"

"Jeremy Sawyer from Biotech," her father said, with a look that told her he didn't like having to repeat himself.

"He was in my class. My workshop with Neill."

"I know, that's why I'm telling you."

"What happened to him? I know, I'm sorry, I was thinking about something else."

"He's gone."

Gone? Was Sawyer dead? No, her father thought euphemisms were tacky. "Gone where?"

"Gone elsewhere. Gone from Ko. Let go. Fired. I believe the standard phrase is 'no longer in good employment standing with the company.' " He showed no expression, but the orange segment he held was in shreds.

She let her fork clatter down onto her plate. "Fired?" She had never personally known anyone who was fired from Ko. Plenty of transfers, sure: Ko was enormous, big enough to change a person's country, class, lifestyle, family dynamics, just by reassigning her to another job, complete with intensive cultural retraining and psychological support. Firing was an utter dismissal, a condemnation: how would Sawyer live, when so many prospective employers were trading partners or vendors that could not afford to take the chance of violating the no-hire clause that was standard in Ko contracts? "Where did he go?"

"He and his family left the island yesterday. Dona wasn't able to find out his final destination. He has people in Burma, I think, but things are very bad there right now. It's his kids I feel sorry for: he was incredibly stupid, by the sound of it."

"What do you mean?"

"You have to disappoint Ko in a very big way to be dismissed with prejudice. It's your Neill's fault, you know," he added.

"He's not my Neill. Why is it his fault?"

Carlos closed his mouth and turned to cleaning the orange pulp off his fingers with his napkin. Jackal and Snow exchanged a look.

"Papa."

"I've said too much already."

The trick with her father was to be quiet and wait. He could no more keep his mind still than his body, and he loved to talk things out.

"He's in my web, did you know that?" She hadn't: it made it more personal, somehow, that her father knew Sawyer so well and now he was gone. "Yes, he's older than he looks," Carlos went on, anticipating her next thought with an eerie precision. "He hadn't done as well as some, but he was a good team lead. His boss, she's another web mate, and she really wanted to find a way to make him successful. This thing with Neill, that was his big chance to shine. But—"

Jackal nodded. Sawyer's struggle had been obvious from that first lunch. She said, "He got to be good at the techniques. When he had to run one of our meetings, he could handle himself just as well as anyone else. But he just never really seemed to get comfortable. He never committed."

"He talked to me about it a couple of times," Carlos said. "He was determined to manage it for the sake of his career. But he said it felt wrong seeing independent, quirky people suddenly turned into well-functioning worker units—I think that's how he phrased it."

"It's not like that," Jackal said.

"Mmm," Carlos said.

Jackal decided to ignore that. "So what happened?" she asked.

"He was given a new project recently—" He stopped abruptly. "The one you and your mother fought about, was it Garbo?"

Jackal nodded.

"That's the one. Jeremy was supposed to handle it until the transfer to Dona, that's why he came to talk to her about it. He didn't know about the reassignment." Carlos tried to smile. "Jeremy stuck up for you. He thought you were very good. He said everyone could see you'd be getting the same amount of attention even if you weren't the Hope, because you were earning it."

Jackal bet her mother had just loved that. She would have to tell Sawyer not to . . . and then she remembered that she couldn't tell him anything, ever again: he was gone, swallowed up by one of the innumerable frightening things that awaited someone forcibly disconnected from the world's most powerful corporation.

Her father said grimly, "He did it to himself. He sat right where Snow is now and agonized over his damned principles, whether he could work on a project that he didn't approve of."

"What was it he didn't like?"

Carlos shook his head. "He wouldn't say anything specific, only that the technology was dangerous. Dona tried to make him understand that she had access to all the records and she could address any concerns, but he just kept saying it was a bad path to walk. He has some pretty strong religious principles. . . . I don't know. But he wouldn't listen to Dona." Carlos pushed his hair back from his face. "It seems that he went to Neill yesterday and begged to be taken off the project, and Neill refused, and so Jeremy apparently went over his head with some kind of ultimatum. And in less than twenty hours the company held the necessary meetings, recorded the authorizations, processed the paperwork, stripped his passwords, deactivated his net status, sent in the packing team, and put him on the tunnel train with all his belongings neatly palletized."

He wrapped his arms around himself. "Mica didn't even have time to say good-bye. Michelangelo is Jeremy's web name," he added, seeing her eyebrows wrinkle. Then, more quietly, "I don't know why I should think of that now, we don't really use them anymore."

"I'm so sorry," Jackal said, and got up from her chair to give him a hug. He returned it fiercely for a moment and then said, "Sit down, finish your food. Here, let me reheat that for you." He whisked her plate away while Snow made a *never mind, let him* hand signal at Jackal below the edge of the table. So she made herself finish her lunch, and then left on a dead run, due in Neill's office to discuss taking over Sawyer's project. Garbo. She found a seat alone at the back of the bus, feeling unsettled, on the edge of an anger she didn't quite understand. It had something to do with the ruin of Jeremy Sawyer, as if he were sliding down a cliff and she was frozen, knowing that one misstep would send her following. Her carrybag slipped as she stood for her stop, spilling her things across the floor so that she had to scramble while peo-

ple laughed and tried to help and only knocked everything farther out of reach. She had a sudden wish to break all their noses:
then she thought of the headlines: HOPE INJURES 12 ON TRANSIT
RAMPAGE: CARRYBAG BLAMED and was able to shake her head and
chuckle. I'm not Jeremy, she told herself. I'm good at this work
and I'm safe, no matter how scared I am. All I have to do is keep
on working.

She made her way to the Executive One building, hoping fer-
vently that she wouldn't run into her mother. She had a hard, busy
afternoon ahead. After Neill, she would go to her global history
tutorial, where she would be expected to provide a précis of the
impact of isolationism on the representative governments of early
twentieth-century Western Europe. She had two media interviews scheduled, and her public-relations team wanted ninety
minutes to prepare her for questions. And doubtless there'd be
more requests waiting for her confirmation that she could squeeze
them in: as the investiture drew near, media seemed to spring up
around her like chokeweed. She was expected at a boutique on the
western end of the island in the evening, to select the formal
clothes she needed for the dozen celebrations she'd be required to
attend on Ko and then in Al Isk. She also hoped to manage some
time with Khofi: she needed his wise eyes and the way he would
wave his hands about, and his advice: how to handle Chao, and
what to do about making things up with Tiger. And she was probably behind in at least one learning module. Yes, she was busy, but
that was good. It would keep her focused.

She took a deep mental breath as the elevator leaped the seventeen floors to Neill's office, trying to let go of her feelings about
Sawyer. It was important to be confident: Neill demanded it, and
she understood that in some way he was her lifeline these days.
The work sustained her, and only Neill could help her grow into
it. Only he could judge her. She looked forward to her private
meetings with him with three parts excitement and two parts fear,

a mix that fizzed through her as she stepped through the office door that was open, as always. He never needed to close his door to keep people from intruding. He simply made them choose to go away.

He stood near one wall-sized window, silhouetted against the Executive Two tower across the plaza, and the iron sky beyond, and he didn't even give her time to reach her usual spot on the maroon leather sofa at the side of the room before he said, "You are a great disappointment."

She knew that words could hurt and frighten, but she had never before had them root her to the floor.

"You broke his nose," Neill said, with a precise, enunciated coldness that made his disgust absolutely clear. "You are an idiot child. Have you learned nothing? Have I wasted all this time and effort on you?"

No, she tried to say, but her throat was too tight; so she shook her head.

"What else should I believe? That someone with your apparent gifts for group management can't control her own emotions for the ten seconds it would have taken to get up and walk away? Or perhaps you think it adds to your credibility as a facilitator to publicly injure someone who can't retaliate in kind against the Hope of Ko?"

She felt her face go hot with shame. "It was a mistake," she stammered, "it won't happen again."

"It certainly will not," he said flatly. "I will not have you perceived as unable to manage conflict. I will not have you perceived as unable to be objective. You are the most important investment that this company will make in this generation. You will do everything in your power to justify that investment. You are the Hope of Ko, and I am making you fit to serve, and you have done well up to now. Listen carefully, Jackal, because I do not generally overcommunicate my praise. You have the potential to excel at this work. You will make every effort to realize that potential and you will use it for the company's benefit, in whatever way the company sees fit. You will control yourself."

She shamed herself further by the fat tear that slid from her eye to the corner of her mouth. She wiped it quickly with the back of her hand.

"Do you understand?"

What could she say? *I understand it all and it's too hard, I can't bear it, I don't want to be the Hope.* But that wasn't true. What she wanted was to be the real Hope. It was a knife-edged yearning that carved her hollow; to feel legitimate, blessed by the accident of right birth and the anchor of demonstrated talent, secure and serene in the face of the future. Bright and shining and safe. "I just want . . ." she said, and then stopped and clenched her hands to try to stuff the longing back inside herself.

"What do you want?"

"I'm trying . . . I want to be a good Hope but what if I can't do it, maybe they should have picked someone else—" *Stop, Jackal!* "I mean—" Her heart was pounding. *Fix it, fix it.* She took a deep breath and made her voice as even as she could. "I just mean that there must be others who could do the job better."

He was silent for a long moment. "Being a Hope has nothing to do with merit," he finally said. He no longer sounded angry, only dispassionate. "You know enough about public relations to understand how associative symbology works. The first children born into the world government visibly dedicate themselves to that government. EarthGov ensures a role for the Hope guaranteed to bring credit and pride to the Hope's people. And then these proud people say, what a wonderful Hope we have; the government must be wonderful too. It doesn't matter that it's specious reasoning. It's still good basic psychology. But let's not fool ourselves—"

He stepped away from the window then and came around the corner of the desk, putting himself on the same side of what had been a barrier. It was a quintessential Neill move, a gesture of inclusion and directness: let there be no obstacles between us. Jackal had seen it, and used it, a thousand times, and still she felt herself leaning in, listening more closely.

"Let's not fool ourselves," he said again. "As this symbol, you are immensely valuable to Ko. We've had the chance to make some small contribution to the development of the Earth Government. Your status as a Hope gives us a greater opportunity for participation, and we intend to use it. This places a great deal of pressure on you," he added, with something momentarily like compassion. "But it doesn't matter how you feel. You are the Hope of Ko. The company supports you and expects your support in return."

She nodded.

He asked again, "Do you understand?" but this time she heard the real question underneath: Do you accept? It startled her—here, now, after everything, to be given a choice. Do you want to be the Hope, or not? She knew it meant agreeing to it all, the conspiracy and the company's ambitions, and she didn't want that; but she did want to be the Hope. More than anything. So what else was there to say but, "Yes. Of course."

"And, of course," he said, matching her inflection, "your continued success benefits your web and your family as well as Ko."

She nodded.

He perched on the arm of one of his guest chairs and looked at her. "Is there anything else on this topic?"

She looked straight back. She remembered to square her shoulders and relax her jaw, and she gathered up every ounce of what she knew of professionalism to say, "No. No, there isn't. Perhaps we should discuss my new project."

"Very well," he said. "Jeremy was stopgapping Garbo until you were ready to take it up. I had hoped to keep him there for another week, but it makes no sense to put someone else in. You will have to manage the additional workload."

She answered, "I can certainly rearrange my priorities and take it on now. I wouldn't want the project to suffer."

She did not expect him to smile or nod, but she knew when he answered, "Please sit down," that she was forgiven, or at least on probation. And not just with Neill. She understood now that he spoke for Ko, and heard for Ko. She did not have to tell him her secret: he was Ko, and he already knew.

4

EXCERPT, KO.CASTLE.COM INTRANET MEMO, EXECUTIVE-level confidential routing to avoid server retention.

From: GC Neill, Executive Vice President, Planning
To: AM Chao, EVP Organizational Development

. . . and I agree with your assessment that she's discovered the true circumstances of her status as a Hope. It's the only logical basis for the obvious conflict she's experiencing. She refuses to verify, so I don't know the source, although I believe Donatella Segura is the most likely candidate for crossing the line of disclosure. If that's the case, then I will take appropriate disciplinary steps. I will speak with you further about this.

In the meantime, I have reinforced to Jackal that the company will not support inappropriate behavior. She has given her commitment, and Garbo should help her re-establish some stability. She's desperate to prove herself, and she should have just enough time to get the project back on track before the investiture. It'll keep her busy.

And another thing, Ana—the poor kid's got enough to deal with right now, so can someone from your end please take Tiger Amomato off into a corner and sit on him hard?

—Gavin

5

SHE LEFT THE EXECUTIVE ONE BUILDING AND FOUND the sun still shining, people moving in their everyday rhythms as if the world had not shuddered to a stop and then restarted. All she could think was that they had given her the choice, and it was not the bright, stainless thing she had once hoped for. And there was no time to sort through what it all meant; she was already late for the next obligation. She ran, feeling five again.

She did not see Snow that night because of their conflicting schedules. Even though she knew Snow was with her study group, her phone turned off, Jackal called her seven times, as if Snow would materialize on the other end once some magic number of attempts was reached. Finally she told Snow's voice mail, "Hi. It's me. I just wanted . . . anyway. Call me. Okay. Bye." But later she was too restless to talk; she turned off her phone and spent most of the night not sleeping, turning the conversation with Neill over and over in memory.

By the next morning she was wound tight with fatigue and ac-cumulated strain. She should feel better—she had a clear direction now, and she had the company's hand firmly at her back, moving her forward. But forward was still a murky place.

Her first meeting of the Garbo project was scheduled for late that afternoon; before that, her weekly advisory session with Khofi. She walked briskly to his office, stuck her head around the door.

"Sorry I'm late, Khofi. What . . . is something wrong?"

He said, "Come in, Zhakal. Everything is fine, but we have some changes to discuss."

"I'm afraid I can only give you a few minutes," Chao said. "I'm expecting someone. You said it was urgent?" She was kneeling on a cushion at a low table, and as Jackal hesitated in the doorway, she picked up the teapot in front of her and poured two cups. The steam smelled unpleasantly of anise and oranges. The table and the cushions were new, placed in the center of the room so they were framed against the window and a view that today was all smoke and blue: inky water that rumbled to itself in deceptively gentle swells, an afternoon sky bruised with indigo thunderclouds, and a widowmaker fog snaking around the north end of the island, the kind that could conspire with a storm to hide a fifty-foot trough from an unwary pilot who might never know her danger until she was dropping down, down, with the sea tumbling on top of her.

"Oh," Jackal said. She had meant to have her say and leave with as much dignity as she could muster: but the sea in its frame drew her across the room until she was within breathing distance of the glass, so that she could see her own eyes reflected against the fog outside. She wished she could climb into it and hide, like a small fish in coral, slipping easily among the sharp edges of the world.

"Beautiful, isn't it?"

Jackal took a breath. "I've just been to see Khofi."

"Yes?"

"He told me that he's no longer my advisor and that I've been reassigned to you."

"Yes, I thought that was understood from our last conversation."

"Well, I didn't understand it. And I don't want it. He's been my advisor since I was thirteen." She stopped, too angry to say anymore. The way he had looked at her and said, "Oh, Zhakal, you have been like a sunflower in a garden to me," with his eyes full of tears.

"It's not what I want," she repeated.

"Jackal, this day was always coming. Khofi knew it, that's why he let you go. He's not fighting the reassignment."

"I'll fight it."

"That's your privilege," Chao said evenly. "But think about it carefully. Dr. Andabe can't provide guidance at the level you need now. He's done a sound and thorough job of making sure you developed a basic skills set. But he can't tell you what to expect in Al Iskandariyah, can he? And time is short."

Jackal turned from the window. Chao still knelt before the table, triangulated by the cups of tea. She took her time to sip from one, and shrugged. "It's not his fault, of course," she continued. "Our negotiations with EarthGov are highly confidential, executive level only. I expect it's the same for all the nations sponsoring a Hope. Everyone's jockeying for the most visible role for their people, something they can point to and say, 'Look what our culture has given the world.' "

"Isn't that the point?"

"It's shortsighted instant gratification," Chao said, with a slight wave of her hand. "It's certainly no way to build an administrative structure for the long term. 'Therefore when thou doest thine alms, do not sound a trumpet before thee.' Matthew. The Christian Bible, Jackal. We'll add a review of comparative religions to your learning plan. What's important is that, like Matthew, Ko believes that service is best rendered unobtrusively. You'll have a less public life than many of the other Hopes. Maybe you'd better sit down for a minute," she said offhandedly, as if she didn't see Jackal's sudden attention. She waved Jackal toward the empty pillow on the other side of the lacquered table, and pulled her phone out of her jacket pocket to punch the intercom button. "Sam, please show Ms. Bey into the conference room when she arrives and let her know I'll be delayed a few minutes." While Chao spoke, Jackal settled slowly, dreamily, feeling the embroidered pillow through the thin cotton of her pants like braille against her thighs. Was someone finally going to tell her what to expect in the new life that she was about to crest into like a wave? She wondered how much this had to do with yesterday's conversation with Neill. She had consented and now they would give her what she needed to know. She clenched her hands together in her lap, below the edge of the table, so that Chao would not see them tremble.

"Of course, there's really no point in getting into this if you'd rather pursue your complaint about the change in advisors."

Jackal bit down on the inside of her mouth. She should say that she was loyal to Khofi and that she'd settle for ten percent of the information if it came from someone she trusted. But she so badly wanted to know.

Chao said placidly, "You should also consider Dr. Andabe's long-term interests. It's a time in his career when he should be moving on to new accomplishments. It's such a competitive environment these days."

Jackal wondered when it had started being 'these days' that were so relentlessly hard. And so lonely: she hadn't been able to reach Snow and they had exchanged voice messages, Jackal's terse and stressy, Snow's concerned and then increasingly irritated at the lack of contact. *I hate it when you don't talk to me* had been the last one. Jackal hated it too, hated the feeling that what she was really hiding from Snow was not Ko's deception, but her own participation in it. And here was one more piece of it that she wouldn't know how to explain.

"All right, I won't argue about the change," she said quietly. "But I want Khofi well taken care of; he's been really good to me."

"Of course," Chao answered, as if she were surprised that Jackal had thought it necessary to mention. She pushed a teacup across the table. "Let me know if it needs warming up."

The tea was cold and bitter. Jackal drank it down.

"Now, then," Chao began.

"Why do people say that?" Jackal interrupted. What am I doing? she wondered, but went on speaking. "Now, then," she repeated. "English is such an awkward language. So many phrases that are empty of meaning. Oh boy. What does that mean? Let's see. Why not let's smell? Or let's hear? That would make more sense, at least. And so many metaphors of control and violence disguised as sports. As if it were a game. I've been thinking a lot about it." She nodded at the sea in the window as if she were talking to it rather than Chao. "I can describe my whole life in metaphors. Stay on target. We're all on the same team. Keep your head above water." Her teacup rattled against the table when she set it down.

"What are you thinking about?" Chao asked carefully.

"Drowning," Jackal answered without a pause, without a breath, not even minding that it was the truth and that she'd already decided never to tell Chao anything that was both important and true. The fog was now firmly banked across the northern headland. She should stop now, but she couldn't: it all rolled out of her like a wave.

"My grandfather was a fisherman out of Torre la Miguera in Spain. He used to tell me stories about the sea until my mother made him stop because they gave me nightmares."

Chao nodded, but otherwise kept still. Good, Jackal thought, you just be very careful, you just let me howl.

"Did you ever hear of Las Tres Hermanas? The Three Sisters. Waves a hundred feet high and as wide as you can see. They hunt ships."

Chao's phone beeped. She thumbed it off without looking away from Jackal.

"They creep beneath the surface, stalking your ship. Then they surge out of the water around you. Impossibly tall. They blot out the sun. Everything darkens in a heartbeat. Las Hermanas try to catch you sideways, to roll your boat over and eat it. So you do your best to turn yourself and meet them head-on, even though there's never any time, because the first sister has opened a hole in the sea and you fall in and she throws herself on top of you. You're overwhelmed. You watch the portholes to see what color the water is around you. How deep you've gone. Green water means you're in the wave's hands: she may just swat you and toss you back to her sister behind her. But if the porthole glass is black then it means you've been eaten, you're deep in the belly of the wave . . ." Was this her voice? Was she the one babbling like this, words tumbling out so fast that she couldn't even take breath between them? "And then you begin to drown. My *abuelo* told me that some people fight as the water climbs their bodies, they swim even though there's no longer a surface they can reach, but other people just give up even though they don't want to die and maybe it's because they're already so tired—"

She didn't seem to have anything more to say. She watched the fog through the window; it was easy to imagine a little boat, perhaps it was called *The Jackal*, riding an ocean that swelled gently, safely, until that unexpected drop into an open mouth. She barely noticed Chao rising from the table, unlocking a door at the rear of the office and stepping through, reappearing seconds later with a small packet that turned out to be a medpatch.

"I want you to put this on," she said. "Give me your left arm, please." Diazepam, Jackal read upside-down. Ten milligrams.

"I don't need that."

"You certainly do. You have your first meeting of the Garbo project in two hours—well, I'm your advisor, Jackal, I've certainly made it my business to know your schedule. Put this on—" she peeled the cover off the patch and pressed it into the crook of Jackal's elbow "—and sit here. I'll make sure you're not disturbed for ninety minutes. That will give you time to rest."

Jackal curled up in the womb chair.

Chao produced a blanket and draped it over her, tucked the edges around her hips and under her feet. It was an unexpected kindness, and Jackal could feel herself begin to tremble again.

"It will be all right," Chao told her. "You are under an extraordinary amount of stress right now. It's situational. It will pass. We will help you manage it. We won't let you fail."

Jackal didn't know whether to be reassured or not. Chao left her. She watched the fog until it seemed to swell into the room and tumble her into sleep.

She woke to the gentle touch of Chao's hand on her shoulder. "You have a half hour to get to your meeting," she said.

"Okay," Jackal said, struggling to wake up. She washed her face in Chao's bathroom and peered at herself in the mirror. Her eyes were bloodshot, and the skin underneath was puffed and sickly gray. But she would manage. The drug gave her a sense of cool distance from herself; she hoped it would last a while. She rolled her sleeve down to hide the patch.

When she stepped back into the office, Chao was there with another woman, fifty-ish, short and dark, soft around the middle. "Senator Bey, allow me to introduce Ren Segura."

"Jackal," she said automatically, and shook hands.

"The Senator is the Asia Regional Director of the Hope Program," Chao went on.

"I have followed your progress for a very long time, Ms. Segura. I know you'll be a valuable addition to our work in Al Iskandariyah."

Jackal answered, "Thank you," and wished she had finished the earlier conversation with Chao instead of rabbiting on about waves. She didn't want to look like an idiot in front of an Earth Congress senator.

"The Senator's interested in observing your project meeting, if you have no objection."

"Umm . . . I guess . . ." She wondered if she could reach into her head and massage some life back into her brain. *Oh, suck it up, Jackal. What would a real facilitator do?* "It's fine with me," she said, "but I will need to confirm with Dr. Neill and the project team. If they have reservations, then I'm afraid I'll have to say no. I hope you understand," she added to the senator.

"Why don't we all go over together?" Chao said brightly. Jackal gave herself another mental shake. Chao seemed very perky; it made Jackal nervous, although the drug patch had smoothed her anxiety into something that she acknowledged but didn't really feel. She watched Chao's body language as they took the elevator down to the lobby and headed toward the cross-complex monorail: Chao talked almost nonstop to Bey about Jackal's work with Neill, giving details of completed assignments and quoting comments from the evaluations Jackal had received. It was confusing, until she realized that Chao wasn't marketing Jackal, but herself, demonstrating her fitness to be in charge of Jackal's transition to Al Iskandariyah. Jackal cruised behind them, watching Chao work. If it weren't for the meds, she realized, she would probably be sharked at being talked about like . . . well, like a project. It showed poor facilitation skills. She would do much better when she—

And then it all fell into place, as if the tranquilizer and the dose of sleep had pushed the clutter in her head far enough away that she could think again. She paused, began to paw through her carrybag for her palmtop. She could use the time on the monorail to review the background on Garbo. This was a Phase Four kickoff, so there was a lot to learn. And her pens, where were—

"Hi."

She looked up: Mist, Ash. Snow.

"Hi!" She dropped everything back into her bag to free her hands so that she could reach out to Snow.

"Where the hell have you been? Are you okay? You look, I don't know . . ." Snow pushed back to arm's length and peered at her.

"I'm fine . . . well, no, but . . . oh, it's a long story and I can't talk now, I have to—" She looked up the ramp leading to the monorail station. Chao and Bey waited for her at the top. "Oh, hell, I really do have to go but I'll call you, honest, and I'm really really sorry about the last couple days, tell me you forgive me?" She kissed Snow hurriedly. "Do you?"

Snow smiled. "You're an idiot."

Jackal grimaced. "You're the second person this week who thinks so. No, it's okay, I like it better when you say it. I gotta go."

"Who are those people?"

"Analin Chao on the left, somebody Bey on the right from Al Isk." She heard Mist's indrawn breath. "Oh, hi Mist, Ash."

"Chao the EVP of Development?"

Trust Mist, Jackal thought. "That's the one. Coming!" she called, and kissed Snow again while Mist rolled her eyes and Ash grabbed Jackal's palmtop before it could wiggle out of the open carrybag. "Oops, thanks Ash."

"Jackal, what's going on?"

Snow's hair was falling out of its clip, and Jackal smoothed it back. "I have an audition," she said, backing away.

"Huh?"

Chao called, "Jackal, the train!" She ran hard and just made it, Snow's "Bye!" trailing behind her. Rushing away from Snow again: one more thing she was going to have to change.

*　　*　　*

She was used to an audience when she worked: other members of Neill's workshops, Neill himself, Khofi (*not anymore, don't think about it*), the bosses and grandbosses of people in the room. Neill was already there; as soon as he saw the two women behind her, he said, "I've already spoken to the team, they're expecting observers." She nodded and parked Chao and Bey in the back of the room, where Neill joined them after he introduced her to the group at the conference table. She wasn't surprised; any evaluation of her fitness in this area would have to include him. She chewed on it a minute while the team members tapped on their palmtops and jostled for table space. Fine, she was being tested—that was nothing new. She scanned the three of them once to make sure they were settled and then forgot about them.

One of the men raised a finger when she asked who was prepared to give a background briefing on the project to date.

"The basic concept is an adaptation of equipment originally used to study depression," he said. "In Phase One we developed a prototype electromagnetic stimulator that generates a shaped magnetic signal. The signal interacts with and alters the brain wave activity in the temporal lobes. It's used in conjunction with a drug that increases temporal lobe sensitivity. In essence, Garbo alters—elongates—the subject's sense of time for a predetermined period.

"Phase Two focused on initial testing of human subjects to integrate control of environmental factors with the time experience, through new applications of existing virtual reality technology.

"Phase Three began about twenty months ago and involves stabilized virtual environmental testing on wider population samples in controlled situations. This testing has been conducted with cooperation from EarthGov and member states. The first round is complete, and the second round participant selection is under way.

"Our goal is a self-contained, active VR environment that delivers a total individual sensory experience. In addition, this experience should be customizable, replicable, and available for indefinite storage and retrieval. Up to this point, we've tested static environments only, with good sensory success. Civil and military applications for a customizable experience are under review by EarthGov. Potential commercial applications include hospital recovery, psychiatric intervention, adventure experiences, and a safe alternative for unpartnered sexual gratification."

Most of the people at the table blushed, which Jackal found endearing. "Okay," she said, "anything else I need to know?"

Shaken heads and shrugs.

"Tell me about Phase Four."

A woman with a harsh voice spoke from the far end of the conference table. "Phase Four is online editing. Phase Five will be shared experience, if we ever get there."

Nods and more shrugs. Jackal put on her best help-me-out-here smile. "Can you give me a little more detail? What's the goal, specifically?"

"The technology seems to work by beefing up brain activity linked to sense-memories. We can replicate places you've been or generate new ones by stitching together old data in new ways. But we haven't figured out how to create a framework that can be altered during the experience. If you go on a virtual cruise and forget to program sunshine, you get a shitty cruise. So right now everything has to be built in ahead of time—front-end customization, which as I'm sure you know is a programming nightmare and way too expensive. But customizing is where the real market value lies, so . . . we need to give people the capability to improve their experience as they go along. Think of it as the difference between a VR arcade and a lucid dream."

"Right," said Jackal. "Then let's begin there. I suggest we get a list of all the obstacles on the board and then see if we can categorize them. I want to start by going around the table so you can each tell me who you are and what your specialty is with regard to this project." Of course, she already knew who they were, that was all in her background notes. But it made a difference to hear how people described themselves, how they perceived their role. "After that, we'll free-for-all. Does that work for everyone? Great, you first."

She was relieved when it became clear this group wasn't going to give her any particular trouble. They turned out to be two research neurologists, a biochemist, two hardware developers, three programmers, three psychiatrists, and a virtual reality game designer. All of them except the designer were typical R&D types—blindingly smart, highly verbal, suspicious of non-technical language, critical of new ideas, desperate for credit, and terminally rude. Everyone was scared of the psychiatrists and compensated by patronizing the designer. Jackal suspected he had the best synthesizing skills in the room, given his work, so she waited until she saw him acquire a middle-distance stare and then opened the door for him to speak. That was the lever that shifted the load; the conceptualizing picked up speed after that and she could begin to work in earnest, helping to clarify and structure their ideas and leading them in the development of an overall project plan. The others were standard-issue behavioral problems, easily managed by any of Neill's students; even the hardware developer with the raspy voice who insisted on putting her bare feet on the table every time she wanted to take over the conversation.

"I'll enjoy this," Jackal told Neill after the meeting. "It's interesting."

She knew she had done well, so she wasn't surprised when Bey said, "I'm glad you feel a connection with the project. It will be easier for everyone to make the transition to direct Earth Congress administration if the activity manager is trusted and supports the change."

"Yes, I'm sure we can minimize the disruption, although it would be best to relocate everyone before the critical path tasks are

under way. I'll work up a time line in the next couple of days,"
Jackal replied, and the other three relaxed: Bey patted Jackal's
arm, Chao smiled, and Neill, standing behind them, met Jackal's
eye and to her astonishment, bent his head in a tiny but unmistak-
able bow.

She ate a late dinner with Snow on the terrace of her apartment,
watching the eastern sky glow with the false dawn of Hong
Kong's night-light as she crunched a piece of fried chicken skin.
She loved the salt and grease on her tongue, and the tang of the
beer that sluiced it down.

"You've had a full week," Snow said.

"I love that nordic understatement thing you do. It's so restrained."

"Hmm."

"What?"

"I'm sorry you've had a hard time."

"It ended just fine." Jackal shrugged, drank more beer. The
meds had worn off, but the feeling of objectivity, of control, had
stayed with her, had even made it possible for her to share another
pot of tea with Chao and finish the conversation about Hopes.

"Even so."

"I just wish they'd told me earlier what they wanted me to do.
It would have saved so much stress."

"Either they thought you might not cut it, or that EarthGov
might not agree to that level of involvement. It sounds like most
of those other Hopes are pretty much for show."

"That's what Chao said." Actually, she had said *Most of the people you meet at your investiture will be little more than circus ponies.
Don't be fooled by the glitter.* "Lots of artists dedicating their lives
to furthering world peace through mixed media. Doctors setting
up free clinics in separatist trouble zones. Scientists whose research

will be funded by EarthGov and given back to member nations. People like that."

"And people like you."

Jackal nodded slowly. "But not many."

Snow raised an eyebrow and went on nibbling a chicken thigh.

"I believe we're going to be presented as project managers."

"Non-glamorous."

"Exactly. Oh, sharks, I don't want to seem ungrateful or anything but I just wish it could, you know, sound better. Everyone else will be highly describable and I'll be the project manager from Ko." She fished in the fruit bowl on the table for a satsuma and began to peel it carefully, concentratedly, so she wouldn't have to look at Snow. "I know it's dumb. And selfish. And I wouldn't tell anyone but you. It's embarrassing to care about it."

"Well, considering you've been raised to take on this big public mantle, I can understand it being disappointing to find out it's just a plain black umbrella after all. Hey, can I have some of that? I love these things."

They chewed contentedly for a minute. Then Snow wiped her chin and said, "Why do you suppose Ko wants to hide what you're doing?"

"Huh?"

Snow gave her a you-heard-me look.

Jackal threw her satsuma peel scraps onto the table. "Can't you just let me have this for a while?" she said, and only then realized that she was angry. And underneath that, scared of the conversation, scared to think too much. "Can't I just have this one good thing without there being something bad about it?"

"I didn't mean—"

"I don't care what you meant. Ko doesn't want a lot of visibility in the investiture because it's not like we're really a nation of our own yet as far as EarthGov is concerned. Okay? So I'm not really as good as the rest of them to begin with, and it's important that we keep that our little secret for as long as possible. And thanks very much for bringing it up."

They sat in bruised silence for minutes. Jackal knew that Snow was hurting but too stubborn to leave. And Jackal was too angry to be the conciliator.

"Fire and ice," Snow said.

Another silence.

"There you go again," Jackal said, "it's that nordic thing."

"Peel another one of those."

She handed half a satsuma to Snow and chewed on a segment. The juice was sharp in the corner of her mouth where the salt had been.

Snow's voice, when she finally spoke again, was quiet. "I didn't mean anything about you. I think you'll be a great Hope, you'll do a wonderful job. I don't want to take anything away from you. But I think you've been really jerked around and I don't understand why you don't want to look at that."

Jackal chewed her way through another bit of fruit. You don't know the half of it, she thought. She wondered how to explain her fear to Snow without telling the rest. Finally she said, "What do you think it's like for Jeremy Sawyer right now?"

Snow sat back and thought about it. That was one of the things Jackal loved about her, that she wasn't jarred by conversational side trails. She assumed that they had a point, that the different threads would wind together in the end. For Snow, they almost always did: her mind worked that way.

"I'd be scared. I can't imagine being cut off from my web and my community. He must feel so alone. And guilty about his family. And vulnerable."

"Of all of those, which do you think is the worst?"

Snow said, even more quietly, "Being alone."

Jackal arranged her second set of satsuma peels into a careful abstraction on the tabletop.

Snow said, "Do you really believe that protesting poor process and bad communication would be cause for . . . whatever you want to call it? Expulsion?"

"The Hope doesn't bite back in public," Jackal answered. "The Hope doesn't embarrass the sponsor. The Hope is only valuable as long as she is perceived to be an asset to the company. Don't look at me like that. It's true for everyone. It's just a little harder for me right now. I'm lucky to be a part of Ko. They take good care of us. Everyone has to compromise to be part of a community."

Snow scowled, but her shoulders unbent a little. "All right. I understand about compromise."

"Yeah. Me too," Jackal said, and they both leaned back in their chairs and looked up. There were no stars, only cloud smeared across the sky like grease on glass. They held each other's hands.

6

A WEEK LATER THE RECALCITRANT HARDWARE DEVEL-
oper began turning up in fuzzy bunny slippers, and Jackal knew
she was back in the groove. The project kicked into higher gear as
the team began preparing for the relocation, and Jackal was in
charge, confident, supported by Chao and Neill, back in tune with
Snow. Her father was preparing to accompany her to the investiture. Her mother had declined to come. Jackal called and recorded
an awkward message, but perhaps she'd left it too late. Donatella
never called back.

There was another issue hanging over her head, and she made
up her mind to attend to it after an earnest talk with Snow. "You
have to," Snow said. "It's not just about the two of you, it's about
the whole web. Everyone's waiting."

So on a Saturday in mid-December, she rolled out of bed and
kissed Snow and took herself off to Tiger's apartment. It took all
her nerve to press the intercom button. He wasn't there. She made
a good guess and found him in the gymnasium, sitting in a half-
lotus, eyes closed, on the thick mat in the area reserved for martial
and meditative arts. His nose was still taped, but the bruising had
gone down.

He opened his eyes as she approached. She braced herself for the conversational barbed wire, but all he did was sigh and say, "I give up, Jackal. Call off your dogs."

"What do you mean?"

He looked at her without expression. "Didn't you hear? I had a little chat with Executive Vice President Chao last week."

Jackal said stupidly, "Analin Chao?"

"Maybe she's Analin to you. She told me to call her ma'am and she handed me my ass on a platter. You say jump, I ask how high."

"Oh, hell," Jackal said. She sat down on the floor next to him. "I didn't know she was going to do that, honest. I'd have asked her not to. I wanted to take care of this myself."

"You already handed me my nose."

A deep breath. "I'm really sorry about that. I got mad."

"You know, I was ready to hurt you back. If security hadn't been there so fast, I would have tried. Chao told me that if I'd laid a hand on you I could have been terminated from Ko. Maybe my whole family."

That chilled her. "I'm sorry."

"No need to apologize to little old me. I'm just a pebble in your road."

"Tiger, can't we just make up?"

"I suppose we can if you say so. You seem to be in charge of everything else around here." He sounded so bitter, and there was a part of her that wanted to cup his face in her hands and try to smooth away all the misunderstanding. But she didn't know how to do that in this public place, when perhaps he felt that he couldn't refuse her touch; and it would kill her if he flinched.

"I wish things weren't so hard," she said, and stood up. "I don't want us to be like this."

"How do you want us to be?"

She opened her hands helplessly. "I'll see you later," she said finally, and left him. At the other end of the gym she turned around and saw him, head down, pounding one fist over and over on the mat.

"Nobody else can make him that mad." She turned back and found Bat next to her, watching Tiger with patient sadness. "Would it kill you to be nice to him?"

"It wasn't like that," Jackal said, and began to move away, but Bat caught her arm.

"There's a trip to Hong Kong next week. To shop for the holidays. Do you want to come?" They both looked at Tiger. "He'd like it," Bat said finally.

"I might." But she knew the right thing to do. She had hurt Tiger and damaged the web, and now she would have to roll on her back and show everyone her throat so they would know she still belonged to them.

She said, "All right. I will."

Jackal and her web mates took the Nan Hai tunnel train from Ko Island to the Apleichau Island Omniport. The omniport was a gift from Ko, a multibillion dollar project that had included extending Apleichau's land mass by twenty-seven percent to make room for the immigration complex and the water, air, and tunnel-train arrivals. No one entered or left Hong Kong without passing through the port. The security network, the immigration computer, and the entire port-of-entry traffic management system were Ko technology. Jackal imagined Hong Kong had been very grateful.

She spent the entire journey trying to get Tiger to meet her eyes, but he wouldn't. He sat close to Bat and acted as if Jackal were invisible. In spite of herself, she was starting to feel irritated. She told herself he had a right to be mad, but part of her just wanted to shake him until his damn nose fell off. Snow would have laughed and offered to help, and eased Jackal's tension: but Snow was on her way to Quanzhou for a three-day conference on macroengineering challenges in Asia. "I'm proud of you. You're the glue that holds the web together," she had told Jackal when they said good-bye.

At Immigration, the web was herded into the ends of several long lines at the row of checkpoint counters that separated arriving passengers from the cavernous main waiting area of the omni-port. Surveillance optics in the ceiling and walls blinked red, green, red, green as they recorded still frames in preset sequences. Guards patrolled the lines and stood at the exits and counters. All were Chinese; no one else was allowed to carry a weapon in Hong Kong or the mainland. The guard nearest Jackal paced back and forth along the last third of their line, talking to himself in an angry voice.

She was always uncomfortable here, although she had regularly breezed in and out of Hong Kong since the age of eight. It was the interminable standing and the sour smell of the room that made her itchy; it was the size of it, the way that she could never quite see the far wall. She usually believed it was her imagination, and lately she had wondered if she would ever again feel confident at any identity check. But today, looking around, she realized that the entire space was designed to make the occupants feel crowded, pushed, hemmed in. Trapped. And, paradoxically, isolated and revealed.

She and Turtle and Mist talked about it. "It's not just the drugs-and-guns people anymore," Turtle said. His voice was low, even though it was hard to hear over the loudspeakers that constantly announced arrival and departure schedules in four different languages. "The Chinese will find them and take them out if they can—" he paused as the guard passed by "—but what they're really worried about is Steel Breeze."

Jackal nodded, and after just a moment too long, so did Mist. Normally, Jackal would pretend not to notice and do Mist the courtesy of letting her figure it out as the conversation went along.

Mist wasn't stupid, after all, just lazy about the world outside Ko. But today was different; today Jackal wanted honest conversations.

"Do you know what we're talking about, Mist?"

Mist looked startled; so did Turtle. Mist widened her eyes and smiled with half her mouth. "Well, of course."

"I don't think so. I'll bet you don't know anything about Steel Breeze." The muttering guard wandered back, and Jackal had a bad moment wondering if he had overheard. Like Turtle, she was trying to keep her voice low. Just talking about Steel Breeze in a government facility could get her a frightening hour of detention and hard questioning before her identity was established.

"Why are you being so mean?" Mist said in a small voice.

"I'm not being mean. Honestly. I'll be happy to give you the short course in international terrorism so you're better informed. I just hate it when you go along with people like that. Some day it'll get you into trouble, *hermanita*."

"People like being agreed with," Mist retorted, surprising her. "Nobody but you thinks there's anything wrong with getting along."

"I get along with people."

"Oh, sure. Don't you mean that the other way around?"

"Mist—" Turtle tried to cut her off, but Jackal could see that there was no chance Mist would stop now. "Everyone gets along fine with you because they have to," she said.

"What are you talking about?" When Mist did not answer, Jackal turned to Turtle. "What's this all about? Turtle?" Her face was hot. Turtle stepped hard on Mist's left foot.

Mist winced, took a deep breath, let it out, and shook her head slowly. "Forget it, Jackal. It's not your fault, you didn't do anything."

Jackal waited.

"It's not your fault. I know you didn't turn Chao loose on Tiger.

It's just that it's hard sometimes, being in a web with a Hope. You're always the most important person. You always get everybody's extra attention. I know you need it, I know that you're going to have this really tough job and everything, but we're all trying to help you and you don't have to be so mean." Mist kept her head down. "Just forget it."

"I'm sorry, Mist. Really, I . . ." Turtle shook his head, and Jackal stopped. She felt hideously uncomfortable and a little shaky. She wanted to touch Mist, but Mist was still clenched in on herself like a fist. Turtle stared at his feet.

Jackal sighed. "I'm sorry," she said again to Mist. "I really am trying to make up with everyone, I'm just doing a worse job than usual." Mist nodded, but there was no more conversation.

The wait was long: she assumed that the system was slowed by the holiday influx. She gave Nat, the entry officer, a sympathetic smile when she got to the head of the line.

"Segura! *Qué tal*, babe?"

"Your accent is still terrible, *amigo*." She handed him her ID, relaxed against the counter as he fed it into the reader.

"Yeah, maybe after the new year I'll have time to breathe and sleep and eat, stuff like that, then I can worry about my Spanish accent in a city full of Chinese-speakers. Everyone else thinks I sound great."

The reader spat out her card. A ponderous electronic voice issued from the computer speaker: "We are honored to have a Hope among us."

"Oh god, Nat, I thought you guys were going to fix that." The voice repeated the phrase in the three other official languages of Chinese business. People nearby had turned to look and were whispering to each other, pointing at her. Behind her, Turtle chuckled. Two ranks over, Tiger watched without blinking.

"Sorry, honorable Hope, but I'm afraid that's way below eating and sleeping on the priority list right now."

"All right," Jackal grumbled. "Just stop calling me that."

"Enjoy your stay in Hong Kong, Your Hopefulness." He returned her card and waved her out of line.

"I hope you never sleep again," she spat.

"Excuse me, what's her problem?" she heard him say to Turtle, both of them laughing.

She walked into the public area of Victoria Omniport. Her face burned. People were still staring. She straightened, stepped harder so that her boot heels rapped. The noise was solid, confident. The problem was, when it came right down to it, she liked being treated like a Hope. She liked it. It made her walk proud, consider her words, look people in the eye. She wanted everyone in the station to point discreetly, tell each other *That's her!*, wonder for a moment what it must be like to walk in her skin, destined for an unimaginable life in the glamour of Al Iskandariyah.

She loved it. And hated it, hated herself for a liar and a cheat, unworthy, trapped; and there was nowhere to go but across the open concourse to the escalator that led to the city trains, to board with the rest of the web, to leap from station to station across the bay to Kowloon in a bullet-shaped firefly that glittered in the coming dark.

She found no comfort on the train, not even room to stand where she did not have to inhale someone else's breath. The crush of riders held her immobile against one side of the car. Something sharp dug into her ribs; she searched behind her with one hand and felt an open plastic container full of leaflets. She tugged one out and pulled it around where she could see it. On the front, three poor-quality black-and-white photographs and a sentence in violent red: HAVE YOU SEEN THESE PEOPLE? On the inside, another headline: TAKE THE WIND OUT OF STEEL BREEZE.

Oh, please, she thought. That made Steel Breeze sound more like a rival sports team than an international cooperative of terrorist groups. She started to crumple the flyer, then changed her mind and reached under a stranger's arm to poke Turtle in the back. When he looked around, she pushed the leaflet toward him.

"Give it to Mist. Don't tell her it's from me, just say you found it."

Turtle raised an eyebrow. At the next stop, when a few people left the train, Jackal caught a glimpse of Mist perched on the edge of a seat, frowning over the pictures with her hair hanging in her face.

The web pushed out at Tsimshatsui stop, but leaving the train brought no relief; everyone, it seemed, wanted to shop at Mirabile. Jackal was carried along in a crowd of chattering foreigners who stopped in all the wrong places to stare, gumming the flow of traffic hopelessly and causing people behind them to step on each other's heels and curse. Moving more easily through the flows and eddies were the Hong Kong executives; the four-to-a-rented-room university students; kids in their street colors. They all moved together through Mirabile, *Wonderful,* and it was wonderful, all glimmer and sheen: Hong Kong's Tsimshatsui shopping district paved over into a mile-square foundation from which Mirabile zigged and zagged and thrust up, enfolding offices and restaurants, clubs, casinos, theaters; level upon level of darkness, color, whitelight, quiet, romantic, wild, exciting, and always for a price. There were mazes of corridors lined with tiny shops that sold herbs, crystals, sex toys, drugs, baby clothes, artificial limbs. There were open expanses of marble dotted with fountains that sprayed colored water. Everything smelled of an improbable stew of sugar, sweat, grease, chlorine, and fruit. An amusement park in the center of one enormous outcropping opened up to the night sky in a seeming canyon of dark glass that reflected the blinking jade and inky purple neon of a massive Ferris wheel. Kowloon Park was gone: in its place, an exercise trail that spanned two levels and a public pool with a ten meter board from which divers with waxed bodies dropped like darts, arrowing into the water not thirty feet from the transparent wall of one of Mirabile's hundred restaurants.

She wanted to find a beautiful present for Snow, something that would surprise and delight with its perfect meaning, but everything she saw seemed tasteless and wrong, so instead she drank too much Dutch beer at a café on the fourteenth level. Her chair faced a shop window with staggeringly expensive clothes worn by live models, who changed position incrementally so that over the course of an hour one woman reached her hand across the space of two feet to touch another woman's. Jackal had plenty of time to watch: all her conversations seemed slightly askew, until she finally decided it was better to shut up.

More beer, and sometime later, movement, the web drawing in around her. Bat knelt next to her chair, particularly little and pointed from this angle, all elbows and collarbones and sharp chin. Her eyes were bright with some kind of excess. "Jackal, hey Jackal . . ."

"Hey, Bat."

"Hey. Let's go up, you want to?"

"Where?" But she knew.

"Up. Up the Needle."

The Needle. The top of Mirabile, one hundred and seventy-eight stories, over two thousand feet, where hundreds of people at a time could crowd up to a view across the sea to Ko in the south, or north into the maw of mainland China. Two thousand feet up, when anything over seventy made her sick. She looked across the plaza toward the Core support shaft, as big as a steel redwood punching through one hundred seventy eight floors. In between the horizontal crossbracing and angled beams, three enormous glass-walled elevators ran up and down like faceted beads. Mirabile staff in aqua jumpsuits handled crowd control at top and bottom. The elevators ran constantly. She had heard that the Needle was never empty.

"Hey, powerful," said Stone. "We can see the holiday lights all over the city."

"There's going to be fireworks," Bat said.

"We may as well have a look." That was Mist, casual, pretending to be bored.

They all looked at Jackal. She took a swallow of beer, wiped her mouth on her sleeve. "No, thanks," she said. "You go ahead, meet me back here." She shrugged, smiled at Mist: somehow it seemed important not to hurt her feelings again. Then she turned and found Tiger at her shoulder.

"I want you to come," he said in a low voice.

She snorted, finished her beer.

"You have foam on your mouth. Come on, you don't have to be scared."

"I'm not scared."

He said, still speaking softly, "I think you owe me this one, don't you? Consider this your public apology. Then we're even. No more hard feelings." His mouth tightened briefly. "I'll leave you alone if that's what you want. But today I want you to come with me up the Needle."

"Tiger, why?"

He said finally, "Don't you know?" Why did he look sad? She had drunk too much. There was a brief moment, his face changing . . . and then it was just Tiger again. He made a great show of pulling out her chair. She let him. He was collecting his debt, and she did not know what else to do except walk beside him, following the rest of the web across the plaza. Then an aqua person was pointing her into an elevator and the doors slid closed.

One hundred fifteen people in a glass bubble going up and up and up. Deceptively simple, as long as she thought about the destination and not the journey, the long trip helpless in the low-bid product of some disgruntled worker's labor; as long as she did not let herself see the distance through the airy glass that looked as though a breath could break it. Tiger stood close behind her, his hand on her shoulder. She made herself see only the LCD counting off the floors; twenty, thirty, forty. She stared unblinking at the display and waited, waited, waited, for the metal beast to haul itself up with little squeaks, changes in air pressure that hurt her ears, small clicks of cables and junctions, a slight shimmy in the climb at around level eighty-five that took fifteen floors to work itself out while she stared and did not blink and never breathed. One hundred ten. No one spoke. Was there a crack in the glass panel there, at the edge of her peripheral vision? The air began to taste of other people's breath, of ketones and heat-activated perfumes. One hundred thirty. Tiger's voice in her ear told her *it's okay, we're almost there, you're doing fine.* She looked up and saw the bulky body of Mirabile narrowing as it stretched. She could see the enormous arches and trusses and beams, the polystyrene concrete skin; and then the walls seemed to fall in around her and the elevator shouldered through its narrow passage up into the night sky, riding now on the outside of the Needle's frame. She looked out; gods and angels, so far up, so far from everything safe. One hundred fifty; one hundred sixty. Kowloon poured itself out in lights below her. One hundred seventy. The cage began to slow. Then they were inside a metal shaft. One hundred seventy-eight. Had they really stopped moving? The doors did not open. They were stuck, she was certain, and her breath hitched under her collarbones. She let herself lean on Tiger, feel how solid he was, how he took her weight and did not let her fall. Then the doors slid apart tiredly.

"Step out, please." Jackal blinked at the aqua-suited traffic controller standing before her. "This way, please."

"We're here," Tiger said gently.

"Right," Jackal answered, and unlocked her knees so that her legs would move. They shook, a little, but they took her off the elevator. She imagined the floating platform, the six cables hanging down underneath it, thousands of feet of steel rope, each waving gently like a manta's tail. She sat down on the first bench she found.

Bear shouldered Tiger out of the way and squatted down next to her. "You okay?"

She shrugged. Tiger bit his lip and then turned away. "I'm okay," she told Bear. He squinted at her, his mouth crooked. "All right, I hate this and I feel like throwing up. If there was an open window I'd probably push Tiger out of it. Is that better?"

He patted her hand approvingly and squeezed next to her on the bench. "That's my Jackal."

"I hate being scared of things."

He nodded.

They sat silent and watched the web push themselves up against the observation windows, seeming to stand on the edge of the black sky; then green and blue light splashed against the glass and lit up their faces, and their collective *ohhhh* came just a second before the echo of the fireworks explosion. When she was a baby, her parents had taken her to Al Iskandariyah for a presentation of the new Hopes. She had a holo of it on her bedroom wall: her father's face so proud, her mother lifting her up so the whole world could see her, and voices had roared out of the night just like the web at the window. There had been fireworks there, too, and it looked in the holo as if the babies were reaching for the light.

Beside her, Bear strained to see across the gallery. "Go on, go watch," Jackal told him. "Really. I'm okay. Really."

Finally, space to breathe. She wished she hadn't drunk so much. She concentrated on shutting out the sounds around her: the mush of noise from the windows; closer voices that might be the Mirabile attendants; the faint drone of machinery behind the walls. But she could not shake the sensation of being too high, slip-sliding over an open space. Okay, let's not do this, she told herself, but it was too late: suddenly oxygen seemed harder to come by, and the room was too warm. Sharks, she was going to be sick. She swallowed air and felt her stomach roll and her mouth fill with saliva. Down the hallway, past the windows on one side and the elevator shaft on the other, she could see the lit sign for the public bathrooms: she walked fast.

The queasiness subsided as she ran cold water over her wrists and scooped some onto the back of her neck. She still felt shaky: the trip home seemed unimaginable, the Hong Kong system and the tunnel train and the bus ride back to her own bed. Around the corner from the sinks, out of sight of the door, she found a padded bench. It was a mercy to lie down and be still. That damned beer. She closed her eyes.

She blinked awake to the last half of a sentence: ". . . one in here?" Another phrase, this time in Chinese; a man's voice, sharp and perfunctory. The door was already closing before Jackal collected her wits enough to realize that she should answer. Had she been asleep? What time was it? She swung herself up to a sitting position and stayed there for a few minutes, leaning back against the wall while her breath steadied.

She still felt drunk, slightly out-of-sync, but she would try to face the ride down the Needle. Get it over with and go home. She splashed water on her face, and frowned at her reflection. She looked strained and tired; she would have to do something about that. Have some fun for a change. Would it be so bad if one or two newspapers on the planet didn't get a personal interview, or if her next global politics class assignment was less than thorough? She frowned again, told her reflection, "Go home, get some sleep, wake up tomorrow and figure out how to get some of your life back. And no more beer!" Well, maybe just not so much beer: she winked at Jackal-in-the-mirror, feeling better, and left the bathroom.

The observation lobby was empty.

She stood at the end of the hallway, confusion bubbling into anger. They'd left her here at the top of this damned high place. She hated them all. Then she rubbed her face, told herself to relax, think it through. Of course they hadn't left her here deliberately. Maybe they didn't yet realize she wasn't with them; or perhaps Bear was even now on the way back up for her. She was lowering herself onto the bench to wait when everything went to hell.

An electronic siren leaped into an ear-splitting *whoop whoop whoop*, and red lights began to flash over each set of elevator doors. She covered her ears, and when that didn't help she retreated back up the hall past the bathrooms. *What is going on?* The combination of the noise and the alcohol made her feel as if the Needle were tipping sideways, swaying in some huge storm. She wondered if anyone was still up here; then she rounded the curve of the tower, and saw an open door.

She stopped just outside the doorway: an operations room of some kind, with a central console of flat-screen monitors and keyboards, wall-mounted speakers, two utilitarian chairs. One chair lay on its side. Two aqua-suited backs bent over the console. Under the cacophony of the siren, she could hear a mélange of voices coming from the speakers, as though hundreds of people were trying to talk on a single comm line.

"Hello?" she said, and wasn't surprised that they didn't hear: the noise was incredible.

"Excuse me!" she yelled, and one of the people turned: a Chinese man, tall and thin. His startled expression at seeing her didn't sit well on the general worried set of his face. He touched the person beside him, who also turned: a shorter man, equally worried, a thin wire headset tucked around his left ear. The second man spoke rapidly to Jackal.

"I'm sorry, I don't speak Cantonese well," she said haltingly in that language. "Do you speak English? *O habla usted español?*"

"You're not allowed in here," he snapped. "Return to the lobby immediately."

She opened her mouth to explain, and at that moment her brain finally began to make sense of the muddy voices in the background.

"Get us out, get us out!"

"Shut up! Everybody just calm—"

"Maman, qu'est qui se passe?"

"I don't like this, I'm scared—"

Mist? That was Mist. Jackal was at the console in three long steps, scanning the monitors: the interior of the Needle elevators, with a digital display at the side of each screen indicating floor location. One elevator was empty except for a middle-aged Chinese woman in a business suit, standing between two large men in loose clothing. The display read 83. The other two were stuffed with people, much more so than she remembered from the ride up. In one, she could see Mist, face clenched like a cramp. And Bear, and Stone: their cage was at floor 117. In the other elevator, Bat and Kea, Turtle: the 120th floor. Back to the other elevator: people shifted and behind them she saw Tiger, looking distant and very still.

"What's happening here?" she asked.

"You can't come in here. Authorized personnel only." He said something in a low voice to the taller man, who stepped to Jackal's side.

"What's going on?"

"You must leave now." The tall man put a hand on Jackal's arm and pointed to the door. Jackal shook him off. "That's my web! Tell me what's happening."

"You are interfering with an emergency situation," he said. "You must leave or I will notify security."

Jackal extended her wrist with her ID meld showing, and he furrowed his forehead so his eyebrows ran together.

"There's no need for security. Go ahead and scan me. I'm Ren Segura, I'm the Hope from Ko Island." She tried to look sober and immovable.

He huffed, then spoke rapid-fire to the shorter man. She caught the word for "Hope," and the two men exchanged a look of resigned frustration. The shorter man began talking into his headset. There was a touchscreen in front of him with instructions in Chinese characters. He ignored it and continued his conversation.

The other man said, "Ms. Segura, you would be more comfortable in the lobby."

"I would not," she said. "Now please explain immediately what is happening." Pointing to the monitors: "Those are my people."

"The elevators have unfortunately become stalled in transit," he said carefully.

"They're stuck?"

"As you say."

"What are you doing about it?" Her stomach wanted to roll over again. On the screen, Mist was crying openly now.

"We are attempting to contact our service contract provider for assistance."

"That's it? You're making a phone call? You have to get them out of there."

"Please, Ms. Segura," he said nervously, "there is no concern. Our elevators are equipped with emergency brakes and secondary rack and pinion lift systems—"

She interrupted him: "I'd like to talk to them, please."

"Excuse me?"

She pointed to the monitors. "I want to talk to them."

He looked as if he might object, so she gave him the Hope look, the blank expectant stare of a VIP accustomed to getting what she wanted. He fetched her a chair and a headset, with a number of anxious glances toward the man still working at the console. Before he sat her down, he pointed up to the corner of the ceiling.

"All activities are recorded for security purposes," he said. "Please confirm for the record that you understand these tapes may be given as evidence of your actions in a restricted area."

"Fine." She waved him off, sat and began to click the headset control through channel frequencies until she found the right set of voices. "Bear, can you hear me?"

"Jackal? What?" He looked around as if he expected to find her standing next to him, and then back up at the place where the speaker must be, just under the camera. "Where are you? Are you on another elevator? Everybody shut up, it's Jackal."

"I'm still up the Needle, I got sick and found a place to lie down. You guys left me."

Mist snuffled and dragged her silk sleeve across her nose. "So you're missing all the fun," she said in a shaky voice. Jackal had never thought of Mist as brave, and she was touched.

"Hey, Mist, what's up?" she said gently. "I thought you're the one who's always saying not to hang around when the party's over."

Mist smiled: only a small smile, but it made Jackal feel forgiven.

"What happened?" Bear said.

"I don't know, they're working on it."

Bear sighed. "Great. You hate heights, I hate crowds. So here we are."

"Where did all these people come from?"

"They shoved us all onto two elevators to make room for some special party coming up. I didn't even get to see the fireworks." He sounded wistful.

Tiger did something with his elbow and slipped between two strangers to stand beside Bear. "Jackal, how long is this going to take?"

"I don't know . . . I don't think they know what's wrong. They're calling the service provider."

Tiger snorted. "What kind of system is it?"

She looked around the console. "Umm . . . aha. Ko HardBrain, Series E."

"Tetraplex processor . . . should be able to run every elevator in Hong Kong at once, never mind these three. So they should look at either the controller or the software. Connective hardware. Maybe a bad interface to the EACS. Are they working on it at Mirabile Central?"

"I don't know."

"Can I talk to someone there?"

"Hang on." She tapped the shoulder of the man next to her, with the headset, and made the request. He shook his head.

"He can help," Jackal said impatiently. She pointed at the HardBrain logo. "He practically lives inside these things."

He put up a hand and turned away.

"He wants to know if you've checked the interface to the EACS?" Jackal challenged. She had no idea what it meant, but it worked: he looked at her and then at Tiger on the monitor, and clicked his headset to the proper channel and began to speak. The first thing Tiger did was to open a panel in the elevator and find a headset: he plugged in and was able to talk privately to the man at the console while the swell of general noise continued to roll through the wall speakers over Jackal's head. Jackal followed them to the private channel and listened: she couldn't understand a word of it, but it became clear that Tiger was making suggestions that the attendant was cautiously following, touching the sensory screen in front of him as Tiger talked him through the steps. It was odd to watch Tiger speaking Cantonese: the sharp edges of the language molded his face into a different shape.

Eventually, the shorter man stopped entering commands on the touchscreen. There was a longer exchange with Tiger; then the attendant left the room with an intent expression, still worried but more focused now. He didn't seem to notice Jackal, and when she turned, the taller man was also gone. It made her uncomfortable that they'd left her here alone; then she glanced up, remembering the security camera.

"Jackal, are you still there?" Tiger said softly. He was slumped directly under the camera's lens, looking drawn and tense, the headset curving along the line of his cheek. The crowd had made some space for him to work: there was a mass of bodies a few feet behind him, a bouquet of frightened faces.

"Right here," she answered. "How's it going?"

"Don't know yet. He's supposed to be checking the EACS connections at the network routers."

She chuckled. "If you say so." And then she realized it was the nicest they'd been to each other in months, and she had to swallow hard.

He must have felt it too, because abruptly he said, "Chao told me that if you needed to break my arm along with my nose next time that they'd let you, that I would just have to take it, that I better back off . . . god, Jackal, I know you probably don't have any idea how that feels, having no choice . . . what?"

"Nothing," she whispered.

"I'm sorry I made you come up here. I know you hate it. I just wanted you to do something because I said so. Because I asked. I thought that if you were scared you would let me . . . I don't know, let me in again." Even though he was keeping his voice low, she could hear it shake a little. "You know, I had this fantasy that we would go back down and you'd be scared and I would hold you, and this time you couldn't pretend that it didn't happen because it would be in front of everybody."

"Tiger . . ."

"I'm sorry. But you—you cut me off after we . . . it was like I was invisible. I just wanted you to see me."

It was so raw and so obviously true that she wanted to reach through the glass and touch him.

"You didn't do anything wrong," she told him. "It wasn't your fault. It was me. I found out—I found out something I couldn't handle and I took it out on you and it wasn't fair, Tiger, I'm sorry. And then everything got so complicated. I shouldn't have—"

"It's okay," he said. He nodded at her through the camera. "I tell you what, let's get down from here and we'll sort it all out, okay?"

"Okay."

And then his image on the monitor shuddered, and people in his elevator screamed and fell about. The digital display flickered and then reset itself to 113. Tiger's headset was pulled off his ear; she rekeyed her comm to the main elevator speakers. "Are you all right? Tiger?"

He had grabbed the side rail, and there were new lines of stress on his face. "We just dropped, I'm not sure how much."

"Four floors. Why's this happening?"

A woman spoke from the group behind Tiger. "We're over capacity," she said bleakly. "We're too heavy. Everyone needs to stay still and try not to weigh so much."

"Has that guy come back yet?" Tiger said. Jackal could hear the strain in his voice.

She shook her head, and then remembered he couldn't see her. "No." She looked up again at the security camera's steady red light, as if she might find help there. Her heart pounded a series of tense paradiddles. It made her feel breathless and jittery, as if she would go mad unless she did something, anything, right now.

"Damn." Tiger chewed his lower lip. "Okay, what do we know about elevators?"

"He said something about emergency brakes and secondary lift systems."

"We stopped normally the first time. So that jerk just now must have been the brakes grabbing when we fell." Jackal suddenly had a clear picture of the elevator cage in the shaft of the Needle, held

onto its cable by a few bits of compressed metal. It wasn't a reassuring image.

"I'm scared," Mist said in a small voice. She was tucked under
Bear's arm.

Me too, Jackal thought, but said, "Don't worry. We'll get you
out."

"Where is that guy?" Tiger said.

"I'll go look." She stumbled along the hall in both directions:
the siren was still screaming in the observation lobby, but she
found no other people. There was an open door leading to a stairwell.

"Oh, great," Tiger said when she got back. "The grid must be
on another floor."

"What do we do?"

"Did he say what kind of secondary lift system they use?"

She wished the damn emergency whoops would stop so she
could think. "Rack and pinion? Does that sound right?"

He stared speculatively up into the camera, so that it seemed he
looked right into her eyes. "Can you read Chinese Traditional
characters?"

"Some." Not very well, but she didn't tell him that. If she was
the web's best hope of action right now, she wouldn't undermine
their confidence in her.

"Maybe some is all we need. Okay, tell me what you see on the
screen right now."

She began to recite the commands, pausing to describe the characters she didn't recognize so that he could translate.

"Right. Go back to the place that says 'Engage backup system.'
Touch that."

"Hang on." She peered at the screen: the resolution was grainy
and it was hard to keep track of all the characters. *If we get out of
this okay, I'll never drink again, I promise*, she heard a voice say
somewhere in the back of her head, like a prayer. She searched,

searched: there, that one. She put a finger on it. Tiger was saying, "You should get some kind of prompt—" and then there was a horrendous triple screech and thud. The sound cut off. Jackal saw in the monitors all the people jerk and stumble over each other. Tiger's head came up. Mist wrapped her arms around herself. Bear closed his eyes.

There was a moment of perfect stillness; and then, one by one, the displays began to flicker through their numbers as the elevators dropped like glass beads running off a wire.

Oh, and it was so quiet, this falling death, *god no no no*, she sees that they are screaming but she hears only silence so how can the screams be real, because this is not the way it ends, not possible, not in a million years, not for the web, *what did I do*, see how they fly and there is Mist beating against the glass as if breaking through it could save her, and Jackal cannot reach them, *I didn't mean to*, and she slaps her hands against the screen and screams for them *no no no*, but they do not hear her, not even Tiger who is pressed face against the glass flying for these last few moments and she wonders how it feels and she is holding her breath and she will never move again, she is afraid to blink because there is no time.

Then Tiger throws his head back. His eyes meet hers. She sees him. And then she sees black; and she does not need the distant explosive sounds to know that they are gone.

PART II

AFTER THE FALL

7

An on-line greeting card to BERT from SCULLY!

**Hope the New Year
Brings You Joy and Happiness!**

Dear Bert—

I know you won't like the card, but I was just thinking of you. And there's nothing wrong with joy and happiness.

Love,

Scully

Dear Bert—

So far the new year is pretty much like the old one. The new paint job is almost finished. Someone has already thrown a grilled cheese sandwich against the wall and made a stain. I haven't decided whether to leave it or not. Maybe I should. The stain on our society or something. Do I really want to repaint every time this happens? I make a lot of grilled cheese.

There's a watcher been coming by who calls himself Razorboy. Nice kid, stupid name. He offered to install a new viewscreen and a program box in exchange for letting him hang around. I didn't ask where the equipment came from, just said sure and told him not to hassle the regulars. So now everyone's watching the coverage on the big case coming up soon in Earth Court. You've probably heard something about it even in Outer East Jesus or wherever you are—Ren Segura, one of those Hopes everyone's making a fuss over, although of course she didn't get to go to their big new year party.

Very busy at the moment. More tourists lately, probably because of the latest with the Lady Butcher. I wrote you about it. The other two should be getting out of the hospital sometime next week. I've told LB it would be nice if she could tone down her response to these things, and she just smiles and asks me how business is lately. What can I say to that?

She and Crichton are the only ones I ever have a real conversation with. It would be nice to find a new friend.
Love,
Scully

Dear Bert—
Between the Segura pre-trial coverage and the stalled hearings on the renewed independence of Hong Kong, I'm hardly selling any grilled cheese. Everyone here is glued to the link. This poor kid, really, B. First a bunch of elevators going down the hard way to the tune of four hundred thirty-seven people (in situ or by debris, bunch of stupids who didn't duck fast enough), and one of the riders was the Chinese Senator to Earth Congress. That got EarthGov and the media ravens going. Madame senator was in Hong Kong on a so-called goodwill trip before the start of independence hearings. Now she and two of her aides are minced beef, so much for goodwill. The hearings

were immediately suspended, no surprise. I'll bet Hong Kong is very nervous.

And the very next day, Sheila Donaghue—you remember Sheila?—turned up on the net to claim responsibility on behalf of Steel Breeze for what she called the assassination of the senator. That made everybody jump around even more and take a much closer look at the whole incident. And what they came up with was Segura, who had just watched a couple dozen of her pack mates, or whatever they're called, drop a half mile and mash themselves into jelly.

Did she do it? How should I know? Maybe Donaghue just knows a slick photo op when she sees it. She's always been good at press relations, Breeze was lucky to get her. And Segura's a Hope. Maybe she'll even get away with it. Who cares, I—

Sorry about that. Had an absent moment, fell down and cut myself. It's okay. It never hurts any worse than it did the last time.
Goodnight, Bert. Wish you were here.
S.

Dear Bert—
LB informs me that Steel Breeze is the best thing to come down the wire since grilled cheese sandwiches. The party line these days is that Steel Breeze is an international cooperative of organizations whose association is based on mutual goals of separatism and cultural preservation in the face of the growing acceptance of world governance and trade principles. She said it all in one breath, straight-faced. And I thought they were just terrorists.

It's hard to picture Segura that way. All the channels here are running profiles of her. Some of them are just those silly canned biographies with lots of publicity stills and dim-witted voice-overs, but a couple have dug deeper than that. She seems like your average young sheltered celebrity person, maybe dumb about most of the world, but nice enough. Certainly not my notion of a global conspirator.

Today they showed Segura's mother on the link facilitating media conferences for Ko Corporation. Now there's a woman who looks like she needs about a half a ton of barbiturate just to get through the day. Seems like Ko is putting as much distance as possible between themselves and Ren Segura, and making best friends with everyone to protect Ko's status during the Hong Kong/China talks. Wouldn't suit Ko at all to find their perpetual lease suddenly revoked by the nice folks on the mainland. And it isn't too hard to figure out that the best way to hold hands with HK and China right now is to find the highest tree for Ren Segura. It's hard to watch.
S.

That's it, B. Stang Karlsson just signed an Earth Congress emergency resolution revoking Segura's Hope status. That's it for her. No hope at all.

8

AND IT SEEMED THAT SHE ONLY BLINKED, THAT SHE
closed her eyes for a fraction of a moment, and when she opened
them again they were all dead and she was to blame, and she
wasn't a Hope anymore, and she was in terrible, terrible trouble.

They kept her in a cold square room with no windows and a
barred iron door. Bright lights shone behind white opaque plastic
strips across the ceiling. There were more lights in the room across
from hers, and in the other cells to the left and right, and in the
hallway that ran between them from one distant end of the holding facility to the other. The lights were always on, and hallway
monitors showed newslink programs and nature documentaries
continuously; it made it hard to sleep, and seemed cruel until she
thought about the alternative of darkness and silence in this place.

The sounds and smells of Earth Court jail were sterile and
cruel, like the light. Ammonia and moans; those were her days
and nights. And the more subtle odors of fear, the smaller late-
hour sounds of despair. They were all around her, and she was
swallowed up. She was too thin. Her hands trembled. Her stomach hurt all the time. She felt swollen with grief. She slept little,
and moved slowly, almost lazily, with little thought from one moment to the next. And that wasn't right; she ought to be afraid.

She was allowed to see no one except her family and her Ko-sponsored defense counsel. Her parents came once and went away quickly, full of grief and a veil of guilt that she could not pierce: she did not understand why her mother looked so ashamed until she saw Donatella on the link. Her lawyers came when necessary and stayed no longer than they had to. They always brought bad news. No one could verify her version of the incident. The security audio record feed had inexplicably failed in the control room and in the elevators, but the control room video clearly showed her dismissing one of the attendants, commandeering the console, and activating the "Disengage backup system" command. One of elevator attendants had been found dead; the other, not at all.

She waited seven weeks to come to trial, assured all the while by the attorneys that everything was moving extraordinarily fast, too fast for her own good. But it seemed interminable. She was so lonely that sometimes she thought she must die of it. She had a note delivered every day from Snow, each one full of an intense, raddled conviction that the stars would all reverse their courses and somehow everything would be all right. The messages, and knowing Snow was so frightened, only made it worse. The lawyers would not allow her to write back.

And finally she came into the light of the immense courtroom with its vaulted roof and ornate moldings and reinforced, bullet-proof windows, blinking like an underground creature rooted from its burrow; and the whole world was there. There were rows upon rows of people, all with spectator passes or media badges, surrounded by a small army of security. The first day, she could not focus on the audience. There were too many of them, and their faces blurred during the two times she was able to force herself to turn around. Mostly, she sat at the oversized table with her three attorneys, looking at her hands folded in front of her, or at the spiral galaxies of the wood grain. Then the next day, returning from the lunch recess for another round of jury interviews, she locked onto Snow's face in the crowd, and she felt as if she had looked up to see a freight train bearing down on her; the breathlessness, the momentary terror of it before the calm and the acceptance. Of course Snow was here. Jackal cried, seeing her, and Snow wept too and reached out as though she could touch Jackal from a hundred feet away.

And that was what finally made it real for her: Snow's face. Suddenly she felt the wheel of the juggernaut, its edge brushing her skin in the microsecond before the crushing weight rolled over her. Snow's face all alone in a row of strangers, without anyone from Ko or the web or their families, told Jackal that she was doomed.

Five days into the prosecution's case, Jackal's lead attorney came to her cell early in the morning. With him was a short woman in a close-woven black suit that made her white skin look bloodless. Her heavy forearms reminded Jackal of Snow's uncle who drove Ko trucks in Italy. The woman was followed by a young Japanese man carrying both of their briefcases.

Jackal's attorney sat next to her on the edge of the cot, leaving the others to stand. "We need to talk," he said. He took a deep breath. "This is Ms. Arsenault. She represents Ko."

Jackal could not remember how people with manners handled these awkward moments; should she stand up, or offer this grim woman her hand? It terrified her that Ko was here in the person of this Arsenault. She twisted her fingers in the loose folds of her trousers. It seemed to her that she should speak, that she should muster some dignity and say, 'Please, tell me what I can do for my company.' But her throat was dry, and Arsenault did not wait.

"Ms. Segura, I'm the Director of Special Projects for the Ko Executive Council." Arsenault's voice filled the room, although she was speaking conversationally. Without looking back, she held her hand out behind her, and the young Japanese man placed a file in her fingers within a half-second; not a palmtop, but a paper document. Jackal swallowed.

"Ko has been very concerned since the unfortunate incident in Kowloon," Arsenault went on. "As I'm sure you can imagine. The allegations of your association with Steel Breeze are particularly troubling." She looked expectantly at Jackal.

"Yes," Jackal agreed. She wished someone would tell her what to do next.

"You are aware that the corporation is sponsoring your defense."

"Yes."

"We'd all like to see a win-win here, wouldn't we?"

Jackal twisted her fingers harder into her trousers, until she thought the fabric might tear. "What are you talking about, please?"

Arsenault chewed on the inside of her right cheek for five seconds before she answered, and her words were directed to Jackal's attorney. "Jesus Christ, Rafael, I didn't realize how young she was."

"Her age is listed in her records."

"I wasn't referring to her date of birth." She turned back to Jackal and her voice became more clipped. "Ms. Segura, let's get this over with. After reviewing your situation, it is the opinion of the Executive Council that you will be found guilty. You may want to check that with your counsel."

Jackal turned to him and he nodded. "We're all going to give it our best shot, but my professional judgment is that you will not walk away from this."

Arsenault continued, "There's been more than enough bad publicity. We're prepared to offer you several incentives to end this quickly and quietly."

Everyone looked at Jackal. All she could think about was the way the lawyer had said *you won't walk away from this*, as if what was happening to her was a prolonged, messy transit accident. She felt herself turning, rolling, endlessly.

Arsenault went on. "Ms. Segura, it has come to the corporation's attention that your status as a Hope was fraudulently obtained. Your birth occurred sometime after twelve-oh-six in the morning, not in the first second after midnight."

Jackal closed her eyes.

"The corporation was shocked to learn that your parents and the obstetrician conspired to alter the delivery record in order to secure Hope status for you."

Jackal opened her eyes and said like a little girl, "The company knew."

"There's no evidence of that. There is nothing to demonstrate that Ko was aware of any irregular activity. There are, however, indications that you as well as your parents were aware that your status was improper. Certain of your training and advisory records from the last few months are particularly damaging in that respect, although no specific mention of your status is made. Much of the content could be used to demonstrate probable awareness."

"Those are my records! You can't use those, they're private. Rafe, aren't they?"

"Those are Ko corporation records, Ren," he replied. "They're only as private as Ko wants them to be."

Jackal's heartbeat skittered and then settled into a steady, panicked pounding. "What are you saying to me?" she said to Arsenault, and the other woman's eyes pinched for a moment before her face settled back into the professional mask.

"You've already lost your Hope status," Arsenault said. "There's no reason to bring this particular matter up in open court unless the trial proceeds and the prosecutor begins to explore possible motives."

"Do they know about this?"

Rafael answered, "Ko has not yet chosen to bring this information to the attention of the prosecution. But they will, Jackal, if we continue."

"So what, Rafe? What if they do? I'm already not a Hope anymore, it's not like they can take it away from me again."

"No, they can't. But they can implicate your parents."

Jackal went still.

Arsenault said, "It would probably go badly for them, Ms. Segura." She did not seem to be enjoying herself, but she sounded official, implacable. "At best, their employment contracts would be terminated and they would be denied jobs, residency, or benefits at any Ko facility. At worst . . . well, the company has enough evidence to file criminal charges."

Everything turned to ice inside Jackal. The skin went cold on her arms, her chest, the tops of her thighs. Her guts gurgled, and then cramped viciously, so that she was afraid for a moment of shitting on the floor in front of them all. She wasn't aware that she had started to shake until Rafe put his arm around her tightly.

Arsenault turned away. After a moment, her young assistant did the same.

"I know," Rafael said. "It's real bad. I know." For the first time, she saw something like compassion in his dark, narrow face.

"They didn't do anything, Rafe. They only did what Ko told them to, that's all they've ever done. Me too. I thought I belonged to Ko, I thought they were supposed to take care of me. Why are they doing this?"

"Shhh," he said. "I know."

"I'm not a . . . I'm not a terrorist, I didn't mean to kill those people, my web, how could they think . . . I want to pay for it so I can forgive myself, but not like this. Not for all this stuff I didn't do. Everybody is so upset about the goddamn senator and nobody even cares about the web, about Mist and Bear and Tiger." The words caught in her throat so that she had to cough them out. It hurt to breathe. "And I couldn't tell anyone that I knew about not being a Hope, because . . . the company had invested so much in me and I was going to manage projects for EarthGov. . . . And I knew I didn't deserve it but I thought, well, I have to try, I have to do my best and just try to act like a Hope. So no one would know and no one could use it to hurt Ko."

"I know you were doing what you thought was best."

"Best for Ko. Because they made me a Hope in the first place. *You* know." She threw the words at Arsenault's rigid back.

"The clock is ticking, Rafael," Arsenault said, without turning around.

"Ren, I'm going to summarize Ms. Arsenault's offer, and then I'm going to advise you to accept it. It includes an Earth Court guarantee of consideration for your age and former status which will almost certainly result in a reduced sentence. There may be special opportunities that could benefit you during your incarceration. There are resources which can be made available to ease your transition back into society. I advise you not to underestimate the value of some hope of assistance on the back end of all this. It's a better deal than anyone else could offer you. And your family and your web will receive guaranteed job security and appropriate career advancement with Ko for their lifetimes."

Jackal could feel sweat under her arms, on her ribs, in her crotch. The soles of her feet were damp and sticky. "What if I want to have my trial anyway? Take my chances with Earth Court. What if I get up and talk all about this Hope stuff? Don't you think they'd understand? They wouldn't blame me or my parents, they'd blame Ko."

Still, Arsenault did not turn.

"I want you to listen to me very carefully," Rafe said. "The court wants this over as much as Ko. The judge has already approved the deal." He paused. "You can't save yourself, Ren. You can only save everyone else."

She pulled her knees up onto the edge of the mattress and put her head on them. Down between her thighs, she could see a crease in the sheet, and a threadbare spot in the heel of her left sock. She breathed in her own smell. No one spoke to her; no one touched her. The room was silent and still. Away, away, she thought, I'll just go away. She thought about the coastline at the southeast end of Ko Island, the wild place that she loved. She let herself wander in the shadows, among the branches and the roots. She scuffed the leaves. She knelt over the rabbit burrow, pressed her head to the ground and felt the pattering heartbeats beneath the earth. She breathed in the cold, salt sky. She lay back on a hill in the sun and the ground rose up around her and she sank down, down through the soil and stones and was part of it forever . . .

"Ren—"

Then she was back, and Ko was gone. It was gone.

She raised her head. "Tell me what I have to do," she said, and Arsenault turned around.

It made headlines all over the world when Jackal changed her plea. Arsenault sat at the table with the prosecutor while he told the judge that the arrangement was acceptable. "We want this over, Your Honor," he said. "We just want to see justice done." Jackal said nothing except yes to all the questions. The only thing she was conscious of was a single outcry, very clear through the hive-buzz of the audience: Snow shouting *No Jackal, no.* The judge dismissed the jury and set her sentencing date. The guards led her back to the bright barred room.

"I sentence you to confinement for forty years in a maximum se-curity facility without possibility of parole," the judge said, and rapped the funny hammer on the desk, and it was over over over over over.

She waited the next three days in mute terror for them to come for her.

She knew about prison. She had seen training movies on Ko that described the rule by discipline and regimentation, the systematic and deliberate dehumanization designed to put a person down and keep her there, and the anthropological parallels between prisoner culture and primate dominance behavior. Her teachers had used the prison model to demonstrate the consequences of Theory X management techniques on worker morale and productivity.

She knew they were here when the guard at the end of the hall called "Segura!" She was standing up, facing the bars, by the time they reached her, her knees locked so she would not fall.

They were two women. One was tall, with dusky skin. The other was as tall, but pale in a way that made her look smaller and weaker. They had the concealed, watchful air that Jackal had come to associate with official people.

"I'm ready," she told them.

"Brave girl." The pale one grinned.

"Shut up," the dark one said, so ambiguously that Jackal did not know who the order was intended for. The hairs on the back of her neck ruffled; danger here.

The bars opened. "Let's go," the dark one said.

"My things—"

"Leave them. Oh, don't look like that. You'll be back in a few hours. Just come on."

So she went.

They took her in a small armored bus to another part of the compound. At least, she thought so; she did not hear any of the sounds that meant outside, market callers or dogs or the wailing of bandurria or hurdy-gurdies. There was only the occasional sound of steel bars moving in and out of their locks.

They led her into a building lobby where a sleek man sat behind a sleek synthetic mahogany desk. He turned them over to a brisk woman who led them along a series of corridors to a passkey-controlled door, to people in badges that showed their pictures and their names, all followed by MD or PhD. Everyone was very polite to Jackal. No one appeared to notice that she wore arm and leg restraints, but no one offered to remove them.

"We'll call you," one of the older men said to the two women who had brought her. "Come on, love. Time to audition."

"What for?"

"Never mind," he said cheerfully. "Just follow the directions and we'll be done before you know it."

"And then what?" she asked, but he never answered.

She was there for fifteen hours. The day was full of tests: physical, psychological, endurance, intelligence. There were personality inventories and reflex measurements, blood analyses, and an MRI scan of her brain that kept her head locked in place inside a tight metal tube for almost two hours. They took samples of whatever they could find in her eyes, nose, mouth, throat, ears, vagina, rectum. People stopped being nice to her. No one explained the purpose of any procedure; no one warned her when something would hurt, or reassured her that it would not. They asked her direct questions only as a last resort. Mostly they acted as if she were not in the room: *Straighten her left leg, please*; *has she eaten today?* And once, to her disbelief, one anonymous tester looked across her to another and asked, "So what did she do, anyway?"

Finally, when she was exhausted, they told her to lie down on a table, and they tied her arms and legs with padded straps. One man lifted her head while a second man fitted a helmet in place.

"What is this?"

"Just relax."

"What is it?"

"You have to relax or the readings will be skewed."

They went away and she was alone. The lights went out. She heard a voice. "Tell me what you see."

She did not see anything. And then she did.

When it was over, Dusky and Pale sat with three of the doctors for a long while in the room next to the place where Jackal had been taken to rest. She could see them through the open door, together around a table, heads nodding, making notes, accessing records.

The women took her back to her holding cell. She only wanted to drop down on her cot and sleep, but they waved the guard back up the hall. Jackal set her teeth and waited for whatever was next.

"Congratulations," the dark one said. "We've just been negotiating an eighty percent reduction in your sentence. Would you like to make a deal?"

In the silence, Jackal could hear the footsteps of the retreating guard. "Goddamn it," she said bitterly, "I wish you people would stop doing this to me." And then, to her dismay, she burst into tears.

She covered her face with her hands, and leaned into a corner until she could get control of herself. The two women were quiet. When she thought she could manage, she took her head out of the corner and saw them both standing at the other end of the cell, giving her as much room as they could. It confused her to find herself appreciating the courtesy.

"Talk," she said thickly. The dark woman moved forward. The pale one stayed by the far wall.

"Short and sweet. We have an experimental virtual confinement program. You're a candidate. Your participation in VC gets you an adjusted sentence."

She cast about for something to say. "Adjusted how?"

The pale one smiled, and the dark one seemed to settle back on her heels as if relaxing some previous tension. Those signals told Jackal that she had been predictable. Standing there, she knew that she was young and stupid and ill-equipped to make life-shaping decisions. She would not ask the right questions, she would miss the important points, and they would win: they would get her, the game-players, the Jackal-molesters of this strange world that she had been dropped into as surely as the Mirabile elevators had dropped her web mates into oblivion.

"Your sentence would be commuted to eight years in VC."

Eight years. Her legs went wobbly and she sat down on the edge of the cot. When she could speak, she asked, "What's the catch?"

"No catch. Eight years, you're done."

"No." Jackal shook her head. "No, that's too . . . it's too easy."

Dusky shrugged. "VC is an experimental technology. You're being compensated for the risk and for your contribution to the advancement of science."

"Tell me more about it."

Pale moved forward. Jackal saw it then, the techie look; it reminded her of Turtle, and that hurt so bad that she missed the woman's first few words.

". . . eighteen percent at any given moment."

"Excuse me?"

"In prison or psych. Some kind of restrictive-rehabilitative setting."

"I'm sorry," Jackal stammered, "eighteen percent of what?"

"The world," the woman said flatly. "On average. Some days are busier than others. But all confinement facilities are overcrowded. And so what happens, you get riots, epidemics, facility disruptions which lead to cost overruns which lead to worsening conditions which lead to more disturbances, and in the meantime recidivism is up." She shook her head. "It's definitely a systems problem."

"Feedback loop," Jackal agreed, unable to resist the impulse.

"Right," Pale replied, mouth quirked as she nodded. "Don't often meet people in this program who understand systems thinking."

"I come from Ko." Then she realized that she didn't, not anymore. Even after she got out of prison—if she ever did, if she didn't die of despair or cholera or a sharpened piece of metal through the throat—she would never be allowed to return to Ko. They didn't want her.

"We want to step out of the loop," Pale continued. "Instead of figuring out how to house more people for longer sentences, we're trying to offer an alternative that produces the same severity of effect in a markedly shorter time period. You'll appreciate the technology." She began to use her hands then, drawing pictures in the air. Jackal sat numbly. "We use a shaped magnetic signal that affects your temporal lobes." She placed her hands like a cap over her own head. "You'll be given a drug that increases temporal lobe sensitivity—sorry, am I going too fast for you?"

Jackal felt her face twisting. "Garbo? You're using Garbo technology?"

Pale shrugged. "Never heard of Garbo."

Jackal tried to get her brain to slow down and think.

Pale was saying, ". . . replace your normal sense of time and place with a programmed template replicating the experience of conventional solitary confinement."

Solitary. "Solitary confinement? You want me to spend eight

years alone in some kind of jail in my head?" She heard her voice thinning and becoming shrill.

Pale put her hands down, regarded Jackal warily. "Actually, you'll spend about ten months in a maximum security psychiatric facility. It will only feel like eight years. That's the beauty of it, don't you see?" Pale spoke earnestly, sincerely. "We can process people faster, more efficiently, no violence, controllable costs, all without losing the punitive effects mandated by the courts. We can handle more people in less space. When that percentage rate gets up to twenty-two, twenty-five percent, we'll be ready. It's a great system solution. Long-term, self-containing, scalable."

"It's more than that," Dusky interrupted. "It's your ticket back out into the world while you still have some time to enjoy it, Ms. Segura. Do the time and come back to the world at the age of sixty-three. Or do it this way and spend your twenty-fourth birthday in the sunshine. In case you're not very good with math, that's an extra—"

"Thirty-nine years," Jackal said hollowly; the number seemed to echo around the small cell. "I'm good with math."

"Smart," Dusky said. "Stay smart. You'll never get this offer again."

Jackal closed her eyes. She heard the dark woman say, "We'll give you a minute to think it over."

She tried to shut her ears to the sound of their breathing, to their whispers in the corner. She wanted to listen only to herself; she wanted to find a small voice between her ears or in the pit of her stomach that would speak to her. But there was only her heartbeat and her stomach groaning; there was only wind and viscera inside her, and no one to tell her what to do.

Thirty-nine years.

She opened her eyes. The two women were watching her.

There were more tears now, spilling gently down her cheeks. "I don't think I can be alone for eight years," she said, helplessly.

Dusky shrugged.

*   *   *

There were six security guards with her on the journey to the Earth Government Rehabilitation and Adjustment Center on the outskirts of Al Iskandariyah. They put two diazepam patches in her elbow, so she felt distanced enough to be amused at the excess of muscle power that quivered around her, ready to uncoil and crush her at the slightest provocation. They bound her with monofilament restraints that bit into her slightly every time the transport hit a bump.

They rode in the back of an armored truck with a financial security service logo on the side. When she asked, one of the guards, a middle-aged latina with soft brown eyes and hard muscles, told her that all dangerous prisoners were ferried in rented money transports. "These're much more secure than your ordinary prison vans. Nobody wants to lose their money. They take better care of it than they do the prisoners, that's for sure." The guard laughed with Jackal, but when the truck arrived at the R&A she was rough getting Jackal out of the van, and she did not answer when Jackal said good-bye and tried to smile.

Two guards delivered her to a white-smocked man with tanned white skin and gray hair. He was solicitous with her, calling her Ms. Segura and asking if he could bring her coffee. She drank it while she signed a stack of consent forms. She authorized the procedures. She accepted the terms. She agreed not to discuss her participation in the program with anyone prior to entering virtual confinement. It took almost forty minutes, and she had to ask him to remove her arm restraints after the first ten. "Oh, yes, of course," he said, and apologized for not having thought of it himself, but he did not offer to take the filament off her ankles.

She did not bother to read the forms. She had already consented.

After that, he took her to a tiny room with a steel door, where he freed her legs and let her sleep.

*   *   *

"You have a call."

She did not know how long she had been asleep. The guard led her to a room with a table, two chairs, an observation camera. A viewscreen. She saw Snow.

"Oh, god," she whispered, and went forward.

"Jackal?" Snow's voice was faint and tremulous. Behind her image, Jackal could see that Snow was in her own apartment, on Ko. Home.

"Jackal . . . Hi . . . Your lawyer got me this call. He said you're being—that when they take you to prison I won't be able to talk to you again and I wanted . . . Jackal, are you okay?"

"Snow . . ." She did not know how to answer. She wanted to put her hands right through the screen, wrap her arms around Snow, pull her close. And she was glad that Snow was so far away.

Snow said, "You look terrible."

"Great. Thanks." Jackal shook herself, tried again. "I'm okay, really. I . . . I'm scared, I guess."

Snow began to cry, a hopeless sound. "Me too."

"Don't cry, Snow. Honey, don't." Snow was sobbing now, dragging in short sharp breaths like a drowning woman about to go back under. Jackal said desperately, "I can't stand it, I can't . . . you have to stop, please stop. Please."

"I'm sorry." There was a long moment of silence. Jackal watched Snow steady her breathing, tamp down her fear, wipe her eyes and nose and then look back at the screen, straight into Jackal's eyes across the miles and the horrible distance between them. Jackal thought, she's so beautiful.

"Oh, Snow," she said softly, "what are you doing?"

"I had to see you. I had to say . . . I don't know. I don't know what to say. I can't imagine saying good-bye."

"No."

"No."

Silence.

"My parents?"

"They're . . . they can't . . ." Snow turned her hands palm up.

"No, I guess not."

"No."

Snow sighed. She was sitting cross-legged on her bed, her hair half in her face. Jackal burned the picture into her brain. *I will never forget*, she thought, *I will never never forget how it feels to touch her and how she laughs and the way she eats apples and the smell of the skin on her ribs and how everything is more clear when I see it with her, I will never forget, I will never* and then the guard put his head inside the door and said, "One minute," and she knew it was almost over—not just the call, but her life as she'd known it. She couldn't breathe. Her life. Her life. What was she supposed to do?

"Snow—" she said frantically, "Snow, I—"

"No," Snow said, "Jackal, no—"

"I'm sorry. I'm so sorry. The web, I . . . please don't hate me, Snow—"

"I love you, Jackal."

"I'm so sorry. I wish . . . I just want you to be happy. I want you to have all good things. I'll miss you every single fucking day." She put her hands right up against the screen, against Snow, and Snow reached out too.

"Don't leave me, Jackal."

"Snow—"

"Don't leave me."

"I love you."

"I love you, too."

"Snow, I—"

The screen went black, and a second later the message *Trans-*

mission terminated flashed in red letters. "Sorry," the guard said from behind her. "Regulations."

Jackal wrapped her arms around herself and held tight, and kept herself together that way until she reached her little cell; then she howled until finally someone came with a needle. She held out her arm and was glad to feel the sting.

9

Hello! My Name Is
Snow Laussen

. . . *I WILL WALK ACROSS THE PLAZA NOW AND THINK only about my project. I will think about how to solve the problem—*

"Hi, Snow."

Nod. Walk—the problem with the incentive program at the vendor in Lyons, how do we reward them for increasing just-in-time delivery volumes without inadvertently encouraging them to loosen their quality standards in order to meet schedules? Walk across the plaza. Ignore the voices around me, all the voices—

"—noodles? There's a place—"

"—miss the train—"

"—see me anymore, she says I—"

"—middle of the meeting!"

"—the garden in summer—"

The garden in summer. The web in the garden in summer. Jackal with her face turned up to the sun, breathing in the smell of the garden. Jackal. I will not think about Jackal now. I will think only about my project.

"—it's just that I've been a little tired lately—"

That's a familiar voice and because I am not thinking I turn, and there is Donatella in a bright blue suit and a startled cosmetic smile: but her eyes are dull.

"Snow! Snow, how wonderful to see you, honey."

"Hello."

"How are you?"

What a stupid question. "I'm okay."

"Me too. I'm good too. I have a terrific new job, did I tell you? My new boss—" *The woman next to her with the still face.*

Nod. Speak quickly. "I have to get going." *I need to keep walking and thinking only about safe things, busy things.*

"I'm sure you can take a minute to tell me what's happening with you. It seems like such a long time since we've really talked."

"Since Jackal was arrested."

"Oh." *She doesn't like that I said that; she looks at the new boss to see how she's taking it.* "Really? I guess we just let the time get away from us. That was wrong. Jackal would have wanted us to stay in touch."

"Why?"

"Well . . . of course she would. She would have wanted us to be family."

I can't begin to imagine what I should say now. Does Donatella Segura know that she's insane? Should I tell her? Sometimes I wonder how Jackal survived this woman's mothering. And I understand why Jackal is so blindly duty-bound and why she is afraid to ask people for help. Why she guards her core so fiercely. It's because she's an orphan whose parents are still alive.

I said good-bye to Jackal yesterday, I want to say. I want to throw it in her face. I want to scream. And what does Donatella Insane Segura want? She wants to hold my hand. "We have to help each other, Snow. Like family. We have to go on. Our Jackal is gone and we have to learn to live without her." *Now she's crying.* "She fell off the cliff and she's gone."

I've just figured out how to solve that problem in Lyons. It's just fallen into my head. I'll propose a contract that deep-discounts the price of the parts we're buying and supplements with huge incentives for quality. They'll only make money if the parts meet standards. Then we'll escalate the volumes over the next six months. That will give them time to figure out how to scale their processes. It's the frog in the stewpot model.

"I have to go."

"Of course," *Donatella says, smiling brightly as if there were no black streaks of makeup starring her eyes.* "Now don't be a stranger."

I will walk the rest of the way across the plaza and down the broad steps, take the right-hand path that leads toward the koi pond. I will hate Donatella Segura for the rest of my life. When I scuff through the gravel of the path, each step sounds like Jackal's name; Jackal Jackal Jackal; and when I run, the gravel whispers don't leave me, don't leave me . . .

10

THE FOLLOWING MORNING, A SECURITY GUARD TOOK
Jackal back to the same conference room. It was hard to look at the
blank screen. She kept her head down. A man came in. He was
dressed in casual trousers and a loud jacket, silk in a multicolored
fishscale pattern that had been in fashion six years earlier. His hair
and his face were too long, and he wore neither well.

"I'm Jenkins," he said in a monotone. He sounded indifferent
and chatty at the same time; it confused Jackal and made her wary.

He sat in the chair across from her. When she kept silent, he
nodded, as if he had been talking to himself and agreed with himself on some particular point.

"I'm the VC counselor at this facility. Here's a brochure about
the procedure, read it at your convenience. It's my job to talk with
you about the program, answer any questions you have. That kind
of thing."

"It'll be the first time since I got here that anyone explained anything."

"Uh huh." He nodded again. There was another silence. "So,
any questions?"

Jackal blinked.

"No? Great," he said, and stood up. "Good luck." He was

halfway to the door before Jackal recovered and said, "Wait!" But when he turned, she didn't know what to ask. She was clutching the brochure he had given her so tightly that it was creased along its length; she held it up so he could see it. "Is this going to tell me everything I need to know?"

"That piece of paper can tell you as much as I can. If you need to know more than that, well . . ."

"What's going to happen to me?"

He spoke as if she were a child. "It's an experimental program. We don't know what will happen. That's why we're doing the experiment. Anything else?"

This time she let him go.

She read the brochure over and over in her cell. It told her she would be subjected to a templated confinement experience. She would be fed intravenously and catheterized. Her head would be shaved for better conduction. Her body would be encased from the shoulders down in a locked medical-minder case "for your own protection." The minder would monitor and feed and clean her out, and electro-stimulate her muscles every two real-days while she was incarcerated. The brochure told her that based on computer model projections, she was likely to experience depression, anxiety, time distortion, and loss of mental acuity; these symptoms were individual in onset, intensity, and duration, and could not be reasonably predicted. She agreed to a post-confinement debriefing so that her experience of the template could be compared to other participants.

When you awaken from virtual confinement, you may experience mild disorientation, the text said. The program would offer her the opportunity to remain after her debrief for forty-eight hours at no expense, including a complimentary session with her VC counselor. That made her shudder.

When it was time, four large men came for her.

She said, "I want to change my mind."

Two of them entered the cell and picked her up from the bed, one holding each arm. "No, you don't understand," she repeated, "I want to change my mind. I'll take the forty years, okay? I'm out of the program." The two men hauled her by her arms to the cell door. "No," she said, and tried to twist away. The other two men each took one of her legs. None of them spoke to her. They carried her like a dressed deer down the hall. "No, goddamn it!" she yelled. "I've changed my fucking mind, I don't want to do this!" But no one was listening. Halfway down a long hallway, she stopped yelling and shut her mouth hard enough to hurt her jaws. Fifteen seconds later, the men released her legs and arms, and she walked shakily between them the rest of the way to the barred gate at the end. She shook while they completed the identity check and let her and the guards in. She shook while they led her to a glass-walled room with a stretcher surrounded by equipment. She shook while they stripped her and shaved her head and laid her out on the cold table and put a drip into her neck and other things into other parts of her. She shook while a woman with a stethoscope took her pulse and listened to her heart; it reminded her of her childhood examinations and she felt just a little reassured. And then the doctor brought a syringe toward her, and all the fear sawed back through her like a riptide. The drug curled inside her. Her eyes fluttered. When she closed them, it seemed that she stood at the edge of something dark and deep. She thought of Tiger, falling free; and then she went down.

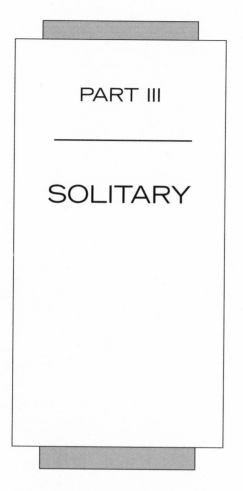

PART III

SOLITARY

11

AND NOW HER EYES WERE OPEN. AND HERE SHE WAS, tucked into a tense-muscled packet, wrapped tight around herself, rocking, rocking, breathing too fast. Trying not to know, not to begin, and above all not to count the days. But it was too late, her mind had already leaped ahead—

—and this was the first of two thousand nine hundred and twenty days.

She thought, what is the next thing to do? And there was a very small voice in her brain that said *Look. See.*

No, that was too hard. She would just stay curled into herself like a snail for a little longer, until she was ready. But adrenaline drilled through her with each heartbeat, and her muscles coiled like something explosive at the end of a burning fuse. So there was nothing to do but raise her head and look around.

Light. Gray stone around her. She pushed herself up onto her elbows and swung her legs over the side of what turned out to be a narrow metal bed. Was there a slight delay between the brain's impulse and the body's reaction? She straightened up slowly; various muscles twitched in odd arpeggios in her legs, stomach, shoulders. She felt as if she were half an inch outside herself, ghosted, like video through a bad link.

She stood in a square cell, with a concrete floor, stone block walls, and a flat ceiling at least twelve feet overhead, out of reach. Everything was gray. The bed frame on her left, pushed into one corner of the room, held a thin mattress, one sheet, a blanket, a flat pillow. A viewscreen covered three-quarters of the far wall. An opaque lighted circle was set into the center of the ceiling, too high to reach. The light in the room reminded her of lukewarm water; the air, too, was tepid, and she could feel no draft or current. Everything was neutral, flat.

Two plastic panels with molded handles sat flush against the wall to her right, opposite the bed. Behind them she found her larder, shelves of simple single items. She remembered the tests she was given, to think of egg and apple and butter, and here were the results. Phantom food. It would not matter to her body if she never ate a bite during her sentence; and if she never opened the larder again, the apples would still be as firm, the cheese as buttery yellow, as she had just seen them. Real; not real. She would never need a toilet here, or a shower. And that led to other anxious questions: would she feel it when her body was exercised in real time? Would her muscles suddenly begin to twitch on their own? What if the medical minder gave her the wrong nutrient mix and she got sick in VC? What if the lights went out and never came back on?

If something goes wrong, how will they fix it? she wondered frantically, turning around and around in a tight circle in the center of her cell. And then, *surely they aren't going to leave me all alone for all these years, they'll check on me, they'll answer my questions, someone will come—*

She stopped herself. She only had to look around to know that no one would ever come. How could they, into a place with no windows, with no doors?

*   *   *

She sat on the floor opposite the blank screen, slumped against the wall with her arms locked around her bent legs. She did not know how long she had been there. Long enough to play the idea of *no doors, no windows* over and over in her mind like a musical phrase. No way in or out, except through the technology in the real-time world. The machines would keep her here inside her own head for an unfathomable length of time while the minutes clicked over on the clock in the outside world. And those minutes would be her hours, and the weeks would be her seasons. Snow's final month of training at Ko would be Jackal's second year of numb gray solitude, alone, alone.

I won't cry, she told herself; and she thought it was probably true. She was hollow now, as if someone had stuck a sponge down her throat and absorbed everything within her. Perhaps it would be easier to get through—and here her mind skipped over what exactly it was she would need to get through, the circumspect voice within her saying *no, not ready*—if she kept that numbness, if she felt nothing. Perhaps she could move through—again, that skip, that space where the concept of *eight years of this* simply would not fit—like one of the balloons she released over the Ko Island shoreline every birthday: self-contained, and empty of everything except the need to rise, rise.

All right, then: get up. She pushed herself awkwardly from the floor. Rise. She still had the sensation of physical movements being out of sync. She ran her hands up her arms, down her breasts and ribs and around her back, across her bottom and down her legs, everywhere she could reach, and it was as if she touched herself through a layer of plastic film. She still had all her hair: it too felt slightly wrong. She thought of her body, the real one, laying loose and unconscious in a medical minder; that body turning soft and rotting subtly from within because her attention, her self, was not there. *Don't think about that*: the small voice was stronger now, and she let herself agree.

She made a tiny sandwich of soft wheat baguette with butter and cheese and a slice of cold ham from the larder. She kneaded and poked it, sniffed it, and touched her tongue lightly to a buttery crumb. She took a bite. The food felt substantial in her mouth, but when she chewed and swallowed it simply vanished somewhere between her throat and her stomach. She could not eat any more. She put it back into the cupboard and shut the panel. Then she opened it again: the mauled sandwich was gone, and everything was new. She closed the larder very gently.

She considered whether to turn on the viewscreen, but the internal voice advised her to save it for tomorrow. She stripped her clothes off, tossed them on the foot of the bed, and crawled under the blanket. Light shone against her closed eyelids. It took a while to remember what she was supposed to do. Then she said, from a scratchy throat, "Dark." The light dimmed. The pearl-sized voice hummed approvingly, soothingly, in her brain, made it easier to lie in the semi-dark and think of nothing at all; and she did not know it when she finally slept.

Day 205

It really wasn't so bad. The Garbo technology was amazing, even in this templated application. She wondered if the engineer was still wearing her bunny slippers.

She had light and dark, room to exercise, a place to sleep, many foods, and the viewscreen with its colorful display programs. She was making the best of it. She sat on her bed and told herself stories from books she had read, making up things to fill the gaps when she could not remember what happened next. Some of the things she invented left her laughing out loud, pleased with her cleverness, her resilience. She played all the parts, created different voices for the characters. She recalled poems that she knew, and music. She sang lyrics and melodies. She imagined performing with her favorite stars, brilliant before an unseen audience. She pretended to be an orchestra.

She stayed busy experimenting with food, finding different ways to wear her clothes. She constructed elaborate sexual fantasies, touched herself for hours at a time and came in one wave after another in rhythm with the colors on her screen. She measured every bit of the cell she could reach, using her hands and her feet as units. Each wall was precisely twenty Jackalfeet long, and more than seventeen Jackalhands high, which was as far as she could reach even standing on her bed. She knew her limits now; she could work within them.

But every once in a while, more often lately, she could think of nothing new to do, no better way to use the time. She worried about running out of stories, of finding no more songs. She began to imagine that the technicians in the real-time world were watching her brain readings spike during her orgasms, laughing at her. She became uneasy with herself. And she began to take comfort in patterns, in repeatable actions, in controlled movements. There was no harm in looking for structure. She would work it out. Through it all she kept herself good company. She really was handling it well.

The comforting, sensible voice within her agreed, and told her so more and more often.

Day 377

"Light," she said. "Screen on."

She woke quickly these days, as if her sleep was so like her waking time that it was no longer hard to slip from one into the other. She got up naked and stretched, ran in place, worked her muscles and tendons. Her motion was smooth and steady.

The viewscreen flickered; she kept it on continuously these days. She turned her back to it so that she would not be distracted by the fractals that ebbed and flowed across the wall. Soon the program would enter the next phase of its long cycle; random rainbow geometrics, followed by stylized morphing faces in primary colors, and then a sequence of animated patterned waves rolling onto a chalk-white beach. She liked the waves best; they made her feel as if she were always on the verge of moving forward.

After her final push-ups and sit-ups, she rose from the floor and rubbed herself with a corner of her blanket. She scrubbed hard to make her skin tingle and turn red. She had learned that physical sensation was important to help her stay connected with her body; to keep it solid against the empty space inside that threatened to eat her one cell, one minute, at a time; against the internal voice that seemed to be growing in power, in intimacy, and how it sometimes gibbered instead of speaking. How it sometimes was too loud. How it sometimes would not stop.

Dangerous ground. She scrubbed her head to wipe the thoughts. When her mind was clean again, it was time to pick up her clothes from the floor at the foot of the bed: socks neatly rolled next to panties, which were folded on top of a generic pullover shirt, which was bundled on top of soft trousers, a little pyramid of clothes. Shoes stood next to the pile, right aligned with left, toes pointing toward the head of the bed, in the direction that she had after careful consideration named north. South was the viewscreen wall. The bed lay on the east wall, and the food cupboard on the west. The north wall was blank, where she used to imagine the door belonged.

She was dressed: time to eat. Today she made her first meal out of granola and plain yogurt. Sometimes it was bread with honey. A few times she simply pulled apart sticky chunks of chocolate cake and licked the frosting off every finger. For a while she had been deliberate in choosing breakfast foods, until it occurred to her that it hardly mattered. There's no morning here, her voice told her: so simple, but it shook her. She had wanted it to be break-fast, so that she would know when it was morning and then after-noon and then evening and then time to sleep, to get up and move through the cycle again. But now she had first meal instead of breakfast, and she ate what she damn well pleased.

She licked her bowl one last time and put it back dirty into the cupboard. Then she folded her blanket into quarters and sat on it cross-legged against the north wall. She began by counting out loud: today by threes, from one to four thousand and two. To-morrow she would count by fours.

After she counted, she paced out the perimeter of her cell, skirt-ing the bed, fitting toe to heel so that her feet measured each pace precisely. It had become a point of reference whether or not she made a mistake in her count, or stumbled in her measuring. Today was perfect. She knew it was a good sign; today would be a good day, an easy day to do.

"Snow," she said aloud.

She was not sure exactly when there had begun to be people in-side her to talk to. She found it easier not to worry about it. It was nice to be in charge of all her conversations, to choose when and to whom she connected, to be able to repeat the best bits over and over if she wanted. On good days, like today, she really could hear people's voices between her ears, and she did not have to rewind parts of the conversation to adjust the responses, to make them sound more true. On good days, her people came to her and she was comforted. She had such wonderful talks with Snow, with Bear. She had forgiven her parents. She understood Tiger so much better now.

"Hi, honey," Snow said.

"How are you?"

"I'm okay. Training's going better now." Snow told Jackal all about the line re-engineering and total quality human resource management program that she had recommended to resolve labor issues at a Ko micro-subsidiary in Aberdeen.

"I miss you," Jackal said.

"How do you like being alone?"

What did that mean? "I try not to think about it too much. Sometimes I feel like I'm not even here, like I'm nowhere. That's good, really. The time goes by fastest when it's like that."

"So you just check out, is that it? What are you afraid of?"

"I—"

"What's the point, then? What good are you if you can't face it, look it right in the eye and rise above it? Rise, remember? I *do*, therefore I am. Descartes was an idiot."

She realized she was digging her fingernails into the skin of her forearms, hanging on tight. Why was Snow talking to her this way? And then she had a bad thought.

"Who is this?" she said.

"Puppy. Cow," the voice said, not bothering to sound like Snow at all now, rich and malicious and perilously loud within her: and suddenly it wasn't a good day anymore, in spite of the tasty meal and the perfect counting. Suddenly it looked like one of the very worst days indeed.

"Moo," the voice said softly, just inside her right ear. It had become her greatest fear that one day she would hear the voice speak from across the room, or right beside her: that it would chew its way out of her brain and she would be locked up with it, and it would eat her alive.

"Moo hoo," soft in her ear. She shook her head once, again, harder. "Go away!" she hissed.

"Moo too." In her left ear, now. Then sudden laughter traveling along the inside of her skull from left to right and back again. She jerked onto her feet. "Stop it," she yelled, and shook her head harder as the laughter rattled around inside it. She swung around to face the screen; distorted multicolored squares and triangles seemed to wink in and out in time with the noises in her brain.

"NO," she yelled. The voice stopped like a jaw snapping tight around the sound, and the colored shapes on the screen winked into black. Her breath seemed to go with them, and she thought she might fall over. She leaned forward and put her hands on her knees to steady herself. When she looked up, the screen was once again placidly running through its fractals as if nothing had happened, as if no time at all had passed since she sat down with Snow.

Snow. How was she going to be able to talk to Snow, after this? How would she know it was really Snow, and not the thing pretending to be Snow so it could sneak up on her, climb up out of her, take her by the throat and shake her until she broke? She stood in the middle of her cell, rubbing her hands around each other, right foot tapping, breathing hard. Goddamn voice. She snorted. Goddamn voice, pretending to be Snow, ruining her day. It couldn't be allowed, she would have to deal with it, show it, show it—

She went rigid and stood still, fists clenched, knees locked, taking in slow deep breaths until she felt in control again. She would find other things to do with her time. Better things.

She asked the viewscreen for the date. It told her that today was Day 377. Her second year.

Day 424

She opened her eyes and saw gray. She did not know whether she had been sleeping or only drifting in some other space, awake but not present, out of her mind. She blinked, and her vision was still full of gray; so she lay without moving and slowly, carefully worked out that she was stretched out on the floor on her left side, with her nose only inches from the stone of one of her cell walls.

That was odd. And she was naked. She rolled over onto her back. The light was on full bright, and she had to squint and turn her head away. Light? When was the last time she had tucked herself into bed and called for dark? When was last night?

She closed her eyes and tried to track some small scent of memory along its backtrail. Nothing. She turned onto her stomach and pushed herself up onto her hands and knees, and then squatted back on her heels. The process took a long time, and was much more difficult than it should have been, because every muscle was tight and sore. Red patches on her forearms and shins were beginning to fade to yellow bruises with blue-purple centers. Her head throbbed. She found a swollen place above her right ear that hurt when she touched it; and it all shocked her so much that she could only pull her hand away from her head and look at it as if she'd never seen it before. She was not supposed to suffer physical pain in VC, any more than she was supposed to feel hungry or sick. But she was sore. She was damaged.

She was very frightened.

She looked up at the screen. Tidal surges of vermilion and naphthol and viridian rolled across a strontium beach; the screen almost seemed to flex under the weight. "Date," she tried to say, and her voice scraped so thick and strained out of her throat that the screen did not understand her, did not respond. "What is the date," she said again, more controlled, and in the lower left corner, amid the swirling colors, a display appeared: Day 424.

She ran her fingers through her hair, wincing when they rubbed across the tender place on her skull. She clasped her hands behind her head so that her elbows were drawn in tight in front of her nose, and her head was tucked into a little cave made out of her arms, a small safe place where she could calm her breathing and think this through.

Day 424. The last day she could remember clearly was, oh, maybe 421 or 422. It must have been 421, because the digits added up to seven, which was a bad number for her. She was very careful on days that added up to seven to observe her routines exactly, to make sure that things went right. She remembered standing in front of the open cupboard, trying to decide what the best middle meal was for a day that added up to seven, and then . . . nothing.

She could not remember. There was a sudden, horrible pain at the side of her head and she moaned and the next instant found herself under her bed, wedged into the corner as far as her body would go. When she scrabbled out from under the metal frame to stand and look at the screen, the left corner display read Day 425.

"What is going on?" she shouted, and her voice cracked around the words.

"Moo, cow," something said.

She yelped, and spun around in a circle. There was no one there.

Oh, this is bad, this is very bad, she thought frantically, very bad, very bad—

"Don't turn around," said the voice, from right behind her.

She froze. Her sore muscles spasmed once, and she winced and squeezed her eyes shut and bit her lower lip.

"Oh, you're a tough one," the voice said, with a sort of syrupy glee, "tough as old boots but I got you, I got you."

No no no, she thought.

"We're going to have some fun. No, don't move," it hissed, as her head jerked back. "No matter what happens you mustn't turn around, oh no."

Her eyes were still closed because she did not want to see.

"I'm the crocodile," it said, thickly. "I'm standing behind you with my big big teeth open over your neck."

And she could feel it behind her, if she opened her eyes she would see the tips of those enormous jaws on either side of her. And now she understood how she must have come by her bruises, fighting unremembered battles. And she had lost. She was lost. Oh, that was such a bleak thought. And she was so scared. But at least she could go down with her eyes open. She would see. She opened her eyes and found herself staring at the harsh colors rippling across the screen, and then they changed—

—and she saw herself. Her face. Just her face, calm in a way that she had never felt, strong in a way that she had never seen in her mirror, not fearless but not afraid. A face made from the inside out. Here it was, looking straight at her; and it was for Jackal as if she paused in front of the open elevator doors of Mirabile, only an impulse away from the fatal step. She was so tired. She wanted to weep. She wanted to lean back and rest in the jaws of madness. But she also wanted to be the face that she saw before her; and it was not a mad face. She was so tired. She bent her head, and the flesh of her cheeks and forehead tightened until she thought her skull would shatter under the force. Behind her there was an indrawn breath, a sound of preparation, a feel of motion in the air: and Jackal threw back her head and screamed from her guts, an ululation of rage and despair, and whirled her body around with her fists punching and elbows stabbing, her teeth tearing at the air behind her. "I won't let you," she yelled, "I won't let you!" She grabbed the air and held it as she went down hard, and then she was rolling, kicking, ripping, bludgeoning, still yelling, and the crocodile voice was barking in anger, wailing in resistance, snarling, pleading and then *snap* it was gone. There was nothing but the sound of her own ragged breathing.

She lay on the floor, winded. When she had the energy to raise her head, she saw that her body was unmarked. The bruises were gone, as if they never had been there. Nothing hurt. She touched herself gently. She felt fine. "I won't let you," she whispered, and then, finally, she began to cry.

*   *   *

Day 500

She lived now as if recovering from a long illness. She treated her body like something that might easily break. She made no casual movement. She breathed shallowly. She tried not to make any noise. She ate small, frequent meals and sipped constantly from the bottle of clear water that refilled itself over and over in her cupboard. She was jumpy. She dropped things. She spent hours staring at the patterns on her screen.

She slept in long stretches during her nights, and in short, hard daytime naps that left her feeling confused. Her first waking thought was always that the crocodile was back, hiding under the bed with its terrible jaws turned sideways to catch an ankle or a dangling hand. She woke every day to fear, and she walked carefully.

One day she ate three meals in a row of cold boiled egg crumbled onto buttered pumpernickel bread, with salt and pepper. It was one of her earliest taste memories, undemanding, comforting. She sat on the floor with the egg-and-bread cupped in her hand, taking half-bites, making it last. She thought about what she had been doing since the crocodile: trying to stay quiet, trying to give little notice to the unfilled moments. Trying to make the small comforts last. She sighed and swallowed the last bit of buttery crust. That was all there was. Empty time between empty meals. Confined in this empty place.

This empty place is my cell, she thought. I am in prison and this is my cell. She felt a sort of cold wonderment, and a sense of standing again on the edge of the long drop. Oh no, mustn't fall. And that idea, fuzzy and inarticulate as it was, gave her something to grip, an anchor. She must continue to walk carefully. She must not splinter and scatter herself again. She must not break. She must endure.

*   *   *

Day 752

It took a long time to understand what she had to do, but when she did it made such sense. The way to endure was to have nothing that could be taken away. And for that she needed control. The crocodile had gotten to her because she was undisciplined and soft; but now she would be tough. She programmed each moment. She was relentless about keeping a meal schedule, but she no longer noticed what she ate. It didn't matter. She exercised once every day, and reined in her restlessness at other times.

She planned it as Neill had taught her at Ko, one step at a time, and when she was ready, when her discipline had hardened, she began to make herself unbreakable. She went about it precisely and with great purpose. First she made a white board in her mind. Then she let a thought draw itself in colored ink on the clean surface, and erased it, and it was simply gone. No longer anything to do with her. Some things were harder to wipe away, but she persisted. It was like a mental fast; she cleaned the impurities from herself until her mind ran like stream water, shallow and cold.

It took a long time. She worked hard. She cut away the grief of the company's betrayal. She burned out the image of her parents, the way her father's shoulders had bowed when he turned away from her the last time, her mother on the net. She stripped the web away, the living and the dead, one person at a time. She cauterized all her memories of Ko Island: the long pebbled beaches; the solid silence of the wood that would grow now without her; the enormous, lucid sky. She put away her dreams and her fears of being a Hope. That was gone.

Then it was time for the last deep surgery. It was time for Snow. Jackal wrote it on her white board. Snow. She considered it for a time. Snow. Wiped it slowly away. And there it was again: Snow, still shining bright, barely smudged, stubborn like Snow herself. Behind it, within the glossy surface of the board, the reflection of Snow's face as Jackal had last seen it the night before her sentence began, wet with tears, puffy with pain. Snow's mouth was open, as if she might speak at any moment: perhaps she would say don't, Jackal, don't. But Jackal did: she erased Snow's pleading face stroke by stroke, over and over and over and over again. And even when Snow was completely gone, Jackal kept rubbing the place in her mind where Snow had been, like polishing one spot on a silver globe until it was shining and smooth. Then she was clean and empty. When she looked inside, nothing looked back.

Day 900

She was stone.

She no longer counted to four thousand. She no longer folded her clothes right side over left. She did not hear voices anymore. She was sea glass, opaque, utterly smoothed by a battering tide.

No, not quite smooth; as she sat on the floor of her cell with the remains of a meal scattered around her, as she thought of being a seashell, the image of the ocean brought her the memory of swimming laps, furious exhausting laps in Ko gymnasium's hundred-meter indoor pool, where the air smelled of chlorine and human bodies, and the noise of people echoed like the music of soft drums; swimming hard in the middle lane and riding the surges made by other bodies. She found herself rocking slightly on her crossed legs on the floor of her cell, her neck stretched as if she were about to turn her head to come up for air before lunging forward into the next stroke. And yet even the small amount of energy to stand and replace her used plate in the cupboard suddenly seemed too much to spare. She sat lotus-legged with her arms loose and her hands cupped beside her knees, her head bent so that her hair hung before her like a curtain almost closed.

Oh, fuck, she thought, with infinite sadness: Jackal, this just won't do.

It was too much for her. There were too many memories. The

lightest touch of her former life, the faintest breath of the Jackal that was, could crumble the rock from her and expose the flesh that hurt, that missed, that mourned. No matter how many times she rebuilt, there would be another memory ready like a typhoon to bring it all down. She would have to wash all her self away if she wanted to stand like stone through the next five and a half years.

She began to breathe harder and faster. Wash it all away. Her chest felt tight. What had she done? She had scrubbed out her home, her family, her lover, her life, like rubbing grease from her hands. She had tried to wash herself away, but here she was, still clinging to herself like a stubborn stain. She had tried to wash herself away. Now she was trembling. How could she have done that? It was like killing herself, or something close to it. It was like finding a dark pit inside herself and pitching headfirst into it, when what waited at the bottom was not that much different from the teeth of the crocodile. She began to weep. I didn't mean it! But she had meant it and it was done. Ko and the Earth Court had taken most of her life away and Jackal had given them the rest, like an earnest child trying to be good.

I am in prison. She reached out and touched the wall nearest her. This is my cell. She touched her fingers to her breastbone. This is my cell. She thumped herself once, hard. This is my cell. Then she stood, looking around her, breathing, turning, looking, breathing, touching herself, for a long time.

Day 1105

She was learning to be alone.

It was not at all what she had expected. She had time; and now she was spending a great deal of it studying each piece of her experience and how it fit into the whole of her. She paced the perimeter of her cell for hours while she reconstructed the year of the crocodile, stopping to stretch, or eat, or rest in front of pastel Mandelbrot sets on the screen. She lay in bed in the dark and recalled her time of stone, and the terrible way that she had flensed her life from her. It was the most difficult work she had ever done; to wrap her mind around those dreadful moments and try to see them clearly. She was not sure she even knew what clear was; but she knew it was important to find out.

She imagined a window into herself, and through the window she looked at Jackal Segura.

She saw only Jackal; and that was the first new thing. She had never before seen just herself. She had always painted herself against the backdrop of Ko, or the web, or the Hope. Was she still Jackal now that she was out of context? That was frightening enough to make her want to stop this nonsense. She cursed herself, and went on.

She found inside her things that shocked her. She was shamed by all her surrenders: the conflicts with Donatella, with Tiger, with Ko; with the crocodile, with the stone. All failures. She had pretended not to be alone, and then she had pretended that it did not matter. But it did. It mattered more than anything.

One night when she had been on her back in bed for hours, blinking up at the dim ceiling, she understood: she had always been alone. She had just never been alone all by herself before. Alone was the ending and beginning of everything she had been, everything she might be if she survived. The realization, the simplicity and the flowing beauty of it, brought her bolt upright.

She took a rest for a few days. She ate, and stretched her body gently. She told herself her favorite stories, slowly, making the telling as plump and round as she could. She sat back against the wall and let herself be overcome by remembered music. When it seemed time to open up the window again, she found all her failures of confidence, of honesty, of will, lined up to display themselves for her, like a blister that had risen within her and burst. She

had so little to show for herself. She was so much less than she had
ever thought.

Another break, this one less restful. She felt toxic, contaminated
by self-discovery. She prowled her cell, measuring its limitations
foot-length by foot-length from her heel at one end of a wall to her
toe butted right up against the other, and then a right turn and do
it again. She became irritated by the way her food lay in its dish,
by her sheet's refusal to stay tucked in. Red and green patterns on
her screen reminded her of Christmas, and made her sad and bitter and so enraged.

More lessons in letting go. It was harder this time. Her anger was
utterly dependable, always on time, always loyal: a best friend with
a loving smile and a butcher knife behind its back. She was tempted
to wall up her anger without looking too closely at it, to put it in a
cell like the one she was in now, with no way in or out. But she
knew that it would only grow until it pushed down the walls.

No short cuts, she told herself grimly, and kept going.

There came a moment in a long line of formless hours when she
despaired of ever feeling good about herself again. She was a bag
of weakness, a half-empty glass. She had made a bad job of herself, and that was the worst of all.

She curled up in a miserable ball and drifted, not awake, not
asleep, until a thought flared in her head, strong and compelling,
like the second voice in an ongoing conversation that she had not
been aware of until it said: So what? Do better this time.

She felt again as if she were standing at the edge of a very high
place. But it was not Mirabile, not the long fatal fall. Do better this
time. She didn't know what this place was, except it was not a
place that she could just fall into like the mouth of the crocodile.
She would have to step out, face forward, arms open wide. She
would have to reach.

Her answer was instinctive and immediate. "I'll do better this
time," she said out loud. "I will do better."

She smiled and fell instantly asleep.

When she woke, she felt curiously rested, and there was something else; something brief that washed through her and left her clean and open. She was astonished to find that she had forgiven herself. She was astonished to find joy. And that was the next new thing.

Day 1170

It was not that solitude was any easier to bear. In some ways, it was harder now than ever before, because there was no one to tell her that the work she was doing was good. She had no one to share those flashes of joy in just being Jackal, in being new and alive. Sometimes that joy made her terribly sad for lack of someone to pass it on to.

But being Jackal Segura was easier now, even convicted and abandoned and alone. It was better in some incomprehensible way to be all those things if she was also still herself. She wasn't sure what it meant, and she decided it did not matter. What mattered was that some days she wept for grief, and some days for exultation, but it was never the crocodile or the stone who cried: it was always the human Jackal.

Day 1279

When she put her foot down in its last step of the heel-to-toe progression along the west wall, there was an inch of space between it and the facing north wall.

That wasn't right. She stood rocking in her tightrope stance, left arm against the wall for balance, and frowned at the wall in front of her. It did not look any farther away; and she was sure that after almost four years of standing nose-to-brick with it, she would have noticed. But there was a difference.

She had an ugly thought, dropped down cross-legged, too hard, onto the floor, and pulled her foot up into her lap. It looked the same as it always had. It didn't seem crooked or suddenly shortened. That was a relief, and a puzzle. She poked the north wall experimentally with a foot, then a finger. Finally she lay flat on the floor and pushed her face as close to the uninvited inch of space as she could without losing focus.

The inch looked back at her, unhelpfully. After a while she stood up and went back to her pacing. The other walls were the same length they had always been. But the next time around, the west wall was still too long. And it stayed that way.

Day 1499

Something extraordinary happened.

She was thinking; measuring out the edges of the floor and remembering how it had felt to visit Al Iskandariyah when she was a Hope and the world still smiled upon her. She was there: the stone square scrubbed to the color of bone by millions of feet, the afternoon sun that made the air ripple and dance, the racket of the marketplace two streets over muted by the buildings of dense stone that squatted around the open plaza, the crooked lengths of date palms and the spiked cactus around them that flowered red and impossible vibrating shades of pink. And there was Jackal, boots and sunglasses, walking tall with arms swinging loose and free, alive and buzzing with possibilities like a young bee hovering just over the cactus before dipping down to the first flower. She smiled and put out one hand to touch the wall of her cell; oh, she remembered how it was to step out strong, it was just like this—

And she pushed out her left foot, expecting it to slide the extra inch and thunk emphatically into the stone in front of it. Instead, it went right through the wall.

She went down hard on her bottom and hip, her right knee

bent and her left leg still stuck absurdly through a foot-sized hole. She sat that way for a very long time, blinking slowly and trying to imagine what she should possibly do next. It was inconceivable that there could be a hole in a virtual cell, where there had been none before. She sat for much too long thinking about how none of it could be true before she realized that her opinion didn't seem to matter at all to the hole. It was there, wrapped around her left ankle. She leaned forward and touched it with her left hand. It was ragged at the edges. It felt like a hole in a wall.

Idiot, she thought, and focused her attention on her left foot. There was nothing special about the way it felt; not hot or cold, no discernible texture difference. She drew it slowly back in. It looked fine, just like a virtual foot should look. She tucked it up under her, in a tailor's seat with the right foot for company, and re-garded the hole. It was where the spare inch had previously been.

What the hell is going on? Suddenly she was frightened, almost as much as that sharp-toothed day of the crocodile. She hauled herself up and backed away from the corner and the light that shone faintly from someplace outside. Outside. "Jesus fucking Christ," she said aloud. She turned in a circle, making fists and pressing her fingers together hard enough to hurt. "Oh god I don't please what is going on GODDAMN IT!" and now she was yelling with her arms fisted out from her sides and trembling, shaking her head and yelling again, "STOP DOING THIS TO ME! STOP DOING THIS TO ME! LEAVE ME ALONE!"

And that was just absurd. Leave me alone, she thought, what a goddamn stupid thing to wish for right now. She didn't know whether she was going to cry or hit something, and then to her great surprise she found that the easiest thing to do was to lean over with her hands braced against her thighs and laugh quietly. Through it all the light went on shining from some place outside her prison cell.

Well, Jackal, what are you going to do now? she asked herself afterwards. Another stupid question: what else was there to do but to stretch herself on the floor, put her face up to the hole, and look out.

She had a good long look. When she finally lifted her head from the floor, she felt that she must move very, very slowly. She opened the cupboard and took out ham and butter and bread, constructed a careful sandwich, ate it with deliberation. She never took her eyes from the hole and the pale light that rippled across the stone floor and into the opposite corner. When the last methodical bite had dissolved down her throat, she put her plate aside and stripped off her clothes, carefully folding the soft trousers and loose shirt that showed no wear from their years of use. She worked her way through her entire exercise routine. She stretched every muscle and flexed every tendon she could. She was thorough. When she was done, she rubbed herself down with her blanket and put her clothes back on. After a moment's thought, she reached under the bed and pulled out the shoes that she had not worn in more than two years. They felt odd on her feet.

Then she took a deep breath, and began to kick down the wall.

It felt good to use her body like this, against something that resisted and then gave way; it was almost erotic, and she forgot for a while what she was doing and simply gave herself over to action and feeling. When she came back to herself, she had broken a hole big enough to crawl through, and her cell was full of a kind of light she had not seen in more than four years.

She looked around at the walls, the ceiling, the floor, the stone box that had absorbed fifteen hundred days of her without a trace. And now she was scared to leave it, scared of what she had seen beyond it; afraid of that final step out over this new edge. She suspected that once she took it, she would never get back to who she had been.

But she could never do that anyway. More than four years alone had changed her irrevocably. The people who put her here had as much as killed Jackal Segura the day they had dragged her screaming into her own head. She was someone new now, or at least she was starting to be. But she wouldn't stay new for long in this one small place in her mind. She would dry up, become stale, if she did not keep reaching. And that was the choice. She could put all the bricks and bits of stone back into place in the wall, and stay safe, and never know what was on the other side of herself. Or she could reach.

Whatever is out there, she thought, is a part of me. It's mine. She took a deep breath; and then she dropped to her hands and knees and pushed herself through.

On the other side of the hole was her bedroom on Ko Island.

She rose slowly. The room was full of morning light, and she could see through the open window that the sky was blue-gray and half-full of scudding clouds. She saw everything discretely, as if items presented themselves to her like a row of cadets lined up for inspection, stepping forward one at a time. There was a scattering of sand on the windowsill. A light, gusting breeze patted her cheek and caught in the folds of her shirt. The built-in bookshelves on the wall opposite the window held the printed books and the disks with all the stories she had told herself over and over in her cell. Her summer quilt covered the bed, bleached cotton with an intricate piecework mandala of sea blue and tidewater green. Small woven rugs lay in a random pattern on the pine floor, which glowed oily gold where the light striped it. When she finally remembered to breathe, the air smelled faintly of salt and lemon verbena. And there was her oldest friend, her Frankenbear, lying on his worn side on her dresser, stitched at his neck and tummy and legs after the neighbor's dog had chewed him to bits. He looked at her with the crooked button eyes that her father had sewn on so carefully.

"Oh," she said quietly. "Oh."

She began to touch her things; the lightest fingertip tracing of Frankenbear's fur, and then full hands flat on the texture of the quilt, the grit on the windowsill, until she was brave enough to lift from the dresser the rounded cherrywood box that had always held her jewelry, to heft its weight in her hand and open the carved lid. It was all there, the everyday beads and silverwork, and the special things: her great-grandmother's opal drop earrings; the tiny braided-gold bracelet that was the first ornament Jackal had ever bought herself; and on a special silver chain, the sea-rock that Snow had found and given her, that looked like a little rounded goddess icon with plump belly and breasts and tiny legs.

She held the little rock until it was warm in her hand, and then she slipped the chain over her neck. The goddess nestled in her usual place just on top of Jackal's breastbone. Jackal curled her body into the overstuffed leather chair by the window, pulled her legs up and wedged them against one of the chair arms. The sky outside the window was enormous. It might go on forever. It was too wide to see it all; and it was so shocking not to be able to see the limit of something that all she could do was look and look and look until it filled her up.

When she was stuffed with sky, when she had as much blue and gray and cloud inside her as she could hold, she touched the goddess around her neck; she looked at Frankenbear with his kind eyes; she whispered, "Home. Home."

She did not know whether to hope that the rest of the apartment would be there. What if it was? What if there was something outside it? If she went there and then returned to find the hole in the wall closed up, herself weirdly imprisoned outside of her cell, that might do it—she might go irretrievably mad. Was she still in VC if she wasn't in a cell? Could they get her back out if she were somewhere else inside her head? Was she supposed to be here?

Could she go back?

She put her head back through the hole just to see the cell again. Just to be sure. It seemed so colorless, in spite of the screen cycling through its fractals. It was extraordinarily creepy to see it from outside.

She pulled her head back into the room, rose and made her way to the door, passing the dresser and closet. The closet; god, she thought, and opened the door; and there were all her clothes, hanging in patient rows, all the cottons and linens and silks and denims that had held her while she went about her life before Mirabile, before. . . . Before she thought too much about it, she stripped and tugged on her favorite scarlet cotton tunic and worn jeans, pulled her boots on and turned without a pause and opened the door.

The rest of the apartment was indeed there. It was empty and still. She did not stay: the need to keep moving was an energy fizz under the skin of her ribs and thighs, that took her through the dormitory and out the side door. She found the rack of bicycles exactly where it should have been, and getting on one was like . . . well, just like riding a bicycle, she thought, absurdly pleased with herself. She rode out into the street and down toward the Sea Road.

Along the south end of Ko, seagulls bulleted across the beach in balletic ricochet-and-return patterns, and the noise they made almost deafened Jackal, who had not heard anything other than her own sounds for such a long time. She had to stop the bike and stand at the place where the road curved down toward the beach, just to lean against the handlebars and take it all in: the enormous, choppy ocean; the rush and suck of the surf; the screech and swoop of the gulls overhead. The Sea Road stretched ahead of her for miles.

She took her time. She rode hard and then lifted her feet off the pedals and coasted with her legs stretched out and the salt air whipping thick and cool past her ears. She stopped to drop the bike on its side and walk the beach, skipping shells across the wash of the tide. Later, she sat on a high dune and stared out across the restless water, letting sand run through her fingers, the grains large and brown-sugary against her skin. She ran along the shoreline with her arms spread out to mimic the birds above her, wheeling and cawing in time with them as they tilted and dipped. Sometimes she realized where she was, Ko but not Ko, Ko-in-her-head, and her brain whipsawed around all the contradictions of real and unreal. But the sun was warm, and the white froth whish-whished cold against her ankles. It was as real as she was, anyway, and that was enough.

It was the longest day she could remember, and the sun began to sink below the horizon only when she decided that it should. It took a long time, because she enjoyed sunsets; and when it was dark, there was an oversized milk-white moon and a hundred thousand stars between her and the darkness. She lay on her back in a soft nest of sand and watched the sky. The night was warm, but not too warm; just right, in fact. Just perfect.

She thought, I'm doing this. What else can I do?

Thinking that, she slept. And when she woke, she made the sun come up, and it was another beautiful day to be alive, to be on Ko Island, to be Jackal Segura, to be for this moment unafraid, to be strong, to be the one who made it all happen.

She left the sea eventually, long after she had lost any sense of VC-time, and worked her way up the center of the island, toward the mountain range of HQ buildings and the training center campus. Riding between the corporate towers was eerie. The sound of her wheels echoed back to her, and her shadow was huge against the white pavement of the plaza; her reflection flashed at her from ten thousand mirrored panes of glass. Yet she felt relaxed and comfortable in a way she had never felt here before. It startled her to realize that she had become used to being alone. She hadn't even thought once of Snow until now, in spite of all this time in these familiar places. She was no longer Snow's Jackal, or the web's Jackal, or the Hope of Ko. She was just herself.

She explored for weeks. She drove a dormitory car all around the island. She walked the woods. She slept for a week in her favorite spot, the one that she had thought never to see again; and when she left it, she did not look back. She prowled the corporate buildings, endlessly fascinated by the mundane: the clutter in desk drawers, the varieties of coffee in the executive dining rooms, the thick carpets full and rich against her bare toes. She wondered if this was the way it really was, or if her imagination simply supplied the details. She sat for hours in the conference room where she had learned so much from Neill, her feet up on the table, staring out the window at Esperance Park. She stood wide-legged in the middle of the plaza outside Ko Prime headquarters, closed her eyes, spread her arms, and imagined thousands of people in the real world, busy and focused, rushing right through her. Then she dropped her arms and smiled, and turned back into the empty lobby, the sun-bright silence. The silence was better; being alone was better.

She lost track of the months. Occasionally she would will a change of seasons, and so she moved sporadically through a long high summer and a chill-edged fall, a clear and precise winter with no snow. She ate and slept, rode, read, spent fascinated hours in the herb garden learning each type of bud and leaf and stem. She danced. She ran naked through the enormous lobby of the Executive One building, and made love to herself on top of the teak reception counter, and the thought of being watched only made her want herself more. She became utterly streamlined. She was certain and serene. There was no need of rigid schedules or rituals to mark the passing of time; not when she was so busy creating worlds within herself. But there finally came a day when she thought of the world beyond Ko.

Hong Kong. She took herself off to Terry's Cliff and sat cross-legged on the edge, looking out to sea. Hong Kong. And then what? Al Iskandariyah? That was a nasty thought, to imagine herself dancing down the corridors of the prison hospital into the room where in another life she was strapped down and hooked up; leaning over the empty table and pressing against the space where she was in that other world, coming that close to herself.

Moved by some unnamable impulse, she returned to her apartment, walked easily to her bedroom and crossed to the hole in the wall in a single breath, knelt and stretched and pushed herself back through, into her cell.

The screen was in its morphing faces phase. The bed was nicely made; the larder cupboard was full. She pulled an apple from the shelf, bit into it: it tasted the same as the Ko apples, as the apples of the last . . . how long? Then she understood what she had come for.

The screen display showed Day 1840.

It was hard to believe that more than a year had passed since she had left her cell, since she had broken out. The Jackal that was had turned to dust in the corners of a virtual cell, under the imaginary skies of Ko. How did she feel now? Pure, serene; as if she moved aerodynamically. She felt powerful. She felt like herself.

*   *   *

It was spring when she finally went to Mirabile, on the Ko ferry that rolled itself gently across the glass-green sea while she stood at the rail and breathed warm wet air that left the inside of her mouth tasting of salt. Gulls and terns kept her company, and she fed them corn chips from the concession stand. While the birds fought over the scraps, she watched Ko become smaller, until she could not see it anymore.

Being empty of people made Hong Kong feel huge, gave her for the first time a true sense of how much space was contained in the buildings that shouldered each other aside for room to thrust up toward the clouds. She felt small, walking in the perpetual shadow of the city's streets, craning her neck to see the sunlight that struck only the uppermost floors of the taller buildings. Anyone who lived here had to reach for the sun.

She jogged down the closest transit ramp into the subway. A train waited, open-doored and humming to itself as if eager to get on with the journey. She let it take her through the tunnels and up the rails that joined the elevated system, and she rode through the ankles of the city until the train stopped, as she knew it must, at Tsimshatsui. At Mirabile.

It felt like entering a cathedral; the vastness of it, the resonance, was holy and terrible. Her steps became measured, the rhythm cadenced and ritualistic. There was nothing but space and silence and, far above her, the dark shapes of birds wheeling around the elevator towers.

One of the elevators opened to her, and she went up.

Mirabile fell away beneath her. She kept her head up. She watched the birds turn slow circles until she came level with them and left them behind. Up and up and up. Her mouth and throat were dry. Her hands trembled. She flew up into the fist that was the Needle, into its knuckletips that scratched the sky. The elevator slowed and stopped, and the doors rolled apart to release her, but she pushed the *Close Doors* button and the metal and glass wrapped themselves tight around her. She breathed in tight gasps that did not seem to reach her lungs. Alone, alone in the place of her fear, with a great emptiness below her.

On the control panel an arm's length away was a button labeled, simply, *Down.*

She thought of Bear, of Mist. Tiger. Was she ready to understand how it felt when the bottom dropped out of the world and you had no choice but to fall and fall and fall until you stopped forever? Was she ready to learn what it meant to die because someone who loved you was a stupid idiot and killed you by mistake? Still a stupid idiot, she thought, wanting suddenly to hurt herself. *You killed your web and you will drop yourself down this goddamn shaft a hundred thousand times if that's what it takes to make you understand what that means stupid stupid stupid god I'm scared I'm scared I wish —*

—and her mouth filled with saliva and rust, and she leaned forward and stretched out her finger for the button, she reached—

And she went down. The world fell out from under her and she flew, like one of the birds that she passed in an eyeblink as she hurtled down, down, down. And it was over so quickly. The car was falling and falling and then, without any transition, it was suddenly still, and she was stepping out onto the Mirabile plaza, stumbling across to the nearest guide rail, hanging onto it while she tried to heave her nonexistent guts out onto the marble floor.

And she knew some of what her web knew now. She knew that when you were dying, you could feel fear and anger and surprise, but mostly what you felt was some version of *wait, wait, I'm not ready!*

She sat with her back to the railing for a long time, watching the birds. Then she left Mirabile, walking through the iron canyons and the steel valleys of shadows, turning over and over in her mind the astonishment of not being ready. But why was she surprised? When had she ever been ready for anything? She wasn't ready to break Tiger's nose or ready to be a Hope or ready to see her life smeared across two hundred meters of Mirabile's pristine floor. She leaned against the bow rail of the ferry and let the wind and the cold hard spray force her eyes into slits while Ko Island grew out of the horizon. Could a person ever be ready for things? The ferry rounded the curve in the channel and headed for the docking tunnel, and the water wasn't so rough now; she could open her eyes and see the Ko ferry station gleaming like a polished silver sculpture, the gulls chattering as they pulled crabs apart on the beach, and beyond it the greenbelt that she hadn't visited in too long. What was the opposite of ready? She remembered feeling like a piece of sea glass tumbled into a muddy no-shape, worn away bit by bit, and how she had welcomed it and even helped to grind herself down. Maybe the opposite of ready was shapeless; well, that was no good, she'd done that and it had only given her a whole new set of things that she wasn't ready for. She watched as the island stretched forward and the arms of the harbor curved around her. The sky was a thick glaze of blue. The air smelled of salt and lemon. She felt as if she were about to understand something simple and important. Light flashed in her eyes; she shook her head impatiently. Something simple and important; she waited for it. Another flicker at the edge of her vision, this time not light but darkness. She frowned toward the beach; dark vertical streaks rippled through the air; one of the gulls winked out.

Suddenly everything blinked into gray tones; the sky, the sea, her hands gray on the gray ferry rail. The air in front of her tore again, and through it she saw, horribly, a huge face in a gray medical mask, a face that filled the world and she began to understand but it was already too late and she thought wildly wait, wait—

PART IV

_____

SOLITAIRE

12

THE WORLD CLICKED INTO PLACE AS IF SOMEONE HAD adjusted the focus on its projector. She was in an institutional interview room, somewhere like a hospital or jail; it had that particular smell of multiple people and uncertain outcomes. She sat at a table with a cup raised halfway to her mouth; she could taste grapefruit juice, with more dribbling down her chin and spotting the robe that was pulled tight around her. *What's happening?* Her right hand trembled as she set the cup down; she misjudged the distance and clunked it hard against the table. And then she saw, oh god, there was another person in the room. She froze. She could see it from the corner of her eye. The first other person in . . . how many years? Surely not eight years already. Surely not. She blinked, blinked again.

"Ah, you're here," it said. "Well. Never mind. We were pretty much finished anyway." A beat. "Welcome back."

Jackal pressed her lips together so it—he—wouldn't see them trembling. She didn't understand. She blinked harder, began to rock slightly. Where was Ko? Where was this? She looked around the room in small snapshot glances, moving only her eyes. Blink. The man in the chair to her right. Was he real? Blink. A small black diamond datagem in the back of her left hand, in the soft place between her thumb and index finger. Was that real? It hurt when she pressed it. Blink. A chewed piece of toast on a plastic plate. Did she eat that? How long had she been here? Blink. No windows. She could see no windows. Blink. She could see no door. Suddenly she was sure that she was still in VC, back in her cell, and this person must be the crocodile come back for some terrible new work, grown so strong that it had taken shape outside her, and this was very bad, very bad, so she tried desperately to make some sound come out of her clenched throat, tried to raise her weak and trembling arms against it, ready to fight again in any way she must. "Oh, criminy," the crocodile said, sounding exasperated, and pulled a phone out of its coat pocket. "She's awake and she's spinning, can somebody get in here please?" There was a noise behind her, a sound exactly like a door opening, and she sagged in relief even before she felt the sting of the syrette gun at the side of her neck.

The tranquilizer smoothed through her. She put her hand to the sore place where the injection had just gone in; my neck, she thought, my hand. She touched her arms, put her hands up to her face and felt her cheekbones and the small scar by her right eyebrow. "Oh," she said. "Oh." Her real body, the one that she had missed wrenchingly at first and then forgotten utterly during the last glorious year on Ko. She made small experimental movements: she didn't need to stand to realize how fragile she was. She wouldn't be kicking down any walls for a while; she wouldn't be walking the Ko cliffs or riding through the campus like a two-wheeled dervish until she was a lot stronger than this—

Then she remembered that she wouldn't be doing those things anyway, because she was never going back to Ko. They didn't want her. She wasn't their Hope anymore. She would never again see the beach or the greenbelt or the fish in the garden pond. No more Frankenbear. She put a hand to her throat; the goddess on the chain, Snow's gift, had vanished back into the runnels of her

brain. She began to shake again in spite of the sedative. "Oh," she
said again, "oh," and then she began to cry for all the lost things.
She was too tired to weep, too beaten to howl out her misery, so
she just sat at the table with her mouth open and let the tears run.
Eventually, someone bundled her out of the chair and into a bed
somewhere, and she cried herself to sleep.

She woke covered in a stinking, cold sweat. Ick, she thought
fuzzily, and rolled herself out of damp sheets.

She found that she was naked and in a small cell with another
person; a woman with hair the color of red clay and a flat, amused
face peering over the side of the upper bunk. The entire wall beyond the foot of the beds was barred; Jackal could see directly into
the cell opposite, where one man lay curled on his side on the
lower bed while another paced back and forth along the length of
the bars, regarding Jackal with no expression. Jackal looked away,
but she was no longer scared. She remembered everything; and
she understood why her heart would be pounding and her body
frantically ridding itself of poisons while she slept. All those
months of accumulated toxins and drugs; no wonder her mouth
tasted like metal and her head throbbed. But she was a bit
stronger; she could stand, and she could hobble the two steps to the
partition that gave some measure of privacy to the toilet and sink
at the back of the cell. Private from the open bars, but not from her
cellmate, who swiveled her head to follow Jackal's progress. Fuck
you, Jackal thought wearily.

She found a thin towel that was rough from too many steriliz-
ing washes; it didn't so much absorb the slick film from her skin
as scrape it away, and she felt raw by the time she was done. She
splashed cold water on her face; then her belly muscles cramped,
and she dropped herself onto the toilet and hoped her guts would
remember how to work. Acrid green urine spattered into the

bowl, and then a stream of thin watery shit that burned coming out. She gritted her teeth and cleaned herself up, and tottered back to the bed. She wanted to lie down and rest, but the sheets were still clammy. So she dressed instead, in a coverall and slippers she found in a plastic storage bag at the foot of the bed.

The woman above her watched interestedly until Jackal pulled her slippers on: then she pulled her head back and disappeared from view. That was fine with Jackal. She did not want to talk; she felt profoundly removed, Jackal-under-glass. She wondered, from her distant interior vantage point, why she had been pulled out of VC early, and how long she might be in this new place, and whether she cared.

Some time later a loud bell rang and the cells opened. Guards lined everyone up, about two hundred prisoners including Jackal and her silent cellmate. Too many people: it was hard to step out of the safety of the cage. Some of the prisoners had the strained look of animals caught in jacklight, trying to be invisible: the others were restless in small, compulsive movements that made Jackal hiss with irritation. She tried to relax, remembering Neill's teaching: model the behavior and expect others to follow. The memory surprised her with a swell of grief. Not now, please not now, she thought, and then the guards were shuffling them along and she gave herself over to the small release of moving forward.

They came to a large room set up lecture-style, cheap institutional desks and chairs facing a table with a projector and keyboard. Everyone sat in silence, and that was an odd thing. In dozens of research activities, she'd never seen a group this size remain silent, even when the researchers made clear that talking would be punished. They'd demonstrated, and Jackal believed, that it was human nature to interact, to seek connection in times of stress or uncertain circumstances.

This is wrong, she thought, I have to talk to someone. She looked to her left, met the bright gaze of her cellmate. It was hard to make herself speak, but she managed to whisper, "Do you know what this is about?" Then there was a guard in front of her saying, "Shut up," and the cellmate blinked equally brightly at the guard and turned away as if she'd heard nothing, seen nothing. No one else even looked their way. The guard returned to his position at the side of the room. Nothing more happened for a while, except that the flat-faced woman began to subvocalize a tune that Jackal recognized after the sixth repetition as The Itsy-Bitsy Spider song. After the seventeenth round, a door opened at the front of the room and two women walked in.

Someone behind Jackal giggled, and Jackal felt her face twitch in sympathy. It wasn't just the difference in height, but the entire jangle of body language between the two. The shorter woman wanted to be authoritative, that was clear from her pace and her jutting chin. She wore what Jackal recognized as a medium-range business suit, in probably the only shade of pink that would suit her sallow white skin and gold hair. Clearly, no one had ever told her that an ambitious person should always have good shoes: she clack-clacked across the floor in her cheap heels, seeming fussy and fraught in comparison with the woman who ambled beside her. This woman was tall; she could stroll and still keep pace with her companion. Her bald head drew Jackal's attention up her body, past the shoulders that weren't quite relaxed. When the head turned, Jackal felt her breath hitch: the woman's eyes were entirely red, shining like animal eyes in her dark face. Lenses, Jackal realized, after the beast-gaze had glided past her; but she was still unsettled.

The white woman settled down in a chair at one corner of the table. The black woman stood in front of the table, reaching behind her to power up the projector and pull the keyboard within reach. "I will have your attention now," she said in a voice that carried without strain through the room. "We're presenting in English today. Anyone who is uncomfortable with English may request an additional session with an interpreter." She continued without waiting. "I am Crichton. I am the case officer assigned to each of you. I am the center of your universe at this moment. Mind me now."

She keyed up a slide onto the projector screen: a list of about sixty or seventy names. "We're going to divide you into groups. The people on the list are the Red Group. You will identify yourself when I read your name, and you will follow the directions of this officer—" she pointed at a guard, who hefted her automatic weapon self-importantly "—to another location. Andressen." She waited until a tall man stood uncertainly. "Over there. Azkhanzin. Brecht." She read through the list impassively. Jackal's name was not included.

The named ones left the room with a large escort of guards. Crichton pulled up another slide—*Virtual Experience Technology Beta Program,* with the EarthGov logo prominently displayed. Her body seemed looser now, although it was impossible to be sure of any expression through the crimson lenses.

"The rest of you are the Green Group. Congratulations on your imminent release from confinement for the criminal activities of which you were convicted. I trust you all find yourselves rehabilitated and ready to resume a productive place in society. Don't insult me by answering," she said unhurriedly, precisely, waving off an attempt to speak by someone in the front of the room.

They're letting us go, Jackal thought. She felt a little as though someone had said *Did you hear about the epidemic in Pakistan?*— news that was real for some other person but not for her. And she had a mild interest in what would happen next: but for now it was fine to sit on this backbreaking chair and let this unfathomable woman tell her future.

"Most of you have been reclaimed from virtual confinement ahead of schedule. This is because of some recent disagreement in Earth Congress about the scope and control of the Virtual Technology Program. Some things have changed while you've been away." Crichton smiled briefly, a show of teeth that made her eyes seem even less human.

"First thing is that at the end of this session, you will be individually processed for probationary release, subject to the conditions of those changes I just mentioned.

"Second thing is that you are still obligated to the program. You'll be interviewed to determine your individual role going forward. Your participation is required for a one-year period starting today. This is considered part of your sentence. When you complete the probationary period, you are considered to have fulfilled your obligation to society and you will be free to take up your lives.

"Third is that you are no longer in Al Iskandariyah." Ko, Jackal thought, like a starburst in her brain, it's Garbo technology, we're back on Ko! But Crichton said, as if it were no great matter, "This program was reassigned to a new oversight committee headed by EarthGov representatives from the Nations of North America. You have been relocated to NNA Zone 17 and are currently being processed for permanent resident status."

Jackal's cellmate jerked hard enough to skid her chair against the floor, and the guards around the room turned as one to point their weapons toward the sound. Jackal kept very still, trying to see as much as she could without turning her head: the woman was standing now, one hand on the back of her chair in a way that would turn it from a support into a weapon with one good heft.

"Please remain seated for the duration of the briefing," Crichton said. She seemed unfazed by the commotion and the possibility of violence. "Any sudden movement is likely to be misunderstood by the security personnel." She pointed out the guards with a head movement, as if the prisoners might not have noticed them before. "Sit down now," she added, and her voice was all the more threatening for being completely uninflected. The woman sat. "Thank you," Crichton said. "If there's anyone else who objects to these conditions, you're free to join the Red

Group. They failed to complete at least eighty percent of their VC term before the final details of the refocused program were ironed out in Al Isk, and will therefore be serving out their original real-time sentences in NNA penitentiaries in Zones 4 and 12."

The room was remarkably quiet. Jackal wondered how many others understood that they were here only because the weeks spent ironing out the details had bought them the time they needed in VC. Saved by bureaucracy.

"So, here's where that leaves you. For the twelve-month probationary period, we will subsidize your housing and provide a living allowance. It's enough to eat on but not enough to fund a revolution, so plan accordingly.

"You will report to me monthly for parole check-in and routine physical and neurological function testing. You have already received cortical implants that will record and transmit your brain's ongoing electrical activity." Jackal's fingers twitched, but she managed not to put a hand to her temple. "Any necessary medical treatment will be managed and covered by the program. We are committed to your continued good health for as long as you're with us. In exchange, you've agreed to release EarthGov, the NNA, and the program from any unanticipated physical, mental, emotional, or social consequences of early reclamation or your status as convicted felons. Any questions?"

Jackal couldn't ignore that; it sounded like something Arsenault might have said. She raised a hand.

"Yes?"

"What—" She didn't have enough air. She had to cough and try again. "What does that mean exactly, social consequences?"

Jackal's cellmate answered before Crichton could, in a voice so low and harsh that Jackal flinched in a sort of physical sympathy for the raw throat behind the offhand words. "It means that they won't be held responsible when we are stoned in the streets, or when no one will give us a job because we're fucking foreign crim-

inals and we starve in the cold." There was a general rumble of
distress from the other prisoners. The red-haired woman looked
straight at Jackal with a sparkle in her eyes that Jackal didn't like
at all, and her voice came stronger and rougher, rising as she said,
"That's what social consequences are, *petite*. Spending the rest of
your life in a place where they have an eye in your brain and a
hand around your throat forever—"

"Let's all take it easy," a man in the back said worriedly. The
guards pointed their guns at the group. Jackal braced to pitch herself out of her chair.

"Oh, I know just what you mean." Crichton smiled, showing
teeth. Everyone looked at her. "You're exactly right about how
stupid people can be. That's why we don't send you back home,
you know, because people get so upset when someone they know
turns out to be a psychotic terrorist or a killer of children. Think
of how much safer you'll be here, where you are more anonymous.
If they throw rocks at you it will only be because you've kicked
their puppy or neglected to pay for your drugs."

The woman blinked at Crichton once, twice; she opened her
mouth, shut it again. Finally she gave a short, sharp laugh.
"Gordineau."

"Excuse me?"

"*Je ne suis jamais anonyme. Je m'appelle Gordineau.* In English
that is Ms. Gordineau."

"Ah, Ms. Gordineau. Yes, I can understand why you might be
distressed at finding yourself back in the NNA. But we're a long
way from the Wichita blast zone. I'm sure nobody here cares
about what happens in the midwest. So how about if you settle
down and we get on with it," Crichton said. "Unless you prefer to
go play with the Red Group."

Gordineau shook her head and laughed again, and it was an
ugly sound, full of bad joy and the promise of conflict.

Crichton continued. "You will have noticed the datagems already provided to you. Implants are standard for all NNA residents. They store identity and credit information, and in your case include your criminal record and function as monitoring devices to ensure that you remain in your assigned region. They will identify you to NNA security and program staff. You can't lose them without losing a great deal of your hand, and even then we can still trace you by the chip in your head, so please let's not be stupid. Follow the rules and you'll be fine. You'll learn more at your individual briefing, which we will begin as soon as we're done here.

"We have one more topic to cover. As Ms. Gordineau has suggested, it is difficult for convicted felons to obtain gainful employment in the NNA. You will find that you cannot work within 100 yards of schools, libraries, medical centers, government buildings, military installations, biotech facilities, financial trading centers, or major tourist attractions. Nothing in a business of more than 100 employees. Nothing that brings you into regular contact with children. Nothing in the technology, weapons, heavy manufacturing, or software industries. No government contractors. No civil service." She stopped and gave them a moment of silence to take it in. "That is why I suggest you listen very carefully to our next speaker. Her name is Irene Miller and she is from the Virtual Technology Program Participation office."

Miller stood and clacked her way to the front of the table. Crichton touched the keyboard and the screen filled with print so tiny that Jackal didn't try to read it. Miller fussed with her hair, pulled down the corner of her jacket, and said, "Well, Crichton's absolutely right as usual, ha ha. It can be pretty grim out there. Unemployment is high and competition is fierce unless you have very good skills. But we can help. We want to help. We are prepared to offer you a two-year research participant contract with option to renew. You agree to take part in various additional research projects and receive regular EEGs and other tests as necessary to ensure a complete understanding of the longer-term effects of virtual technology. You'll draw a reasonable salary and receive great benefits." She began to recite them, but Jackal was too distracted to focus on the particulars. Her brain was trying to get her attention.

"Of course, you really should commit now. Participation is limited, and I'm afraid we don't have room for everybody. We strongly suggest you reserve your position today. I'm going to hand out contracts and give you a few minutes to look them over."

When the sheaf of documents came to her, Jackal took a set and passed the rest on to Gordineau, and then skimmed through the text. Miller was right, it was a standard term-limited research agreement: no bio-invasion without informed consent and additional compensation, no tests that were known to have a better than ten percent chance of irreversible physical or mental damage not already incurred through a pre-existing condition.

"Excuse-moi, petite." Gordineau leaned toward her and said, almost politely, "Do you understand this crap?"

Jackal raised her eyebrows.

"This part." The woman pointed a calloused finger at the pre-existing condition clause.

Always use vivid examples, Neill's voice said inside Jackal's head. Why was she thinking of Neill? She wondered if she would spend the rest of her life having inconvenient conversations with people who weren't really there. It made her tired to think it, and the weariness was in her voice when she said, "If you're already a quadriplegic, it doesn't really matter what they do to your spinal cord." Gordineau nodded, shrugged, clucked to herself, continued reading.

She couldn't sign this, Jackal thought. It would be giving them license to root around in her brain, and she certainly didn't want them to know that she'd essentially escaped from jail. That would be too tasty a puzzle for some engineer. And then she suddenly put it all together: gods and angels, it's Garbo Phase Four and I did it: I edited the environment.

She put the contract down shakily. How could she not have realized? She was going to be in serious trouble if her brain didn't start working properly. And what was she going to do? Here came Irene Miller working the room, Crichton trailing her impassively. Miller spoke earnestly to each parolee. Jackal could chart each decision process by the body tensions she saw: the tight neck muscles, the hands rubbing each other or rolling up into fists. It was like a physical surrender when each person finally signed and Miller moved on. Jackal's anxiety grew. All her Ko-trained instincts screeched at her to sign, sign anything to avoid the nightmare she'd imagined for poor old Sawyer or anyone else forced out of Ko. She pictured herself in some cold and hostile NNA city trying to find work and a home where she might be safe (with no web, but she wouldn't think about that now, that was just too hard). If she signed, maybe she could keep them from finding out about leaving her cell. But how? She wasn't feeling detached anymore: she was almost as afraid right now as she had been when they slung her by her shoulders and knees down the hallway toward the black hole of VC. Miller had reached her row. Jackal heard murmurs of *guaranteed income* and *one-time offer* and she thought god, it's not like any of us have a better choice, she doesn't have to push so hard—and then her brain went suddenly, completely quiet as if to say *About time you woke up!*

Then Miller was standing over her, holding out a pen, with Crichton looming behind. "Okay, are we all set here?"

"I haven't read it all yet."

"I've explained the important points."

"I'd like some more time to look it over."

"You'll be best advised to commit now if you want to take advantage of the offer. Otherwise we might not be able to guarantee a space for you."

Jackal said carefully, "Perhaps you'd like to refresh your memory about Cranes versus NNA. I'm sure you want me to be fully informed."

A beat. Then, "Certainly," Miller answered, equally carefully. "I do want to be clear that at no time have I stated that employment status is unequivocally based on immediate acceptance of the offer."

Another beat. Jackal swallowed. "I'll just look it over and return it to you. Is your address on here somewhere?"

The blond head nodded fractionally. "Or Crichton knows how to reach me. I'm sure you'll have noticed that the document carries a date and time stamp. The offer is void after—"

"One hundred twenty hours, yes, I know."

"Which one are you?" Crichton asked, with no particular inflection.

"Ren Segura."

"Ah," Crichton said. "Ko. Of course. I'll look forward to our little chat later, Ms. Segura. Come along, Irene." They moved along to Gordineau, who scrawled across the signature line without any comment, and then settled back into her chair with an exaggerated sigh as Crichton and Miller moved to the next row. She turned her head to look at Jackal sideways, like a bird. The sparkle that Jackal did not like was back in her eye.

"*Très intéressant*," she said. "What did you just do?"

"I just reminded them that pressuring anyone into a bio-research contract is illegal. Everyone's entitled to a five-day review period during which the offer status remains open. Once your name's on that document, they have to hold the position for you until you turn it down or the time stamp expires. They also have to give you a two-day remorse and rescission period if you sign."

"So you have just gained five days to figure out how bad it really is."

"Right."

"And if it's bad, what then?" Another silence. "How else will you live?"

Jackal said finally, "I don't know."

"Hah," Gordineau chuckled. "You are young and amusing, *petite soeur*. Sign and be done, and use their money to buy the knife that you will cut their throats with in the future."

That killed any impulse Jackal had toward conversation. She sat wrapped in her own thoughts for some time until Crichton appeared in the front of the room again and said, "You'll be brought back here in groups of ten, in alphabetical order. You will participate in follow-up tests to determine any variances from your pre-VC baseline. Then we'll have a consultation. The results of your tests may require us to assign you to twenty-four hour residential status in the program facility for any length up to the duration of your probationary commitment. If that's the case, you'll still be reimbursed at the usual stipend rates. Any questions? Good. Behave while you wait."

Crichton left by a door at the back of the room. The guards rounded everyone up and herded them back to their cells. To amuse herself, Jackal did the math and worked out that given the probable alphabetical distribution of last names of the prisoners, and assuming an eight-hour total schedule of tests with time built in for the testers to eat and sleep, her turn would come at about two P.M. the day after tomorrow.

Gordineau was moved out right on schedule, about six hours later. Jackal lay on her back on the bottom bunk, staring at the molded mattress platform above her, enjoying the psychic silence that Gordineau left behind when she took away her disquieting laugh and her dangerously bright eyes.

She didn't want to think: about herself; about the NNA, whose convoluted regional governmental system and inconsistent, issue-reactive legal structure had provided innumerable case studies throughout Jackal's educational career; or about what she would do if the tests showed enough variances that they decided to keep her here for a year while they probed and prodded and maybe, finally, turned a corner in her brain and found an empty cell with Ko Island beyond. No, better to drift, the only noise in her mind a quiet background hum through which she noticed everything and responded to none of it. She knew when the man across the hall resumed his pacing, and when he was taken away in one of the groups. She knew that an unseen prisoner was weeping in a choked and desperate rhythm. She knew when someone slid a tray through a slot in the bars, and later when someone came back and retrieved it, untouched. Her nose told her that the dinner she had not eaten was vegetable soup and cornbread and something caramel-sweet. She lay in her bed and her brain hummed, hummed, and eventually she became aware that the groups were still being marched out although it was well into the evening now. Apparently no one on the processing team was getting a break; the guards continued to take prisoners out all through the night. The noise on the hall dwindled and muted with their departures, until Jackal could hear her own breathing and the slow drip of water from the tap in the sink next door.

Late the next morning they took her.

The first thing was a cursory medical examination: she thought dourly it was probably only to certify that she was fit to make it out the door on her own, no matter what happened after that. A bleary-eyed doctor listened to her heart and took her blood pressure and temperature, and then gave her an equally sketchy neurological exam: she touched her fingers to her nose, walked heel-to-toe across the room, closed her eyes and stood on one leg. He noted her responses in his palmtop, announcing them for her benefit: "Normal. Mm hmm. Okay, fine. Normal. Good." He removed the bandages under her left arm and inside her left thigh, and behind both ears, where the machines had entered her body. "Routine physical reclamation from VC. No obvious physical anomalies. Reflexes normal. The percentage of muscle mass you've lost is within acceptable parameters. None of the invasion scars should be too noticeable unless you decide not to grow out your hair. You may have episodes of insomnia and rapid-onset fatigue for a few days. Don't operate any heavy equipment until your sleeping patterns are re-established. Next."

The tests that followed were in many respects the same as her VC screening test, but much less thorough. No one strapped her down, but they didn't feed her either, and she became surly and dehydrated as the day wore on. The technicians were indifferent and sloppy; one gave her a bad needle bruise. The equipment was less sophisticated, and there wasn't the same sense of excitement that she'd felt from the program staff in Al Isk.

Her group was shunted from one room to the next. There was plenty of waiting time while people disappeared one by one into some new and unexplained experience. No one spoke much, although as the day went on, and the group became more familiar, they began to communicate through looks and body language; wrinkled noses, scowls, shrugs, shared expressions of contempt for the process and the people managing it.

They finally came to a waiting area where, when someone left, they did not return to the group: whatever this was, it was the final stage. Jackal sat next to an older man with tribal scars on his face; he must feel very lost, having no one to recognize his lineage and help him find his place here. On his other side, a younger man who had spent the day chewing his upper lip ragged said, suddenly and to no one in particular, "I'm scared."

No one answered. Jackal sat back in her chair and didn't look in his direction. She wasn't scared. She didn't really feel much of anything at all, except that ongoing sense of mild, detached interest. She should be thinking about what to do next, but she couldn't seem to care. She understood with some backroom part of her brain that she was simply removing herself as much as she could, like the first day in her VC cell when all she wanted to do was sleep—

"Segura," a light voice said, and she stood with a sigh and let her escort shuffle her down yet another corridor, into a small windowless room with stale air and greasy walls that turned out to be Crichton's office.

Crichton looked at home, her feet propped up on a metal desk, hands cradling a mug with an obscene cartoon and steam that smelled of coffee and cinnamon. Stacks of paper files threatened to slide off the desk's edge to join the piles on the floor. Jackal assumed Crichton had been at this without a break: there were grooves running from her nose to the sides of her mouth that hadn't been there before, and her skin puffed underneath the red eyes; but she showed no sign of mental fatigue, and her muscles were relaxed, without the swelling and apparent stiffness that Jackal associated with exhaustion.

Also in the office was a man in a lab coat and a badge. He did look tired, and out of sorts. "Do you have the results on this one?" he said testily as Jackal came in.

"Nope, just the baselines." Crichton answered. "We'll just have to sign her out and bring her back if you find something interesting when her test data finally gets into the system. Don't start with me, Bill, the bright idea of bulk processing these people came from your shop, not mine." She was staring at a point on the wall, and didn't turn her upper body to acknowledge Jackal's presence until Jackal was seated and the guard had left.

"Segura." Crichton drank a deep swallow from her mug and then put it down. "Aren't you a little young to be the silver medalist?"

"Excuse me?"

"Well, Gordineau is still the heavyweight, of course, but four hundred thirty-seven in one fell swoop is almost a Steel Breeze record. Hah, fell swoop, not bad. Do you get a ribbon or something?"

It was a kick in the stomach. *Bear, Mist, Tiger. Mirabile*. It poked right through her smooth detachment. Her throat clenched and she ground the words through it, "My web was in that elevator and you don't know what the fuck you're talking about."

There was a moment of silence. "Maybe not," Crichton said, and made a long arm to retrieve the top folder from the leaning stack. The man clucked disapprovingly.

"Segura," Crichton said again, reading this time. She tapped the fingers of her left hand against the desk as she read, stopping every few sentences to draw a breath and peer at Jackal over the top of the file. "Former Hope of Ko, convicted of terrorist activities against a Member State, premeditated murder of four hundred ten citizens. Presumably people from non-member states don't get murdered, they just get in the way. Oh, also conspiracy, fraudulent use of governmental status, and destruction of property. No prior convictions or arrests. No prior known criminal associations. Best defense that money can buy. Guilty by reason of voluntary confession." She regarded Jackal expressionlessly as she took a sip of coffee.

"Doctor Bill has some questions for you that you are required to answer, after which we will complete our interview and you may proceed to the convicts-want-to-be-free portion of today's schedule."

Jackal was recovering some of her equilibrium. She enjoyed Crichton's sly impromptu riffs on business-speak. It felt companionable. *Hah*, her internal voice said, sounding unnervingly like Crichton for a moment, *don't get stupid. No one here is your friend.*

"Oh, fine," Bill said. "We'll just cover the basics." He fished a palmtop out of his coat pocket, plugged it into a network port on the top of the desk. "Crichton, where's that file? Oh. Uh huh. Please describe your cell."

There was a pause. Crichton said, "He's not talking to me."

Jackal rubbed her eyes. "Sorry. Okay, the cell. It was square . . ." She talked him through it, carefully and with as much mundane detail as she could muster, watching his response closely as she talked. He seemed to be waiting for something. Finally she said, "Maybe you could give me an idea of what you're looking for."

"Anything atypical."

Now she was nervous; she was positive that kicking down the wall and running around on Ko Island for a virtual year would be considered atypical.

"I don't know what atypical means in this context," she told him with a completely serious face. "Can you give me an example?"

"Faces coming out of the walls. Unexplained noises. A feeling that the air is leaking out of the room. Bleeding food."

"Ugh. Somebody's food bled?"

"It was a very interesting anomaly," he agreed. "And of course, we have continuous EEGs on all of you, and we try to match these kinds of anomalies with pattern variations in the data."

Oh, now she understood where this was going. She imagined the needle had probably gone off the scale when she broke through her cell. But no, on second thought, he wouldn't be so casual about this if her EEG line had been too spectacular. Or would he? Was he smarter than he looked? She thought quickly about what to tell him. Her voice wanted to tremble a little. She let it.

"Nothing weird happened except . . . stuff I did myself. I got a little . . . I think I got a little unstable. Sometimes I tried to, um, pound my head unconscious against the wall. Maybe a couple of times I tried to hurt myself other ways."

"Did you manage to damage yourself to any extent?" he asked with interest.

She shook her head, not trusting herself to answer.

"Hmm. Well, that's in line with what some of the others have reported. And your confinement data isn't really that far outside of the average baselines." He stood. "I don't think we need to spend any more time on this. If you have any interesting pattern spikes in this round of tests, we'll bring you back in. Make sure

Crichton knows where you are. Crichton, I think we should assume that we won't have results available today on the rest of the group, so I'm going to get back to work. Get the data to me as soon as you can, will you?" And he was gone in a flurry of white, muttering and looking irritably at the time readout on his palmtop.

"Asshole," Crichton said dismissively. She stretched, watching Jackal. Jackal shifted, rolled her shoulders. She was good at the silence game, but she was very tired and it was better to let Crichton win.

"Are we done?"

"Not quite." Another silence. Jackal waited. "So, what are your plans?"

"Plans for what?"

"Life. A job. A hobby. Learn to play the violin. Build a fusion bomb with four or five friends. I don't know, that's why I'm asking. What are you going to do with yourself?"

"I haven't really thought about it."

Crichton leaned back in her chair. "So it's a year from now and you're at a party and someone says, nice to meet you, what do you do? And you say—what? I used to kill people for political reasons, but I gave it up a while back."

"What difference does it make what I do next?" Jackal said abruptly.

"None." Crichton smiled. "Identity is an illusion that brings comfort to the struggling mind." And added, "It's not polite to be too surprised."

"I didn't mean to look surprised," Jackal said as convincingly as she could. "I don't know much of Chang's work, but I recognize that one. Have you read—"

She stopped herself. *No one here is your friend.* She was too tired to affiliate, and she doubted that Crichton really cared. In another life she would have jumped at the chance to talk more about Chang Yijao's theories of the social politics of waning cultures; she might have learned something, and it would have been fun. She wondered if there was any fun left in the world for her.

She came back from her brief reverie to Crichton's red gaze on her face. Right now Crichton was the world, pushing at Jackal, waiting for an answer. But there were no answers, only hard questions. The blessed cool distance that Jackal had preserved throughout the day was collapsing under the pressure of all those questions waiting to present themselves. Any moment now the wreckage of her life would burst through the protective bubble she'd created, and she would have to start thinking about all the answers she didn't have.

Crichton asked abruptly, "Why didn't you sign the contract?"

That one she could answer. "I haven't read it yet."

"Everyone else signed it."

"Well, I didn't."

"You have a better offer?" Crichton asked, and it was a clear challenge.

There was no point getting angry, but Jackal couldn't help it, anymore than she could help her fatigue or the fear that was lurking just outside her shrinking composure. "I didn't sign the contract because ever since I got out of VC I haven't been able to give a damn what happens to me, and that tells me that I'm too tired and too scared to be anything but stupid." She began to shake; the bubble was bulging now, almost ready to rupture and let in all the unimaginable truths. "I don't have any room left to be stupid. So I have, what, about another ninety hours according to contract law. I'll get through whatever I have to with you and find a place where I can sleep for ten solid hours and then I'll decide about the goddamn contract. Gordineau asked me how I would live and I told her I don't know, but I'm still going to read it and I still don't know if I'm going to sign or not. If you have a problem with that, tough. It's one of the few fucking rights I have left."

"I see," Crichton said, less ferociously. "So it would solve all your problems if you had an interest-bearing NNA Central Bank credit account with a sizeable balance."

"Well, it would be a good start," Jackal retorted, still angry. And then, two beats later: "Are you . . . do I?"

Crichton named a figure that stunned Jackal into silence because it was probably enough for years of careful life.

"Are you sure it's mine?" she asked finally. And then, "Where did it come from?"

"The original deposit was wired into the NNA by Magister Asiae Bank in Hong Kong. Any theories?"

The bubble rent apart with a force so explosive that Jackal was sure it must be audible; she half-expected Crichton to ask *what was that?* while Jackal's carefully constructed detachment imploded. She looked up, hoping her shock didn't show. Crichton's red eyes studied her, waiting, and Jackal remembered Neill saying *truth is a tool*.

She answered honestly, but not completely: "Someone from Ko. Magister is one of Ko's primary financial partners in the Asia-Pacific region."

"So you have a friend."

"It looks that way. I'm surprised. And grateful." Which was true, in a pathetic way: she was grateful that Arsenault had lived up to the agreement made all those years—no, she kicked herself mentally, those few months ago. Rafe had told her, *Don't underestimate the value of some hope of assistance on the back end of all this.* She'd had no hope at all, and now, pitiably, she wanted to think of Ko as still honorable because they had given her some. That was followed by a fierce longing to get back inside her own head, back to VC-Ko, even if she had to be alone to go there. Maybe especially if she had to be alone; so safe, the bare beach, the empty plazas, the open cloudless sky . . .

"What is it?"

She came back to the weight of Crichton's red regard, heavier now that Jackal's safe shell was blown away. *Nothing I can tell you.* So she only bit her lip and said, "I wish things were different." All the long hours fell over her like a thick blanket; she hadn't realized how tired she was. Rapid-onset fatigue, the doctor had said.

Crichton watched for another moment and then rooted through an open box on the desk and produced a palmtop with a stuck-on label that read *Segura, Ren* followed by an alphanumeric string. Jackal took it: it turned out to be a cheap Ural State knockoff with a limited battery life.

Crichton said, "Courtesy of the NNA. It wipes itself in a week. Get your own before then and transfer all the preference settings. Bring that one back to your first parole meeting. The palmtop includes an auto reminder for your parole appointments, second Tuesday of every month, eleven A.M. sharp. That's less than two weeks from now, make sure you put it on your calendar. Anything more than ten minutes late is grounds for immediate arrest. My office brick and e-mail addresses are stored in the palmtop; you have three days from today to report a permanent residence address to me with a verification e-mail address for the landlord. Failure to report residence is grounds for immediate arrest. Your datagem accesses your credit account and you can download the information anytime into your palmtop, make sure you get one with a reader. Don't overdraw your account under any circumstances. Indigents are subject to immediate arrest. Any questions so far?"

Jackal shook her head.

"Good. The basic theme is immediate arrest, so don't screw up. Here's a list of rentals that accept convicted criminals as tenants. Not everyone does. You try the one on Perdue Street, the Shangri-La. The manager will probably say he doesn't have anything available. You tell him Crichton asked how his mama is doing. Hah. See what happens then."

"I—"

"You have a problem taking advice from me?"

"No. No. Sure, I can try to find it."

Crichton gave her a sharp look as she put the file folder on a different pile. "Do it or don't do it, no tears from my eyes either way. You're entitled to one free session with a VC counselor, do you want it?"

Jackal blurted, "God, no."

"No one ever does. Get to my office on time for your appointments or find yourself in a real prison for a change. That's all. The guard outside will tell you where to go."

Jackal wanted to say, *Why are you angry with me*, or *I don't know what to do*, or *I'm afraid*. But Crichton had already closed up her face and turned away. The chat was over.

The guard pointed her to a processing area where a clerk gave her a plastic-wrapped parcel of the clothes and boots she'd worn for her transfer to VC. She was surprised to see them. They didn't seem like hers anymore.

The clerk pointed her to a changing cubicle and stared at her through the gaps in the curtain. It seemed to take a long time to get dressed. Back at the counter, she thumb-printed a handful of screens and signed her name electronically seven times. Then she waited until the clerk said dismissively, "You're done. There's the door."

She began to turn and the man said, "Well, take this with you," and pushed over her palmtop. "Bunch of fuckin' zombies," he said, and someone else laughed, but she didn't care. She almost agreed with him. Sleep seemed a remote imagining, something she had perhaps done once a long time ago. She understood that her body would struggle on until it could not function anymore;

then in the simple way of machines it would stop working, and she would tumble wherever she was into a heap of broken parts until someone came to repair or dismantle her.

She let the body-machine carry her through the heavy steel-plated door that, without warning, dumped her onto the street and into a current of people that whirled her in a rush of color and noise and smell off to her left. For the first moments, she saw only an enormous blur; then the jumbled images coalesced into buildings streaked with grease and graffiti, people on crowded stoops, and more people in open windows, as far up as she could see, until their shapes were lost in the shadows that the giant structures cast on each other. It was cold: she'd worked out during the endless waiting of the day that it must be roughly late October, and she'd expected the weather to be warm, like home. But she wasn't home anymore.

Voices echoed in layers from the street to the sky; the noise spun around her as she stumbled along the edge of the crowd, close to the road that was packed with mass transport, commercial carriers, private cars, and even a few people on battery-powered scooters, small and vulnerable among the heavy traffic. The air was gray with industrial fumes, and many of the people on foot wore filter masks. The rest trudged barefaced through the smoke, gasping or wiping their eyes; many of them coughed openmouthed, as if it were such an habitual reflex that they no longer noticed they were spreading spit. Jackal thought of disease vectors, and tried to turn her face whenever someone passed close by.

She saw a young man and woman who even to her untrained eye were obviously misplaced tourists. Their clothes gave them away: much too trendy, the sort of thing that suburban people who read too many fashion magazines thought city people would wear. Jackal had seen others like these on the streets of Hong Kong, in the terraces of Mirabile, on the playas of Madrid.

These two looked young and uneasy; their body language broadcast *lost* and *afraid*, and the street noticed. Already they were drawing a crowd of hustlers, and kids who yelled *hey lady let me carry ya bag!* and then dashed away, hooting. Up ahead, a group of young men all wearing red berets and matching earrings swiveled as a unit, scanned the crowd, and drifted back toward the disturbance and the two bewildered people at its center. Jackal checked her body language, tried to walk straight and loose, to relax her face and remove herself from the scene. She passed the tense young man, the tight-lipped woman, the cluster of red hats and flat, interested eyes without a sideways glance or a flutter in her pulse rate, and she tried not to hear as the trouble started behind her.

Now what? Which way? Around her, the buildings rose up and up, and the voices echoed, and then the sound receded like slow water down a drain, and she was shivering against a pillar of some cold stone, lost and too tired to find herself. The slow-swimming schools of people eddied along the sidewalk, ignoring her for the moment, but she thought of the tourists and knew she could not afford to be still. The shadows were longer on the sidewalk, and she had to be somewhere safer than this before dark. She took a deep breath and rapped her head back against the stone behind her, hard enough to jar what was left of her brain against her skull; it hurt, but it didn't help. A block away, the red hats moved in her direction.

"Do you require assistance?" the pillar said.

She blinked. The pillar repeated its question in a pleasant mechanical voice.

"Um," she said. "I'm lost?"

"State your destination."

"Perdue Street, Shangri-La Apartments."

The pillar told her that a map would print out at the port on its other side; that she was required to recycle the paper upon reach-

ing her destination; that failure to comply was grounds for a stiff
penalty; and that it had been a pleasure serving her. The map told
her that Perdue Street was two kilometers away. You can make it,
she told herself; she whispered it all the way there.

13

THE MANAGER OF THE SHANGRI-LA SPIT ON THE STEP two inches from Jackal's right boot when he heard Crichton's message, but he gave her an apartment, less dismal than she expected—four tiny rooms in the back of the building, with a few pieces of worn furniture and a small window in the main room from which she could see slices of the several canals that crosshatched this part of the city. They were industrial canals, thoroughfares for barges, bounded by maglev train rails and huge crossdocking warehouses, and constantly busy with the roaring backspin of diesel engines and the bossy busy tooting of the tugboats that shoved the big vessels around like small dogs herding sleepy hippos. When it rained, she imagined, the window would run red and green and white with the reflected lights of the barges and the harsh halogen spotlights of NNA customs boats.

He cleared the front door and apartment door locks so that she could set her thumbprint and access code; then he accepted a credit transfer of three months' rent and a hefty security deposit. Jackal didn't argue; she added something extra, "for your trouble."

He snorted; and he took it, nodding once at the amount. Then he told her, "This one's only open because the tenant died day before yesterday, some kind of wicked infection." He said it with a

sideways look of nasty hope, as if she might flap her hands in horror and change her mind. She didn't; she smiled and closed the
door in his face, locked it all three ways, wiggled into the most
comfortable position she could find on the sprung couch, and fell
immediately asleep.

Later, she roused muzzily to the clangor of raised voices in the
hall, and wondered if she had in fact poached someone else's deal.
She didn't care. Let them find another place. She was safe. She
turned over and went back down into the dark.

She woke alert and hungry in the small hours after midnight, and
propelled herself into a marathon of activity. The first street vendor she found taught her how to use her datagem in the credit
reader, and she bought a steaming sausage on a sourdough roll,
slathered it with mustard, and ate it where she stood, not bothering to catch the brown drips that spattered her and the sidewalk.
She carried a second back inside and ate more slowly while she
plugged Crichton's palmtop into the apartment's network port
and puzzled out the unfamiliar operating system; then she began
locating city services on the net to arrange for utilities and e-mail.
She wasn't surprised to find that the net service provider for her
zone was Ko, but she didn't like it. The only surprise was her own
hesitation over her choice of e-mail address: finally, she shrugged
and requested *jackalsegura*; and smiled wryly to herself when the
database told her that she was *Accepted*.

She registered her apartment and virtual address with Crichton. She sent Irene Miller the most rigorously formal e-mail she
could devise, declining the program's employment contract; she
had to rewrite it four times to filter out the obvious fuck-you sub-
text, and she was remotely interested to find herself still weighing
these sorts of concerns.

She saved the most difficult transaction for last. She located the web site of a nearby storage facility, negotiated a month's rental; then she took a deep breath and, still in her most formal style, sent a request to Ko Facilities Management to release and ship her personal goods. She shouldn't waste the money on storage—she didn't intend to leave anything in it—but she couldn't bear to give Ko her actual address. It was an odd contrast, her physical secrecy and her open, almost contemptuous presence on the net; she didn't understand it and decided not to try. When she'd worked up the nerve to send the message, she became aware that it was full day, and she was hungry again.

She ventured a little farther from the building this time, and found a small grocery shop relentlessly stocked with prepackaged meals and processed foods. "Vegetables?" she asked, and was pointed to the row of cans and vacuum-sealed plastic bags in the middle aisle. The combination of low availability and high prices told her a lot about her new situation. She knew that as she explored her immediate territory she would find it a mosaic: determinedly proud neighborhoods, worn and tired but well-scrubbed and inching toward economic security in two or three generations, divided along inexplicable sudden lines from hardscrabble angry poverty and areas of aggressive despair. There would be a large, crumbling public clinic somewhere in a five-mile radius, the only one that would offer public health services. There would be two or three trendy clubs where locals served upper-class patrons who parked their cars in guarded lots while they enjoyed the frisson of the danger zone. There would be some really good ethnic restaurants where she might or might not be welcome. Power outages would happen here first and be repaired last. The police would always ride in pairs; and, indeed, she saw her first matched set cruise by as she returned to her apartment with two carrybags of provisions and the most expensive can opener she had ever owned.

She had messages waiting, and that was a tremulous moment. It made her too aware of where she was: sitting on a rickety chair

in a room that smelled wrong and was still her only place in the
world. All the energy she'd generated from being brave about the
shopping, competent about the apartment and the utilities, vanished utterly and left her deflated and sad. Accepting the messages
meant accepting it all: that life had turned around and broken her
when she wasn't paying attention, and that these e-mails were for
some new Jackal who had to find a different shape from the
pieces.

She stared at nothing for several heartbeats; then she heard a
particularly insistent tugboat toot-toot-tooting on a near canal,
and it sounded so like a harassed caretaker saying *no no no!* to a
maniacal two-year-old that she had to smile, in spite of everything.
And then she saw that the drab room was speckled with sunlight,
and she pulled herself out of the chair and opened the window.
The air smelled faintly of sausages, and there was enough breeze
to stir the flap of one of the carrybags. She could paint the room
a pale yellow to catch and hold the light; she could put a small
desk there in the corner; when they sent her things, she would
have music again, and her set of wooden spoons, and maybe even
the thick wool socks that she had always worn in place of slippers.
Everything did not have to be different; she did not have to be entirely new. Okay, she thought, okay; and sat down to read the
mail.

There was a confirmation from Crichton that her address information had been recorded; no arrest today, Jackal thought almost cheerfully, and saved the message to a folder she labeled Stay
Out Of Jail. There was a return message from Ko, which she
opened before she had time to get too scared. It was unsigned and
generic, and told her that her request for retrieval of stored material would be granted upon receipt of advance packing and shipping charges, as quoted, and that her goods would arrive at her
location within two weeks of payment verification. She paid the
bill. That wasn't so bad, she thought, she could deal with Ko; but

maybe that was only because for her, Ko was now an empty place. She had rubbed out all the people while she was in VC. Snow and the web and her parents were gone. No more people for Jackal. Don't think about it, she told herself, and felt like crying again, so she made herself get up and put away her food. Then she heated some vacuum-packed fettuccine alfredo and ate it with a roll; she didn't like the taste, but the carbohydrates steadied her. She'd have an hour or so before she got tired again. She should have bought some beer, and she needed to get back on a protein-rich diet if she didn't want her blood sugar freewheeling. And she had to get a new palmtop, and maybe a low-end desktop. She'd have to find other places to shop if she wanted to have any money left. That meant transport schedules and city maps. She needed paint. A phone. Newsnet access. A microwave. A budget. She made herself a cup of tea and started a list.

And so she entered into a time of strange, dislocated freedom; she ate and slept as necessary, and in all the moments between, she worked fiercely and with the clean satisfaction of getting things done. She made herself into a project: the reconstruction of Jackal Segura. Her wish list was enormous. She categorized it and then began to explore the city, on-line and by transport, finding her way to one neighborhood after another, comparing prices and weighing alternatives, making notes on her new palmtop: it took much longer than it should have, because she would suddenly get the shakes in a busy store or on a crowded sidewalk, and would have to find her way back to her apartment in a controlled panic.

When she had enough data, she ran a draft budget and sliced the list in half. She agonized over the shade of yellow, the white and green for the bathroom: she picked a deep muddy blue for the bedroom because as a little girl she had always wanted a room like an underwater cave. She held a brief memory of that other Jackal; then the hundred things still to do pushed it almost casually from her mind and she went on with her spackling and sanding.

Occasionally, someone would pound on the wall or underneath her floor, and she would know it must be late. Then she would turn to quiet chores—configuring her new desktop, washing down the kitchen shelves, haphazardly hemming curtains for the window, so badly that she had to rip out the stitching and redo the entire job. She could not rest until everything was done.

Her belongings arrived from Ko, and it took her almost a whole day to move them from the storage space to her apartment, one crate at a time on a rented hand truck that she maneuvered slowly along the sidewalks. She was managing the crowds better now; there were whole days when she didn't get scared by the press of other people. Today she was able to nod to the Laotian grocer sorting canned goods in his shop window, and raise a hand to the sausage vendor each time she reached her building. A group of neighborhood gang kids watched her interestedly throughout the afternoon from their place on a stoop four buildings west of Shangri-La. On her last trip, one scooted out to meet her, right hand casually riffling a butterfly knife through its paces.

"Ho," the young woman said, slender blades fluttering.

"Hello," Jackal answered. She did not want to stop, but the girl had placed herself in the middle of the sidewalk. Jackal braked and silently cursed the loss of momentum.

"Whatcha got?"

"My things," Jackal said economically.

"Nice things?"

"Not really. Nothing you'd be interested in."

"You never know," the girl said conversationally. "What will you do if I am interested?"

"I will dislocate your left knee," Jackal answered immediately and as calmly as she could. She could hear Neill say good, Jackal, specific examples are always more convincing.

The girl grinned. "Okay," she said. "Welcome to the neighborhood." She stepped out of the way.

"Thanks," Jackal said. "Delighted to be here." She grunted as her sore shoulder took up the strain of restarting the hand truck. She left the kids whooping on the stoop behind her, their laughter punctuated by the castanets of the flicking knives. It was the closest thing she'd had to a personal conversation since she had left Crichton.

She unpacked and arranged all her precious things in a seven-hour burst of adrenaline focus, smiling in delight to see them emerge from their wrappings. She opened a box and found Frankenbear, and was overcome by the memory of her first minutes in VC-Ko, reliving the astonishment and the way she'd felt as if a huge wind had blown her wide open. Then she sat Frank on her dresser and went on with her unpacking. There were some interesting omissions: all of her jewelry, many of her books, a letter opener that had belonged to her *abuelo*, other small items. Well, she would write to Ko and get someone in Facilities Management on the case. Or maybe not; maybe better to be grateful that the price for this particular reclamation was no higher.

And then, quite suddenly, it was over. The clock on her desk told her it was two forty-seven in the morning; she wasn't quite sure of the day. There was nothing more to do. The list was complete, the work finished. The apartment smelled vaguely of new paint and lemon cleaner, overlaid with street grease borne on the night breeze that belled the new curtains slowly in and out. It was very quiet: no tugboats, no transport engines whuffing along the street, no shouts or laughter or screams. There was a faint sound of music from far away, a bit like flamenco guitar. She turned off the lights and sat in the chair that she had placed so that she could see both the door and the window. She breathed; and the quiet filled her up.

14

SHE WOKE IN THE CHAIR THE NEXT MORNING WITH A stiff neck and no feeling in her right leg, her desktop calendar gently beeping to remind her that she had her first parole appointment with Crichton in two hours. She panicked and tried to dash for the shower, and yipped as the prickles ran up and down her leg with the returning circulation; she saved herself from falling at the cost of a wrenched wrist. Then she forgot to double-check the transport route before she left, and had to guess where to transfer. It made for a tense ride.

She finally found herself about a half mile from where she needed to be: in spite of the bad start and feeling like a wrung-out paint rag, she had enough time to walk the rest of the way. She felt a bit like she had been running at top speed and just smacked into an invisible wall; stunned, and not quite sure that she had stopped moving. It took a while to realize that no one was paying her any attention. Perhaps it was her clothes, rumpled and musty from their journey in a Ko shipping crate; or maybe the stoop of her shoulders and the way she had straight-armed her hands into her jacket pockets. She lifted her chin and stood taller. It made her feel better, and no one pointed or stared. As she made her way through the trickle of shoppers and couriers and businesspeople rushing to appointments, she finally noticed that it was a beautiful day; thin white sun washed over the dense blue sky like yolk inside an eggshell; light flecked the glass-fronted buildings; the air was cold, especially at corners where the wind tumbled about before gathering itself for the next run down one of the canyon streets.

Crichton's office, when she eventually got through the security checkpoints, was the shabby room she remembered, still devoid of any personal touch save the same mug, with what looked like a fresh chip along the base, and a number of self-adhesive notes stuck to the wall, curling at the edges from the heat pumping out of the floor vent beside the desk. There was also a new filing cabinet in the corner, by far the nicest piece of furniture in the room. Jackal assumed it held the folders that had been threatening to take over the office. She wondered why people still used paper files; she herself was very happy to manage all her information electronically, but most people she had known at Ko still kept some paper records. And, in fact, there was Jackal's folder, primly closed on Crichton's desk.

"Right on time," Crichton said. "Shut the door. Sit."

No arrest today, Jackal thought again, coming perilously close to saying it out loud in a chirpy, singsong tone.

You're tired, her little voice said, be careful.

"I ask questions, you answer them," Crichton began. In spite of her bad sleep and her case of nerves, Jackal found herself enjoying Crichton's lack of concern for the niceties. Crichton's eyes were gold today, the shiny color of foil wrapped around cheap chocolates. She looked like a fierce machine.

She went on, "After our little chat, you get a once-over from the doctor down the hall so that we can tell EarthGov we're taking care of you. That'll include the usual basic neuro exam—follow my finger, that kind of thing. Any questions? Good."

She picked up her phone and punched in a number. "Segura's here." A beat. "If you want to talk to her, come to my office. If you don't, don't. Well, I told you that, didn't I?" She closed the phone hard enough to make Jackal's ear twitch sympathetically. "Idiot." She propped Jackal's open file against her stomach and leaned back in her chair.

"Okay, Segura, Segura. You're living at . . . Shangri-La." She gave Jackal a look over the top of the file. "Good. No performance ratings from your program supervisor because you're not an employee. Fine. Credit's good. Hah, I guess. It halfway pisses me off that you've got more money in the bank than I do." The gold eyes gleamed.

Jackal kept her mouth shut.

"Made any friends?"

"Excuse me?"

"Have you made any friends?"

"What do you care?"

"Play nice, now," Crichton said, showing some teeth. "I ask, you answer. I get to ask anything I want, that's how this game works."

The enjoyment was starting to wear off. "No, I haven't made any friends."

"Any sexual liaisons since your reclamation?"

Jackal set her teeth together. "No."

"I should point out that prior to entering into a sexual relationship with a guardian of a minor child, you're required to divulge your felony conviction status and are not allowed unsupervised access to that child."

She couldn't help flushing. "I don't hurt children."

Crichton gave her a flat look. "You killed ninety-eight of them less than a year ago. The NNA does not consider you a good risk."

Jackal rubbed her hands across her face. "I didn't . . ." But she had. She had killed ninety-eight children. She had been about to say, I didn't mean to hurt anybody, but what difference did that make? It was strange that only the deaths of the web had seemed real up until now, that it was always Tiger and Bear and Mist that she remembered. She hadn't been thinking about ninety-eight children.

"What have you been doing with yourself?"

Jackal wiped her eyes and wrapped her arms across her chest. "Getting settled in. I don't know. I bought stuff, I got my things from Ko yesterday and unpacked them."

"So what's next?"

I don't know, I don't know. "I'm pretty tired. I think maybe I'll just take some time and learn my way around."

"Then what?"

"I don't know, okay? God. Unless you have a post-prison checklist you'd like me to follow?"

"No, but that's not a bad idea," Crichton replied calmly, making a note and irritating Jackal even more. Then Crichton said, "Your test results are back."

Jackal put on her best politely interested face; it felt a little crooked, but she hoped that didn't show.

"One of the advantages of all this paper—" Crichton twitched Jackal's file, but she wasn't looking at it; she was watching Jackal very carefully "—is that it's very private. Everyone assumes the electronic files are complete, original data. But when I see something that interests me, sometimes I'll just put it in one of my messy old outdated folders so I can chew on it for a while."

Jackal nodded cautiously.

"I'm not Doctor Crichton, but I've handled more than four hundred VC cases and I've reviewed a lot of test results. I know an interesting variance when I see it. I just don't know what it means yet." She picked up her mug and drank, never taking her eyes from Jackal.

Jackal worked to keep her expression appropriate; it was hard to look relaxed with all her facial muscles rigid and her heart jammering in her chest. She tried now for a still-cooperative-but-slightly-puzzled look. "What kind of variance?"

"Don't waste my time," Crichton said. "You've got no game face. You can fool these program scientists because they're morons, but you can't fool me. Something happened to you in VC. All of you come out changed, we expect that by now. But there's something different about you, and I want to know what it is."

Jackal took a slow deep breath, through her nose so that it was silent, down into her diaphragm. A strong, steadying breath. There had never been more need for care. In, in; and out as slowly. Then she let the fear express itself as anger. "I sat in a square room in my head for six years. I went a little nuts just like everyone else. Well, maybe not exactly like everyone else, how would I know? But exactly like me. I don't know if I'm different or not. I'm not even sure I remember who I was before I went down the rabbit hole. I don't know what you want me to say. I killed ninety-eight kids and they shoved me into my head and I stared and stared and stared at the walls and then one day I was back here and my whole fucking life was gone—" Her voice had risen; she closed her mouth on whatever else might come out. It was too easy to make mistakes when she was afraid.

Crichton folded the file closed and placed it on the desk. "I didn't expect you to tell me. So let me tell you: almost everything about you is in my bedtime reading pile right now. You interest me. You had influence and money, you've never been remotely political in your life, and you gave it all up without a squeak to plead a charge that any decent lawyer could have beaten with half their brain excised. So I have to wonder what that's about?"

Jackal could feel her face smooth into a tight mask of grief. Damn Crichton. She shook her head fiercely, trying to hold back tears. Crichton waited in silence.

"I am guilty," Jackal finally said in a low voice. "I killed those people."

"If you did drop those people down the well, I'm guessing it was an accident. Oh, please," she said exasperatedly as Jackal looked up in shock. "Do I look stupid? You're about as much a terrorist as the lab nerds with the white coats. You wouldn't get two feet inside the door with Steel Breeze."

Jackal felt numbly scared and, weirdly, just a little insulted. She didn't know what to do.

"So is it just that there really is a hard-wired criminal brain-wave pattern and, since you're not a criminal, you don't have it and so your readings are different? Or did something happen in VC that you don't want Doctor Bill and his merry band to get excited about? My money's on door number two."

Jackal opened her hands: "I don't know what you're talking about. I can't help you." And then she waited for the inevitable: the phone call, the security escort back to the lab. The new tests. The remand to facility custody. And then what? It was like being back in her cell in Al Isk, listening to the footsteps in the hall and knowing they were coming for her.

Crichton's smile was a brief, thin slash. "Don't fuck with me, little girl. I can make you miserable in ways you haven't even thought of yet. Now scram."

Jackal was startled into immobility; but not for long. She got through the door without trembling, but following the guard down the hall to the security door, she began to shudder. "Is there a bathroom?" Her bowels were loose, as shaky as the rest of her. Afterwards, she ran a cool stream of water over her wrists until she felt a bit more steady. Her reflection in the mirror was shadow-eyed with fatigue and shock, and the beginnings of consideration: what does she want with me?

Some days later, she came awake with her own voice fading in her mind, as if she had just finished answering Crichton's party question from that first interview: *I'm an executive-level project manager.*

She lay still, and the room held its breath around her. Project manager. If she were in Al Isk right now, that's how she'd be identified. Boring but safe. Maybe it would feel safe enough to businesspeople here that they would overlook the small matter that she was a convicted criminal.

Oh, wake up, her voice said. Of course they won't overlook it. But what else could she do? What else was she good at? Just shut up and let me think about this, she told herself, and then wondered if this was a bad sign. She still had occasional night terrors about the crocodile; she had become used to having conversations with herself, but she was always vigilant for that sly, sliding change in tone to tell her that her head was no longer safe.

Whatever Crichton's intentions, she'd really stirred things up. Jackal dressed, gobbled two fried eggs and a cup of Irish breakfast tea, scooped up her palmtop, and grabbed a transport downtown.

She spent the day walking the main commercial district in a purposeful grid pattern, locating tier-one service businesses and the corporate operations of luxury product developers, the types of companies most likely to spend money on her skills. She needed to get a sense of where the power lay—who had the best real estate, the hippest icons, and who was sponsoring what at the downtown museums. Where did they eat their deal lunches? How did they dress? In the early evening, she drank fizzy water in two different bars, listening intently to the conversations of people just coming off work, the stories they shared as they decompressed from the day. Coming back on the transport, standing shoulder-to-shoulder in the aisle with commuting workers, she studied everything: the periodicals people chose to download or read in paper form, their shoes and haircuts, the unexpected amount of corporate insignia jewelry. Clearly, executives and senior managers wouldn't be riding transport; but Jackal began to make some cautious, preliminary assumptions about status markers, and the clothing and presentation cues that would be reassuring to potential clients. She was hopeful that even after she filtered the list based on the restrictions Crichton had outlined, there would be several good candidates for her services. She wondered if any other convicted terrorist had ever expressed an interest in business contracting, and she had a hair-raising vision of Gordineau in Irene Miller's pink suit trying to blind a room of vice presidents with a laser pointer.

That night and the next morning she did the necessary on-line research, and narrowed her initial targets to three companies, all of which were in a rapid-growth phase and fit her parameters: a travel agency that designed custom adventure packages and luxury tours; a downtown art gallery that specialized in corporate consulting and commissions, and was currently second in market share to a larger, more stuffy operation; and an upscale event planning service for corporate charity functions.

The next step was a résumé: it needed to be particularly effective, since she wouldn't be getting interviews on the strength of personal contacts. But she couldn't hold a layout in her head; the concept kept fragmenting into confused bits. She was distracted by the troublesome, inevitable question: *Ms. Segura, why are you no longer with Ko?* Should she just come out with it right up front, do her best to minimize it? No, that was stupid: it would be hard to minimize four hundred and thirty-seven dead people on the ruined floor of Mirabile. She had to make them see her as an incredibly competent person before they saw her as a homicidal terrorist.

She decided to fudge a little and slant her Ko experience as if it had been on a contract basis rather than full-employment terms: she would talk about projects rather than career path, and forego any mention of Hope status. It wasn't ideal, but she could think of no better strategy. She began to build the résumé. She started lists of the particular executives she might want to approach. But every time she thought about calling or e-mailing for an appointment, or actually putting on nice clothes and walking into an office reception area, she became so restless that she could barely sit at the computer. She decided to take a break, and curled up on her chair—the best and most comfortable she could afford, she had scrimped on other things to work it into her budget—with a book loaded into her palmtop, only to find herself skimming the paragraphs and jumping ahead. It wasn't a satisfying way to read. She made Brunswick stew and dumplings and left it half-eaten, the little flour balls congealing into paste. She wandered aimlessly through cyberspace, using a randomizer to pull up web sites that were only interesting for the time it took to scan them. Finally, immensely irritated, she took herself for a long walk.

It began to rain, a light patter of drops that settled into a soft, steady rhythm. She had already resigned herself to being cold, so being wet as well didn't seem much of an extra burden. She pulled her jacket close around her and kept walking, head down, hands jammed into her pockets. It was early afternoon, and the streets were not so crowded now, so it was as if she were a drifting jellyfish occasionally brushing past other sea creatures in the current that carried them all. Eventually she let herself weave aimlessly back into her neighborhood, the now-somewhat-familiar streets and alleys, the storefronts, the dirty facades of the apartment buildings. She felt tired and grubby, as if the rain had washed her with a fine layer of soot. Shangri-La was only three blocks away, but she wasn't ready to face the ramshackle state of her life. Impulsively, she turned left at the next corner, heading north on a street that she'd never explored carefully because it dead-ended into a canal, and had looked, the one time she'd ventured down, like a tired industrial zone.

She thought she would go all the way to the end this time and try to find a place to sit by the canal, a scrap of grass or even a little park. It wasn't impossible: she'd found small public parks scattered throughout the city, although none close by. It would be nice to have a green space to walk to, with a bit of water to slosh soothingly against the retaining wall when a tugboat went by. She did not pay close attention to the buildings she passed; she had already categorized them as warehouses or perhaps small manufacturing operations, although now she noticed how quiet the street was, without the mechanical rumblings and oily smells she'd expected. She passed a blank-fronted building to her left with a large iron gate at the entrance, and heard music, faint and muddled, somewhere inside. It made her curious and more alert. Further along, she smelled something baking, wheat and warm fruit and sugar, and her mouth flooded with saliva. I want some of that, she thought, and realized with a small shock that it was the first specific thing she'd actively hungered for since she had come back from VC.

She followed the baking smell a third of the way down the next block to a wooden structure of two or three stories holding its ground between two taller buildings. The door was propped open by a brick, and next to it was a sign framed in steel:

Solitaire
4pm to 2am
every day

Not a bakery, with those hours. A restaurant then, or maybe a bar: there was a definite tang of hops underneath the doughy smell that she was almost sure was *apfelstrudel*. She peered through the doorway, but could see nothing except a wide vestibule that led to another door, also propped open. Through it drifted the soft echoes of low music and muted voices.

Other people. Suddenly she wasn't so inclined to go in. This was different from shopping conversations or excusing herself when she bumped someone on the sidewalk; this was too much like walking into the corporate conference room or any other place where strangers would be noticed.

Oh, so that's what it was; being noticed. She had been faceless since she came to the NNA. Maybe it wasn't time. Maybe she should just go back to Shangri-La and wait a while longer before she made herself visible in the world; *another six years sounds about right*, her internal voice jeered. But when she imagined herself boxed in her small safe space, it felt too much like climbing back into her cell. She had to do better than that.

She took a deep breath and let it carry her across the threshold and the entrance hall, shoulders back in the old proud way, the Hope walk that had always helped when she was in a new situation. Then she was through the doorway and inside.

It was as if she'd knocked over a bucket and spilled Solitaire out in front of her. She stood in one corner of a large rectangular space that flowed out over wood floors and up over colorful walls to windows set near the ceiling. They doubtless looked over an alleyway or the next street, but from inside they showed clean slices of sky rather than the city that hunkered around them. She thought the ceiling must also be glass, until she saw that the light and clouds were painted, with the clear afternoon sky above her fading in one direction to dusk and evening and night, and in the other to the thin brilliant colors of summer dawn.

Small square tables were scattered across the floor, each with a single armchair; more chairs were stacked in tidy rows in the empty space just behind the doorway where she stood. Several oversized booths lined up along the opposite wall, under the windows. To her right, a dozen steps led up to a second level not quite as long as the main floor, screened along its entire length by vertical wooden shutters that reached high enough to give privacy without losing the light from the windows. The louvers were open: she could see more tables and chairs, and a padded bench running along the far wall. A sign at the bottom of the stairs read *Private*.

The focal point for the color and light, the trails of tables and chairs, was the bar that arced across the far corner of the room. It had perhaps a dozen chair-backed stools fronting it, and it pushed out into the room far enough to include a workspace with a small grill and convection oven and refrigerator, as well as the beer taps and the racks of bottles and glasses. Wire baskets of drink-fruit dangled over the bar—lemons and limes, oranges, bananas—interspersed with pin lights that pooled the long counter into individual islands. The near end rounded into an order-and-pickup counter; she could see a board with what she assumed was a menu, and a datagem reader. Even empty as it was, the place felt comfortable and welcoming. She liked it already.

At the center of the curved counter, two people were talking. A man stood behind the bar, cloth in one hand, busily drying and stacking glasses as he listened to the person who sat on the stool opposite him, back turned to Jackal; she could see a very long ivory shirt of soft flannel with a high collar under nape-length straight dark hair, and elegant low-heeled boots under what looked like the kind of olive-drab pants her *abuelo* had worn fishing, baggy and full of pockets, tough enough to resist hooks and fish blood. The man nodded at something, still focused on his work; he had a tanned, broad anglo face and blunt hands, brown hair tied back. He turned and bent out of sight, standing up a moment later with a bottle of wine that he used to refill the glass on the counter.

Beads of water ran from Jackal's wet head; the man saw her when she moved her arm to wipe her face. The other person turned; a woman, already half off the stool. "It's okay," the man told her calmly, holding out his left arm in a sit-down gesture. And then, to Jackal, polite and impersonal, "I'm sorry, we're not open yet."

"Oh," Jackal said. She felt the first creeping of depression up the inside of her skull. "Okay. Um . . ." She meant to ask, "What time is it now?" but what came out was, "When can I come back?"

"An hour or so," he answered. "Four o'clock."

She nodded and gathered her jacket around her. She was about to turn and leave when she saw the wall at the far end of the room.

"Oh," she said, and moved forward for a closer look, forgetting she was not welcome.

The wall was whitewashed, like a primed canvas, with a rectangular grid laid across it. Some of the sections were still blank; the others had been filled in different media. What unified them was not style, but theme. One panel framed a charcoal drawing, delicate and precise, of a human figure slumped in the corner of an undefined space. Another panel was painted in the style of Munch's *The Scream*, a raging swirl of blue and green and gray and white; but this picture showed only a head, mouth open in a howl, two ghost-gray hands plucking at the temples and stretching the skin just to the moment of splitting. In the second row of the grid, a clay mask of a stylized human face, features only suggested, was trapped behind a set of gray bars. And in the lower center of the wall, the image that had drawn Jackal forward: a crude white shape of a face, stark against a black background, with the contemptuous suggestion of mouth and nose, and where the eyes should be, a broad black smudge that could be a blindfold or a window or a wound.

It was as if someone had captured her very worst days of VC and hung them up before her: the fear, the madness, the despair, the stubborn endurance; the hopelessness, the inevitable crumbling of herself. "Oh," she said again and then she felt dizzy, the air flashed, and the colors of the room grayed around her and there was a terrifying wrench in her head—

—and she stood in her VC cell facing the viewscreen as it cycled through its morphing faces. Adrenaline blasted through her and she lost all breath and all she could do was turn, turn, and it was as if she had never left, the larder and the bed and the screen. *What . . . what?* She touched the wall nearest her, tentatively, unbelieving. It was solid; so were the others, and they did not give at

all when she began to beat on them with her fists, first incredu-
lously and then in horror, whimpering *no, no*. But it was real, she
was there, with no doors, no windows, no way out and she yelled
"What is happening to me?"

—and another flash—

—and she blinked up at the man from Solitaire who knelt over
her, the painted ceiling above him like dusk on Ko just before
moonrise.

"It's okay, you're back," he said.

"I don't . . ." She gulped down a breath and started again, in a
small voice, "I don't know what's real anymore." She felt slow
tears on her cheeks.

His face twitched in sympathy. "It's all right now. You're back.
Just lie there until you get your bearings."

When she was ready, he helped her to a table. He gave her his
bar towel to wipe her eyes, and pointed his chin at her nose to let
her know it was all right to blow it. She was horribly confused and
embarrassed. If she ever came here again, this wasn't how she
wanted to be remembered; and she wasn't even sure she'd have the
courage to return. Already she mourned the loss of this place. "I'm
sorry," she managed. "You're closed. I'm okay now, I'll come back
later."

"Never mind about the time, I thought you were a tourist. You
should have told me you were a solo." He knelt down beside her,
looked at her more closely; took a breath, and his voice changed.
"Segura, right?"

She blinked. *Recognized*, her internal voice skreeked, *run run
run!*

"It's hard to tell without the hair. Still, I should have known
you." And then he said the most astonishing thing of all: "You're
welcome here. Can I get you something to drink?" And before she
knew it, she found herself alone at the table with an imperial pint
of cool bitter ale, a baguette with a plate of soft goat cheese, and a

box of tissues. The man was back at the bar polishing glasses; she hoped he was using a different towel. The woman was gone. It was quiet except for the occasional bright clink of a glass on the counter. Silence spread smooth through the room like the afternoon light and the smell of baking apples, heavy and comforting.

She drank the beer slowly, enjoying its bite and the contrast with the smoky cheese. She had two swallows left when the man came back to the table.

"Mind if I join you for a minute?"

"Please."

He pulled a chair to face hers. Before he sat down, he said, "I'm Scully."

"Jackal." He had not put out his hand, so she did not offer hers. He nodded, sat.

"Feeling better?"

She was, although her head ached fiercely. She drank another swallow of beer. "I'm sorry about all that, I don't know what happened to me."

He startled her again. "It was a virtual technology aftershock, by the look of it. First time?"

She nodded mutely.

"Big shiny flash and poof, back in your cell?"

She nodded.

"Yep, classic aftershock. Everybody gets them, it's one of the little residual benefits they don't tell you about in your debrief. Lousy pricks." He spent a moment looking off into the middle distance. "The first time is scary. It'll almost certainly happen again, but you always come back. Sometimes it takes a while. You just have to keep telling yourself that it's only been a few minutes in the real world and that you'll wake up soon."

"It's happened to you?"

"Lots of times." He looked bleak as he said it.

He's like me. The thought was too big to digest all at once. Of course there were other VC survivors, she'd been on a cell block with a couple hundred of them, but this was different: a man tending bar, a real person out in the real world; and he's like me. She put the thought away for later.

"This is really good beer, thanks."

"Don't thank me, you're running a tab." He smiled.

She smiled back. "Then I hope it's not as expensive as it tastes. Can I have another?"

"One Redhook, coming up. From here on in you'll need to order and pick up at the bar, I don't normally do table service. And I brought you this, I'll put it on your tab as well."

He handed her a skin meld the size of her thumbnail; a tiny replica of the white face with the black slash. "The bond is reversible if you don't want to wear it in public. Just use the switch here on the side."

She frowned at it: it was disturbing, and she wasn't sure why she should put it on. "What's it for?"

"It's sort of the secret funny handshake for solos. It's specially coded, so don't lose it; it's a pain, but we get too many people trying to pass otherwise." He looked at her quizzically. "Didn't they have one?"

"Who?" She could feel her blink rate getting faster again.

"Whoever sent you here."

"Nobody sent me, I just . . . I was out walking . . ."

It was his turn to be shocked. "Tell me you didn't just wander in here by accident."

"I wanted to see if there was a place to sit by the canal and then I smelled whatever it is that's baking. It smelled like apple strudel."

"It is. I'll save you a piece." He rubbed one hand across his forehead and gave her a lopsided grin. "My, my. What are the chances? Okay, here's the drill. The main floor's open to everyone, it's how I pay the rent, but the upstairs is private for solos and their friends—" and he added cryptically, "—which I'm still waiting for, but you never know."

"What's a solo? Is that some kind of slang?"

"Oh, my dear, where have you been hiding?" He said it nicely, but she could tell he was nonplussed. "You're a solo. You've participated on an involuntary basis in the Virtual Technology Program that's now under the full control of god-bless-the-NNA. We come in all flavors—virtual solitary confinement, state-sponsored drug withdrawal, schizophrenia research, social conditioning for non-employables who have run out their aid allotment, terraforming simulations, terror studies using prisoner populations. Other stuff that I can't think of right off the top of my head, but you're bound to meet someone on the network who's been through it.

"Any solo is something of a celebrity these days, but VC is where the glam is, especially after the program shake-up in Earth-Gov. All that publicity. No, really," he said as she wrinkled her nose. "Well, you'll see for yourself. I really would put that on, it'll make a difference and you can always take it off."

"Why 'solos'?" She made quote marks with her fingers, made a face: stupid word.

"Everyone goes in alone."

"Okay, I get that, but we're out now."

"You think?" he said gently. "Look what just happened to you." He eased himself out of the chair. "I'll get you that beer."

He had to start a new keg; it gave her time to reflect. He set the glass on the end of the counter when it was ready and waved her up, had her swipe her datagem through his credit reader to set up an account. He didn't directly acknowledge the meld on the back of her left hand: he only said, "Solos come in at all hours. Tourists usually show up mid-evening. Anyone bothers you, deal with it efficiently. People who start trouble or prolong it are permanently barred, once they recover. People who stop trouble get a free grilled cheese sandwich and I will personally escort them to the clinic if they need attention."

She nodded. "A first-strike rule." She saw his raised eyebrow, and waved a hand while she searched for the right phrases. "You punish offense, not defense. It's not violence you're worried about, it's escalation."

"That's right." She heard in his voice interest, and the beginning of approval. She thought of Tiger in the park, hands over his nose: her fault, that day. Her offense. She drank more beer. He did not speak, only waited while she wrestled with herself: so, he understood the value of silence. She was beginning to approve of him, too. She nodded thanks for the beer and carried it back to her table.

A few minutes later, Scully hefted a hinged sidewalk board out to the street. The first person came in the door five minutes later, a man with the solo meld on his hand and a bruised right eye. Scully had a drink waiting for him, something tall and improbably red. The man took it without a word and carried it up the stairs, giving Jackal a narrow-eyed look but not otherwise acknowledging her. A moment later, the louvers closed across the solo level.

People arrived in a steady trickle over the next half-hour while she drank her second beer. She stayed alert, uneasy with the public identity the meld gave her, glad that her table was out of the traffic flow. As time passed with no challenge, no pressure, she relaxed a little. But she reached her limit when the main floor was about half-full: she had the jitters, and her headache worsened, so she waited for a moment when no one was at the order counter and told Scully, "Coffee and that piece of strudel would be great. Then I think it's time for me to go." She didn't want to offend him by walking out on the strudel. Consideration was a feedback loop; good feedback built good relationships. If it worked in conference rooms, she didn't see why it wouldn't work here.

He busied himself with the mug and the coffee urn. "Milk and sugar on the end there. I hope you'll come in again."

She smiled; it was small and went quickly, but in some important way it was the first real smile she had given anyone since the horrible day at Mirabile. "Is tomorrow too soon?"

He smiled back. "See you then."

She walked slowly to Shangri-La, thinking in spirals that always led to a blank place at her center. *People like me*. Back in the apartment, she let herself be drawn into a movie on fiberlink, letting it unfurl on her desktop screen while she stretched out on her chair and ottoman. It was a thriller about a team of scientists investigating the inside of a supposedly defunct volcano: a large number of the explorers died in satisfyingly gruesome ways before the final sequence, a spelunking chase through tight cave passageways in near-darkness, a monster in pursuit. It helped take some of the edge off, and after the scenes in the caves, her rooms didn't seem quite so small; some of her restlessness had gone. Maybe tomorrow she could settle to those résumés. But tonight, she had to think.

Her headache had faded. She poured herself a glass of orange juice and took herself through the evening again, the aftershock, Solitaire, this solo identifier that Scully had pinned on her: she flipped the meld through her fingers like a coin. Aftershock was worrying, no matter what Scully said. How often would it happen? How long could it last? What catalyzed it? And would she be able to break out of her cell again? The thought of finding herself back there, with no warning and no control, was frightening and depressing: but it was different to imagine being back on Ko Island. She'd been trying to put that time away, to make herself understand that she was back in the world now and that she would never return to Ko. But what if she could?

She needed to know more, so she spent a couple of hours online. She didn't find much about aftershock, but the search led her to a wealth of solo-related sites that gave her pause because of the quasi-cult markers they contained: a crude but consistent caste system of solo categories, with, as Scully had promised, VC solos at the top; the elevation of individual solos to the status of idols; and a fascination with interactions between them, particularly solo-on-solo violence. There was a lot of personal bio data, some of it at a level of detail that Jackal thought could only have come from program personnel files or solos themselves. It was morbidly interesting to read about other people who had been through some kind of virtual technology experience; not a generally nice crowd, but certainly a distinctive one. She resolved after reading a few of the personal testimonials to never find herself in a confined space with anyone who'd undergone a terror induction study.

She couldn't resist accessing a few of the references to herself. It was believed she'd been exported to the NNA, but no one was entirely sure. She was even-tempered; no, she was quick to anger; she supported a dozen conflicting political causes; she disliked dogs. She shook her head: where did people get this stuff? Then she found selected bits of testimony transcribed from net recordings of her trial, and a "kill list" that named all the people who had died at Mirabile. That made her turn off her desktop and climb into her too-small bathtub, feeling sour and unsettled again. Maybe she shouldn't go back to the bar: she didn't want to sit around with sick fans and talk about body counts. But the idea of Solitaire was so appealing—a place for solos, no matter how unwelcome she might be in the rest of the world. Those web sites might be fucked up, but they were right: she was a killer. What was it worth to have one place where she didn't have to be afraid of that? Just about anything, her voice told her; she said out loud, "You're damn right," and began to wash herself before the water got too cold.

*   *   *

But she still had trouble sleeping, and she couldn't settle to her work the next day. She told herself it was excitement, nervous energy, and took herself off early to Solitaire; it would be better to stake out a space before the crowds rolled in. She was determined to stay longer tonight, to increase her tolerance for being among people again. It would be useful when she began to interview; it wouldn't do to bolt from the visitor's chair in some sleek office in the middle of a conversation about project structure or team norming.

She bonded the solo face to the back of her hand as she walked up Marginal Way toward Solitaire. Scully said hello in a friendly way and remembered that she'd liked the Redhook, and she tried not to be shy with him. She was determined to do well, to be accepted, to belong.

It didn't take long to suss out the ground rules. The social dynamic defaulted to single-person activities and minimal involuntary interpersonal contact; if you wanted to be part of a group, you had to work at it, by bringing together tables and chairs in configurations that would not disturb the individual areas already staked out. The solos split half and half between the main floor and the private zone; of those she could see, some gathered in nearly silent groups of two or three, but most sat alone at tables or the bar. There were no servers; the only negotiation for drink or food was with Scully, and solos always had right of way at the counter. Every so often, Scully dashed from behind the bar and raced through both floors to haphazardly bus tables. As the room became more crowded, the dishes piled up, and the wait for food and drink lengthened considerably, but no one complained. Jackal had never seen a more quiet or patient line in a bar. The only nervous moment came when a man who had finally worked his way to the head of the line—Jackal was already learning to recognize tourists—failed to give way to a solo. It was the woman in the long shirt, and when he protested she turned on him and said a few words in a voice too low for Jackal to hear. The man paled: there was no room for him to step back, but he made himself very small until she left with a wineglass in one hand and a bottle in the other, held by the neck as if she might use it on someone. As she passed, Jackal saw the meld on her right cheekbone; the tourist would not have seen it until she had rounded on him.

Some time later, three young people commandeered a triangle of tables and chairs next to Jackal, giving her a little extra space when they noticed her meld. She ignored them, and hoped they would behave; she tended these days to regard younger people as more socially inept than she remembered being. And then she imagined someone looking at this part of the room and seeing the four of them, all about the same age. She choked slightly on her beer. How old was she? She felt twenty-nine. But she wasn't, she was a twenty-three-year-old who was in some weird way ahead of herself.

She rubbed her face and put the topic on the long internal list of things to figure out. In the meantime, she was aware of the young people trying to identify her: they were doing their best to watch her without looking and talk about her without being obvious. They resorted to low conversational voices and a strained metaphorical code that was so transparent she almost felt sorry for them, even though she wasn't inclined to help. At least she wasn't running screaming into the night because someone was paying attention to her. Or sending someone else out that way: belief in the solo potential for violence was clearly widely held, whether or not it was true, and she guessed it must account for some of the care that people took with the solos here. She chewed on that while she went up to the counter; and she wasn't sure whether to be delighted or appalled at how easy it was to take the front of the line just by saying, "Excuse me," and waving her meld under the nose of the person in front. He looked at her nervously, and she realized he was the same man that had run afoul of the woman in the long shirt. She had to bite her lip to keep herself from reaching out and saying, "I won't hurt you, really," and scaring him even more. It was hard to accept that she was this man's brush with danger. She'd been watched by millions of people all her life, but never as if she might eat them.

No one bothered her. No one spoke at all except Scully and various people excusing themselves for being in her way. Other solos were polite enough; some of them were the most openly curious, which she supposed made sense given that solos set the standards for behavior here. She understood why they had a funny handshake to identify each other; without it, some of these people wouldn't know whom to acknowledge and whom to ignore. As a caste system, it wasn't so different from the corporate hierarchies she used to navigate.

She stopped by for a couple of beers or dessert and coffee every day for the next week, arriving at different times and trying to sit in new places. She treated it as a sort of acclimatization therapy. She became much more comfortable sitting by herself in a room full of people. It was a curiously free feeling, this sense of company without interaction. Group solitude. She didn't go upstairs to the solo level, she didn't feel ready somehow, but at least she could be alone with lots of other people now. That had to be some kind of improvement. But she hadn't approached any businesses about a contract, and the restless itch was still with her.

Every night she went home and looked at solo web sites, which all agreed that her whereabouts were still unknown. "Are you people blind?" she found herself saying irritably to the screen one night. "I'm right here."

She wasn't sleeping well at all. Everything pissed her off: her idiotic personal publishing program that wouldn't scale her fonts correctly, the substandard whitebread pseudo-flamenco bubble-pop that the woman next door played too loud, the rain that would never quite stop. She went food shopping and snapped at the clerk who miskeyed her zucchini as cucumbers; on the transport coming back, a burly woman stepped on her foot and, when Jackal complained, replied, "Oh, get a life." Jackal trembled with rage; she wanted to scream out, *You have no idea who I am! You have no idea what I did!* She couldn't even muster a smile for the sausage vendor.

She limped into the apartment and put away her food, and then forced herself to return to her desk; she had finally finished customizing résumés for each of her target businesses, and she was determined to pick one at random and do something, anything, to get herself through this useless, dithering place she'd somehow got herself stuck in.

Her mail icon was blinking: a message from Crichton. *Report to my office tomorrow 1 pm. Failure to report is grounds for immediate arrest.* Jackal jam-clicked the mouse on the *Close* button so hard it hurt her finger. Great, wonderful, terrific. Just what she needed. What did it mean? She paced the room, finally coming to a stop at the window, where she braced her arms against the sides of the frame and stared out. The city twitched and shimmied busily outside. She was still Jackal-under-glass. She sighed, watched a contrail fluff out across the sky like an angry cat's tail and then thin into a cirrus cloudbank. It was all out there, and she had no idea how to get to it. She could no more reach any notion of her life than she could reach up and touch that cloud. She wished that Snow were here; Snow would look at Jackal with that particular tilt of her head and ask a couple of sharp questions that would point Jackal in exactly the right direction, and they'd have a beer and maybe go over to Ypsilanti Street for Mongolian stir-fry.

Snow.

She had tried so hard to avoid thinking about what was lost. Snow was a big shiny blank spot in her soul, where Jackal had rubbed her out in VC; what was the point in hurting herself with something that was gone?

She's not gone, she's right there on Ko where she's always been, her inside voice suddenly said, in the matter-of-fact way it had told her in VC *do better next time*. She went cold. *You can talk to her anytime you want. Send her an e-mail. Pick up the phone.*

She wondered how she looked, standing at the window, staring at nothing, mouth open like a fish in a tank. She felt as if she might crawl right out of her own skin if she didn't move, didn't get away, but she forced herself to stay still and think about it. She tried to bring Snow's face into her mind; as before, she couldn't, not really. She could only get a complex stew of feelings and the sense of shared experiences now remote. That was the tedious tragedy of it, that those moments were gone, or scared into hiding, now that she wanted them back.

But Snow was still real; and Jackal understood with a deep pang that Snow would never have rubbed Jackal out like a stain in an awkward place. Snow was somewhere in the world outside this window, working, talking with her hands in motion, scattering toast crumbs at breakfast, alive, with the memories and thoughts of Jackal equally alive inside her. *And I haven't even thought about her, not really.*

And now her face was hot with shame, and she pushed herself away from the window to curl up in her chair. Talk yourself through it, she told herself.

Okay. How about this? She won't want me back.

How do you know? You haven't asked her.

She's loyal and brave and she has no idea what's happened to me. She doesn't know that I killed the part of her that lived inside of me. How could she forgive me for that?

And what if she did?

It wouldn't work. I'm not me anymore.

And there it was: she was not the same Jackal Segura who had drunk wine on the cliffs and eaten oranges in her father's kitchen and wept with Snow through the video link between Ko and Al Iskandariyah. She had gone too far down the powerful road of isolation. She wasn't Snow's Jackal anymore, and now she had to figure out how to explain that to Snow. What was she going to do?

She didn't know, and there was no one to help her. She had no people anymore. The three sisters—maybe they were called Ko and VC and NNA—had eaten that little boat, *The Jackal,* and now it was struggling in the belly of the sea. All this work, making the apartment as nice as she could, being brave about the shopping and the neighborhood, the hope of a fingerhold at Solitaire—all this, and she was still simply trying not to drown.

And there was the matter of Crichton, her suspicions and her brilliant eyes that saw too clearly. What could Crichton want with Jackal tomorrow that could be anything but trouble? Maybe her patience had run out and she would pull the plug on Jackal, hand her over to the brain-strippers. Or maybe she wouldn't: so what? If not tomorrow, then someday.

Jackal hugged herself, made herself into a tight ball. So here it was: she was doomed. The only choice she had was how she went under and who she took with her. Well, not Snow. Never Snow. So now I have to do something about this, she thought, with a sudden deep sense of bitter anger. Why do I always have to do something?

Because you do, she told herself. Well, she would do it. Then maybe she could stop being so torn and twisted. Then maybe she could get some fucking sleep.

It took hours to write the pages and pages of e-mail, the whole story of VC, the frightening solitude and the madness and the eventual joy; the current danger and the thin strands of hope still left to her; and her resolution to go it alone. When she was done, she made a cup of tea and cried while she read it through. It was a beautiful letter. It explained everything. It would bring Snow right inside Jackal's head.

Then she deleted it all and sent the necessary message, a ten-second burst of words whose only possible result was distance. She used a transient account that she canceled as soon as she was reasonably sure the message would not bounce for any reason. Then she sat in the growing dark. She was hollow: waves pounded her and filled her full of echoes that sounded sometimes like *Snow* and sometimes like *don't leave me, don't leave me*. But it was done. After a while, she put on her coat and went to Solitaire.

Snow,
I wanted you to hear from me that I am out of prison instead of finding out some other way.

We can't be together anymore. We can't be in touch. You won't hear from me again.
Good-bye.
Jackal

15

THE BAR HELD A BUSY CROWD, LOTS OF MOTION AND
rising voices, laughter full of alcohol or some other high. She put
her meld on her left cheekbone where it would make a white
shock against her skin and the unrelieved black she wore, long-
sleeved tunic and trousers and boots; and she used it and the force
of her yawning emptiness to carve a path to the bar.

She didn't return Scully's hello, only said, "Can you give me six
pints on a tray?"

"Did you bring a friend?" he asked, almost hopefully. She remembered his remark about solos and their friends; maybe she
would ask him about it one day, if she ever cared.

"I have some thinking to do."

"Ah," Scully said, "the kind of thinking that makes a person
want to drink a hundred and twenty ounces of beer in one evening."

"That's the kind."

"It's your liver." But he said it with the particular stamp that she
was coming to recognize as his impersonal kindness, comforting
because it required no response. And he gave her a dish of olives
as well.

She found a table on the outer ring of the room and set her back
to the wall. Solitaire staged itself around her. She put the beer

away slowly and methodically, and thought about the strange skewed dynamics of anonymous grief in a room full of strangers, people who would notice but not share. Witnesses. She stripped the olive flesh from the pits with her teeth and made sure to suck all the pulp and oil before she dropped them back into the dish. She drank her beer and imagined a huge bowl full of beads that had been dipped in various paints and tossed in together; a giant hand shook the bowl and the beads mixed, bounced against each other, leaving a dent or a streak of color behind. Soon all the beads would be little lumpy rainbows, shaped by each other but still discrete. Millions of them, each one alone in a universe of beads.

She imagined the giant hand reaching into the bowl to pluck out the Jackal bead and put it in a box of its own where it could roll unimpeded, no more friction, no more pain.

She drank. When Scully came by to bus the tables, she told him solemnly, "I know what Solitaire is. It's a special little box for broken beads."

"Are you okay?"

She thought about it, shook her head.

"Time to go home, maybe."

"Not done thinking."

He didn't answer, just hefted the tub over to the next line of tables; a few minutes later he set a mug of strong milky coffee on the table and went away before it occurred to her that she should thank him. The coffee wouldn't make her any less drunk or angry, but it was meant to be comforting and she was touched. She didn't drink it, though. It didn't really go with the beer. She closed her eyes and let the noise of Solitaire spin around her, a tidal pool of words and glassware and background music, voices breaking against her like waves on a reef.

She opened her eyes to find a young man standing a careful distance away.

"Excuse me," he stuttered. "Can I ask you a question?"

"You can ask," she said deliberately.

"Are you Ren Segura?"

She put both hands on the table, her heart pumping faster; she wasn't ready for this, not tonight. She thought of the kill lists and the breathless accounts she'd seen on the web sites; and then she saw herself as he must see her, the solo meld defiant against her skin. She wore the badge; she looked at the web sites every night for her name. She had already consented.

"Jackal," she said.

"Um, sorry?"

"I'm Jackal Segura."

His eyes opened wide and his mouth jerked in excitement. "Ayo! It is so crisp to meet you! You've been number one on the spotter's list since Mario saw Jeanne Gordineau at HeadSpace last week!"

She had no idea what to say to that, so she picked up the last olive. He seemed to take it as a routine dismissal.

"Well, um, thanks. Um, if you need anything, I'm Razorboy, I do stuff for Scully sometimes." He managed a certain dignity with the introduction, which he promptly spoiled by adding, "Wait until I tell Cy and Drake about this!" before he faded off toward the back of the room.

The buzz started to spread no more than two minutes later. Grateful for the distraction, she put her training to work charting its course through Solitaire, the one-to-one progress of the news of her identity, followed by a slow I'm-not-looking scan of her sector of the room and the equally slow think-I'll-just-wander-over-to-the-bar stroll that inevitably offered the chance for at least one *guess what I know!* exchange with someone along the way. She pretended not to notice the curious eyes, or the breathless way the crowd shifted to let her up the line when she decided to go get some more olives, but she did make sure to stand up straight and look as scary-but-not-too as she could manage.

"Welcome to the party," Scully said. "Razorboy is absolutely delighted with himself. And business will pick up even more the next few days, thanks very much."

"How thrilling to be useful," she said. Then she smiled briefly to show him that she wasn't trying to be rude.

He studied her more closely. "How about something else to eat? Grilled cheese sandwich?"

". . . sure. Okay."

He built a fat sandwich with orange and yellow cheeses and thick brown bread, and set it to sizzle on the grill, slathered with butter. Jackal stared around the room, and the art wall caught her gaze. She hadn't looked at it closely since the first day and the aftershock, but now she was curious and the sandwich would take five minutes; so she left the olives on her table and, beer in hand, wandered toward the back of the room. People got out of her way a shade more quickly than on previous nights.

Standing close to the panels made her head feel like it was trying to expand, and she didn't think that was just the beer. The images were brutal and direct, but not simple: they spoke to her of the lonely journey that a person's soul could make when it was faced, unprepared, with itself. There was a new picture that she liked, a forearm and hand reaching out of a hole, caught in a moment that might have been the beginning of a grip or the end of a letting go; it was left to the watcher to decide whether the person inside would pull themselves up or not.

But as nice as that one was, she returned again and again to the panel that was the basis for the solo meld. Whatever else it was, this was a face that shouted, "Here is what VC is like."

"What do you think?"

A woman stood to her right, so close that her shoulder nearly touched Jackal's arm; the woman from her first day, who tonight had approached so silently that Jackal hadn't sensed her. Jackal managed not to spill her beer.

"Well . . . at first all I saw was pain . . ." She hunted for the right words. "But now I think there's more to it. This one could be a face with no more humanity in it. Or it could be a face that has had so much experience, so much contradiction, that it's the complete face. Like it's saying that we can be nothing or all things. And the common thread is anger and endurance: this has both, whether you see it as an empty face or a full one."

The other woman tilted her chin up, as if considering. Tonight she wore the same fisherman's trousers with a long black priest-collar jacket over a white ribbed T-shirt, a combination that gave her a compelling air of being both brutal and severe. *"Muy bien,"* she said finally, with a trace of Euro accent. "That is a graceful thing to say to an artist."

"You did this?"

The woman shrugged, but in a way that told Jackal it was hardly a casual subject.

"It's very powerful. It makes me feel lonely and strong."

The woman smiled a strange smile. "A poet," she said. She turned to face Jackal. As with the last time Jackal had seen her, terrorizing a tourist, the woman's meld was on her right cheek-bone, a mirror of the one on Jackal's left. She saw the other woman register the similarity and be flattered. Good; the imitation certainly was a tribute to her style, and this was not a person Jackal wanted to offend. There was no wine bottle tonight, but she remembered the practiced grip she'd seen. And from her time on solo web sites, she had a name to put to this face like a hungry cheetah's under the straight black hair.

"You are Segura," the woman went on, managing to convey simultaneously *Here's some news for you* and *Why was this not brought to my attention before?*

Jackal nodded, a formal up-down of her head.

"Estar Borja," the woman said, and even though Jackal had known it was coming, she couldn't help the thrill she felt. It was different when the legend named itself.

"Everyone knows the Lady Butcher," she answered, sounding like nothing so much as a goggly-eyed fan watcher: she could have kicked herself. The other woman's eyes narrowed: Borja was deciding whether she had been insulted or not.

Jackal said quickly, "I'm sorry, I meant no disrespect. You're such a good artist, I should be talking about that instead of . . . well, anyway, this is really powerful, like I said. It's beautiful, it's really really beautiful," she added, surprised at her own intensity. She waved her glass at the wall, and then, finally at a loss, raised it in a toast and drank down half the remaining beer in one gulp.

The muscles around Borja's eyes relaxed. "There's no harm in being known for many achievements," she said. "You may appreciate me with a drink."

And it was that easy. They went back to the counter, where two stool-sitters melted away under Borja's stare. Scully gave Jackal her sandwich and Borja a glass of rioja. "Why don't you give me a glass too, and leave the bottle," Jackal said; Scully's face set into an expression that Jackal couldn't quite fathom, as if he were trying to decide whether to smile or shriek. "Relax, my friend," Borja said lazily, "I will drink wine with this ferocious child and then she will walk me home safely." That didn't seem to reassure Scully, but he left them alone with only one last hard look at Jackal.

"What was that all about?" Jackal said.

"He worries too much," Borja replied unconcernedly, and began to talk of the panels on the wall. Her hands were small and strong, with slender square-tipped fingers that sketched rapid, expressive pictures as she spoke. Jackal found herself telling Estar of her own clumsy attempts at painting and the sadness she had felt when it was clear she had no talent. "This was about ten years ago," she said, and then fumbled, recovered, "No, of course I mean about four years ago . . . well, you know what I mean—"

Estar nodded, and Jackal went on, rolling the wine around in her glass, "It was more than just no talent. It was anti-talent. The more I practiced, the worse I got. It was so frustrating to have a picture in my mind and only be able to create something stupid and completely joyless. And to know that the vision would always be a prisoner in my head, there was no way to get it out into the world. Does that make any sense?"

"Yes, of course. Visions want to be real. There is the vision and then there is the act of birthing it." She touched her meld absently. "We are here because we realized our visions too well."

Jackal blinked and decided to let that one pass; instead she drank the lees of her wine. It seemed that Estar was finished too: "Walk me home," she told Jackal, and slid off the stool without waiting for an answer. Jackal followed more slowly, and when a movement caught her eye she turned to see Razorboy slide Estar's dirty wineglass into the pocket of his voluminous madras jacket. He reached for Jackal's: "Don't even think about it," she said, pitched just loud enough. He jerked his fingers back and blinked at her like a startled owl. Scully plucked the glass off the bar on his way by without missing a beat, then paused long enough to say, "Take her straight home. It's just down the block on the right, the one with the big iron gate."

Borja was waiting at the door. Jackal waved to Scully and headed out.

They walked in silence to Estar's gate. As usual, Jackal could hear muffled music inside the building. She opened her mouth to say good night, but Estar spoke first. "Come to dinner tomorrow."

"I'd like that." She tried to dredge up some pre-VC manners. "What would you like me to bring?"

"Ah," Estar said, widening her eyes dramatically, "something delicious." She grinned. "Seven," she said, and then the gate was closed and Jackal was left on the doorstep grinning in her own turn. Then she remembered, and she almost rattled the gate and shouted, "If I don't show up it's because they're scooping out my brains downtown." But she didn't. Instead she walked home full of grilled cheese and the beginnings of a classic hangover.

Before she reached the corner of Perdue, a voice said, "*Hola,* neighbor!" Out of the darkness came the knife-wielding young woman she'd met on the street the day she moved her belongings into Shangri-La. There were others with her, but they lagged at the edge of the shadows rather than circling Jackal in the way she would have found immediately threatening.

"*Buenas noches a ustedes,*" she said politely.

The girl lifted a finger at Jackal's cheek. "You are Jackal Segura."

"That's right." She braced herself; she didn't really expect trouble now—it would have come already—but she couldn't help remembering Gordineau's morbid predictions.

"Chacal. *Es un nombre bueno.*" There were soft noises of agreement from the dark around her.

"And may I know your name?"

"You may know me as Jane," she said graciously. "Good night, Chacal."

"Good night, Jane." But they were already gone.

She felt calmer now, heavy with alcohol but also ready to face whatever was next; the curiosity at Solitaire, Crichton's intimidating behavior. Oh, and all the different versions of 'not in a million years' from prospective employers: she hoped they would be polite, but most executives didn't have compassionate confrontation skills. And she would hope for a lovely dinner with Estar Borja.

She was distantly amused, back at her apartment, to find that Razorboy's web site was already updated with the news—*Segura spotted!*—including, to fully round out her day, one good digital photo of Estar Borja in mid-gesture, hand blocking Jackal's face, and a second fuzzy one of Jackal with her nose in a glass and five more piled up around her. Still, she could expect to be recognized from now on. It was about time.

She touched the meld on her cheek lightly, and left it on when she went to bed.

The guard at the security door to the administrative section let her in, but didn't bother to escort her to Crichton's office this time. "Just knock," she said, and went back to the seemingly unmanageable task of keeping one eye on her security monitors, one eye on the door, and one eye on everyone in the hall.

Jackal was wound up. She rapped on the door and pushed it open without waiting, and found that Crichton wasn't alone: Jeanne Gordineau perched on the edge of the visitor's chair. She turned when Jackal came in, and the look on her face made Jackal back out of the room.

"It's okay," Crichton called out. Her eyes were the clear green of laboratory emeralds. "We're done here."

Gordineau swiveled her head back toward Crichton and watched her fixedly, like a cat staring at some small prey just out of reach; Jackal could practically see her tail twitch when Crichton spoke.

"You will follow the instructions of the program managers," Crichton said. "Failure to cooperate will result in your immediate return to real-time prison to complete your sentence. When your year is up, then rebel all you want. They'll fire you, but that's not my problem. Until then, you behave."

"Je comprends," Gordineau replied. "I understand. You own me and you amuse yourself now by listening to my thoughts with your little machines in my brain, and you use me in your research. *Bien.*" She flashed a look at Jackal; she radiated an unsettling, bruised cheer, her eyes bright inside their dark circles as she turned again to Crichton. "So now it is your turn. This is how the world works. Soon perhaps it will be my turn again and then we will learn what your jewel eyes look like from the inside. *Je mangerai tes beaux yeux.*"

Crichton smiled. "Never happen," she said. "And now it's time for you to be somewhere else." Gordineau winked broadly at Jackal as she left the room.

"She's a wacko," Crichton observed. She looked at Jackal sharply. "And she's trouble. You stay away from her."

"I thought you wanted me to make some friends."

"Don't start with me, I've had a hard day," Crichton said, surprising Jackal; Crichton looked a little surprised herself. "Close the door," she added.

Jackal did. Her heart hammered in her chest.

"You had a brain spike last week. What about it?"

"I'm sorry?"

"You had a neurological event at three oh four Sunday afternoon. I'm required to follow up on any such incident."

"God," Jackal said involuntarily, and put a hand up to her temple; she had forgotten about the transmitter.

"Well?"

"Is that what you brought me in for?"

"It's routine."

Jackal blinked and tried to relax her shoulders. They wouldn't move.

"What happened?" Crichton said, relatively patiently.

She took a breath. "Okay, well, I was just standing around and then I was in my cell. I was there for, I don't know, about three minutes? VC time. And then I was back."

"And the cell was exactly the same as your original confinement?"

"That's right."

"Were you alone when this happened?"

"No," she said slowly. "I was with someone."

"And did you discuss this event with this person?"

She still spoke slowly, trying to work out what the right answer would be. "They told me that it's called aftershock, that it happens to all solos, and that I shouldn't be too scared because people always come back."

"Now that wasn't so hard," Crichton said. "In a few minutes, Doctor Bill will be along to ask you all these questions again. Please answer him with the same level of cooperation."

Jackal wondered if Crichton was being ironic; it was impossible to tell.

"The interesting thing about this aftershock is that it fits your early VC readings like a glove. Totally vanilla. Same alpha and beta wave landscape, same Magnesson curves. Your confinement readings start to wobble about two months real-time, and by five months your whole baseline shifts up above the original by a few points. More temporal lobe activity, more everything. Boy Bill would have seen all this if he'd taken the time to look at the graph instead of relying on filtering software to find his anomalies for him. But this aftershock, this was just what anyone would expect. You're giving me a lot to think about."

There was a knock at the door; Crichton opened it for Bill.

"I don't have much time," he said to Crichton. "Please describe the event."

"He's not talking to me," Crichton said after a moment.

"Oh. Sorry." Jackal told him about the aftershock.

"First time? Hmm. Nothing unusual, don't be worried if it happens again."

"Have you ever had one?"

"Me? No, of course not."

"Well, it definitely is unusual. It was terrifying. So what is it, and why does it happen, and what do you intend to do about it?"

"It's simply an adaptive response of the brain. It should fade in time and there's no reason at this point for any kind of intervention."

Meaning we don't know, we don't know, and we don't know, Jackal thought sardonically. It must have showed; Crichton grinned suddenly, a flash of white that was gone quickly, but not before Bill saw it. He gave Crichton a sour look, said, "Is her recent test data finally in the system?"

"Coming right up." Crichton tapped her keyboard; she didn't look at Jackal, and her face and body were relaxed. Jackal waited.

"Okay, got it," Bill said. "Hmm. Yes, hmm, well, this all looks pretty average. A few variances maybe, but nothing special. And you've had your first post-confinement random event—" Is he kidding? Jackal thought "—pretty much on schedule. So there's no reason for extended participation. I don't know what you thought you saw here," he said to Crichton, "but there's really nothing special."

"You're the expert, Bill. I just like to make sure that you have a chance to see anything that might be unusual. After all, isn't that the kind of teamwork we expect from each other?"

Jackal's mouth all but dropped open in admiration of the sheer brass.

"Hmm, well, yes, of course," Bill said seriously. "I appreciate it. But there's nothing here to be concerned about. We'll keep her in the control group, and if you see anything unusual come across the scope, then you just bring her back in and we'll take another look at her."

He left without acknowledging Jackal further. Crichton closed the door behind him, then resumed her seat behind the desk and leaned back, very much at ease. "Cretins run this program," she said with a tone of absolute satisfaction.

"I appreciate what you think you're doing," Jackal said. "But I really don't have anything to tell you."

"You have no idea what I'm doing, and it's killing you," Crichton replied. "And you will tell me when you're ready or when I am, whichever comes first. Our business is done, go home."

"I just have a question." She had debated hard with herself about whether to ask or not, until her internal voice had said, so what's worth going to real-time prison for? And the clear answer was: nothing. So she asked: "What's the policy on being around other convicts? Am I going to get arrested if, I don't know, if I happen to fall into a chat with another solo?"

Crichton answered neutrally, "You enjoying Solitaire?"

Jackal nodded warily.

"Glad to hear it. And don't look like that, I'd have told you by now if you were in trouble. The NNA no longer has regulations about criminal associates, mostly because there are too many criminals in the world these days. You can't turn around without bumping into one. So we control it at the back end. We'll add an automatic lifer clause to your sentence if you commit another crime with another convicted criminal. So talk all you want, but don't be stupid. Your whereabouts are always recorded and there are plenty of eyes watching you."

That was interesting. Jackal wondered if Crichton was talking about security officers hanging around places like Solitaire, or if she was referring to the network of solo watchers. If Jackal had Crichton's job, she would recruit as many watchers as she could. Who better to notice behavior changes and association patterns?

Why's she telling me this?

"Now disappear." The green eyes glinted in the flat overhead light, but there were no answers there.

16

SHE HAD FORGOTTEN TO TELL CRICHTON ABOUT HER
job search, but she wasn't about to go back or even send e-mail:
right now she wanted as much distance as possible between them.
And she didn't need Crichton's permission to look for a job, she
told herself, even though part of her wanted nothing more than
the other woman's approval and support, maybe the offer of a private word in an executive ear because Crichton was so impressed
with Jackal's determination and grit. She told herself to grow up,
but she daydreamed about it on the transport back to Shangri-La.

It was time to do some work. She set herself to analyze each
company on her shortlist. It quickly became clear that the art
gallery was the best choice, because of its size and competitive
stance, and because according to the business news it was taking
on a number of major installation contracts in a short period of
time. The gallery was urgently commissioning sculpture, painting, mobile, holographic and audio/olfactory art. Jackal didn't
know anything about sound/smell pieces, but she would bet that
facilitating the design and approval processes between artists and
clients was not a beginner's job.

She pulled the Director of Human Resource's e-mail address
from a net article. She wrote a polite cover letter stressing her

skills, describing in general terms a few of the projects she had last worked on, and announcing her immediate availability on a contract basis. She put everything under the name 'R Segura,' and she double- and triple-checked that the résumé was utterly professional. They might turn her down, but they were damn sure going to take her seriously first.

She sent the e-mail before she could worry herself out of it. Then she stood and stretched in front of the window, enjoying the crisp blue of the sky and the precise planes of the high thin clouds. She felt the satisfaction of forward movement.

She arrived at Estar Borja's door at seven oh two with a brightly colored paper bag with string handles. She had spent the rest of the afternoon shopping, agonizing over what to buy. Something delicious: the first test. She rang the buzzer and waited. And waited. She rang again. Somewhere over her head, a speaker fuzzed into action. "You should be careful whose door you knock at."

"Um . . . hello? It's Jackal."

Silence.

"Jackal Segura? You said to be here at seven . . ." Oh, sharks, had she misunderstood? Maybe she could simply find a way to sink into the sidewalk so she didn't have to be so embarrassed.

Then the voice said brightly, "Segura! Dinner. Is it so late already?"

The gate clicked open, and a tiled walkway led her between high whitewashed walls to massive double wooden doors that were beautifully hung and swung open with a touch. She came into a large central courtyard that opened to the sky, elegant and utterly private, like the old Spanish houses she remembered from visits to her *abuelo's* friends. Three moorish-arched doors were set into the courtyard walls, one leading in each direction: this was a huge house, not the apartment or small wing she'd expected.

She went further into the courtyard, past enormous plants in clay pots glazed with intricate designs, and at the heart of the open space found a gentle fountain that plinked like liquid chimes into a circular pool bounded by a low stone wall, perfect for sitting. So she did, enjoying the smell of water and green growing things. The music was louder here, but not more distinct; she couldn't tell what it was, but it played weaving games with the notes of the water in a way that made the garden more luxurious and exotic.

Estar came around the side of the pool, wearing a long raw-silk dress that reminded Jackal of mediterranean sand, the color and the way it moved as if individual tiny grains flowed endlessly over one another. Estar's feet and arms were bare; as if she read Jackal's thought, she put out one arm and said, "It's cold. Come inside."

She led Jackal into the wing to the left of the main entrance. Jackal tried to orient herself—right now she was walking toward Perdue Street—until she stepped into the first room and any sense of direction disappeared in wonder.

She had never seen anything like it. Each wall was fully covered, floor to ceiling, by a different, vivid mural. The first one stopped her speechless: a photo-realistic pair of french doors opened onto a balcony that overlooked a wild seacoast under a turbulent sky; the water had receded from the beach, stranding sea creatures and revealing disturbing objects—a golden mask, a rusted car with algae-filmed windows, a set of tossed human bones entangled in a net. On the horizon, a huge wave swelled toward the viewer.

"Oh, my," she said, and stepped forward for a closer look, only to be distracted by the next, a quasi-expressionistic rendition of a bullring, all swirls and suggestion, where the matador was a small girl in a plain white shift, her sword nearly as big as her body, surrounded by a dozen circling bulls with bright blue eyes and human teeth.

Ugh, she thought, and turned to the right to find a painted extension of the garden she had just left, that led from planted beds and disappeared down a tiled path into a jungle. The tangle of green and black parted slightly at the curve in the path to show golden animal eyes peering through.

Estar was waiting at the door into the next room. "Come along. If you stop to look at everything, we'll never get our dinner."

Multicolor rugs layered the wooden floor, piled three deep in some places, so she had to step carefully. She also had to navigate the furniture: it was large and stuffed and there was a great deal of it, chairs and couches and ottomans positioned for conversation or quiet contemplation of the artwork, or in a corner under a bright reading lamp. Muted music played from concealed speakers, sitars and some kind of reed instrument wailing at each other.

"It's just so—" Jackal began, and then opened her hands to show she had no words for what it was.

Estar took her down a short hallway past several rooms stuffed with color and texture and sound, the same technique of decorative overload. Different music drifted from each open door, loud enough to fill its particular room and blend into a gentle stew in the overlap areas: now Jackal understood the muddle of sound she always heard outside the gate.

The kitchen was at the end of the hall, a large L-shaped room with a thick dark wood dining table at the far end. There was a cooking island in blue and orange tile; on racks and shelves, copper-bottomed pans competed for attention with patterned dishes, thick-stemmed glasses in dark berry colors, crockery jars, an entire rack of glass spice containers. An opaque golden film covered the kitchen window and made the room seem bathed in olive-oil light. The walls were painted in a checkerboard of eggplant and kale green and nectarine. More music, this time a deep, throaty female voice accompanied by acoustic guitar. Something bubbled on the stove: Jackal breathed in garlic and sautéed onions.

"It's fantastic," she said spontaneously. "I am completely happy to be here."

Estar looked pleased. "So," she said, "reward me for being so clever as to have invited you. Show me what you have brought."

She studied each item that Jackal produced: a bottle of rioja and one of barbaresco, wines that would taste of earth and sun and, Jackal hoped, would complement whatever meal she was offered in this wonderful, mad house; a container holding two steamed artichokes wrapped to keep warm, with little pots of garlic butter and herb mayonnaise; a loaf of banana bread, homemade and only slightly burned in one corner; a bunch of cheerfully ragged sunflowers.

Estar opened the pot of mayonnaise and sniffed it, then wrinkled her nose. "This is foul," she said. "The rest is very nice. You'll find a corkscrew in that drawer." She waved a hand towards a sideboard near the table, and then began to arrange the flowers in a tall blue vase. Jackal opened the barbaresco and poured a taste for each of them while she set the rest aside to breathe.

Estar rolled the wine in her mouth for three or four seconds, closed her eyes and breathed the fumes out through her nose. "You chose well," she told Jackal. "Tell me where you found this adventurous wine." So Jackal told her about the little shop in a ripe-for-gentrification zone just within walking distance; how the shop owner noted whether customers came in from the east or west of the shop and treated them accordingly, and how satisfying it was to subvert his expectations by choosing better wine than the middle-class customer he was being nicer to; how he'd approved of her choice in spite of himself. Estar was curious about every detail. At some point she poured the wine and served the artichokes in eggshell porcelain bowls with a matching platter for the discarded leaves, all the while asking questions: How did Jackal know where to find such places? How did she feel about being taken for, how did they say it here, a risky element?

And Jackal was somewhat astonished to find herself answering honestly: "It made me feel bad about myself. And that made me mad. I spent more than I meant to just so he would treat me with respect."

"Ah. Then who has won?"

"We both did. He got more money and I got better treatment and some great wine."

"Pah. He got more money and you got a snide remark behind your back as soon as the door closed on it. The merchant classes are the same everywhere, bourgeois and stupidly elitist because it is the only thing they have to cling to."

Jackal said admiringly, "You say the most outrageous things with such authority."

Estar snorted. "I say everything with authority. Why not? And outrageous thoughts harm no one. History is not shaped by such thoughts, no matter what the sociologists say. Only needs make history. You don't agree?" She smiled beautifully. "Imagine if I had only thought about killing all those people, if I had not needed to make my vision real. But for me it is never enough to keep the picture in my head. As you see." She waved in a gesture that included the whole house.

Jackal didn't know what to say to that. Her mouthful of artichoke turned to string on her tongue.

"You understand, of course," Estar said, eyes half-lidded like a lizard across the table.

"Of course," Jackal said, and Estar grinned like a child who has just been told, Yes, I'll be your best friend. *"Bueno!"* she said. "More wine."

After dinner they walked to Solitaire. Everyone noticed them come in together, and Scully again put on that peculiar expression. Jackal would have gone to the bar, but Estar put a proprietary hand on her elbow and said, "You have never been upstairs? You must come. Wave politely to Scully and see him later." So Jackal waved as if to say, *what can I do with her, she's determined!* and allowed herself to be drawn upstairs.

Dozens of eyes watched them go; it was a relief to pass behind the closed louvers and shed the weight of all that attention. The shutters dampened the noise as well. The space was dim except for a few wall sconces over the padded bench along the wall, and more of the hanging pinlights spilling faint pools over the floor. It seemed as if she had walked into a maze of light and shadow; then she saw that folding screens were set around some of the tables, giving the effect of a puppet show as shadowy shapes moved behind them. Other solos had chosen to remain visible, and there were several tables with two or three people talking in low voices, looking in her direction as she paused behind Estar.

"Over there." Estar pointed to several chairs grouped in front of a viewscreen. Five other people were already watching the newsfeed, the largest group of solos Jackal had ever seen. No one exchanged names. For the most part, they watched silently, with occasional, usually cynical comments that neither required an answer nor opened any doors to real conversation. The program concerned Steel Breeze, and Jackal didn't enjoy it. She tried to dampen her restlessness; finally, she leaned over and whispered to Estar, "I'm going to go get some coffee. Do you want some?"

Estar waved her off without answering, intent on an interview with a woman named Sheila Donaghue who was precisely and dispassionately justifying the most recent Breeze atrocity in Cairo. Jackal was glad to get downstairs.

It didn't take Scully long to come out with what was bothering him. He said, as he poured the coffee, "You know who she is."

"Well, sure."

"You know what she did."

Jackal nodded.

"You know she's the first and longest VC prisoner. Eleven years."

Jackal didn't bother to agree, she just waited for him to get to the point.

He leaned close so he could speak without being overheard. "Come on, Jackal. You've read the web sites. You know the story. VC made her crazy. She's wonderful, I adore her, and she's completely unpredictable. They started capping VC at eight years when they saw how she came out. You've been lucky. She could just as easily hand you your own eyeball as feed you dinner."

Jackal sipped her coffee. There was a lull at the bar, so she pulled up a stool and sat down. "I certainly agree that she's a little peculiar," she said quietly. "And I can handle her. She's been very kind to me and it's nice to talk to someone again. To have an interesting conversation. You know what I mean. You and I can talk like that, at least I hope that's what we're doing now," making a back-and-forth motion with her hand between them to show that she meant the circularity of real communication, the active connection. "But you're busy here and god knows the watchers don't have much quality conversation to offer so far. And the other solos are . . . I don't know what they are. I just sat upstairs with a bunch of them for forty minutes, and if that's what passes for social activity . . ." She shook her head.

"I understand what you mean."

"Solo isn't just about being in VC, is it? It's about what comes after."

He began to polish a glass she was sure was already clean. He said finally, "It seems like there's a direct relationship between the amount of time people spend alone in virtual space and their—what would you call it—maybe social stability afterwards. The longer you go in, the more disconnected you are when you come back out. The biggest exception to the rule so far is you." He raised his eyes to her face without pausing in the polishing; the cloth squeaked along the edge of the glass. But Jackal felt warm and soft from the wine and the evening with Estar, unassailable in the way that alcohol sometimes fostered. His speculations didn't worry her; *what does he know? What do any of them know about me?*

She replied, "You do fine."

"Sure, but I wasn't in that long. Eight months, a little less. I'm just a garden-variety criminal." He smiled a private smile, and she wondered for the umpteenth time what he'd done and how he ended up running Solitaire. "I'll tell you about it some time," he added casually, but the glass squeaked again from the pressure of his grip.

"I'd like that," she said. "Maybe we can trade some stories."

He set the glass and rag aside, and then reconsidered and took the glass back to pour himself a beer. "So where I was going is that I think there's a threshold of alone that most of us can't pass beyond without some kind of profound change."

That silenced them both for a long time. "Well," she said with a deep breath, "that's a big one. I'll have to think about that."

"It makes some sense out of why they've rounded up all these people for that two-year research program of theirs." He squinted at her. "Are you in it?"

"No." He gave her a funny look and she wondered what he'd heard in her response; but she knew he was too polite to poke at it.

He went on, "Well, rehabilitation is still the goal of the prison experience, at least in all the political speeches, and having people come back whacked out and antisocial from VC doesn't play well. So they're trying to fix that part. Then they'll go make lots of money and put lots of people through a whole new kind of hell. Unless the researchers can spin it out longer by making it look like something really interesting is happening here, in which case they all get to keep their high-priced jobs a little longer. Hence the program—fix the bugs and maybe find some new ones and everyone stays employed for as long as possible."

"They have to fix the aftershock too."

"They don't give a shit about that. Who cares about the occasional bad day for a bunch of convicts as long as it doesn't directly contribute to recidivism? Want some more coffee?"

"Yes, please. Scully, that's a really cynical attitude." She said it with a certain admiration.

He fetched the coffee. "Cynical is just a grouchy word for right," he said when he returned.

"Maybe. But in this case, I think there's more to it. I think it's worse."

She waited to see if he was interested; he made a questioning face, so she went on. "This stuff is intended for a lot more than just prison applications. They're going commercial."

"How could they? The technology is way too unreliable for respectable citizens. I'm guessing they're just trying to meet what passes for humane treatment criteria in most of these judicial programs."

"I don't think so. There's nothing in those regulations that would stop them from rolling out now. None of the anomalies have proven to be fatal or result in permanent damage."

"Maybe," he said quietly. "But I've run Solitaire for over two years now, and I say the damage is all around us."

They shared another one of those silent moments. Then Jackal said, "Maybe one of the reasons solos don't talk to each other much is that we're all so fucking depressing."

"Or depressed."

"Same damn difference. Oh, hell, I'm sorry. I believe you. I know you're right. Look at me: I won't even tell my lover where I am. How well-balanced is that? But I don't . . . I don't want to be damaged."

"I know you don't, sweetheart," he said. "None of us do."

His hand rested on the bar between them, and he started to move as if he might reach out and touch her, and she wondered how she would react; no one except the testers had deliberately touched her since she went into VC. So many years without touch. The internal voice tried to say, no, it's only been a few months really, but she told it to shut up: if Scully was going to reach out to her, she did not want to be distracted. But he did not reach: instead, he made a nasty, strangled noise and his eyes rolled up into his head so that for one horrible moment they were solid white, like a pair of Crichton's lenses. He turned boneless and went down behind the bar.

"Oh, shit," she said, and in an instant had climbed over the counter and swung herself down next to him. He lay in a heap on the floor, looking much smaller than himself. His body, when she touched him gingerly, was pliant and relaxed, and his eyes were open; they moved in rapid small jerks back and forth, as if he were looking around himself quickly. And she knew: he was in aftershock. At this moment he was in his cell, perhaps pounding on the wall as she had done, perhaps curled up and crying, perhaps simply resigned.

She could move him in an emergency, she was strong enough, but there were too many sharp edges and hot surfaces between them and the back stairs to his apartment. She bundled some clean bar towels into a lumpy pillow, and used another towel to mop up the beer he'd spilled on his way down. Then she stepped over him and began to serve the customers who were piled up three deep at the end of the counter, alternately gawping or politely looking somewhere else. She knew how to draw the beer properly, and she managed to find an open bottle of house red; but when a scrawny tourist openly leered at Scully on the floor and then demanded a tequila sunrise and a turkey sandwich, she gave him a withering look and said, "On your bike, son," and jerked her head for him to leave the line. "But . . . but," he sputtered, and Jackal gave a nod to the person behind him, a big man who got the point immediately and growled, "You heard the lady."

"Thanks," Jackal said economically, and gave the big man his beer free.

When the line had cleared, she turned and found Scully on the towels, eyes open, watching her.

"Hey." She squatted beside him. "You okay?"

He wasn't; he was shivering and his eyes brimmed with tears.

"Can you walk?"

He gave her a tentative nod.

"Okay, hang on just a minute." She stood and scanned the bar. "Ho, Razorboy! Yes, you. Come over here."

He did, looking confused and a little excited.

"Can you pour beer?"

"Sure, can't everybody?"

"Okay, get back here and serve. Beer and wine only, nothing fancy, no food. Make sure the tourists pay. If they don't, tell that guy over there." She pointed at the big tourist with the intimidation skills. "I'll be back as soon as I get Scully upstairs."

Razorboy swallowed. "Are you sure? I mean, nobody ever runs the bar except Scully."

"Well, right now I'm running the bar. Do you have any concerns you'd like to express about that?"

"No m—" He caught himself, and she kept her smile off her face.

"Good. Then I'm putting you in charge. Any solos give you a hard time, you tell them they can talk to me when I get back. I won't be long. I really appreciate your help." He straightened up at that, and she wondered with a pang what Neill would think about her using her management skills to put a boy in charge of a bar full of tipsy ex-convicts. Never mind about that now; it was time to get Scully off the floor.

He stood with help and managed the stairs with little problem. She hesitated at the landing as he fumbled with the print lock on the apartment door: she'd never been up here, and she did not want to intrude on his privacy.

"It's okay, you can come in," he said. "I . . . I'd like it if you did." Then he pushed the door open and shuffled inside, slightly bent as if he were hurt. She followed and closed the door behind her.

He was already easing himself down onto the couch in the front room. He reached for a blue-and-green patterned blanket folded over one arm of the sofa; she took it and spread it over him and, after a moment's hesitation, tucked it around his sides and feet. He was still shaking, but he didn't flinch from her touch.

"Can I get you anything?"

"No." His jaw and the muscles around his eyes were tight. "Could you sit with me for a minute?"

"Sure." There was an armchair at the corner of the sofa. She tucked her legs up in a tailor's seat so she wouldn't be so obtrusive; that would make it easier if all he wanted was the comfort of another human in the room. And at first it seemed that was how it would go: he closed his eyes, and she waited for his breathing to slow and deepen. She would leave when he was asleep.

She looked around the room, curious about the kind of place he would make for himself. The sofa was good brown leather, now worn and battered. He had an entire shelf of paper books with colorful spines; their musty smell mixed with incense and the faint residue of grease from downstairs. The walls were painted the muted green color of forest light, and the illusion was strengthened by the painting on the wall by the door: a cathedral of giant, straight trees, painted as if the artist were standing head back, looking up at the trunks and the distant treetops, and beyond them, the coming dusk. It reminded her of Estar's work, except that it was so serene.

He spoke, his eyes closed, his face completely still except for the smallest movements of his lips: a talking stoic mask. "That was a bad one. I only notice the bad ones anymore." A breath. "Most of the time I just bounce into my cell for a second, maybe two, just a flash of the walls and then I'm back. It's only a microsecond in real time, not even long enough to pass out."

He was silent long enough for her to work out what he meant, and to feel a deep wrench of horror and pity. "Scully, how often does this happen? How many aftershocks do you have?"

"Huh," he said, in a hopeless imitation of a laugh, "I've lost count. It's a really good day when I don't go back four or five times. I had a really good day last week." Silence again, and then a sigh. "But usually I just take a deep breath and go back to whatever I was doing. Nobody ever notices." And as if that were the saddest thing of all, he began to cry.

She unwound herself from the chair and found his bathroom, brought back some toilet paper and pushed it into his hand. "Thanks," he said, eyes still shut, and wiped his face until the tissue was a soggy lump that he dropped uncaringly onto the floor.

"They scare me so much." His nose was clogged; he breathed through his mouth and spoke in short sentences, his voice thick. "I was in the first phase of VC testing. Like Estar, but a much shorter sentence. Eight virtual months . . . that's where I found out how claustrophobic I really am. I was scared all the time. And I was so lonely. I just sat there every day by myself in this room that was too small, feeling myself going crazy. They have a viewscreen now, right?" His mouth tightened. "We just got four walls and a shelf of food and this horrible grinding quiet. Finally I invented a friend so at least I wouldn't be alone." His face moved briefly into a small, sad smile. "Forty years old and I have an invisible friend. He's called Bert. I talked to him every day for the rest of VC. And it made a difference. It was still horrible, but it was better.

"And then they let me out and I had some money from . . . well, I started to make Solitaire. I had my first aftershock one day while I was painting the place, that's how I got this scar." He put his fingers above his right ear. "Fell off the ladder and hit my head. And then I was back in my cell and I didn't know what was happening, no one had told me, and I was terrified. And Bert wasn't there. I couldn't hear him anymore. He never came back. And I'm so scared of being trapped again all by myself. One of these days I'll have an aftershock bad enough that I really will be crazy when I come out. It's just a matter of time."

He sighed. "You know what I've been doing? I've been pretending that Bert's on a long trip somewhere. I write him letters. He doesn't write back because he's not allowed to. He's on a secret mission, and even though he can't be in touch, getting my letters is really important to him." He sighed again. "You probably think that's weird, but sometimes I just need someone to talk to."

"I don't think it's weird," Jackal said softly.

He opened his eyes. "No one's ever helped me with an aftershock," he said. "The tourists don't know what to do, and other solos either can't deal with it or it just doesn't occur to them. Usually I just wake up on the floor and hope that people haven't stolen too much beer while I've been out. Oh shit, is the bar still open?"

"It's okay. I took care of orders while you were out, and I put Razorboy in charge until I get back. Turns out I'm good with beer and wine, but you might want to teach me how to make a tequila sunrise sometime."

This time his smile didn't look quite so sad. "It's a deal."

More silence. Then he said, "Thanks for taking care of me. But I think I'd like to be alone right now. Jesus, now there's an irony for you." His face cramped, and she knew there were more tears pushing up behind his eyelids.

"I can stay," she said, but he was shaking his head no; so she patted his arm gently and said, "Don't worry about the bar, I'll take care of it, okay? You just rest." She let herself out and made sure that she pulled the door shut firmly, so he would hear the noise and know that he was safe.

Downstairs, she found Razorboy pale but coping.

"You okay?"

He nodded.

"Any trouble?"

"Nope."

"Good. Want to help some more?"

He thought about it. "Okay."

"Great. Take this tub and go bus the tables."

He did; and he stayed until two-ten when she finally shooed the last straggler out the door. She hadn't seen Estar leave: she wondered what Estar would make of Jackal's disappearance and their sundered evening. Nothing, probably, she thought crossly, and realized how tired she was.

Razorboy brought in the signboard. "Where should I put this?"

"Just leave it there inside the door. Scully can put it away tomorrow."

"You want me to do anything else?"

"No. You go on home. Thanks for helping."

"Yeah, it was pretty crisp. We kind of worked together, didn't we?"

She suppressed the amusement and just let the gratitude show in her smile. "We sure did. It would have been tough doing all this myself." And she wondered what kind of headlines she would find on the web site tomorrow: *Segura Up Close!* And the coy text. Well, fine. It was a small enough price to buy Scully a little peace of mind tonight.

She was mopping the floor when she heard him come down the stairs.

"How are you feeling?" she said without looking up from her work.

"Okay. My head is killing me."

"Try some Redhook, it works great for me."

"Thanks, I might do that. Join me?"

"Sure." She figured the floor was clean enough; she put the mop away in the small closet by the back stairwell and sat across from him in one of the booths. They each stretched out full length and savored the beer in appreciative silence.

"It was really nice of you to do all this," he said. "Why did you?"

She put her glass down. "What do you mean?"

"I mean, why did you do all this?"

"Because we're . . . I mean, I thought . . ." She was surprised at how vulnerable the question made her. "I want us to be friends." Now she felt like she was about six years old.

"Oh. Well . . . me too," he said, equally nervously, and it was suddenly important to her to be very clear.

"It matters having friends. Maybe we aren't so good at it anymore, but that doesn't mean we shouldn't do it."

He looked at her. "Okay," he said finally. "Okay."

"Okay."

He drew parallel lines in the condensation on the side of his glass. "Don't tell anyone about Bert."

"I won't. Anyway, I think it was a great strategy. Better than mine."

He looked up. She knew he wouldn't ask; she would have to give. She was tired from mopping and wiping tables and stacking chairs, but he was her friend and he needed to hear her story. Not the breakthrough: she couldn't afford to talk about that, especially now that she knew how frightening it was for him to be trapped. It would only be cruel to tell him that she'd had a whole world to explore inside VC. But she found that she wanted, she needed, to tell someone about the rest of it, the battles she had fought and the way that solitude had compelled her to dismantle and then reassemble herself.

"Do you want to hear about it?" she said; and instead of the yes she had expected, he answered, "Please. Please."

17

SHE SHUFFLED HOME ABOUT SIX-THIRTY IN THE MORN-
ing, worn out with beer and hours of digging up handfuls of herself. She had told her story of the crocodile, and the different kind
of madness that led her to turn herself to stone. And she had finally spoken of Snow and the web and her training with Neill;
and the discovery, just before it all ended, that she wanted nothing
more fiercely than to do the work Ko wanted. But in spite of the
beer and the special buzz that came from revealing herself, she'd
had the wit to withhold the information about her false Hope status and the deal she'd struck to protect her family and her web. It
was the last job they had given her, and she would do it well. In
that way, at least, she still belonged to Ko.

Her desktop cheeped softly at her: mail waiting. She came
within a breath of shutting the whole thing down and going to
bed: she didn't think she could bear any bad news on top of the
emotional rib-spreading she'd done tonight. But she opened the
mailbox and found a single message, from an address she did not
recognize at first, until she read *Dear R Segura: we are currently
seeking a project manager and have reviewed your qualifications with
interest in further discussion. Our search is winding up, so I must ask if
you are available on short notice for an interview.* The gallery: good,

her instincts had been on target. She pulled up her calendar program to record the date and time, squinted, checked the e-mail
again, squeaked "Oh, *sharks!*" and ran for the shower: she had two
and a half hours to clean up, eat, print some leave-behind copies of
her résumé, and try to gather some semblance of brains.

The rushing around gave her less time to be nervous, and she
made it to the gallery as much past on-time as she could get without being officially late. She was grateful for the ten-minute oblig-
atory let-the-candidate-stew holding pattern to steady her
breathing and let some of the sweat under her arms dry in the cool,
faintly coffee-scented air. It was strange to be wearing formal
business clothes after so many months of Neill-style loose dressing,
and there was nothing she could do about her too-short hair, but
she'd caught the right overall tone, judging by the people she saw
in the hallways: including the one who stepped through the glass
doors off the lobby area and came purposefully toward her. She
straightened and then stood.

"Ms. Segura? Thank you for coming in. I'm Mark Levinson,
Ms. Oronodo's assistant. If you'll come with me, the interview
team is ready."

"Certainly," she said, took a deep breath, and followed him in.

She arrived back at her apartment tired and hungry, her bladder
full to bursting with all the sparkling water she'd been politely offered, and had politely accepted, during the three hours of various
group and individual conversations. She wished she had someone
to talk to; then she thought about Scully's friend Bert and marched
into her bedroom, where Frankenbear sat on the dresser, his
crooked-sewn eyes steady and reassuring. She knelt down so that
she could look straight at him.

"I was great," she said. "You should have seen it. They loved
me." She carried him with her while she peed and ran a bath, and

she told him all about it: the behavior-based group interview approach, a screening process she approved of and knew how to manage well from both sides of the table; the project stories she'd told to illustrate her ability to keep people focused and motivated; and the subsequent tour of the office that was really a thinly disguised series of one-on-one meetings with key staff, to determine her connection-building techniques and assess her communication style in action. At the end, Jennifer Oronodo had shaken her hand and said, "It's been a pleasure to meet you, Ms. Segura. We'll be in touch by the end of the week. I assume that your availability will hold until then?" Jackal had solemnly assured her that she would juggle her schedule to keep herself open, and restrained her grin until she was more than a block away from the building.

The only tricky point had been the gallery's insistence on references. "It's part of our standard contract with clients that we complete reference checks on anyone working on their projects. It's a necessary formality," Oronodo had said. "If you'll give Mark three local business contacts, that should be sufficient."

"That's a problem," Jackal said candidly. "I'm new to this area and am only now lining up business for myself. Is there another way to meet your needs?"

She hoped that Oronodo would follow a typical corporate pattern and dismiss the check on the basis of 'my seasoned executive gut tells me that a person who fits my needs so well must be a fine individual.' Unfortunately, Oronodo was a better manager than that. "I'm sorry," she said, "I do need some kind of verification. Tell you what, how about a reference from one of your projects with Ko? If you can give Mark a director-level or above contact, I can justify the lack of local experience. But I will need two local personal references to confirm that you are you, and that you haven't mugged any old ladies lately." Oronodo smiled to show that she was sure Jackal understood. Jackal smiled back as best she could.

Oronodo said good-bye and disappeared into the core of the office complex: it was a compliment to Jackal that she'd come all the way to the lobby. Levinson waited. Jackal chewed her lip. The local references took no thought: she only knew four people in town, and it would be professional suicide to name Estar or Gordineau, although it was tempting in a macabre way. She provided Crichton's and Scully's e-mail addresses: Scully could represent himself as an established business owner, and Crichton—well, Crichton would think of something unexpected and utterly convincing, if she was in the right mood. Then, with outward assurance and a huge inward flutter, she told Levinson, "The best contact at Ko is Gavin Neill at Ko Prime. He's the Executive Vice President of Planning for Ko Worldwide."

Levinson raised an eyebrow and then broke his corporate demeanor long enough to grin. "I guess we'd be happy with his recommendation," he said with a chuckle.

"Do me a favor, will you? Give me the afternoon to let the local people know that I've provided their names." There was no point asking for time to contact Neill; either he would support her or he wouldn't, she told herself. Begging wouldn't work with him, and what other reason was there to call?

But now, after the bath to slough off some of the stress, she said to Frankenbear, "The thing is, I'd be scared to call him anyway."

Frank regarded her solemnly from his perch on the cold water faucet of the sink.

"Because if he's going to say no, I'd rather find out from Oronodo."

Frankenbear waited.

"Because it matters to me what he thinks." She hugged her knees in the tub. "I do not want to cry anymore, Frank. I've cried enough about this stuff. And it would make me cry to have Neill cut me off."

How come? Frank seemed to ask.

"Not because he would be mean. He wouldn't have to. But we were . . . I was . . ." She flopped a washcloth into the water and trailed it around her like a fish. "Okay, because I was special." It sounded almost defiant. Frankenbear didn't seem to mind. "And I'm probably not special to him anymore and I hate that, you know?" She crunched the washcloth into a tight ball in her fist and scrubbed her face with it. Then she climbed out of the tub to dry herself, coming down now from the interview high, trying not to feel sad. Frank looked at her with button-eyed staunchness; you are special, she imagined she heard him say. She kissed him on the nose and kept it in her mind—I am special, I am special—while she called Crichton.

Her phone didn't have a view option—one of those budget trade-offs. She clutched Frankenbear against her chest, and heard Crichton say, "Hello."

"It's Jackal Segura."

"What?"

It was reassuring that Crichton on the phone was so consistent with the in-person experience. "I applied for a job today and gave you as a reference."

Silence.

"Someone from Calabrese Galleries will probably e-mail you in the next couple of days. I've applied for a contract position as a project manager. I had to give a couple of local references."

"I see." Fleetingly, Jackal wondered what color Crichton's eyes were today, and whether the lenses made her see the world in the same color. "Are they aware of the nature of our professional relationship?"

"If you mean, do they know that I'm a carefree killer in the triple digits, then no, I left that out of the conversation."

This silence was different. Jackal could almost see Crichton's mind working. "When did you last eat?"

"What? I don't know. Dinner."

"And when did you last sleep?"

"I don't know. Night before last."

"You go fix yourself something to eat and then take a nap. We'll talk about this later."

"Why? What difference does it make if I'm tired and in complete insulin cycle mayhem? Seems like a perfect time for you to hold me up for that nonexistent information you think I've got." She felt a long way from herself; it was interesting to hear all that anger bubbling up.

"Oh, I'm thinking about it," Crichton said evenly. "But you're in no shape to negotiate with me right now. Go to sleep." There was a click and then nothing: Jackal listened to the *bzzz* of the open line for almost five seconds before she realized that Crichton was no longer there.

She'd known in her head that she was tired, but telling Crichton had made her body realize it too. She weighed too much, and it seemed like a very long way from her brain to her legs. She chivvied herself into the kitchen with the promise of a sandwich, but she could only muster the energy to gum down a slice of turkey. Then she climbed into bed and nestled Frankenbear on the pillow next to her, where she might see his loyal lopsided face when she woke up. She would sleep, and then she would go to Solitaire and have some food and tell Scully all about her interview. Perhaps Estar would be there. They could make plans for another dinner. Jackal wanted to see all the walls in Estar's house, all the beautiful and frightening and unfathomable corners of Estar's brain. She wanted to stride into Solitaire beside Estar and drink a bit too much wine, be just a little dangerous. Maybe that was wrong to want; or maybe it would simply be nice to have some fun for a change.

She dreamed of the investiture at Al Iskandariyah: Stang Karlsson introduced her as the leader of projects that would shape the future, and voices across the earth roared their approval; she was

the star of the show, the favorite daughter of the world, and everyone loved her again.

She was more tired than she thought: she slept well into the
predawn hours, and then had to get up and eat right *now*, her
hunger so sharp that she fell on whatever came to hand in the
kitchen—three slices of turkey, a fistful of pickles, a quarter cup of
leftover white rice—until she felt able to think a bit more clearly.
Then she made a cup of tea. Solitaire would be closed, and she was
too wound up to go back to sleep, so she watched three hours of an
overnight marathon video series she'd never heard of, about a dys-
functional family running a boarding house along the Yangtze
River. Possibly because of her fatigue and the late hour, she found
the program almost unbearably funny. When she finally crawled
into bed, the sun was coming up: she dropped into sleep like a lead
sinker into still water.

She spent the morning and afternoon weaving back and forth
between deep sleep and an almost-waking state that never loosened its grip enough for her to become fully conscious. By the time
she surfaced, it was late afternoon and she felt wrung out and ap-
athetic. She sent Scully an e-mail about the reference and told him
she would see him tomorrow.

She checked the web sites before she went to the club, and indeed,
there was a long article by Razorboy: *Segura Steps IN at Solitaire*.
He'd done a fairly objective job of describing Scully's aftershock,
and he made Jackal's response sound positively heroic as opposed
to the simple stopgap measures she'd actually taken.

He'd also posted a picture of her and Estar on their way up the
stairs to the solo level, captioned only with *Estar Borja and Jackal
Segura at Solitaire*. It had been copied over to other sites with less

flattering descriptions: *Lady Butcher Trades Tips With Killer Hope!* was undoubtedly her least favorite. She should start having a word with some of these people.

She stopped outside Estar's gate for a few uncertain moments, shuffling in the cold air that was spiced with jasmine and the mélange of muffled music from within. Then she rang the bell, waited, rang again. Finally she went on.

Solitaire was unusually full, and she wondered if she would find a place to sit. She checked upstairs: Estar wasn't there, and she didn't want a dark corner to herself. But it seemed that celebrity had its rewards: back downstairs, two strangers each stood her to a beer, and someone else gave up his stool so that she could sit and talk to Scully in half-sentences as he bustled up and down the length of the counter. She wanted to tell him about the interview, but the crowd made her shy, and he was busier than a grove of grasshoppers.

"And here's another offering from a fan who prefers to remain anonymous. They don't know whether to throw themselves at your feet or run away," he said, placing a third beer before her.

"Scully, this is weird."

"You're used to being famous." He didn't sound very sympathetic.

"Okay, maybe I am. But I'm not used to being Most Admired for Casualty Rate, or whatever it is these people are goobing on."

He said, almost jovially, "You committed the second biggest mass murder of the last forty years. You're a six-year VC veteran. You're establishing a rapport with the most notorious solo on the books. They wonder if you're going to turn out like her. I wonder too." He went on before she could respond, "And then you turn around and perform a small-scale humanitarian act. It's the combination that's got them excited. If I could get you to take your clothes off and dance on a table, I'll bet my business would double for a year. Or maybe you could punch an obnoxious tourist. Didn't you break some guy's nose once? Blood on the floor, then we'd see some real money. You can be my secret retirement plan."

He chuckled and went off to serve the next ten people in line as she stared at him, open-mouthed and dismayed. He must have sensed it, because he turned back, pointed a just-a-moment finger at the would-be drinkers, and leaned one arm on the counter to say, "Jackal, either you take this stuff with a sense of humor or you take it totally seriously—the VC, the aftershocks, the violence, the disaffiliation from most of society, the complete fuckup of your life. So you choose whatever you want; I've been thinking about it a lot today, and I choose to laugh. And thanks again for talking to me, and for listening, it really helped. Hey, do you want to have some coffee and cheesecake after the bar closes? I promise, you don't have to do any work. It would be nice to have the company." He took her hand and held it for just a moment; then he went back to the line with some cheerful comment for the next customer.

Yeah, well, you sure weren't laughing last night, she almost said to his back, and felt a thick, choking dislike for him. She looked around at the crowd: the solos like matchflames, blazing brightly but so small; the watchers, their clever knowing eyes measuring the burn. And then there were the tourists, thrilled by a dash of danger in their lives. She understood in a cynical flash where the power was in this room. They make us real, she thought, it's because of them that we're solos and mysterious and exotic. Without them we'd just be a bunch of criminal failures with parts of our brains turned to cottage cheese; and so they get to eat us little by little, like moose at the salt lick. She realized that each person in the room had positioned themselves so that if she moved, they would notice. They had oriented themselves to her the way she'd seen them do with Estar, with Duja McAffee who had horrible scars on his arms and neck from one of his own napalm devices. Did that explain the odd look that Duja had given her when she

said hello? Was she in some kind of misunderstood competition
for the top slot on the solo "A" list? It made her claustrophobic:
what a miserable thing to be doing with her life.

She turned to slide off the stool and met the eyes of one of Razorboy's retinue sitting quietly next to her, a young latina with bad
acne and shocking pink hair. "Drake, right?" Jackal guessed, and
the young woman's eyes widened with surprise and wary delight.

"Tell me something," Jackal said, leaning a little too close,
"when you die, are you going to look back and think gee, I wish
I'd spent more time at Solitaire watching broken people huddle in
corners trying to hold on to some semblance of a life? Or are you
smarter than that? How old are you anyway?" It was a rude question, rudely asked, and she didn't care: she was full of heat and
ready to howl. "How old are you?"

"Um . . . twenty-two?"

"Twenty-two. You know how old I am?"

Drake shook her head: no.

"Yeah, I'm not sure either anymore. But let's pretend that I'm
old enough to tell you that this isn't a life you're having here, this
is just a pale reflection of something you should run screaming
from. Life is out there. Go get some."

Drake looked at her blankly. Jackal sighed. "Forget it." She had
one foot on the floor when Drake put out a hand, not quite touching Jackal's arm. "What?" Jackal snapped.

Drake pulled her hand back and circled it in front of her as if it
would help her find the right words. "I . . . you . . . no, wait. Please,
I really want to say this to you."

Oh hell, she'd said please. Jackal sat.

It seemed that Drake had used up her courage in the one moment of eye contact; she looked at the floor and spoke so softly that
Jackal was forced once again to lean in.

"I've been coming here for nine months and you're the first solo
that ever knew my name. I'll bet you're the first one that ever even

really looked at me, you know? You probably don't know what that's like 'cause you've been famous all your life, but it's really hard and all. I'm not trying to get you to feel sorry for me," she rushed to add, with an intense, shallow dignity that Jackal recognized from her own last confused months as a Hope. And she did empathize, so she clamped down on the urge to say any number of ill-tempered things like, okay, I've seen you, can I go now? Or, are we getting to the point sometime tonight?

"It's just that you're different. So maybe you don't know that a lot of life is really lonesome and mean. I already get that, you know, I don't need to go back out and get some more. It's okay here. I fit in. I'm a watcher, I know how to act with solos, people respect me. I got a good web site. You're on it a lot. I don't know if you ever looked at it." Now she was shy and vulnerable.

"I've seen it. It's nice." She was glad it was the truth, because Drake asked eagerly, eyes up, "What did you like best?"

"I like that you talk about what you see but you don't make assumptions about what it means. You're really careful to separate out the facts from your opinions about people."

Drake thought about that. "And that's good?"

"Yes, it is."

Drake nodded. "Okay. Well, I'll keep doing it then." Then she opened her fingers and grabbed handfuls of air as if the words she wanted were flying like moths around her. "See, this is what I'm trying to talk about. I thought you would say how you liked the design or the photos. But instead you talk about this other stuff." She was bouncing up and down in tiny bursts in her seat, trying to catch the thoughts. "You're different. It's why I watch you all the time now. You're not like Duja or Estar or even Jeanne Gordineau, they're all more scary than you but it's like that's all they are. They just walk around being scary. But you know things. Last night when Scully went down, you knew exactly what to do. You bossed everybody around."

"What I did wasn't special," Jackal said gently. "Anybody could have done it."

"Nobody ever has before," Drake said simply. "I've seen aftershock like a million times and I never knew what to do. But next time I will. And I'll put it up on my site, too. I'll say to get the person in a safe place and try to make it so they'll be comfortable when they wake up, and then take over whatever they were doing if it needs to get done. Is that right?"

"That sounds fine," Jackal said, still gentle, watching Drake work her way through to this new place.

"That's why I watch you most of all. You do things. You're not mean and you're not scared."

Jackal made a face; Drake said, firmly enough to surprise Jackal, "If you don't act scared or mean then that's what counts to the people watching." Then Drake surprised her even more by saying, "This conversation we're having, can this be private? I mean, just between us."

"That would be fine."

"Cy and Razorboy will want to know what we talked about. I'll bet they're dying over there, we don't know anyone who's ever talked to a solo like this. But I just want to think about it for a while."

"I don't mind if you don't talk about it," Jackal said. "You should do whatever you think is right. I have to go now, okay?" She caught Scully as he stopped to reach into a hanging basket for a banana and a lime. "I'll be back before closing. See you later."

"Great," he grinned, and she found that she remembered how to like him. She looked back at Drake, who was sitting up a little straighter on the stool with her pink hair blazing like a tuft of cotton candy at the summer fairs that Jackal had dragged her father to every year of her childhood. People are amazing, she thought, but to Drake she only said, "Thanks for talking to me."

Drake smiled. "Sure. Maybe . . ." But her courage skittered

away again and her eyes went down. Jackal was relieved. "Well, anyway, bye," Drake said.

"Good night."

Marginal Way was empty. An icy sodden wind from the canal chilled her hands and the back of her neck as she walked south toward Perdue. She passed Estar's gate; then she stopped and turned back to try the bell one more time. Was the music a bit louder? She was tired and knew that staying up late was stupid; her sleep cycle was already so far out of alignment that she would probably have to resort to melatonin. Did they sell that here? There was so much she still didn't know about the city, the NNA, this new universe to which she'd been consigned. She pushed the bell again. Damn it, I know you're there, she thought irritably, ignoring her own advice to go home and sleep and apologize to Scully tomorrow for standing him up.

The wet wind turned into light rain on her uncovered head. Perfect. She pulled up her collar; it didn't help much. Time to go back to her apartment before she was soaked through. But wait—there was a flicker at the edge of her vision, and she thought it was Estar come to open the door at last, to let her in to the warm, colorful heart of a place that was someone's home, to drink wine or coffee in front of a fire while it rained on other people, people who had nowhere to go. The vision was so clear in her head that she was already smiling as she turned. But no one was there. She frowned, and the flash came again, and she said, "oh, no," and reached for the bell, but it was too late: the world pulled itself inside-out in the gray negative tones of aftershock.

18

SHE WOKE IN A SURGE OF LIGHT *THE DOOR,* A RUSH OF energy that propelled her from VC into the waking world between one eyeblink and the next, *the door I,* and Scully was leaning over her, saying, "What? What is it?" She wanted to exult, to open her mouth and let out the vast blue sky, the sea, the wheeling birds inside her. Home. Ko. Lost and found again. She wanted to shout, but she was so weak and she could only whisper, ". . . found the door, I found the door—"

Then she came fully awake and shut her mouth hard. She squinted up at him. "Nothing. I don't know. Oh, my head hurts."

Someone else was helping her sit up: Estar. The two of them propped her up on some pillows. She must be in Estar's house: the walls were covered with dozens of overlapping quilts and tapestries and printed cloth hangings, and a cello cantata thrummed from hidden speakers, clashing only slightly with the faint sound of thrash rock from the next room.

"How are you feeling?" Scully asked. He looked genuinely worried, and she was touched, and sorry that she'd been grumpy with him earlier.

"I'm all right."

"If you wished so badly to see me again, you could simply have called," Estar said lightly. "These dramatics on my doorstep are not necessary."

"I don't have your number, that's why I rang the bell," Jackal said. "Ow, careful, I think I landed on that arm. Thank you for letting me in."

"I didn't," Estar replied. "Jane found you unconscious on the street and, being a sensible young woman, brought you immediately inside."

"Jane? Oh, you mean . . ."

"Yes, you've met her, the one who is so competent with knives."

"Oh." She tried to work out why Jane was letting herself into Estar's house.

"She lives here," Scully said, exchanging a look with Estar that Jackal could not interpret.

Now Jackal was thoroughly confused. She blurted, "Isn't she a little young for you?" before she thought about what she was saying and who she was talking to. Scully bit his lip. Estar, thankfully, only laughed.

"Don't be jealous, *chacalita*. That is her wing of the house," Estar waved an arm vaguely off to the right. "She is an employee of sorts."

"A kind of bodyguard," Scully added. It took Jackal a moment to work out that he meant protecting other people from Estar.

"I didn't realize . . . I've never seen her with you."

"Sometimes I don't tell her I am leaving the house. It is very wicked of me," Estar said complacently. "Now, can you stand?"

"Oh, sure, if you need me to go I can—"

"Don't be so ready to slink away." I wasn't slinking, Jackal thought, I was just being polite, but Estar had already continued, "You are clearly in no shape to leap up and run from my house. You should demand that I show you to a hot bath and then feed you, which is in fact what I am intending to do. Scully will help you into the bathroom while I find something that is passable for a late breakfast." Estar looked at them, her head cocked to one side, and added in a curious voice, "You are both entirely too nice."

"What did that mean?" Jackal asked Scully when she was sure that Estar was out of earshot.

"Oh, you know what she's like." No, Jackal didn't, but she was all ears. "She thinks if you haven't sent someone to the clinic in the last three months, you must not be trying hard enough to assert yourself."

The bath was the best she'd had in years, in a soaking tub with just the right slant at the back. She would get herself a bath just like this the next time she was in VC.

She had found the door. She had been in aftershock for almost four virtual days, and on the second day she had opened a door from her cell into Ko. It was as if she had developed some muscle during her confinement that had been easily rediscovered once it was needed. Just like riding a bike: she laughed and splashed some water around. She would know exactly what to do next time: there would be no moments wasted in that terrible gray box they had tried to lock her into. She had not lost Ko after all. It was inside her.

A knock on the door. "Breakfast in ten minutes," Estar said.

"On my way." She closed her eyes and took a deep breath, pushed herself underwater so that, for an instant, she floated free. Then she sat up warm and relaxed. And hungry; she sniffed, smelled ham and something baking which, when she got to the kitchen, turned out to be biscuits, along with an amazing gravy and slices of ripe cantaloupe.

"This is great," she said around a mouthful of buttered biscuit and gravy. "I've never had anything like it."

"It is called redeye gravy, a recipe from old-style United States Southern cooking. There are coffee grounds in it, if you believe such a thing."

"If you say so. How'd you find the recipe?"

"My nanny was from that area, the recipe is from her grand-mother."

"Is that how you grew up bilingual?" She saw Scully's face. "I beg your pardon, Estar," she said. "I'm certainly not trying to pry into your private life. I just . . . you're such an interesting person. Please feel free to tell me it's none of my business."

Estar smiled. "And why should I take offense at interest so charmingly expressed? Eat your biscuits, Scully, and relax. We are three comrades having a lovely breakfast, and our Jackal may ask anything she likes." She bit a chunk of melon in half, and a trickle of juice ran down the side of her mouth to her chin; she wiped it away and licked her finger clean. On someone else it might have been simply poor manners, but Jackal recognized it as perfor-mance and was charmed in turn. She enjoyed the other woman's precise flamboyance, her assurance, her gusto; Estar was so defi-nitely herself. She remembered watching Jordie and Jeremy and the others the first day of the workshop and wondering how they knew what they wanted to be, and now she understood: you knew what you wanted to be when you saw someone else being it.

"I speak five languages," Estar said matter-of-factly. "I learned my Spanish in Spain and English from my mother, and French and German and Italian at school. My mother believed that chil-dren should learn languages and so we did. Between us my brother and sisters and I spoke fourteen of them. My mother got these notions from reading too many fantastical novels. We all had names that she found in books. It was a great difficulty when we moved to Spain, the children laughed at my name. *Tu nombre es un verbo!* But my mother had read a story in which Estar was a word for soul, so Estar I must be. In Spain I made them call me Ana. Now, of course, they called me *La Carnicera*." She kept her eyes fixed on Jackal, and very slowly cut a slice of ham and put it into her mouth, closed her lips and chewed. Jackal didn't know whether to be flattered or appalled.

Estar swallowed and smiled, said confidingly, "The long knife is a wonderful tool, you know, especially with the good steel one gets in Spain. Of course, they took mine away. I had to get another one. It was very inconvenient. Tell me, why aren't you acting like a solo who just came out of a long and difficult aftershock?" She said it with no change in tone; but her smile had left her eyes. Jackal put down her fork with the last bite of biscuit still impaled.

"I'm sorry if I'm acting strangely," she said carefully. "I do feel shocky, but I'm enjoying being with you, and having the bath and this nice meal and your company really helps."

"When I come out of my cell, I come out screaming," Estar said flatly. "Scully whimpers. Duja fights. You eat ham and biscuits and flirt with me at my own table. I have met no other solo like you, *chacalita*. Why are you different?"

"You know what, Estar? That was a terrific breakfast," Scully said, wiping his hands on his napkin. "Why don't we help you clean up and then I'll walk Jackal home so she can get some rest."

"I would prefer to talk."

"And I think it would be better if we all took a break."

"Buenos días," Jane said from the kitchen door. "Chacal, Scully, good morning. Are you feeling better?"

"Yes, thank you," Jackal said automatically, although she was feeling alternately numb and on alert. "And thank you for bringing me inside."

"It was raining," Jane shrugged. "You were getting wet. But I see you're leaving. You've had a hard night, or whatever. I find it hard to talk with solos about time anymore." She shook her head. "Is that cantaloupe?" She had moved to the table and now inserted herself into the sight line between Estar and Jackal.

"Let's go," Scully said privately. "Bye, Estar, Jane. Thanks. See you later."

Outside the gate, Jackal said, "It's okay. I can get home on my own."

"I'd be happy to walk with you. Really. It'll help me clear my head." He sighed. "I just sat up all night with you. Humor me."

It was still raining. They walked in silence up to Perdue Street and turned the corner into a cold wind that pushed icy drops into Jackal's eyes and made her face ache.

Scully pulled his jacket tighter around him and said, "Look, Jackal, I'm sorry for hustling you out like that, but she was starting to get into one of her places and it's just better not to be around when that happens."

"I appreciate it, but I've dealt with weirder people than Estar."

"You've never seen her when she's like . . . You need to know, especially since you're getting close to her. She—"

She really didn't want to talk about this right now. She interrupted him: "Scully, I know that Estar is—" she took a breath "—I know she's damaged. But I've told you I can handle her. I'm not going to do anything to frighten or confuse her. I know how to manage egos and paranoia and abrasive communication styles, okay? It's what I was trained for."

"I'm sure you are, but that's not the point. She's fascinating, I know, especially when she turns on the charm like she's been doing with you, but she's *dangerous* and—"

Jackal put an edge into her voice. "If I was good enough to run EarthGov projects, I imagine I'm good enough to cope with Estar or Duja or anyone else in our little club. I like her, I am not fascinated by her. And I know that solos are unpredictable. Give me some credit."

Scully raised his hands in the universal don't-shoot-the-messenger gesture. "I'm just trying to make sure you have information."

Jackal raised a hand in a mirror of his move. "Okay. Fair enough. I'm sorry, I guess I'm still wound up. Say what you need to say, and then I'm going to sleep for a week."

He opened his mouth, and perhaps he even spoke, but she no

longer heard him: she was looking up the street to Shangri-La on the next block, where the sausage vendor leaned on her cart, speaking to someone resting on the building stairs. The morning traffic faded, and she did not feel people pushing past, cursing as they threaded their way around the obstacle that she'd made of herself by stopping in the middle of the sidewalk. Scully caught himself a few steps beyond her and backed up: faintly, she heard him saying, "Jackal, what's wrong? Jackal?" but she paid no attention. She stood absolutely still, and she felt as if her head had become hollow in the immensity of the moment: *wait, I'm not ready*. But this was how it happened: the big things never announced themselves, you just turned a corner and there they were, before you'd had time to order your life to meet them. Choose right, she seemed to tell herself, choose well. Everything now depends on this moment. And then in a heartbeat her choice was made, and it was just like the old days: a path cleared in front of her and she walked it straight into Snow's arms.

It was like drawing a breath that came in and in and in, stretching her, filling her with Snow, etching Snow back into the space that Jackal had rubbed smooth. This is what she looks like; this is her smell; this is the feel of her shoulder blade under my right hand; this is how tight she holds me when she has no words, when the body must speak for itself. I remember it all. I remember Snow.

"Snow."

Holding on. Holding on. Hard to breathe, the brain stumbling over itself, caught in this moment of contact that felt like a homecoming. She felt Snow tremble through the thick cloth of her quilted jacket, heard the deep breath that she took before she spoke, her voice shaking even though the words wanted to be casual: "Someone sent me an unbelievably stupid message with your name on it, so I thought I'd better find out for myself what was going on." Then Snow clutched her even more tightly and said, with a hopeless stubborn resolve that tore at Jackal's heart, "You can't send me away, Jackal. Please. I don't know what you think you're doing here, but you have to talk to me. Don't send me away."

They stood for another moment: over Snow's shoulder, the sausage vendor stared in frank curiosity. Scully had disappeared.

She sighed. "Come in. Come inside." She picked up Snow's duffel bag with one hand, and used the other to draw Snow up the steps and into Shangri-La.

She watched Snow take it all in: the five-foot-square elevator with the bad air quality and a control plate crimped from the last time someone had tried to pry it off; the threadbare carpet in the hallway, and the paint that was obviously ancient latex-based because it was peeling rather than repairing itself. Snow said nothing, but Jackal saw the line of her mouth and knew what she was thinking.

Inside the apartment, Snow's face relaxed. She stopped just inside the door for a good long look. "Well, this is nice," she said, and the mix of "we can work with this" and dismissive disapproval of the rest of Shangri-La was absolute, essential Snow.

"God," Jackal said in a small voice. "It really is you. You're really here. You're here." She felt a bit dizzy, and she let herself drop onto the sprung sofa that she'd kept in hopeful anticipation of guests someday. She rubbed her eyes and her forehead, pushed her hair back from her face.

"Are you okay?"

She should say *I'm fine* and then she should do the polite make-the-guest-at-home things: pull out pillows and a duvet for Snow to use if she wanted to curl up on the sofa; point out the bathroom and the tea kettle; put Snow off with *you must be tired, why don't you rest, we'll talk later.* Then she should start figuring out the most efficient, least hurtful way to get Snow back on a plane to Ko, before anyone learned she was here. Before Snow got any wrong ideas about staying.

Snow was still waiting for an answer, studying Jackal's face with that total attention like a spotlight that always made Jackal feel completely seen.

"And don't say 'I'm fine,' " Snow said.

Jackal closed her eyes, feeling a jolt of something surprisingly like anger. Angry at Snow? Well, maybe I am, she thought. What am I supposed to say to her? I've been locked in my own head for ten hours or four days, I'm not really sure, and I've had no fucking sleep, and my apartment has mold in the bathroom that makes my nose run every morning, and VC did something to my brain that I don't understand, and I spend my evenings with people who think it's cool that I smashed our web all over Mirabile's marble floor and you know what, sometimes they convince me that I really am that cool and that makes me wonder about myself, and maybe if I try hard enough I can find one person in this whole lousy city who will give me a job and someday I'll get out of this building that doesn't meet your exacting scandinavian standards. Other than that, I'm just peachy. And who invited you here anyway? Why is it any—

"And I know you didn't ask me to come here, but please don't tell me it's none of my business," Snow went on with an edge in her voice.

And Jackal couldn't help it, she had to chuckle and shake her head, and speak the truth: "I never have to tell you anything, you already know I'm not okay," and then she was sobbing and Snow's arms were around her, holding her, and Jackal was saying, "I'm not okay, I'm not okay," and Snow was saying, "I'm here."

She woke in the late afternoon tucked under a blanket on the sofa, with the sun painting a warm stripe across her legs and the smell of marinara sauce filling the apartment. Her eyes were still sore from crying, but she felt better, lighter and cleaner, as if some particularly nasty toxin had been flushed from her system.

She stretched, and then hauled herself into a sitting position. Snow stuck her head around the frame of the kitchen door and said, "How are you feeling?"

"I'm okay." She got two seconds of Snow's searchlight glare and then a nod. "I'm gonna take a shower."

"Beer after?"

"That would be great."

And it was, as was the linguine and the sauce and the garlic toast that Snow had made with the last of the bread. The conversation was casual and arrhythmic, lots of silence and then a spurt of talk about projects Snow had worked on, favorite meals they had shared, a competition to see who knew the most alcohol toasts in the greatest number of languages. Jackal won, but the fun went out of it when Snow said curiously, "Where on earth did you get that one?" and Jackal realized she'd heard Duja say it one night in Solitaire: and that brought back all the ugly realities she'd put aside for the last hour. But bless her for that hour, she thought, bless Snow.

She took a breath and let it out hard, the way she might before hefting a heavy weight. "Okay. What are you doing here?"

Snow leaned back in her chair and folded her arms across her chest, looked at Jackal for a long moment.

"I got your e-mail," she said slowly. "I don't think you can imagine how that felt. I didn't know about the program, I didn't know that you were in it . . . I've been staying off the newsnet, particularly anything to do with EarthGov. I thought you were in the Earth Court prison in Al Isk. I even went and found their web site and got a picture of it so I could try to imagine what it was like inside, what you were doing. I wrote you e-mail every day and sent it to the prisoner drop address. I started trying to find out about visiting procedures. Finally Analin Chao called me into her office and told me that Earth Court prisoners weren't allowed to send or receive messages or have visitors. And she'd read all my letters."

Snow reached jerkily for her beer and seemed surprised to find it empty. "Do you mind if I have another? You want one?" She kept talking as she went into the kitchen. "She was a real pig. She wanted to talk about my conflicted feelings, and she suggested that clinging to a one-way relationship with you was not in the best interests of my long-term emotional health."

She came back and handed Jackal a bottle. Jackal could picture it clearly: Snow in the womb chair, not conscious of the design cues but not falling for them either, straight-backed and stubborn, mute with anger.

"Did you know your mother's working for her now? I ran into them once in the plaza." Snow looked as if she might say more, and then shook her head and took a sip of beer.

"What? What's she—no, never mind, tell me about it later."

"Anyway, after that I just tried not to think about anything except my projects. I mostly stopped talking to people. I kept writing you e-mail but I didn't send it. It made me feel a little better, because I was still thinking about you. You were still there, even if you couldn't talk back. I finally realized that I was depressed, but I didn't care. I was going to stay connected to you no matter what anyone said. That went on for a while." She pursed her lips and looked up over Jackal's shoulder, toward the window that showed a thin ribbon of sunset orange under a wide belt of evening blue.

"And then I got your message. I was just checking e-mail and there it was. I sat in front of the screen for ages, trying to understand. It wasn't really you who sent the message. It was you but something horrible had happened to you and you didn't want me to know, you didn't want to be a burden to me. Somebody was making you do it. Prison had made you insane and they put you out and you were all alone. But I knew it was you, and I knew you weren't crazy, and at some point I just thought, Jackal is telling you that she doesn't love you anymore." She looked at Jackal with hurt hollow eyes. "And I was so sad," she said simply, and Jackal bowed her head.

"And then I got smart. Finally. I just thought, no, damn it, she does so love me so what the fuck is going on here? And it finally occurred to me to wonder what you were doing out of prison. So I did a net search for your name, which I hadn't done in ages because . . . well, I'd seen all the trial coverage and it was too hard to read about Mirabile. . . . And there you were with practically no hair drinking beer someplace. So I did a bunch of research on the program and that's when I knew that you must be in trouble and that I'd better come."

She stopped, took two big swallows of beer, and looked at Jackal as if that explained everything.

"So you just got on a plane and flew to the NNA."

Snow nodded.

"Even though I said not to. Without giving me any warning."

"I was afraid you might say no."

"Oh, so instead I just don't get a choice?"

Snow folded her napkin into a tidy packet and shifted her body somehow so that she appeared to become rooted to the chair. It was a trick that Jackal had often admired and could never imitate, the act of becoming unmovable. "Do you want me to leave now?" Snow said icily.

"I . . . no."

"Fine, you just got to choose."

Jackal raised both hands. "Sorry. Never mind. It's just . . . unexpected." She wrinkled her forehead. "And how did you find me, anyway?"

Silence.

"Snow?"

"It's a long story."

Jackal settled back. "I have time."

Snow swallowed. "I learned enough from the research to understand that you shouldn't have been in the VC program—what?"

"What do you mean?"

"The demographics are skewed. Didn't you look into this?" She
frowned. "Ninety-five-plus percent of the participant pool are
nonviolent criminals up on regional charges. More than sixty percent of them ended up serving one virtual year or less. The rest
never went over four virtual years. The only exceptions I could
find were you and five others: McAffee, Smetyana, Borja—"

"Estar Borja?"

"Yes, and Jeanne Gordineau and Eric Ronn. The six of you are
convicted of international crimes, high profile, not the kind of
cases that should be eligible for a standard research protocol. So I
kept looking and I found out that the common link between the
other five is money."

"Huh?"

"Borja's mother is worth two hundred and seventy three million pounds, give or take. Gordineau's father is the head of a
military-industrial manufacturing firm in Rouen, which explains
how she got hold of all that stuff. Ronn's grandfather owns half of
Burma. And so on."

"You think they paid to be in the VC program?"

"I think their families bought an Earth Court verdict and this
program was part of the deal. I'll bet a big chunk of the program
funding comes from these people. But the big indicator is the
length of sentence. The six of you are the only ones I could find
with sentences longer than four virtual years."

"That's not right. I've met other people who were in for as long
as that."

"Maybe in some of the social rehab programs, but not in virtual
solitary confinement. And not on an involuntary basis."

Snow sounded so definite that Jackal closed her mouth and
thought about it. She said eventually, "You might be right."

"I am right. Go do the analysis yourself, it's all there on-line or in EarthGov public reports, although you have to be really determined to get through those things. But I was." Jackal smiled. "And I found something else: all the deals for the lower level participants were a matter of public record, whereas the big six were barely announced, even with all the publicity about the program transfer to the NNA. You had to be really paying attention to find out. I've never seen something so successfully minimized in the major news media. I read a little about Gordineau and McAffee on these watcher web sites they have here. These are scary people."

Jackal nodded.

"I couldn't understand what you were doing in this group. Your family doesn't have that kind of money. So I had to assume that Ko paid for you."

Jackal became very still.

"And then it made sense to me why you said you were guilty. You made a deal. They made you say it and then they got you in the program."

Jackal barely breathed. Snow was looking off into the middle distance now, and Jackal recognized her tone, the vocal equivalent of the thousand-yard stare: Snow was using the part of her brain that dissected things and turned the pieces over to see all sides of them, and then put them in order, like fitting stones together to build a bridge.

Snow continued, "But why would you do that? You didn't murder those people, so it must have been some kind of accident. Surely that's easy enough to prove, so why would you take the deal? And why would Ko want you to? Why wouldn't they want you to be proven innocent?" She stayed quiet for a moment, still in the analysis zone; and then she came back to the moment and looked at Jackal. "There were lots of different scenarios I could build around that," she said. "None of them were happy. They all added up to you being in trouble. I knew I needed to find you but

I didn't know how, so I—well, I don't know what you'll think
about this, but I had some help."

Oh, god. "You told someone about this?"

Snow nodded.

"Someone at Ko?"

"Gavin Neill."

Jackal put her face in her hands.

"I had to talk to someone. I couldn't go to Khofi. When you . . .
when you were gone he's the one I talked to about visiting you, I'm
pretty sure he turned me in to Chao. So I tried to think of who you
would trust the most, who you would go to for advice."

And now Ko was aware of whatever Snow knew. Jackal
wanted to leap up and throw some clothes into a bag and run
away. But that was silly: there was no more running to be done.
She took a deep breath, held it, exhaled. "Okay. I want you to tell
me everything and I need another beer."

"There's two left."

Jackal took the dirty plates with her into the kitchen and
brought back the beer and some pre-sliced jack cheese that she absently shredded into bits while Snow told her about Neill.

The idea had occurred to her in the middle of a strategy meeting and, being Snow, she'd simply walked out while her boss was
in mid-sentence of a discussion about one of their critical decisions. She'd gone straight to the Executive One building, heart
pounding, cheeks flushed, and didn't stop to think about what she
was doing—bearding an EVP in his own office and confronting
him about the company's most sensitive public-relations issue—
until the elevator doors were opening onto Neill's floor. She almost did not step out: easy enough to let the doors close, to take
some time, to think it through. But she imagined Jackal in the
NNA, alone, maybe homeless or cold, certainly afraid; she held
Jackal's face in her heart like a flag and let it lead her to Neill's
open door.

He stood at his work table, head bent over a large process flow drawing, making pencil notes around the edges. He looked up, his face expressionless, pencil poised.

"May I speak to you?" she said. "My name is Snow Laussen, I'm—"

"I know who you are," he said. He would, Jackal thought.

Neill looked at Snow silently, long enough that she thought he would refuse, but he said, "Come in."

He stepped around the desk and waved her to the sofa; then he closed the door behind her. "What can I do for you?" he asked, when they were both seated.

"Jackal is out of prison," Snow said without preamble. Neill leaned back in his chair.

If he was current on his e-mail he had already known, Jackal thought, working out the timing. But she knew he would have reacted the same either way, leaving all his options open until he knew why Snow was there.

Snow continued, "She's been involuntarily reassigned to the custody of the NNA. I don't know if she has any money or a place to live, and I think something bad might be happening to her."

"You've heard from her directly?"

She explained about the message and the lack of backtrail.

"And what can I help you with?"

"I want to find her and make sure she's all right."

He regarded her evenly. "Her message said that she wanted no further contact."

"She's trying to protect me from something."

"What makes you think that?"

How much should she reveal? She'd debated with herself all the way up to his office and still had no answer. Now she tried to read his face, looking at him in a way that could have been rude if he hadn't seemed so unruffled by it. She could see integrated in him all the things that Jackal had been practicing so assiduously and so unevenly: the ease with waiting and silence, the total invitation to speak and be heard, the open-ended questions that gave her no sense of his own thinking. When she opened her mouth, she had no idea what would come out; she had decided to let her heart speak, and she waited to hear what it would tell him.

"Jackal admires you more than anyone on Ko," she said, and watched the muscles around his eyes change subtly. "When she understood what she'd be doing as a Hope, she was so determined to be the best. Partly because that's what she's like, but it was also for you, because you gave her this work that she loves. And something happened to her a while ago, I don't know what it was, but it hurt her and she had a hard time, and work was so important to her then. It kept her going."

She paused; he nodded, and she took a breath and went on. "She wanted to be special to you. I don't know if she is or not, but I hope so because it's the only reason I have to ask for your help. She's the most important person in the world to me and I think she's in trouble and scared and all alone. And I think she believes that she can't see me because the company doesn't want her to. If that's true, then I guess you'd know about it. So you would have to decide if you wanted to punish me for bringing it up, or if you wanted to help."

"I see," he said quietly. He rested his elbows on the arms of his chair and steepled his hands. "And you think I might be inclined to help Jackal after her crime against humanity and her betrayal of her company."

"Someone did," Snow said simply. "Someone got her into the VC program. I thought maybe it was you. If I'm wrong, then I'm guessing I'll be terminated from Ko within twenty-four hours and I will have to get to the NNA and find her by myself. I can do that, but it will take a long time and I'm afraid of what might happen to her by then. Even if you won't tell me where she is, at least let me give you some money to send her so that she can take care of herself. Or let me arrange to have part of my salary credited to her. Something. Everyone keeps telling me to forget her as if she were, I don't know, a bad meal we all had at a restaurant, as if we should be finished with her. But I love her and I'm not finished."

Jackal watched her as she told it; Snow's face was so pure, so brave, and Jackal was filled with shame and self-loathing. *She fought and I didn't. She held on and I let go.*

"What's the matter? What is it?"

"No, it's okay. I'm okay. What did he do?"

He had studied her for a long stretch of moments: she counted the time by her heartbeats, slower now, more steady. Her heart had done its best to be heard; now she waited.

He said, "You appear to be very clear about your priorities. You'll have to give me a little while to consider mine. Until later today."

She hadn't realized how tense she was until she stood and found so many tight muscles. "Thank you for your time," she said. But when she reached the door, she found she had one more thing to say.

"Jackal loves you," she said. "That's really why I came here, I guess. Even if you could just make sure that she's safe, I would be very grateful."

He smiled, just as politely as he had when she arrived, but with no more depth, no indication of what he might be thinking. "It's been very interesting meeting you, Ms. Laussen," he said, and she left unsure that any of it had mattered.

Snow paused in her story and drank some beer, and pointed across the table: "Give me some of that before you wad it all into cheese balls." Jackal pushed over the entire package, thinking about Neill. Snow had painted him so clearly that she felt she could see him, or that he had just left the room and something of his presence still lingered like a scent.

"Anyway," Snow said, "I got a call that afternoon from my

manager that I was being sent out to do a complete systems and efficiency evaluation of a subsidiary facility. Apparently the plant engineer met me at the Quanzhou conference and thought I might be able to help her with a couple of issues. It's a two-week assignment. I got my itinerary and had just about enough time to pack and check my e-mail, and there was this address." She waved her arm around the apartment. "Anonymous sender, a non-Ko account."

"And where's this plant?"

"If I've read the maps right, it's about three kilometers on the other side of that canal that I saw from your window."

"And you never heard back from Neill."

"No."

"Wow." Jackal slumped in her chair. Maybe this really was Neill's way of helping. Maybe she didn't need to panic, although she shuddered at the risk that Snow had taken. But what to do now? She needed time to think. She looked at the table: four empty beer bottles lined up in front of each of them, the table littered with scraps of cheese. And Snow, across from her. Snow.

"You're amazing," Jackal said.

Snow shrugged, but looked pleased.

"When is the plant expecting you?"

"Tomorrow morning."

"Do you have a hotel?"

Snow hesitated. "Well, sure, they got me a reservation. And I registered before I came here, in case anyone checked. But I thought . . . I hoped that I could stay with you."

Jackal sighed and sucked a cheese crumb off the tip of one finger. "I think you should stay at the hotel," she said finally. When she looked up, Snow's eyes had filled with tears. "I'm sorry," Jackal said miserably. "It's just . . . there's a lot you don't know about what's happened to me. I . . . VC changed me. Being alone for so long. . . . One of the things that happens to solos is that we have a hard time being around people after we come out. I know for you it's what, eight months since you saw me, maybe nine—" she didn't stop to count the weeks since Mirabile "—and I know it's been hard. But for me it's been six years since I've seen you. I've been alone for six years. You have to try to understand what that's like."

"I spent most of my time alone."

"No, you didn't." She saw the hurt and confusion on Snow's face but she kept going; she had to. "Refusing to interact with people is not the same as being alone. Alone is when there are no human noises except yours for six years. Alone is a box no bigger than this room with no windows and no doors, that never changes year after year. Alone is having no context except yourself. And the thing I found out is, that's not enough. I couldn't keep the context when it was just me."

"I don't understand."

"I don't know if I do either. And I want to try to explain it. But at least for now it's better . . . I need to be by myself. It's not about you."

Snow wiped her eyes. "Okay," she said. "I don't understand, but I don't have to. I know you're not trying to hurt me. If you need me to stay in the stupid hotel, then I will. Shit," she said, and sniffled. "I don't know why I'm complaining. I wanted to see you and I have. I wanted you not to send me away and you haven't, at least not yet. You have a place to live, you have food. Do you need money? You're going to have to explain that part of it too."

Jackal nodded. "But not tonight. Tonight I'm going to get you to your hotel, and tomorrow evening I'll take you someplace that will help explain. I hope."

The transport was nearly empty this late, and Snow's hotel was just far enough away to be in a better neighborhood. Jackal walked her to the entrance.

"Call me when you get back from the plant tomorrow and I'll come pick you up."

"Okay."

"Be brilliant. Impress the engineer."

Snow grinned. "Okay."

Jackal took her hand. "I just want to tell you—" She couldn't find the words; she looked up as though they might be hovering overhead, but there were only the few stars bright enough to shine fuzzily through the night-light of the city. "You came for me," she said, and her voice quavered. "It means so much that you came for me." She felt as if her heart turned over with a jerk, like a long-silent machine struggling into motion. Its new, tentative rhythm stayed with her all the way back to Shangri-La.

19

THE PHONE WOKE HER LATE THE NEXT MORNING FROM the first decent sleep she'd had in days. No one had ever called her here: she didn't recognize the noise, and it took her a full fifteen seconds of insistent beep-beep-beep to work it out, get untangled from the blanket and find it in her coat pocket where she'd left it last night. She was grateful for the lack of video.

"Hello?"

"Are you trying to piss me off?"

"Crichton?"

"If you think I won't have you arrested, you'd better think again. I hate it when people don't take me seriously."

"What?" She sat down hard in the desk chair. "What'd I do?"

She knew she still sounded half-asleep as well as confused: it seemed to make Crichton pause.

"You were due in my office an hour ago. Get here. And get an alarm clock."

"I was?" But Crichton had already disconnected. Jackal blinked at the phone and then found the ringer control and turned it to low, wondering why factory settings always trended toward the most obnoxious delivery of any function. Workers' revenge.

She realized she hadn't checked e-mail since before her last aftershock. Oh sharks, that was it—the aftershock readings had come through and Crichton was probably sharpening up the drill right now. To be sure, she opened her e-mail box, and there it was, right on top: *Failure to report*, etc. She had a bad moment imagining the official knock at the door; or maybe the police would have gone straight to the landlord for the override code to her lock, and she would have woken to the sound of boots and loud voices in the living room. And that might still come. Crichton's patience would eventually run out.

She hit the delete key, and then stilled. There was another message waiting:

Ms. Segura:
I've been trying to write this e-mail in standard business English and have come to the conclusion that there are no adequate euphemisms for this situation.

Your skills match our needs extremely well. However, we have learned of your conviction on charges of international terrorism and murder. Our policy in this regard is non-negotiable: I'm unable to offer you the contract, and would be unwilling to even in the absence of the policy.

I am puzzled and concerned by your application for the position, and have instructed my legal department to forward details of your interview to NNA Security Services. We may choose to seek a restraining order barring you from our premises or any further contact with our staff. We will also notify our affiliates in the business community.

I apologize if your application was in good faith. I won't expect you to appreciate my concern, although I am sure you can understand it.
Jennifer Oronodo
Vice President, Corporate Accounts

She couldn't even feel surprised, only deflated and stupid—how had she believed this would work?—and ashamed. She had liked the people at the gallery: it made her queasy to think of them gossiping, recoiling at the news, picking her apart. *She did what? Oh my god, I've heard of her, I thought she looked familiar. What kind of person do you have to be to do something like that?*

She dressed carelessly, decided it was worth an extra five minutes to clean her teeth, and then left a voice mail message at Snow's hotel: *My parole officer wants to see me. I'm going over there now. If you can't reach me tonight, call this number and make her tell you where I am.*

After some thought, she re-recorded the message and revised the last sentence to *she can tell you where I am*. It seemed less melodramatic. Then she went.

Crichton had a surprise for her. Jackal walked in braced for more probing, prepared to resist, and Crichton looked up from the desk with eyes the flat no-color of a blank viewscreen, absolute black. They were the most unsettling lenses Jackal had seen; Crichton looked as if someone had eaten her soul. That wasn't the surprise: Jackal was completely prepared to believe that Crichton might be missing a few key spiritual components. What caught her off guard was Crichton's apparent good cheer. For a moment there seemed to be sparkles in the alien eyes, like little stars.

"Ah, Segura," she said. "You beat the drop-dead time by two minutes. Don't ever stand me up again."

Jackal resisted the urge to warble *no arrest today*. "I'm sorry, I wasn't checking e-mail. I didn't know about the appointment. Are we going to have to do this after every aftershock?"

"Maybe."

"Is that standard policy? I mean, if it was, you'd have some people in here practically every day."

"You're lucky you're not flat on your back in an MRI scanner right now. These are exactly the kind of readings I was waiting for. Now, would you like to tell me what happened to you in there?"

Her heart began to slam. "Nothing unusual. It was just like being in VC always is."

"How's the job search going?"

Jackal bit the inside of her lip. "You know I didn't get the job."

The lids blinked briefly over the disconcerting eyes. "That's too bad."

"They found out about my conviction. I assumed you told them."

"No, I gave you a glowing reference. I want you to have something you want to keep badly enough to trade for. Well, you keep looking, make me proud."

"There's nothing to tell."

"Beep! Wrong answer. Would you like to try again?"

Jackal sat mute while her heart tried to crawl up her throat.

"That's okay. It's only a matter of time. It's very interesting watching you try to put your life back together. If you do, you'll finally have something to protect. And if you don't, then you're going to need my help eventually. Either way, I'll be there with my best listening face on. And it won't be so bad, you'll see."

She grinned briefly and then turned her attention back to her screen. Jackal counted silently to thirty.

Crichton looked up with her galactic eyes. "Are you still here?"

She wanted to yell yes, I'm still here, you manipulative ratfuck jerk! But she remembered her training and the debit value of frustration in the long term. "No," she said, biting down on it, "I'm gone."

Jackal enjoyed bringing Snow along Perdue Street in the early evening, with the weight dropping from the faces of the passersby as they made their ways home, voices calling children for supper, the lighted windows framing people in moments of living. The air was crisp and still, with a faint tang of salt as they turned down Marginal Way and drew closer to the canal. As they passed Estar's gate Jackal said, "I don't know if I told you that Estar Borja is a friend of mine. She lives here."

"Here's another friend," she said a minute later as they approached the counter in Solitaire. Scully gave Jackal a piercing look when she introduced Snow, and then clasped Snow's hand gently and said, "How wonderful that you came." It seemed they liked each other right away.

Scully already had Jackal's beer on the counter: Snow squinched her mouth at the taste, and Scully asked, "Do you eat lobster?"

Snow nodded, a little uncertain.

"What's your favorite fruit?"

"Satsuma oranges."

"And your favorite color?"

"White."

He took a bottle of golden wine from the refrigerator and poured a glass. "Try this." Snow sniffed at it suspiciously, looked at Scully, tasted, and gave him a delighted smile.

"Never fails," he said smugly. "First glass is on the house."

It was a slow evening and everyone seemed relaxed about their food and drink, so Scully had time to keep the tables bussed, and paused every so often to talk. He asked smart questions about Snow's work, and laughed at her jokes.

"Everyone's watching us," Snow commented at one point.

"Jackal has a habit of exploding people's expectations of solo behavior," Scully said with a grin. "I've already had at least two watchers summon up the gumption to ask me who you are. None of them have the nerve to ask why you're getting the red-carpet treatment from a solo."

"What have you told them?" Jackal asked.

"That if they want to know who she is, they should ask you."
He laughed. "It seems to be an effective deterrent."

When he was not there, Jackal and Snow drank and ate hummus and pita bread, and talked about Snow's day at the plant, about Crichton and her monster eyes.

"Why did she want to see you?"

It was the sort of innocent question that needed an hour's worth of answer: Jackal mentally bellied up to the bar and started in. "Because I had something called an aftershock, and I have to go in after that happens." She held up a hand to forestall the next question. "Before I tell you what an aftershock is, I need to explain what VC is like."

Snow put on her now-we're-getting-to-it expression, and Jackal began.

It took more than an hour because Snow wanted to go back and ask about the screening process, and poke at the link to Garbo. "It's really sick that they would put you as a participant into this program that you'd been leading."

"I don't think the program people have any idea about that. No one here does."

She also told Snow about the nasty mess that she'd caused with her interview at the gallery. "They'll spread it all over the community. I won't be able to get a return e-mail from these people, never mind an interview. I guess they're afraid I'll take them all to dinner at the top of the Hengler Building and throw them off the balcony."

Snow looked startled, either by Jackal's words or the bitterness behind them. Then she sat up straighter and applied herself to the issue. It only took her a minute to say, "You're a project manager. Go get a project."

"I've been trying to get a project."

"No, you've been trying to get a job."

"What's the—" Jackal stopped. If Snow thought it was different, then it was. She put it into a mental corner where it could ferment for a while, while Snow wandered up to the bar for more hummus. Jackal stared at the tabletop and tried to work out what to do. She had not told Snow any details of her time in VC, only about the technology and the cell itself, and then about the early reclamation and her life since then—judiciously edited to exclude Crichton's bloodhounding. What if Crichton decided to pressure Snow for the information she wanted? Better that Snow know nothing: Jackal would just have to keep that secret. But it made her anxious.

She watched Snow now at the counter chatting with Scully, politely making room for a solo as if she'd been here a thousand times. Then a shadow fell across the table, and Jackal looked up as Estar took the seat across from her.

"There you are." Estar seemed particularly alive tonight, her face alight and attentive and slightly amused, as if she had some piece of special news reserved for exactly the right moment. She wore black trousers and boots, and a soft jade-green tunic that curled around her body when she moved. "Jane and I were here last night to see you, but you were absent. I imagined the mugger or the wayward bus, but I see that you are fine." She noticed Snow's glass and picked it up, sniffed at it and then took a sip. "Pah," she said, "tell me this isn't yours. Who would drink this?"

"I would. It's good, actually," Snow said from behind Jackal. Estar's head came up sharply and she raised an eyebrow. "Then this would be your seat."

"Yes."

Estar relaxed farther into the chair. She said to Jackal, "And who is this beautiful girl, *chacalita*? A new friend?"

Oh, wonderful, Jackal thought, Estar picks the perfect time to become jealous. "This is Snow, from Ko. From my real life. *Mi amada*." Oof, her internal voice said, the "real life" remark probably isn't the best choice of words. And now Snow was looking at

Jackal speculatively. Jackal didn't blame her: it was a bit of a mixed signal to call someone your beloved in public and send her off alone to a hotel when no one was looking. But at this awkward moment, Jackal understood that she had not erased her love for Snow. It wasn't that simple. Perhaps what she had scoured away in VC was her capacity for daily love, the dozen hourly acts of will that bound people together; she did not know if this new Jackal could build those links. And that meant she didn't know if she and Snow could be together; at this moment, it certainly seemed a bad bargain for Snow.

Nevertheless, she caught Snow's hand in hers to put the public seal on it. Don't you be mean to her, she thought to Estar: if I have to choose, this is the way it will go.

"I see," Estar said, and stood gracefully. She put an elegant hand out to Snow and drew her into the chair. "Snow. A perfect name. And I am Estar."

"It's Estar's house we passed on the way here," Jackal said.

"Yes, of course. And Jackal tells me you're an artist."

Estar smiled. "Among other things. Would you like to see some of my work? Chacal, fetch me something rich and red. Snow, come with me." She pulled Snow up again and toward the back of the room. Snow put on her best good-manners face and followed without resisting.

Jackal shook her head and strolled up to the counter, barely registering the way the tourists crowded back to give her room. "Another beer?" Scully said over his shoulder from the grill.

"Yes, and whatever you think Estar would like."

"What did she ask for?"

"Rich and red."

"Oh, she's feeling dramatic."

Jackal snorted. "She's always dramatic."

Scully nodded to concede the point. "Still, you know how she can get herself into trouble with people. Is Jane here?"

"I don't know."

"She should be. Estar has to stop sneaking off on her."

"I'll find out."

She carried the beer and Estar's wine back to the table and panned the crowd until she spotted Estar, one arm lightly resting on Snow's back, pointing out the various panels in the mural. Jackal sat and sipped her beer until they returned, Estar touching Snow gently and possessively—fingers laid briefly on her wrist, or a soft bump of Estar's shoulder against Snow's arm as they moved through the room that was becoming more crowded now, warmer and louder.

Jackal found a chair for Estar and placed the wine in front of her. "Thank you," Estar said dismissively, and then turned her full attention back to Snow. Snow's face was impassive, but Jackal could see the amusement deep in her eyes and in the slight curve of her mouth. I know her, Jackal thought; it's so good to know someone again. She winked at Snow behind Estar's back and kept sipping as she listened to their conversation. Estar was being charming, and Snow was being polite, but she wasn't giving much back.

"What's wrong?" Jackal said when Estar left the table for the bathroom.

"She's absolutely fascinating and very smart, and she's a loon," Snow said flatly. "A loon on a timer. One day soon—" she extended both hands, fingers fanned out, and mimed a mushroom cloud.

"She's already done that. You read about her on the web."

"She's not finished."

"I think she's different now. VC did something to her. She's always been fine with me, although everyone here is shit scared of her."

"I'm not surprised."

Jackal felt oddly defensive of Estar. "She's been kind to me, Snow. She and Scully are the only people I've met in this whole

city that I can talk to. I recognize that they're a little nonstandard,
but so am I now."

"I see that you've changed, if that's what you mean."

She didn't want to ask, but she had to. "What do you see?"

"You really want to talk about this?"

Jackal nodded, because she did not have enough breath to
speak. Of course she didn't: she was sure that most of the news was
bad. But the best kind of knowing went both ways: Snow understood her better than anyone.

Snow ran a finger around the rim of her glass, marshalling her
thoughts. When she returned her focus to Jackal, she was wearing
her looking-under-rocks expression.

"You drink more than you used to, but you don't seem to
enjoy it as much. Tonight, in here, is the first time I've seen you
move with your old confidence. I don't understand your body
signals anymore; I can't tell when you do or don't want to be
touched. It seems like much of your passion, your enthusiasm, is
in a box somewhere in a back room. It's hard to know whether
that's because you don't have your work to bring it out right now,
or whether it's the price of all those secrets you're keeping so
hard. You're compartmentalizing yourself. If you keep doing it,
then you're right about us—we won't make it." She put up a
hand to stop Jackal speaking. "I know you haven't said that, but
it's perfectly obvious. You still show everything on your face. But
you're so guarded that it's hard to ask about things when they
show." She reached across the table and took Jackal's hand. "I
wish you'd let me help you. I wish you'd tell me what was going
on last year and what really happened in VC. I'm not someone
you have to hide from. I'm not going to judge you. God, Jackal,
of all the people in the world, I'm the one who isn't going to punish you—"

Estar appeared from the crowd and put a hand on Snow's
shoulder. "You both look entirely too serious."

"We really—"

"We must spend more time together someplace where we can talk uninterrupted. My home, perhaps. Snow, you will agree?"

"It's up to Jackal."

Jackal asked, "Where's Jane?"

"She is home already."

"Why don't we walk you home if you're ready to go," Jackal offered, mindful of Scully's concern. She added to Snow, "Then maybe we can go back to my place and talk some more about this." Snow gave her a beautiful smile.

At her gate, Estar turned and said, "You'll come in for a glass of wine? Snow, I want to show you the picture I told you about, the one of Mondarruego."

Jackal said, "We really need to get going."

Estar tipped her head to the side and smiled up at Jackal. "Of course you do. You have serious things to discuss with this snowflower of yours. But because we are comrades, and because I am interesting and somewhat tragic, you will give me the favor of fifteen minutes of your time. Besides, I have something special for you."

It's okay, Snow's face said.

"Fifteen minutes."

Estar left them in a room deep within the house, a small space, intimate rather than confining, with the usual conglomeration of expensive furniture and fine rugs, color and scent, and some unfortunate music with indecipherable lyrics and multiple clashing guitars. The painting she had spoken of was another of her wall-sized murals. In it, a woman had just launched herself from a mountain cliff over a vertical drop of brown and gray rock bordered by greenbelt; far below her was a village, an old stone church surrounded by slate-roofed houses. The woman's arms were spread, her face lifted, so that it was not clear whether she was falling or flying.

"The inside of her head is very different from mine," Snow commented. But when Estar returned with three large bell-bowled glasses on a tray, Snow told her, "It's beautiful. It's as if you've painted adrenaline and something else—hope?—in with the brush strokes."

"Another poet. I'm glad you like it. Here, drink this interesting wine." She handed a glass to Jackal, and one to Snow. "To visions," she said. Jackal wasn't entirely sure she wanted to drink to that, given what she knew of Estar's thoughts on the subject, but she mentally crossed her fingers and raised the glass. The wine was good, if a bit sharp.

"Mmm," Snow said. "Lovely."

"Not as nice as your wine from Scully."

"It's different, but good. Very smooth."

Jackal drank again.

"Sit down for a minute and let me tell you about Mondarruego. It is a grandmother of a mountain, with many of its bones show-ing. This village that cowers beneath it is Torla . . ."

Jackal sipped her wine and let herself drift. The voices faded into a background hum. It was nice to relax, to feel pleasantly heavy and calm. Her mouth was a bit dry: she drank again, rolling the tang and the tannin around her tongue before swallowing slowly.

She heard her own name. "Let us see how Chacal is doing, shall we?" Estar's voice seemed far away.

So did Snow's. "We've already stayed past time. She's tired. We should go now. Jackal? Let's go."

She tried obligingly to raise herself from the couch, but she couldn't seem to make her arms and legs work properly. "What's wrong?" she heard Snow say, and then Snow *oofed* and Estar said, "Sit there while Chacal and I have a little chat. I need to talk with her about something, and then you can go wherever you like. No, *stay there*."

Snow made another, weaker noise, and was silent.

Estar settled herself beside Jackal. The music evolved into a single guitar seemingly searching for the highest audible note it could find.

"What's happening?" Jackal said.

"We never finished our talk about why you are not like other solos. It's a mystery, and I dislike mysteries. There are enough unanswered questions in my world that I do not willingly make room for more. So I brought you here to finish our conversation."

"I don't want to talk about that."

Estar stroked Jackal's forehead; her hand was cool and dry on Jackal's skin. "I know you don't. You're afraid. But I have given you something to make you brave. Don't fight it, it won't hurt you. No, don't fight."

She wanted to, but she couldn't. All her muscles felt as if they belonged to someone else.

"Now," said Estar, "you were talking as you came out of aftershock in my house two days ago. You said, 'I found the door.' Explain what that means."

Her brain no longer had control of her mouth, which answered on its own, "I found the door back to Ko."

"Explain."

"Ko is a global multi-corporation with impact on approximately seven point four percent of the world's economy. It's based—"

"Stop," Estar said testily. "Explain to me what the door back to Ko is, and what it has to do with your virtual confinement."

As Estar leaned in, the soft green fabric of her shirt pulled creamy and rich across her shoulders and breasts: Jackal watched the play of light and shadow across the material while her mouth talked easily on, not resisting at all, as if it were happy to reveal the knowledge that Jackal had been guarding so fiercely; the secrets that she had made the center of her world.

Her mouth said, "After a while in VC I went mad." Estar only shrugged; but Jackal heard Snow make a small, sad sound. "So I had to try to fix myself as best I could, but I was changed, and one of the changes was that I broke down the wall in my cell and stepped out and on the other side was Ko. A virtual Ko. It was all there. Just like the real one but with no people." She did not need Estar's urging to go on: now that the gate was open, the things she had kept silent were eager to push through and have their turn in the light. "I was there for over a year. I didn't want to come back."

"And what did you do for a year in this Ko of yours?" Estar's voice was soft and emotionless.

"Everything. I did everything. I rode my bicycle. I watched the birds swoop over the ocean. I made the day and the night. I was as big as the world." She shook her head. "I was free. Just being myself. Not Jackal the good web mate or Jackal the bad Hope. Just me. Just Jackal Segura. It was amazing. It was . . ." She discovered that she was crying; she blinked up at Estar through watery eyes. Estar's face was like marble, cold and still and intent.

"It's not like that here," Jackal said. It was important that Estar understand. "I don't know how to be that Jackal in the real world. And then I had that aftershock outside your house and something clicked into place like a gear in my head, and I knew how to get back. I made a door in my cell and I walked out." She smiled through her tears: her voice was thicker now. "I was on the beach on the south end of Ko just before I woke up, it was early evening, warm, I was barefoot and I could taste salt when I breathed and I was big again, as big as the world . . ."

"And how did you make this door?"

"Big as the world. Big big big . . ."

"Chacal!"

"I'm tired. Let me sleep, I'm tired."

"You can sleep as soon as you tell me how this thing is done."

"Wouldn't you like to know?" She felt slyly pleased with her clever answer. "Crichton wants to know too. She pushes and pokes but I'm not telling her. Never never. Can't tell anyone." She peered at Estar. "I can't tell anyone." That was stupid; wasn't she telling Estar? "You can't tell anyone," she amended. There, that would take care of it. "If they knew I was editing on-line, they'd dig tunnels in my brain and there'd be no more me left. No more Jackal." Her chin trembled, and snot made a slimy trail along the corner of her mouth. "Estar, don't make me do this."

"Tell me how you make this door."

"I don't know! I don't know how I do it. If I knew, I would tell Crichton and she would tell the techs and they wouldn't need me, they would leave me alone. Hah. That's funny, leave me alone."

"Chacal, you must tell me. Look at me!"

Jackal compressed her mouth into a straight line, like she remembered doing as a child to exasperate her mother, and shook her head exaggeratedly.

Estar looked at her for a moment. *"Muy bien,"* she said. "Then we must find some other way to encourage you."

She shifted her weight, rose from the couch: a gust of cool air swirled in behind her. Jackal closed her eyes. Her internal voice was locked behind a door somewhere at the back of her brain, pounding with staccato fists, horrified at what was happening: but that didn't matter. She had to answer Estar's questions; it was necessary. I've always done what was necessary, she thought; I should have been doing what was right. She suddenly understood what Snow had been trying to tell her earlier.

And there was Snow now, standing before her. She was more pale than Jackal had ever seen her. "You were right," Jackal said earnestly. "I have to stop waiting for people to give me things. I don't need someone to give me a job. I have the money from Ko. I can make a project myself. I can do what I want. Is that okay, to do what I want?"

Snow's face twisted. "Yes, honey," she said, sounding breathless, "yes, that's okay."

And then Jackal saw that Estar stood behind Snow, slightly to one side; her right arm reached around Snow's ribs, and her left arm held Snow's left wrist so that Snow's arm was pulled back. Estar's right hand held a long knife.

"Do you love this snowflake?" Estar said.

"Oh, yes," Jackal said.

"Can you live without her?"

"Yes." Snow did not move, but tears began to run down her face. Jackal went on, "If I absolutely have to, I can live without anyone except me. I know how to do that. I learned it in VC." She told Snow solemnly, "I erased you and that's why you shouldn't love me anymore."

Snow continued to cry without movement or noise, a weeping statue with steel at her heart. Something's not right here, Jackal thought; it was hard to work things out when she was so tired.

Estar's hands shook, and the knife tip wavered over Snow's diaphragm. She said, "I was in my cell for longer than any of you and I know what it is to go mad from facing oneself." Her eyes rolled back slightly and she laughed, a terrible tight noise. "Did you ever truly come face to face with yourself, *chacalita*? Did you ever turn one day with an apple in your hand and meet yourself covered in blood from the knees to the teeth, looking much as you might have done on a particular day in your past? Do you know what it is to fall asleep with your doppelganger hunched in the corner, to wake with her bloody voice gurgling in your ear?"

"That's the crocodile," Jackal said. "You have to fight it, or it will eat you."

"Too late," Estar said, and smiled.

Jackal said, "I'm sorry the crocodile got you, Estar. You are so beautiful and so much yourself. But that's how it works. It's really not fair, you know." She wished that she could speak more clearly.

"It's not fair," she said again. "After everything, after the crocodile, when I was alone on Ko, I was so happy. I liked myself there more than I ever have, more than I do now. . . . But the real world is different. . . ." She tried to find the right way to say it. "The world is full of people. We bang into each other like beads in a bowl." Estar made an impatient sound. "We have to learn to make it all fit together. I have to find a way to be myself and still let other people leave marks on me."

That was sad, but it was true. "It's not fair," she repeated. She shook her head. "But there it is."

"You find the way if you must," Estar said. "You are the fighter. You are the one who struggles against fate. You are a light in our shadowy little corner of the world, Chacal, and you do not even know that you shine. And you have what I need. I need a world where even my crocodile cannot follow me. I want—oh, Chacal, I want to walk on the beach while the motherwave gathers herself on the horizon, and stand on the sand while she howls into shore and throws herself over me. I want to sink and sink and never drown. I want to make all my visions real and then tear them down and make them over again. I want to be all the things I see within me. But I cannot do that here. I try to remember that you other people are as real as me, but often I forget and then it is too easy to hurt you. And then the crocodile returns." She made a shrugging gesture with the knife in her hand as if to say, *You see?*

You don't want to hurt me, Jackal wanted to say in fond exasperation, and then the drug loosened its grip slightly, pulled one finger back from inside her brain, and she thought, it isn't me she'll hurt. Snow is in terrible trouble.

"So you must tell me how you opened the door," Estar said, and pulled Snow's wrist higher behind her back; Snow gasped.

"I broke myself open," Jackal said harshly. "I turned over every single rock inside myself and found all the worms. And then I ate them. I took it all back in and then I took it with me into the sunlight. And you can't do that. You don't have the guts."

There was silence.

"You may be right," Estar said finally, in a voice that was almost completely sane, without any overtones of performance. "You may indeed be right. And if you are, then you have made my point for me. If I cannot do it for myself, then you must. Now tell me how to open the door before I disjoint this person that you love." She jerked Snow's arm up and Snow shrieked.

"Stop!" Jackal yelled as best she could in her drug-roughened voice.

"Tell me!"

"Don't hurt her!"

"Tell me!"

Snow screamed and sagged to her knees. Her arm looked wrong, and she was gasping, short shallow gulps of pain. Estar let go, and the arm dropped: Snow screamed again, as much as she could with no breath.

"It's only dislocated," Estar said mildly. "Now tell me what I want to know, *mi amiga* Segura, or I will cut it off."

Jackal tried to think of what to say, and she braced her weight against her hands to launch herself off the couch. A shape appeared in the doorway behind Estar: Jane mouthed *Keep talking* as she moved slowly into the room.

"All right, Estar. All right. I'll tell you. Please don't hurt Snow anymore. I'm sorry, I should have trusted you. I want you to have your visions too. I understand. So here's what you have to do. When you are in VC, you have to face the viewscreen, and then you have to jump up and down and say, Door, door, open wide, let my body go outside—"

And Jane plucked the knife away from Estar with one hand

and slapped a syrette gun against her shoulder with the other. Estar said, "No, Jane—" and then she melted into a puddle, her eyes showing almost completely white.

Jane paused briefly to check Estar's pulse and to straighten her neck: Jackal was both touched and repelled by the gesture. Then Jane crossed to Snow, who was on her knees holding her left elbow in her right hand. Jane raised her to her feet and walked her carefully over to a straight-backed chair.

"Jackal, come help me."

Jackal levered herself off the sofa, swaying slightly.

Jane scanned her. "What happened here?"

"She gave me something. Tranquilizer, maybe. Made me want to talk a lot."

"Then you shouldn't try to help with the first aid. I want you to stand over here and talk to her while I fix her arm. Your name is Snow, right? Snow, we're going to put this arm back. Okay?"

Snow nodded, her eyes closed against the pain: Jackal could see the sweat on her forehead and temples.

"As soon as it's back in the socket, it will stop hurting. I promise. All right?"

Another nod.

"The bad news is that it will hurt worse while I put it in. Can you handle that?"

Snow clenched her jaw. Then she opened her eyes and nodded again, looking straight at Jane.

"Good," Jane said. "We're going to straighten the arm out, then pull it across your chest, and when it finds the socket we will fold it back up toward the shoulder to show it the way in. And that will be all."

Snow whispered, "Okay, let's do it." She grabbed Jackal's left hand with her right and squeezed hard.

Jane began. Snow's eyelids fluttered. "Breathe, honey," Jackal said, kneeling beside her, fighting to keep her balance. "It's going to be okay. You're going to be all right."

"Told you . . . she was a loon." Snow was panting now. Jackal looked up at Jane, whose face was set in utter concentration as she hefted the weight of Snow's arm and started the bone back on its journey home.

"Honey, I'm so sorry. I'm sorry she hurt you. When this is all over, I'm going to take you back to Solitaire and buy a bottle of that lovely wine, and we'll sit upstairs where it's quiet and dark and private, we'll eat grilled cheese sandwiches and drink wine until we can't drink anymore."

"I don't know," Snow said raggedly, "we can drink quite a lot." She was trying to smile: it was more of a terrible rictus than anything, but Jackal admired her courage profoundly. Snow clamped down hard on Jackal's hand as Jane worked.

"Who's the smartest?" Jackal said.

Snow huffed in mingled surprise and pain. "It certainly isn't you. Must be me."

Jackal nodded. "And the bravest."

"Well, that still leaves you—" and then her body jerked with the jolt of the arm finding the socket, and there was a series of terrifying crunching noises as Jane folded Snow's wrist up and over and the arm slid snug into the shoulder.

Jane gently placed Snow's hand in her lap. "How is it?"

Snow blinked. "It's fine. It really doesn't hurt anymore." Already, the color was returning to her face. She flexed her fingers experimentally, and then took a deep breath. "That's amazing. Thank you."

Jane nodded, her face drawn into planes it might achieve permanently when she was fifty years older. Jackal realized that she'd shown no sign of stress until this moment, now that everything was over. "Jane, you should sit down."

"Not yet. I need to get her to bed." Jane pointed her chin at Estar, snoring gently on the floor.

"Let me help." Jackal pushed herself to her feet too fast; the room shifted and she had to sit down again.

"You'll drop her and it will be more work for me. Help me get her up on her feet and I can take it from there. You look after Snow. I'll be back with some hot tea in a few minutes."

Together they hauled Estar to her feet; Jackal steadied her while Jane put her shoulder under Estar's ribs and lifted her up into a rescue carry.

"You're strong," Jackal said, impressed.

"Not really. She is mostly bones and sadness, and those don't weigh so much."

Jackal and Snow were both silent as Jane left the room with Estar over her shoulder.

"Well," Jackal said finally, "Another conversation stopper."

"Would you put your arm around me, please?" Snow said.

Jackal did. Snow was trembling slightly, clammy and cool, fragile in the crook of Jackal's elbow. Estar's music groaned around them.

"I love you," Jackal said.

"I love you too."

Jackal smoothed Snow's hair with her free hand.

After a few moments, Snow said, "Who is that girl?"

"That's Jane. I . . . I have no idea who she is." Jackal wasn't sure she knew anyone, anymore. She still felt off-balance from the drug and the fear of seeing Snow with Estar's knife against her skin. She squeezed Snow's hand tighter.

"I'm okay," Snow said. "I'm right here."

"I'm so glad," Jackal answered shakily. "And I'm so sorry. It's my fault she did this to you."

"What, this was your idea? I don't think so," Snow said sharply.

"It's not your fault. Don't you dare apologize." She sighed. "Sorry. I'm pretty tense. I can't believe any of this happened. But at least—" She stopped, bit her lip.

"What?"

"At least I got to hear some of those things you've been keeping locked up."

"That stuff I said about us—"

"Was true," Snow said quietly. "Of course we can live without each other if we have to. I didn't kill myself when I thought you would be in prison forever and I won't die if you send me home in two weeks and tell me never to come back. I'll just want to die. But they aren't the same." She sighed. "It's hard to know that. It's hard to even think about it. It would be better if we could figure things out."

They sat like that until Jane returned with a tray of tea and honey and shortbread. Jackal sniffed at the mug Jane handed her.

"It's only tea," Jane said, with most of her usual aplomb recovered.

"Right. Sorry." It was hot and bracing, and she began to feel less like falling down or throwing up.

"I found this in the kitchen." Jane held up a prescription bottle. "Her amobarbital. She is supposed to take it every day, but sometimes she doesn't. She probably gave you her regular dose, you should be fine once it wears off."

"She functions on that? She must have the metabolism of a hummingbird."

"Will you press charges against her?"

Jackal blinked, then looked to Snow. "She hurt you. Whatever you want to do, I'll go along with it."

Snow very carefully rotated her arm through a small circle. Her voice shook a little when she spoke. "She's a fucking menace. She can't be allowed to just go around doing this to people."

Jackal bit her lip. It broke her heart to think of Estar in prison. She wished that Snow was the kind of person who could march into Estar's bedroom and break her nose while she slept, as a way of evening the score.

Snow continued, "I don't know. I have a pretty good idea that if we call the police tonight, she'll spend the rest of her life in a box somewhere. I'm not sure . . ." She shrugged with her good shoulder.

"The responsibility is partly mine," Jane said. "It's my job to prevent this."

"I wish I'd listened to Scully," Jackal said. "He was trying to tell me this might happen. And I told him I could handle it. I am ten different kinds of idiot."

"This wasn't even about me. It's you she was trying to hurt," Snow said to Jackal. "She was just using me to do it, like I was your favorite toy that she was going to break. That almost makes it worse, you know? I'm not even real to her." She put a hand to Jackal's face. "And she's your friend. You say you'll back me up if I press charges, but how will you feel when they lock her up for the next sixty years?"

Jackal rubbed her eyes and told the truth. "I'll feel bad. And I feel bad that she hurt you." Then, to Jane, "Assuming we don't do anything, what happens now?"

Jane handed her a piece of shortbread. "She'll wake. She'll remember that she's wronged you. She'll play loud music and refuse to eat. Then she will lock herself in her studio and paint something beautiful and bring it to you for a present. And then it's over for her."

"She did that with Scully, didn't she?" Jackal guessed, remembering the cathedral of trees.

Jane raised an eyebrow. "Yes."

"Great," said Snow. "I get my arm yanked off and you get a present." She began to cry.

"You should put some honey in your tea," Jane said. "It's good for shock."

"I don't want any damned honey. And I sure don't want an art collection from Estar Borja. Is she going to try something like this again?"

No one answered. They all drank more tea. Snow said, "Could someone please turn that damned music off?"

20

JACKAL PAID FOR PRIVATE TRANSPORT TO SNOW'S HOTEL; a cold, slow walk would have helped clear her head, but Snow was still shocky and needed a quiet, safe place to lie down. And a quiet, safe person: Jackal came upstairs without any discussion, and the only thing they said was "good night." They slept tumbled together like socks in drawer. Jackal woke in the small hours and watched Snow sleep, her body still and loose under the blanket, her smell a mix of freesia and old warm leather. I love her, Jackal thought. I'm scared.

The next morning, they both treated Snow's arm as if it were likely to disintegrate at any second, until Jackal lobbed a bottle of shampoo at her and Snow stretched to catch it.

"There," Jackal said, "it didn't fall off, or anything."

Snow humphed, but she smiled as she dressed.

"Are you okay, really?" Jackal asked.

Snow shrugged. "No. Yes. I don't know." She sat down on the bed, one sock in her hand. "I didn't know that my body could come apart that easy. That probably sounds weird. . . . Some moments, I had no idea what was happening. And other moments I was right there, focused and thinking. I was trying to figure out how to get my fingernail out." She held up her left little finger. "I was visualizing sticking it into her eye, all the way up to the knuckle."

Jackal sat down next to her. "Would you have?"

"I don't know. Would you?"

"I don't know if I could do it for myself. I hope I would always stop somebody from hurting you."

"Sometimes you can't," Snow said. "Sometimes you can't even stop yourself." She studied Jackal for a moment. "I'll be okay," she said, and kissed Jackal's cheek and then went back to putting her sock on.

Jackal walked back to Shangri-La and decided that it was a beautiful day even though it was cold; the weather was on the spiral toward full winter, and today was perhaps one of the last of the blue-and-orange days before the corner turned toward gray and brown and white.

There was an e-mail from Scully: *I heard about it from Jane. Are you and Snow okay?*

She replied: *We're fine. Thank you. We'll come in tonight and tell you all about it.*

Then she poured an enormous glass of orange juice and made herself two slices of buttered toast, and curled up in her chair to mourn for Estar, and to think things through.

They decided that Scully should hear the whole story, including the truth about Jackal's last year in VC. "He's your friend," Snow said.

"Not to mention that he's Estar's friend too," Jackal said. "I'd rather he heard about this from me."

It was not quite four o'clock. Snow had "worked like a demon," she told Jackal, to get through her meetings and leave the plant with a palmtop full of data to analyze. "They won't expect to see me again for a few days," she said. "Let's go get drunk." So they had turned up early at Solitaire to give themselves some conversational privacy with Scully.

"Jesus Christ," was his first comment. He leaned on the counter and peered at Snow. "Are you sure you're okay?"

"I'm fine. As Jackal has already pointed out, my arm didn't fall off."

"You should still go to the clinic."

"I'll have it looked at when I get back to Ko."

Scully made a face. "You're going back?" It was obvious he was making an effort not to glare at Jackal.

"We're working on it," Snow said.

"What are you going to do about Estar?"

"Nothing right now," Jackal said, checking Snow's face to make sure she had read the signals right. "I'm still thinking about dragging her out into the street the next time I see her and throwing her under a truck, but other than that . . ."

"I may come back from Ko with a gun," Snow said. "A gun beats a knife every time."

He nodded. "Wouldn't blame you."

"It's weird," Snow said. "There's one part of me that is so outraged, I want to hit her and hit her until she screams. And the other part of me knows she's already screaming. And she's Jackal's friend, and yours. It's hard to know what to do."

"Isn't that the truth," Scully said.

"Scully," Jackal ventured. He looked at her. "I'm sorry that I didn't tell you about VC."

He looked down. "I don't blame you. There wasn't much point. If you can't tell anyone how to do it, why should you put up with everyone being jealous?"

"It's not just that. I don't . . . I can't let them draft me into the research program and suck my brains out through my nose."

"They might not. Anyway, it's only a two-year commitment."

"Oh, come on. The whole goal of the project is to be able to customize the environment. I should know. They won't care how long the contract term is, they'll keep me as long as it takes. They'll threaten me with finishing my sentence in prison. Or now that it's an EarthGov program, they'll find some legal loophole about the greater good or some other happy bullshit, and I won't have any choice. I'll be eighty-five years old and still living in that building under Crichton's nose. No thank you, very much. The only reason I'm telling you is because we're friends and I thought you should know why Estar came after me. But you can't tell anyone."

Scully nodded, but he looked unhappy.

"We can talk more about it later, if you want."

He nodded again, and then stretched to the refrigerator for a new bottle of the chardonnay he'd poured the previous night for Snow. "Here you go. Come back whenever you're ready for that grilled cheese."

They went up to the solo level and pulled two tables together in a corner. Jackal set a screen around them, and liberated a handful of candles from around the room.

Snow opened the wine with her little finger, and for a moment Jackal was back on Terry's Cliff, talking about people growing up to be themselves. She waited for Snow to pour the wine. Then she said, "I want to tell you some things, but I don't know how."

"I want to hear them." Snow looked at her with compassion. "But I can't say them for you."

Jackal nodded. Took a deep breath. Drank some wine. "I'm scared," she said finally.

"I know. But you're brave."

"I'm not brave at all. If I was brave I probably wouldn't be here right now."

Snow waited.

I don't know if I can do this, Jackal thought. She bent her head over her wine. Perhaps she should say that she needed more time to think. They could talk tomorrow. You're a fucking coward, she told herself; then like a clear, distant bell she heard her internal voice say *Do better*. The answer welled up within her immediate and urgent. "I will," she said out loud, "I will do better."

And without pause, before Snow could ask what it meant, she began.

"Halloween last year—" she did not say, "the day with Tiger," but both of them nodded as if she had "—my mother and I had a fight, the worst one ever, about me being assigned to Garbo. It was supposed to be her project, but Neill gave it to me, and when she found out it was his idea . . . she's always been so competitive about him. When I first started his workshop, she would ask what I was learning, and she always had a story about what happened when she'd been in that part of the training. It was all about how she'd been there first." She frowned. "I think she wanted me to do well, but another part of her really minded when I did. Do you think so? Or am I crazy?"

"No." Snow said. "I think she minded a lot. Your mother isn't much of a grown-up."

"Anyway, that day she . . ." Jackal waved her hands, trying to find the right words, sloshing wine on the table. "She just went berserk. She said that I got everything I wanted, I was spoiled, I was taking opportunities away from other people." She drank some wine, remembering clearly as she told it to Snow: the two of them in the office, Donatella's face twisted, breath hitching as she shouted *they give you everything and you're no more a Hope than I am!*

Snow gasped. Jackal said, "I went completely cold. I said, what do you mean, and she told me they induced me to have me on time, but I was too late, and so everyone had lied all my life to give me opportunities that I didn't even deserve."

She stopped and waited. Snow did exactly the right thing: she blinked once, twice, and then her eyes filled and she put her hand on Jackal's, saying, "Oh, honey, that must have hurt all the way through."

Jackal said quietly, "I do love you," and went on with the story. The complex stew of feelings that brought her up the Needle at Mirabile; the horror of the last moments before the screens shattered into static and the web was gone. The arrest and the trial. When she came to the deal with Arsenault, Snow hissed fiercely, "I knew it. I knew it was something like that. Those bastards. But why—" She stopped herself. "Never mind, that's a side trip. I'm sorry. Please keep going."

VC. Having told the story to Scully, she found more coherence to it this time, and she could see its powerful impact on Snow. She traced the first disorienting days, her systems and rituals, and the gradual descent into the time of the crocodile; fighting against madness; and finally crawling back from the edge of someplace maybe not too far from where Estar lived now. Snow drank it all in, her eyes wide.

Then it was time to talk about erasing things.

"I don't know how to begin this part. I don't know how to tell you this." She gulped her wine, poured some more, and then said, simply, "I had to protect myself. The crocodile scared me so much. And I had to admit that my old life was over. I was never going to be the Hope or part of the web or part of Ko. I could either fight it or accept it. So I decided that if I was going to survive, I would have to let go of it all. I made a list in my head of everything that could hurt me, and I erased everything on the list. Just like wiping a white board."

Snow said softly, "I don't understand."

Jackal was so frightened: she wanted to shout, You should understand, what's the matter with you? Why do I have to spell it out for you? But she reached through the fear for the right words. "I disconnected myself from everything I cared about. I couldn't allow those things, those people, to hurt me anymore. I thought if

I rubbed everything out of me. . . . So I did. All of it. I cut all ties. I put it all away. I made myself stop caring about everything because it was all done, all gone, and I was never going to get any of it back. And I only understood a long time afterward that I had gutted myself. But I didn't know what else to do. It was like that old joke about surgery, where it's successful but the patient dies. I cut away the web and Ko and my parents and Neill and everyone else I could think of."

She stopped. Her throat felt too thick to talk. She stared down at the table miserably, at her own stupid hand on the stem of the glass.

"And me," Snow said gently.

Jackal nodded. Tears dripped down onto the table. All I ever do is cry anymore, she thought. Boring, stupid Jackal. "You were the hardest. You wouldn't go away. I had to scour you out." She sighed. "And I did. That's the thing. I did it. I scrubbed you out. I made you disappear. I went into Ko and was so happy by myself, without any of you. Then I came back to the real world and suddenly things weren't so simple anymore. But I had already . . ."

Silence. More tears on the table.

"Already what, honey?"

"I betrayed you," Jackal said. "You would never have abandoned me like that. You didn't. Look at what you did for me; you went to Neill and you came all the way here even after I sent you that message. You fought so hard for me, and I just wiped you out and left you behind. I didn't hold on. And I couldn't tell you because you had come all this way, you told yourself 'I know she loves me' and you came. You trusted me to be the same, but I'm not, and I did this terrible thing and I let you go. And I still love you but there's this distance and I don't know if I can heal it. I don't know if I can undo what I did. And I think that makes me bad. I'm bad, Snow. How can you trust me to love you now?"

Snow was crying too. "You aren't bad," she said. She shoved the wine bottle and the glasses aside so she could reach for Jackal's hands and hold them while she said, "You listen to me, Jackal Segura. You are not bad." Jackal tried to pull her hands away, but Snow held tight. "Listen to me, damn it! I will always want you to survive. You do whatever you have to do. You hear me? Whatever it takes. If it means you have to drop half of Ko off the cliffs, then you do it. You were brave enough and strong enough to survive your own fear. That's an amazing thing. Look at what happened to Estar, and then look at you. You did fine."

"But what I did to you—"

"Oh, bullshit. I wasn't there. You didn't do anything to me. But that doesn't mean you have to keep doing it. You're not alone now, and you don't have to kill me to save yourself."

Snow let go of Jackal's hands and repositioned the bottle and glasses carefully, precisely.

Some time later, Jackal said, "Have I told you lately that you astonish me?"

"It's been a while."

"How'd you get to be so smart?"

"I'm not that smart. You're just really dumb about this kind of thing."

"Oh," Jackal said.

"You want to make it up to me, go get us another bottle and some grilled cheese sandwiches."

They devoured three sandwiches between them, as well as half a bowl of blue corn chips and salsa, and were making inroads on the second bottle of wine, when the screen moved and Crichton appeared at the table.

Jackal was so surprised that she said nothing as Crichton put down the chair and wineglass she was holding, and sat. Her white lenses turned her eyes to stone. She grinned at Jackal, then turned to Snow and held out her hand. Jackal saw for the first time that Crichton's fingers were long, and her hands were beautiful.

"I'm Crichton."

"I guessed. I'm Snow."

"All of you people have such appropriate names," Crichton said conversationally, as if it weren't completely unnatural to be here on the solo level of Solitaire with a client. "Close your mouth, Segura, your food is showing."

"What are you doing here?"

"Looking for you."

Jackal said, with controlled exasperation, "Why?"

"Well, there's no reason for you to come to me anytime soon unless you have a convenient aftershock, and they're never around when you need them. Hah." Crichton pincered a chip out of the basket and dunked it in the salsa.

"What do you want?" Jackal could feel herself almost grinding her teeth around the words.

"I'd like to chat about what we're going to do with this little vacation paradise you've made out of VC."

Jackal and Snow froze; Crichton ate another chip and leaned back in her chair, grinning. The white eyes were the most malign effect Jackal had ever seen on her; she looked in need of exorcism.

"I don't know what you're talking about."

Crichton leaned forward so quickly that her face simply seemed to appear inches away from Jackal's: Jackal blinked and remembered in time not to let herself jerk away. "Just stop this now," Crichton said earnestly, without irony or amusement. "I know everything. So think it through, Segura. Why am I here?"

She's here to arrest you! Jackal's internal voice babbled. *Slice up your brain!* But, think it through, Crichton had said: so Jackal set the voice aside. She stared at the boiled-egg eyes while she worked it out, and Crichton stared unblinking back. Jackal was aware of

Snow filling everyone's wineglass, and spared a moment of surreal appreciation for Snow's priorities.

"Okay," Jackal said slowly, rubbing her forehead. Nothing to lose, she thought. "You can get me to your office anytime you want. You don't need a real reason. So you came here because this is an off-line negotiation and you don't intend to turn me over to the Bills of the world."

"A for accuracy. I heard you were good at this, I'm glad to finally see some evidence of it."

She was feeling her way now in delicate steps. "So let's assume for a moment that whatever you've heard is true—"

"And I'd like to know where you heard it," Snow bristled.

Jackal put up a hand and then changed the gesture so it became a touch on Snow's arm. "We can get to that in a minute. First let's make sure that we're all playing in the same sandbox. So, if it were true, what would you do about it?"

Crichton sat back a little and put both hands on the table. "I would ask you to come to a private location, enter VC through a verified link, and do your party trick for a period not to exceed twenty-seven real-time hours so that we can get a complete set of diurnal hormonal, brain wave and body chemistry cycle readings. In exchange, we will arrange for your permanent removal from the EarthGov program, and will try not to need any more participation from you on the research side."

" 'Try not to need' is a little non-specific."

"We would negotiate a fee-for-participation contract. We would only activate it as the final option available to further our research. It will be a standard contract with right of refusal."

"And the goal of this research?"

"To bring Phase Four Garbo to market within twenty-four months on a commercial franchise basis."

Jackal said slowly, "And who are 'we'?"

Crichton tilted her head and replied, "We are Ko, Jackal. What did you think?" She picked up her wineglass for the first time since she had come to the table, and drank.

Silence.

"You work for Ko?"

Crichton drank again.

Jackal and Snow exchanged a look.

"Perhaps you'd be kind enough to explain," Jackal said formally.

"Certainly," Crichton answered, as if surprised the need existed. "I was assigned early last year to strategic analysis of Garbo through direct observation of participant behavior. Emphasis on short-term and long-term effects of various applications of the technology. We structured the study so that the purpose of my observations was masked from participants by my function of case officer. It's also a role that lends itself to my particular personal style."

"I'll say," Jackal commented involuntarily.

Crichton grinned. "I am our teacher's least orthodox student, but I'm very good at what I do."

Jackal traded another look with Snow. *She means Neill.*

Crichton continued, "When the senator hit the marble in Mirabile and you were alleged to be responsible, both Hong Kong officials and the mainland Chinese government moved to sever all ties with Ko. They were twenty-seven minutes away from immediate revocation of all leasehold rights and the biggest liability suit in the universe when Smith finally agreed that you would be stripped of your status and offered up to EarthGov justice as an unaffiliated individual, and that the company would not bend over backwards to defend you. If you had chosen to be more active in your own defense, the company might have found itself in a bind; but it was a calculated risk. Why should you choose to reject a Ko-sponsored defense? And in fact, you didn't."

Even though it had already happened, it was horribly hard to hear it all laid out so coldly. "So the company made a deal."

"Yes, they did. They traded you to guarantee the flow of revenues and patents and executive bonuses, and the continued livelihood of two million people. And EarthGov got much more direct control of what could prove to be the most lucrative entertainment and social technology yet devised—they demanded it in exchange for expediting your case and offering you program placement. That was a near one for you. You should be flattered that Smith agreed: the company believes that Garbo could change the essential social dynamic of Western-model culture in the same way that the automobile did, with a massive economic return to the holder of the technology."

"And you were part of the package."

"I was assigned to Garbo in Al Iskandariyah. That's where I managed all my case load until we came here. If you'd come to Al Isk as planned, we would have been working together. You would have had to put up with me in meetings. Hah."

"So . . . I don't understand. How were you involved in the negotiations?"

"Heaven forfend," Crichton said with a laugh. "I'm just a storm trooper like Snow here, do what I'm told and try to have some fun along the way." Jackal darted a look toward Snow to see how she took to the comparison: Snow was wearing her under-rocks face again. Crichton continued, "I'm telling you the story as it was told to me."

"So this is Ko's chance to sweep the technology out from under EarthGov."

"I'm glad you're finally letting those brains come out to play. You haven't been the sharpest tool in the shed since your arrest."

"And thank you very much for your fucking support."

"Now, now," Crichton said, at the same time that Snow put a hand on Jackal's arm. Jackal flexed her shoulders and poured herself and Snow some more wine: she pointedly did not refill Crichton's glass. Crichton smiled and did it herself. "At any rate, you're correct. Ko can truthfully say that your participation data was rejected by EarthGov's scientists as non-contributory, and we will exercise our option to form a small subsidiary to explore alternative applications of such data. And if we just happen to stumble onto the editing sequence on the way, well, there's a handy bargaining chip to renegotiate the entire contract with EarthGov."

"And let me guess who's running the new show."

"Aw, shucks," Crichton said, batting her eyelids over her cue ball eyes to stomach-churning effect. "Little ole me will get my chance to shine."

"So your ability to be successful depends on my cooperation."

"And your ability to have a life depends on mine."

Jackal nodded. "As long as we know where we stand." She rose abruptly. "I'm going for a walk. No, by myself," she said as Snow pushed back her chair. To Crichton: "Do you want to wait for me, or would you like me to come to your office tomorrow?"

"I'm fine here. Snow and I can get acquainted. I'll bet we have tons in common."

Snow tried to smother a smile, but it didn't work. Jackal understood. "You really are a pain in the ass," Jackal said as sternly as she could.

"It's my special gift. If I'm a good pain in the ass tonight, I get my own company tomorrow. I'm happy to wait for you."

Jackal wiggled her eyebrows at Snow to ask if she was okay. Snow nodded, and did that trick of appearing to become one with her chair. "Did you know that many people are incapable of raising just one eyebrow?" she said conversationally, helping herself to a corn chip. Jackal headed for the stairs.

Once outside, she turned left, toward the canal: perhaps she would finally find that green space at the end of the road. The street was dark, the buildings like faces with closed eyes; there were only faint sounds of traffic behind her, and the thrum of barge turbines in the waterway ahead, to tell her that there were other people in the world.

The street ended abruptly in a rib-high stone wall and a razor-wire fence along the canal bank, with an orange-cast halogen streetlight off to one side. No park, no bench. No place to rest. She stood at the wall and watched the water traffic with its white and red and green lights. A half-moon was up, like a bowl tipped sideways.

There were footsteps on the street behind her; she turned, guessing who it was.

"Hi."

"Hi."

They stared together at the water running with light.

"I told her," Scully said. "I'm very, very sorry. I don't expect you to forgive me. But I hope you'll take Crichton's offer. What you can do—solos need it, Jackal. I need it. I know it's not fair to you. But I thought, here's a chance for someone to get that technology who'll actually do something better with it, who will put it out there so that we can use it; and here's a way to get Jackal out of danger. Crichton doesn't want to give you up to the brain-slicers. She just wants to know how you do it." He opened his hands. "And so do I. The idea that there might be even a scrap of good in this hole they opened in my brain. . . . Do you know, I've been in and out of my cell twice just since I left the bar? I don't know if they'll ever find a way to fix that. But maybe someday I can be in and out of Maui instead of that damn tiny box."

He turned to look at her directly for the first time, smiling weakly, with affection but without hope.

She said, "I assume you've been watching solos for her ever since the program transfer." She didn't wait for his nod. "I should be angry. I should shout at you or break your nose or something. But that would be . . . I can't seem to drag up a whole lot of outrage, you know? I understand doing things because you think you have to, even when they hurt someone else. I wish you'd trusted me. But why should you? I've been keeping my own secrets." She sighed.

"I wish I'd trusted you too, now. But I didn't."

They watched the water move slow and black under the orange fingers of the halogen light. She wondered if fish lived here; she'd been thinking of it as industrial water, but maybe something survived it. She thought she heard a faint *plosh* out in the dark, the sound a scaled belly might make slapping the water.

"Who's minding the bar?"

"Razorboy and his friend with the pink hair. They both look scared as rabbits, I promised I'd only be gone for twenty minutes. But I just . . . I understand that you might not want to be friends anymore, but I thought I would come out and see if there was anything you wanted to say to me, or anything I could do to help."

"I'm still making up my mind about Crichton. But you've given me an idea." She told him what it was and watched his face smooth out and then crease into a smile.

"You'd do that?"

"Don't you think it would be a good thing?"

"It's—yes, it's great, Jackal. She'll agree, why wouldn't she?"

"There's something else. I think you owe me something for all this."

His face became solemn again. "What do you want?"

"It's fine to have Razorboy and Drake for emergency backup, but you need real help in the bar. I want the job."

He frowned, and asked, "You want to work in Solitaire?" as if he thought he hadn't heard her correctly.

"We can figure out some overlapping shift work. Maybe we could be open more hours. I think people would like that."

He looked thoroughly confused and, strangely, a little scared.

"I . . . look, I said I would do what I could, but I can't afford to hire anyone. I can barely take care of myself with this place."

"I know that. That's the point. If you could take care of your-self better with it, maybe you wouldn't have to be a goddamn cor-porate spy on the side." He flinched, but she didn't worry about it: he deserved it. "Anyway, I don't need the money right now, I need the work." *Thank you, Snow.* "Pay me in grilled cheese sand-wiches. We can figure something out. Maybe we'll work out what it takes to run the bar and pay you a living wage, and I'll take thirty percent of any profit above that. That way we'd know for sure there was enough for you and the club before I got any. I can do that for at least a couple of years, especially if I get my working meals free." She looked at him frankly. "No one in the real world is ever going to give me a job. And I need to be doing. You've made a good thing with Solitaire, a place where people can come and be themselves, even if their self is really weird. That's a great gift. But there are so many of us damaged people, like you said, and we need more help. I have some ideas about that too, but first we have to get the bar in shape and part of that means more hours. And that means more people. Me."

He said suspiciously, "You're not planning to turn my bar into some kind of social services organization, are you?"

"No," she said with a certain sense of discovery, of dawning de-termination. "Into a web."

They walked back together. He wanted to argue about schedules and who was in charge of the menu, so she knew he had already agreed and was just working himself up to saying so. When they stepped back inside, Razorboy was squaring off with Duja McAf-fee, looking a bit like a schnauzer nose-to-nose with a rottweiler: as Jackal drew near to the bar, she heard Razorboy saying, ". . . sorry, but Scully said only beer and house wine until—oh, here he is now. Scully, this gentleman would like something that I have no idea what it is—"

"It's okay, I've got it. Sorry to keep you waiting, Duja. Razorboy was just doing what I asked him. This one's on me." Duja's forehead unwrinkled and Razorboy visibly relaxed. At the other end of the counter, Drake was happily plucking olives out of a large jar and portioning them into bowls.

"Gotta go upstairs and do some business," Jackal said. "I'll see you later."

"Okay. But don't hold your breath on that deli sandwich and soup idea, we have no place to store that kind of inventory."

"We'll see."

"It's my bar."

"I know, Scully. You're the boss," she answered, feeling suddenly every bit as cheerful as Drake with her bubblegum hair.

Upstairs, she found Snow and Crichton almost exactly as she'd left them, except with less wine in the bottle and all the corn chips gone.

"Drugs, hah," Crichton hailed her. "I should have thought of that."

"I'm sure you did."

"Nice walk?"

"It did the trick. I have some proposals of my own to make."

Crichton straightened herself. "Fire away."

"I'd like to outline my entire plan before you respond to any of the specific points."

"Fine."

She'd marshaled her thoughts on the way back, with the part of her brain that wasn't trying to persuade Scully that soup and sandwich combos would pay back on the extra refrigerator storage investment within ten months. Now she let everything click into order at the front of her brain.

"It's my intention to work with you on springboarding the online editing function of virtual technology, if we can agree to terms.

"Here's the thing. I'm aware that I'm outside the regular research demographic subset for this study—" a quick glance to Snow "—and I'll bet my screening records will show me outside the psychographic subset as well. I'm guessing that you'll be able to route my data out of the program on that basis. I'm also guessing that there's something about my particular profile that makes on-line editing possible for me."

She checked to make sure that Crichton was with her so far; the white eyes flashed *go on*.

"That means that my pattern, my profile, is the intellectual property that I have to contribute to this undertaking. I will agree to license that intellectual property to Ko for a fee commensurate with its value to the company. That's the only way I'll work a deal.

"Part of the payment for this license will be in kind rather than in cash." Crichton shifted and blinked; good, she was paying a different kind of attention now. "First, if Snow wants it, I want her to be permanently assigned to the start-up, with a guaranteed no-recall clause."

Snow reached her hand out and placed it over Jackal's for just a moment.

"Second, I want only voluntary paid contractors used in your research, at least for the first year. The test subjects will be drawn from a program that you'll seed for that year: if I can't make it run on its own after that, then you can get your participants wherever you want. My program will do a couple of things: it will offer solos an opportunity for paid employment with recourse, and it will also offer free biofeedback training to teach solos how to alter their patterns to match mine, and therefore give them the ability to edit aftershock. This training will include use of your facilities for supervised practice sessions. You'll provide the equipment and technicians free of charge to me and program participants.

"And I want Gavin Neill and me both on your advisory board."

And there was the little voice inside her, saying, Jackal, do you

really want to be involved with Ko again? Look what happened
last time. And the answer was *no, not really, not the same way. I'll
have to do better this time.*

She looked across the table at Crichton, who watched her
soberly in turn. Time to close. "I don't want revenge on Ko. I
won't make unreasonable demands; if you think these are unreasonable, you need to help me understand why. But this is more
than strictly business for me. It's a chance for me to make some
good out of something that's been almost purely bad up until now.
I'm not padding my requests and there are no giveaways in here.
I don't like to negotiate that way. All these points are deal-
breakers for me."

She sat back and folded her hands to show she was finished, and
let her breath out slowly through her nose. She'd done her best.

Crichton gave her a flat white look for a minute, and then said,
"Just for the sake of discussion, suppose I simply negotiate with
the NNA for the pattern information from your last aftershock?"

"You wouldn't have come here if you didn't need me. You've already run the pattern and something went wrong, or there's some
data missing. That's why you're here. You probably weren't even
sure I was editing until Scully talked to you."

Crichton nodded. Another moment of silence.

"And suppose I don't want a bunch of solos running around my
offices moaning about aftershock?"

"Then you can set up someplace else for them to do it, and staff
accordingly. Damn it, Crichton," she said, leaning forward, "no
one deserves what Scully gets in aftershock or what Estar Borja
got in VC. It's not going to kill Ko to give them some skills to cope
with it. And it's just more data for you."

"About Estar Borja," Crichton said carefully. "It's my understanding that, given editing ability, she might be amenable to a
long-term assignment in a virtual environment. I'll need extended
term data to justify life-support applications of the technology. Is

this something that would be permissible under your program arrangement?"

Jackal regarded her thoughtfully and then turned to Snow.

"I've been making some proposals of my own," Snow said evenly.

"I see."

"You should. It's your damned win-win scenario that I've heard up, down and sideways since you started Neill's training. Estar gets to realize her visions and I get to sleep a little better most nights."

Jackal put a hand up. "She . . . well, of course she'd want this. But it's risky, especially for her. What happens if something goes wrong with the technology and she gets trapped back in her cell and no one lets her out for another bunch of years?"

"Then I guess she'd have to deal with that crocodile of hers after all," Snow replied, without much apparent sympathy.

"You don't know what it's like. It's too dangerous."

"She's a grown-up. Who are you to make these kinds of decisions for her?"

"Who are you to do it?" Jackal retorted.

"I'm not making decisions," Snow said with an edge, "I'm creating opportunities." She relented, leaned in toward Jackal. "Just don't stand in the way of it. If Estar wants it, let her have it. She wouldn't think twice about stepping right on top of you to get it, you know that. You're too nice sometimes."

"That's funny," Jackal said quietly. "That's what Estar said."

Snow didn't respond.

"Okay," Jackal said finally, "I won't oppose it."

Crichton smiled. "Then I think we can come to an arrangement. I'll give you a call within the next two days to let you know what the current status is." She swallowed the last of her wine. "Snow, thank you for a most enjoyable conversation."

"My pleasure."

"I like her," Crichton told Jackal. "I might even like her better than you. And I should tell you that Gavin Neill sends his regards."

Oh, she missed him: the long, sometimes frustrating hours of learning, the meetings and practicums when she soared on his approval, the sheer joy of watching the expert at work. And she missed his keen eye and the knowledge that on some level he had cared for her.

"And my best regards to him," she said. And then, unable to help herself: "Will I hear from him?"

"You've been hearing from him all evening," Crichton said. She smiled with her moon-white eyes, and disappeared around the screen as unexpectedly as she had come.

They did not speak for a long while, as if Crichton had taken all the words with her and left them only able to hold hands and sip wine and occasionally sigh. Jackal's shoulders gradually relaxed, like iceworks melting into a softer shape.

"You did well," Snow said finally. "She'll go for it. I'm really, really proud of you."

"It's the only way I can go through with it. The things that have happened to people in virtual space . . . when things go wrong . . . well, it's just horrible. Did I tell you that one guy's food bled every time he tried to eat for a month?"

"Ick."

"Big ick."

Another silence. She liked being quiet with Snow; it was a rich and comfortable thing. Then she remembered: "Hey, I got a job!" She recounted the conversation with Scully.

"Great. I'll expect you to keep this nice wine in stock."

Another quiet moment.

Snow said abruptly, "This thing with Estar . . ."

Jackal shook her head. "I know that I can't protect her. I don't even know why I want to. But what she did to you—it made me want to hurt her back, you know? Like Tiger that day in the plaza. So now if something bad happens to her because of this, I'll wonder if it's my responsibility. Letting someone walk off a cliff because they want to isn't that much better than throwing them off."

"Of course it is. It's entirely different."

"You sound very sure."

"Of course I'm sure. You would be too, if you weren't so twisted up about making everyone's choices for them."

"That's not fair."

"Isn't it?" Snow pushed her hair back from her eyes. "I love you, Jackal, and you have consistently excluded me from all your choices. The only thing I got to consult on was whether you should go to Mirabile with the web, and you can bet I feel great about that piece of advice. But the rest of the time you just go off and do what you think is best for other people. And I'm tired of it. Your theories about how people behave may work in meetings, but I'm not a theory and you don't have to manage me."

"I'm not trying to manage you." She had been feeling so good a few minutes ago, and now she was angry and miserable.

"Then look me in the eye and tell me what you want. Do you want me to stay here? Or do you want me to go back to Ko and never darken your door again?"

"They'll make it hard for you—"

Snow held up a hand. "That's my choice. You make yours."

"What happened in VC—"

"Just tell me what you want. Tell me what Jackal Segura wants."

"I'm trying to tell you that I'm different. I've changed. I'm not the same person I was at Ko. If you come here, you won't be the same." *What if we don't like each other anymore?* her internal voice wailed. "We're different now."

"Of course we are." Snow shook her head and reached across the table with both hands. "We'd be different even if you'd never gone to Mirabile. That's what people do, they get different together."

Snow took one hand back and drank the last of the wine, and Jackal took a deep breath. She wondered if all of life would turn out to be making choices that she wasn't ready for. She breathed again and said, "Snow, will you come back and find your own place to live that isn't too far away and help me figure out how I can live in my head and in the world at the same time?"

"Is that what you want?"

She nodded. "More than anything."

They took the empty bottles and all the rest of the dishes and glassware downstairs to Scully.

"Thanks for saving me a trip," he said.

"Just building job skills."

He peered at her. "You've been crying."

She nodded.

"You look happy."

She nodded again. He looked at Snow.

"I'll be going home to pack my things."

He beamed: then he tried to beam even bigger. "That's great. That's terrific. It's . . ."

"About time," Snow said, and they all three laughed together.

"More wine?" Scully said, reaching for another bottle.

"How about some coffee?"

"Sure, and I've got some lovely strudel," he said. Snow made a happy noise.

Jackal carried everything on a tray to a table Snow found near the center of the bar. Solitaire was crowded with people Jackal recognized: Razorboy puffed up with pride at his twenty minutes of close encounters with solos; Duja climbing the stairs to the solo level with another bright red drink; Drake with a shy nod to Jackal, blushing furiously when Jackal raised her coffee cup in acknowledgment.

"You're going to clean up here," Snow said contentedly. "You'll own the place in two years."

"I don't want to own it, just run it."

"That's my Jackal," Snow said, and Jackal had to agree.

A week later they sat at the same table. Jackal was wearing an apron, with a bandanna tied around what hair she'd managed to grow so far.

"I have to get back to work."

"Mmm," Snow said. She was mapping a plant systems problem on her palmtop, and Jackal knew that she was lost to meaningful conversation.

She was about to kiss Snow's neck and get back behind the bar, when Jane came into Solitaire with Estar behind her. Although Jackal had been expecting it, waiting for it, it was still a shock to have Estar in the room.

"Snow," she whispered, and Snow looked up and became very still.

Jane came ahead to their table. "She'd like to talk to you," she said to them both. "Will you?"

Snow said nothing. Jackal answered, "Yes, of course."

Estar looked like a beautiful child, dressed in a long sea-blue dress and boots, her face as soft as Jackal had ever seen it. *"Buenas noches."*

"Hi, Estar," Jackal said. Snow nodded, more civilly than Jackal had expected. Jackal looked around for a chair. "Do you want to sit down?"

"No," Estar said. "I will not stay. I will go home as soon as I have done what I came to do, and I will wait to hear from Crichton that this gift of yours is now available to me. And then I will make a home for myself inside my head." She looked serene, almost peaceful. "I am grateful to you. I hope you will accept this."

She handed Jackal a package. Inside the wrapping was a small framed painting, exquisite and fine: an outdoor café at the edge of a *playa*, full of people painted in dashes and strokes of color, all suggesting motion and sound and a density of humanity. The only people distinguishable were two women at a table, one with olive skin and dark hair, the other fair like summer wheat, subtly pooled in light, hands clasped, talking, laughing, happy. Connected.

"It is my vision for you," Estar said.

Jackal almost wept. "It's beautiful, Estar. Thank you so much. I love it."

Estar smiled. "*Bueno*. Then I will go home happy and begin to wait." She bowed to Snow. Then she said to Jackal, "They tell me that the next area of study is shared virtual experience. I am counting on them to fail in this for a long, long time. But perhaps one day I will have my fill of being alone, and then they will send me a friend. Perhaps it will be you, *chacalita*."

She stepped very close and they looked at each other: then she kissed Jackal suddenly, fiercely, and was gone.

Jackal wiped her eyes and turned back to the table. She found Snow studying her.

"What?"

"I remember telling you what a good Hope you would be. And I was right."

"I'm not a real Hope. I never was."

"That doesn't matter, and anyway, yes you are."

Jackal said, with a frown, "I don't get it."

"I know," said Snow. "But you will."

Acknowledgments

MANY PEOPLE HELPED, AND I'M VERY GRATEFUL. FORE-most are Nicola Griffith, Shawna McCarthy, and Jennifer Brehl.

Special love to Sharon and Larry, my mother and father, and Celeste and Arthur, who are also my parents and family.

And for various reasons—support, candor, knowledge, joy, or just plain love—Ronnie Garvey, Chuck Munro, Steve Swartz, Liz Butcher, Cindy Ward, Ed Hall, Mark Tiedemann, Pierce Watters, Gretchen Hastings, Vonda McIntyre, Therese Littleton, Bill Eskridge, Ben Eskridge, Neil Eskridge, Ken Saint-Amand, Vince Caluori, Peter Adkison, Tina Trenkler, Juliane Parsons, Dave Slusher, Darlene Slusher, Timmi Duchamp, Amber Fullerton, Bryan Kinsella, Casey Leichter, Dave Schwimmer, David Serra, Donna Simone, Doru Culiac, Jan-Maree Bourgeois, Jarrod Nack, Jennifer Dirksen, Jill Waller, Josh Fischer, Karen Kapscady, Larry Weiner, Leeds Chamberlain, Lori Heric, Marty Durham, Mendy Lowe, Motoaki Nagahisa, Nelson Chang, Pat Robinette, Tamara Grunhurd, Wendy Wallace, Yasuyo Dunnett, Kathy Acey and the Astraea Foundation, Jeremy Lipp, Ellen Datlow, Rob Killheffer, Kris Rusch, Center Theatre, St. Paul's School, and U2.

Jackal's story of Las Tres Hermanas was inspired by Sebastian Junger's *The Perfect Storm*.